The Meridian Fiend

NICK DOYLE

The Meridian Fiend

ISBN: 978-1-7751987-0-3

Editing by Katie McCoach / Standoutbooks Ltd
Cover Illustration and Interior Design © 2017 Alana Lawson
Published by Nick Doyle
www.nickdoylewrites.com
First Edition

ACKNOWLEDGEMENTS

Special thanks to Alana Lawson. Her immeasurable support and work made this book possible.

The Meridian Fiend

PROLOGUE

Underneath a sign reading "St. Boniface's Cemetery" stretched the shadow of a man. Meridian City was choked by the heat of high summer, but the man wore head to toe black. A cracked 'MU' for Meridian University marked the center of the hoodie he wore. Its faded and chipped nature suggested many years of use. Across his face, he wore a black balaclava, leaving only his eyes bare. On his right shoulder, hung a hunting rifle. On the left rested a shovel, which he gripped loosely with his left hand.

The figure ducked low as he entered the cemetery. He hadn't brought a light, and cloud cover obscured the moon. This left precious few lights as his guiding posts in the darkness. One was a lamp halfway down the main path toward the office building. Another shone further down after the turn off to the grave markers. This light leaked into the night through the windows of a structure – the night watchman's shack. As the intruder approached the shack, he pulled the rifle off his shoulder and balanced it awkwardly in his hands with the shovel. He kept his breathing short, as he rested his shoulder on the side of the building, below one of the shack's windows. The familiar music from a 70's sitcom introduction blared in his ears. The man slowly stood so he could peer in the window. Inside, the night watchman leaned back in his chair, laughing quietly to himself. He was an elderly man in flannel and jeans with a nameplate on his breast that read 'Stanley'. No way Stanley was going anywhere soon. The intruder took one look back down the main path he'd come from before he began creeping down the path toward the rows of tombstones.

When he was far enough away from the night watchman's shack, the man rose from his crouch and walked with a brisk pace past the identical markers. Although there were no lights to guide his way, he moved with confidence. Near the wrought-iron fence in the rear of the cemetery, the figure stopped. He leaned his rifle against a nearby tombstone and drove his shovel through the ground beside him. The man squatted, took off his gloves, and placed his hands on the ground in front of him. He kneaded the dirt. It gave way without much effort – a fresh grave, exactly what he wanted. A smile crossed his lips. He pulled his gloves once more over his hands, and reached for his shovel. He sighed, kicking at the dirt, knowing exactly what efforts he was about to expend. Any hesitation he had broke way when the satisfying *thunk* of metal on soil filled the air as his shovel made contact with the grave.

The man worked frantically, knowing he was more likely to be caught during Stanley's hourly round than by the noise he made – night watchmen were the type to dismiss noises as rodents or dumb kids. This one was probably old enough to need a hearing aid. The stench of iron and ammonia filtered through the balaclava he wore. A heavy sweat covered his skin . He created a well-practiced rectangle in the ground as he uncovered the casket, as he had done many times before. It opened without much trouble. His hands fell into the box, grasping at the corpse's face and neck. Everything was intact. The man silently exhumed the body, pulling it onto the grass. He threw the shovel into the hole, grabbed his rifle, and turned to leave. He stopped. A nagging thought tugged at the back of his mind. He turned back to the grave and scooped up a clump of mud that caked the casket. The man rubbed the soil on the grave stone, making a crude pentagram.

His task complete, the grave robber grabbed the corpse's shoulders and dragged it back toward the main path. He slowed to a crawl as he approached the watchman's shack. The formulaic noise of scripted comedy no longer seeped from the structure. Instead, he heard the dour tone of news anchors and the jangling of keys. The intruder stumbled forward. He rushed over to the bushes, shoving the corpse out of sight as he knelt down, gripping his rifle. The door to the shack opened, and Stanley stepped out into the warm night. He stretched up in the air and looked to his right then left, as if trying to decide where he should start. The watchman let out a cough, cupping his hands over his face. He took a step toward the tombstones. The figure in the bushes watched carefully as Stanley turned on a flashlight and shone it down the path.

The night watchman continued coughing as he walked down the path, only a few feet from the man's position. He passed by, ambling further down into the cemetery. When his coughing subsided, Stanley stopped. He spun on his heels, holding the flashlight up to eye level.

The grave robber jumped to his feet and darted forward.

Stanley screeched.

The butt of the intruder's rifle slammed into his face. The old man went down. The man pointed his weapon at the pleading watchman and fired two rounds into his head. Brains sprayed across the cobblestones of the path. He retrieved the rifle casings and fished the corpse out of the bushes, careful to avoid stepping in the expanding pool of blood. The news broadcast coming from the shack almost drowned out the grave robber's ghastly work. He smiled to himself when he heard the subject matter.

"Another body was stolen from a local cemetery last night. The Meridian City Police Department has yet to release a statement concerning the crime, or say whether it was the work of the serial grave-robber known as *The Snatcher*."

The Meridian Fiend

CHAPTER 1

About midway down a steep hill in Meridian City was a two-story home. Its dull, yellow paint stood out as a little off in the line of suburban houses in the neighborhood with their bright, white siding and identical black roofs. The hill was in a cozy, residential district in central Meridian, just far enough from the port that the salty, east coast waters didn't stick to the lungs on each breath.

A car pulled into the driveway of the home at precisely 6:30 a.m., as if even a second's delay would not be tolerated. From the car emerged Luca Russo, a woman in a stark black suit with features chiseled by four decades of a harsh life. She walked to the front door and inserted a key in the lock. It turned effortlessly – a sure sign it hadn't been locked. A grimace formed on her face at the realization. The expression stuck as she pressed inside. As she walked through the home's sunken living room to the kitchen on the other side, she took off her blazer and neatly folded it in her arms. Without a jacket, her shoulder holster and firearm were in plain sight. Luca sat at the kitchen table and waited, browsing the news on her phone.

Not long after Luca arrived, she heard a scuffle coming from upstairs. Her gaze didn't falter from the phone even as heavy steps clumsily landed on the staircase.

"Today's the day," Luca said as she finally looked up at Cecil Delacroix, her business partner and childhood friend.

Cecil let out an exaggerated yawn, stretching his arms up high.

"The fridge is stocked and ready to go. I'm going all out on breakfast today," he said. "It is special, after all."

"Coffee first." Luca extended her right hand until Cecil filled it with a mug of coffee and sugar. Luca took a sip before lowering her phone. "You forgot to lock the door again."

"Oh yeah?" Cecil said as his hands blurred in the kitchen, forming a pile of food in his usual madcap fashion. Bits and bobs inevitably ended up scattered along the floor. "What's the worst that could happen?"

"Someone could break in."

"I'd like to see that. Could be fun." Cecil fell into a fit of giddy laughs.

"Have you planned out what you're going to say? They're not going to take it well, especially Chris. You need to be very careful," Luca said.

"Yeah... is there any way we could tell them in a week or so... you know, after they get settled in at college?"

"No."

"But..."

"No." Luca slammed her fist on the table. "It's today. You can't put it off anymore. Someone could get hurt – even killed - and neither of us will be around to fix it."

"I guess." Cecil's shoulders fell as he let out an exaggerated groan.

"No, not *I guess*. They've been in danger for two years – two years. We've been lucky, plain and simple. It could happen any day now, and I'm not going to be around to protect them soon. They'll be on their own and they need to know."

"Couldn't you tell them?" Cecil asked.

"You're their father. It's your job." Luca checked the time on her phone. "Call them."

Cecil marched up to the foot of the stairs.

"Chris? Alice? It's time to wake up." His call was the same as every morning, with the usual singsong character reserved only for long-repeated phrases. When scuffling and the telltale sound of the shower reached his ears, Cecil returned to haphazardly creating a mountainous breakfast.

* * *

Christine Delacroix was first downstairs, as always. Her cropped, black hair was still dripping from the shower. She never bothered drying it, preferring the chaotic mess that settled after it dried naturally. Chris threw herself down next to Luca. The chair barely uttered a creak as her lithe form landed soundly on it. Chris's hands tapped wildly on the table and a giddy smile sat proud on her lips. She had never been energetic in the mornings, but today was special: within a few hours, she'd be at the Meridian University dorms and her life would be changed forever. No more dealing with her bossy sister, or her smothering father. Luca didn't look up at Chris's arrival, but Cecil did. Abandoning the precarious balance he had going in the kitchen, he ran over to her and tapped her on both shoulders, his teeth bared in parental affection.

"First day. So excited," he said. "Where's Alice?"

"Sleeping, probably," Chris replied.

"Alice, breakfast. Hurry up!" Cecil shouted up the stairs. He turned back into the kitchen to see black smoke rising from the toaster. He threw the blackened bread and the rest of the food onto four plates and tossed them haphazardly on the table.

Luca rearranged the food to set four places. Chris smirked as Cecil ran to silence the high-pitched squeaking of the fire alarm in the hall that had been triggered by all the smoke in the kitchen. Slow, pained thumping almost drowned out the fire alarm as Chris's fraternal twin, Alice, trudged downstairs. A static scowl plastered on her face, she lurched toward the kitchen table.

"Wow," Chris exclaimed when she saw her sister stomp into the kitchen. "I guess that explains why the bathtub was stained pink. I figured a unicorn threw up."

Alice's naturally brown hair was slathered in bright pink blotches. The uneven assignment of color pointed squarely at a bad dye job.

"Do you like it?" Alice asked.

"Your hair was fine the way it was," Luca said.

"Come on, Luca. Isn't it pretty?" Alice pleaded, trying to look innocent, as if that would win any favor from the stoic woman.

"Cecil, say something about your daughter's hair," Luca said.

"Looking good," Cecil said, poking his head in the room.

"Don't encourage her," Luca replied.

Cecil had a bad habit of letting his girls get away with anything, something that irritated Luca to no end. Though she was not their mother, she had been heavily involved in raising the twins. She had no problem being the disciplinarian, but Cecil's soft touch constantly undermined her strict rules.

"Encourage me?" Alice said with mock disgust. "Chris is the one throwing her life away in the liberal arts. At least I'm going to be able to get a job."

"I'm taking Criminology. Last I checked, lawyers can get jobs," Chris said.

"Oh yeah? How many other prelaw classes are you taking?"

"I'm keeping my options open." Chris waved her hand dismissively. "When you find out you hate Biology, you'll wish you'd have taken a single non-science elective."

"Not going to happen."

"Sure it won't, just like how you were going vegetarian forever."

Alice shuddered. "Whatever. I'll admit that was never going to work, if you admit Psychology is useless crap."

"Nope."

"Bitch," Alice said.

"Watch your language," Luca said, putting her phone down on the table and giving Alice a customary glare.

"Hey, I extended the olive branch," Alice said.

"Is there anything interesting in the news?" Chris asked Luca, no longer interesting in sparing with her sister.

"Oil prices are fluctuating."

Alice let out an audible groan. "Something interesting, please Luca. How about the Snatcher?"

Chris sighed when Alice brought up the serial grave robber that had been plaguing Meridian for months. Morbid as usual, she thought.

"He killed someone last night," Luca said.

"I'm so sick of that guy," Cecil said.

"Why?" Chris asked.

"Oh, nothing, Honey. It's just that people at work never shut up about him."

"At least he's not boring like the rest of this place," Alice said.

"Hey, it's not that boring around here," Cecil said.

"Really, Dad? When was the last time you dug up a body or killed someone?" Alice asked.

"Who can keep track?" Cecil laughed as he returned briefly to the kitchen.

As the foursome worked through their breakfast, Chris picked at her food. She tried to take in all the details. Alice shoveled food into her mouth with the care and grace of a garbage compactor, her other hand sneaking across the table toward Luca's coffee. Luca smacked the young woman's hand away with her fork.

It was the usual scene, but not for long. The thought caused Chris's giddy smile to return.

"You guys excited?" Cecil asked.

"Yeah," the twins said, almost in unison.

"Eat more than instant noodles and please exercise," Luca said.

"Doesn't that defeat the point of university?" Chris asked.

"Yeah, stop suffocating us," Alice shouted, banging her hand against the table in mock disgust.

"Don't you have something to tell them, Cecil?" Luca said.

"Right... that." Cecil rubbed the back of his head, a nervous grin making Chris's stomach churn uneasily. "So, like, there's this thing I – we've been meaning to tell you girls for a little bit now. It's not really that big a thing. You probably won't care at all actually."

"Get to the point, Cecil." Luca kicked him under the table.

"Okay. Yeah. It's not really a big deal. We can laugh about it later. So, you guys know where I work, right?"

"Somewhere in City Hall," Chris said, her heart rate jumping as Cecil's ramblings increased.

"Is that where I...?" Cecil shook his head. "Anyway, so about that..."

"Did you get fired, Dad?" Alice asked.

"No. It's not that," he said.

"You can tell us if you got fired," Chris said. "A lot of people change careers in their forties, and you have years of civil service experience."

Cecil laughed for a solid minute, avoiding every worried glance from Chris. When he finally stopped, Chris saw his hands continue to twitch, fingers flailing wildly in every direction.

"I've... I'm being transferred to a new department. It's not important really, so I didn't want to bring it up on your last day, but Luca thought I should share the news. Right, Luca?"

"I can't believe this," Luca said. "Finish getting ready and head out to the car." She stood suddenly. She grabbed her jacket and walked back to the front door, taking one look back before leaving.

"What was that about?" Chris asked, watching Luca disappear.

"Nothing. Everything'll be just fine," Cecil said, balancing himself by grabbing onto his daughters' shoulders.

He kneaded and clawed his fingers against them, only stopping when they grew too unconformable and squirmed away from him.

"Just fine," he repeated, as if he needed convincing himself.

CHAPTER 2

Chris had trouble keeping the heavy boxes in her hands from falling as she stood in front of the northern Meridian University dormitories. Luca, easily managing more than twice the weight Chris was carrying, finished pulling the remaining bags out of the car's trunk before tapping on the roof.

"I'll pick you up once I get Alice settled in the townhouse," Cecil yelled to Luca out the window as the car sped off.

"He's going to be a wreck for the next two months because of this, and I'm the one who's going to have to deal with it," Luca said.

"Oh, Luca. That's what you get for being so damn indispensible," Chris teased, too excited to worry about her dad missing her.

"For that, you're carrying another box," Luca declared as she effortlessly lowered one of the boxes she was carrying to the ground before marching into the dormitory.

A large smile broke out on Chris's face as she clumsily grasped her belongings and followed the older woman. She was on the precipice of a new life.

Chris had been assigned a room in what was affectionately known as the Old Dorm. The name rang true and the pastel blue paint did little to cover the stains and holes peppering the plaster. It didn't much resemble the college of Chris's fantasies, but she was too excited to notice. They passed several broken and worn chairs leaning up against the walls as they moved toward Chris's new home.

"I hope you weren't expecting privacy," Luca said as they entered the room.

It was tiny. There was a single bed and a desk pressed against the left side wall and their mirror image on the right with only a thin, floral curtain separating the space.

"Do you know who your roommate is yet?" Luca asked.

Chris looked up, panting and covered in sweat. The boxes had been too much for her.

"Her name's Cindy Bell," Chris said. She noticed the boxes piled near the bed on the right side of the room. "I guess she's already here."

"I'm going to go find the RA. Start unpacking."

Chris stretched out on her bed, reveling in the hard, uncomfortable mattress, because it was *her* hard, uncomfortable mattress. She heard a few gentle taps on the door. A teenage girl with impossibly bouncy, blonde hair stood in the doorway with a naïve smile plastered on her face.

"Oh my God, you must be my roomie. We are going to have so much fun this year," she squealed, bouncing up and down on her heels and clapping her hands.

"I'm Christine, but most people just call me Chris. You're Cindy, right?"

"That's right," Cindy said gleefully before flinging herself onto the bed opposite Chris. "What classes are you taking?"

"The metaphysics of applied discrete poetry." Chris rattled off some of the confusing terms she'd come across during registration, hoping to get a laugh out of her new roommate.

"Wow, you must be really smart."

Cindy seemed totally earnest. Embarrassed, Chris fished around in a box until she found her actual schedule.

"I was just joking. I'm in Introduction to Psychology, Criminology, Political Science, English, and Symbolism and the Occult."

"I'm in that class, too!" Cindy jumped up. "I hear Professor Moore is really good. My sister, Emily? She took it first year and she said it was the best class she's ever taken."

Luca marched into the room without a glance to Cindy.

"They're having orientation activities tomorrow. I have a schedule for you," Luca said.

Cindy ran over and violently shook the older woman's hand.

"I'm Cindy, and you must be Chris's mom. You two look so alike."

Luca freed herself from the excited girl's surprisingly firm grip.

"I'm not her mother, just her father's partner." Luca remained expressionless.

"That's okay, too," Cindy said with a tight nod. "My sister, Emily? She always says that the institution of marriage is overrated anyway. I'm sure you two are very happy."

Chris's hand shot to her mouth in an attempt to dam the wave of laughter that threatened to spill out.

Luca often forgot the word 'partner' had other meanings. Cecil enjoyed playing her lack of insight for laughs, especially on Valentine's Day, which the perpetually single friends always spent together.

"His work partner," Luca corrected the girl with an unimpressed frown.

Cindy hung her head like a confounded child.

"She's a family friend," Chris added, hoping to help the bewildered girl.

It was a common mistake. Luca had been taking care of the twins their entire lives. It was usually Luca who showed up to parent teacher conferences or came to sporting events. That was far more than Chris could say for her actual mother. Though she had died only ten years prior, she hadn't been part of her children's lives even before then. Luca had always been there to fill the void.

Luca turned her attention to Chris and thrust the orientation schedule into her hands.

"I'm heading out. Call me if you need anything else." Luca gave Chris a quick hug, then was gone.

Chris froze at the rare display of physical affection. When Luca left, Chris felt different, like piles of pillows were taken off her head and she could breathe freely at last. She lay back on the bed and closed her eyes for a moment as she tried to get her head around her newfound freedom.

* * *

A few miles away, Cecil pulled into the driveway of a white townhouse on a street adjacent to the university that functioned as unofficial student housing.

"I really wish you and Chris would stay together," Cecil said.

"Don't worry so much," Alice said.

"How do you know these girls anyway?" Cecil asked as he and Alice carried boxes into the house.

"The internet, duh."

Alice ignored the worry in her father's eyes. She was too busy planning the rest of the day in her head. Luca had tried to talk her into staying in the dorms, but there was no way Alice was going to let herself get stuck in one of those boxes. The last thing she wanted was to be closely supervised.

Once inside the town house, they were greeted by five young women. One of the pack, a blonde shrouded in blinding pink athletic gear, bounced up to the pair and extended her hand.

"Are you Alice?" the girl asked. "I'm Sam. Thanks again for taking the room. I don't know what we'd have done if we couldn't get a sixth."

"You're all first years too, right?" Cecil asked.

"Oh no, we're all in our third year. One of our friends transferred to Berkeley, so we needed someone to take her room."

Alice's shoulders lifted as she began to laugh uneasily. Cecil joined in, muttering something under his breath. When he stopped he kept a wide, strained smile on his face.

As soon as father and daughter reached Alice's new room, Cecil's fraudulent smile vanished.

"Why didn't you tell me that these girls were in third year?" Cecil asked.

"I didn't think you'd be okay with it, so I just kind of forgot to mention it." Alice was wringing her hands, avoiding her father's gaze. "Are you mad?"

Cecil placed his coat on the desk and leaned against the wall.

"I'm not mad. Luca will be. How about we wait a week or so before we break it to her?" He let out another chuckle. "Hey, maybe they can help you with your homework?"

"I don't think so, Dad." Alice laughed. "Remember, I'm the God of Science, and that pink girl probably doesn't know the first thing about skinning lab rats."

"Yeah, speaking of which, I've got a few questions for her before I go," Cecil said, darting out of the room.

Alice's smile was stretched as far as it could go as she unpacked her suitcase. It was full of recently purchased clothes that she knew Luca would never let her wear – scandalous tops and shorts of gaudy, clashing colors. She was putting them away when she heard a noise coming from near the desk – inside Cecil's discarded jacket was his cell phone and it demanded attention. She raced over to his jacket and reached into the pocket.

"Ow!"

She quickly withdrew her hand. A glistening red bead had formed on her finger. It ran down her wrist and made a break for the floor, leaving a tiny, round spot. Alice put her bleeding finger into her mouth, then reached carefully with the other hand back into the pocket. She smiled as she pulled out the culprit: a scalpel.

"That's weird," she said to herself. "Maybe Dad's been skinning lab rats, too." Thrusting her hand back in, she grabbed his phone. "Hello?" She heard Luca's voice. "Yeah, don't worry. He's almost finished up here."

Alice carefully returned the phone and scalpel, though part of her wondered exactly why her father would be carrying around something like that in his pocket.

CHAPTER 3

"It's time to wake up, Chris."

Chris's eyes flickered open at the faint whisper of her name. She couldn't see anything. The world was enveloped by darkness. She was lying on her back, and it ached terribly. She tried to turn to her side, seeking relief from the pain, but found herself utterly incapable of moving. Something rough was cutting into her wrists. She tried to kick out her legs. Nothing. She tried to shift her body and felt heavy resistance around her shoulders and waist. She was fully bound.

"Hello?" Chris yelled into the void. Her heart beat violently against her ribcage.

The darkness ate her voice the same way it had eaten all light. Everything felt hot, and Chris became aware of tiny beads of sweat on her forehead. She pressed her palms flat on the bed, seeking leverage, but found no traction. There were no cotton-soft sheets to buoy her up. Instead, her hands discovered cold, hard steel beneath her. She beat on it as strongly as she could without moving her wrists, but the hollow metal clangs only intensified the feeling of helplessness now overcoming her.

"Please, somebody help me," Chris screamed. She waited for a response, an echo, anything to show there was something left in the world besides darkness. Nothing.

Panic overcame reason. Chris threw herself into a mad struggle against her bonds, tearing her skin against the restraints as hard and fast as she could. The compulsion to fight coursed through her body like a drug. How long she writhed fiercely against the void was impossible to know. It felt like forever, but it accomplished nothing. When she came down from the heights and lay still once more, she had gained not one inch of freedom. Breath flew too fast up her throat, and she gasped audibly. It was the only sound in the room. What had happened? How did she get there? Questions sliced through her head, but her mind was a disorganized mass of fear and anger.

There came a new sound. It wasn't coming from her – it was something else, something within the room. It started as a tiny hum, barely audible, then grew louder and louder to a pervasive buzz, as if there was a beehive hovering just above Chris's resting place. A light flickered on. The sudden luminescent invasion knocked her eyes closed; they had become too accustomed to the dark. Slowly, she pried them open again. The light was coming from a single naked bulb suspended in the middle of the ceiling. It illuminated very little, leaving the shadows to regroup in the room's corners. Chris strained her eyes down to see that her slight frame was still covered by her red flannel pajamas. To the right, she could make out the faint outline of a side table with a leather pouch unrolled beside her. Chris squinted, trying to see the contents of the pouch. It held a row of scalpels, glistening in the dim light.

Chris felt her terrified blood surge through her veins. The light sound of tapping metal rang out again. Her hands were trembling against the table.

"Please," she begged.

Something answered her call. It was a deep, horrible voice, speaking words she didn't understand. It bellowed its inhuman, guttural tones with such force that the light bulb dangling from the ceiling began to creak back and forth. When the voice went silent, the bulb gave a final, decaying flicker and went out. Chris felt tears roll down her cheeks as her sobbing filled the darkness. The light, the voice, the hum – they were gone, as quickly as they had come.

"I don't like it here," another voice shot past Chris's left ear.

She could feel breath rub against her skin. The light returned, only this time it filled the room with a dim shade of green. A screeching metal sound fought the sound of her cries for dominance in the room, but there was no contest. Soon she couldn't even hear herself cry. Chris's eyes again searched the room for help. To her left she saw a wooden stool, sitting benignly beside her. It hadn't been there before. Its tiny innocence seemed warped by the twisted green light. As she gazed at it, she realized the screeching metal was starting to fade. She listened raptly for a hint of the voices from before. At first, she was only aware of the growing silence as the screeching faded fully away, but then there was a tap. Then another, then another. The tapping intensified - the sound of fingers rapping against steel. Chris jerked upwards, arching her back as far as she could against her bonds. She couldn't just hear the taps – she could feel them, too. They were coming from beneath the table.

She tried to rock herself to the right, then to the left, to somehow escape, but the table stayed firm, like it was bolted on the ground. Chris choked on her own breath as her ear caught the hint of scratching creeping up beside her body. Her head twisted, looking down at her sides. Two long, joint-less arms made of some sort of black metal, glinting in the sickly green light, rose from underneath the table from her sides. Chris screamed again, bucking against her restraints, contorting her body in a hopeless attempt to escape the black appendages. The fingers on the hands were easily twice the size of her own and each one ended in a razor sharp point.

"No, no, no, no, no," Chris repeated compulsively as the black metal claws caressed her ribs.

The fingers tore away long streaks of fabric as they moved up her torso, leaving tiny red scratches on her bare flesh in exchange.

"Get off me," Chris screamed.

The hands reached her stomach. They circled it, rubbing it, prodding it. Then one of the black metal digits ran down from Chris's collar, taking off the first two buttons of her pajama shirt. Chris jerked still – if she moved in the wrong way, just an inch, she would find herself wheezing up blood.

The buttons on her shirt clinked to the ground. Chris heard the squeaking of a door opening. The invading metal hands froze. Bright white light entered the room, chasing the green glow away. Chris looked over as a figure stood against the light in the middle of a door's threshold. She squinted through the blinding light. Was this figure a savior in the dark? She immediately begged for help as the door closed. The dim green light once again overtook Chris's world. The hands, however, remained still, silent on her chest. But Chris wasn't looking at them anymore. The man who had entered the room now filled her vision, and burned his image into her eyes. He wore a set of surgical scrubs, whose exact shade was impossible to tell in the green. Above them was his face, a terrible face. Affixed to his head was a pure, white porcelain mask. The mask bore an indifferent visage with painted red lips and wide, terrifying eyes. They gazed hungrily upon the trapped girl on the table, and Chris realized with horror that they were not part of the mask – they twitched with reality.

The man moved with too much grace and ease through the sea of green light. He reached over toward the black metal hands and slapped them. Chris could feel the hands quake and tremble against her skin. They slowly receded down her sides until they left her sight. They were still here, though. She felt them tapping underneath the table. She sensed that they would never leave her again. The surgeon walked over to her right. He leaned forward and rested his elbows on the table next to Chris's face, cradling his head in his hands. The eyes looking back at her were devoid of love or hate. He reached for one of the scalpels. Chris remained still, but tears welled up in her eyes. This man was going to kill her. She hadn't even had a chance to begin her life, and it was already over. The man pulled at her pajama top, shaking his head in mock dissatisfaction. He raked the scalpel through the remaining fabric, finished the job the clawed hands had so tentatively begun.

With all the care of gutting a fish, the man cut through Chris's clothes and yanked the garments from her body. Chris's chest expanded and contracted in uncontrolled haste as the green light coated her pink flesh. The tapping from underneath the table intensified, crawling up and down like ants playing on her spine. Chris clenched her hands, clawing her fingernails into the slick steel. The surgeon lifted a curved saw from the table, one that couldn't have been there before. He raised it above Chris's sternum and dragged it to and fro through the air, pantomiming the splitting of her ribs. Chris could feel the intensity of the smile behind the mask's porcelain lips.

Chris felt a needle-like prick on her back. Then another, and another. The black metal claws had pierced the table and were making their home inside her flesh. She gasped at the pain, inching its way like a knife dragging across her spine. The green light shuddered. The surgeon noticed and grabbed the light bulb with his gloved hand. He tossed it to the side so that it swung in circles like a perverse carnival ride. The surgeon faked noiseless laughter before becoming stiff and jagged. His arm flew over to the table, grabbing another scalpel. He leapt onto the table and straddled her torso. He pressed one of his fingers to her lips. Chris whimpered for mercy. He didn't seem to hear. The scalpel pressed against her skin, and blood began flowing to the surface.

Chris flew out of bed. She was covered in sweat and had to grasp her chest to catch her breath. Everything around her was different. It was wrong. Where was her room? She spotted movement to her left. Turning, she saw a very concerned Cindy kneeling beside her.

That's right, Chris thought. *university*.

"Are you okay?" Cindy asked. "You were shouting in your sleep."

"I'm sorry. It was just a nightmare."

"You want to talk about it?" Cindy asked.

"I don't know where I'd start. It was really weird, but... I don't know. It felt familiar somehow."

"Weird. I got this book on reading dreams last year. Do you want to check it out in the morning?"

"Sure. Thanks, Cindy."

Chris fell back in bed. She closed her eyes and prayed that the darkness would stay away.

CHAPTER 4

The heat from the summer months lingered as two men approached the office of the West Blair Cemetery. It was a tidy, brick building whose entryway was flanked by two beautifully groomed bushes and dozens of flowers. Julian Morales, the younger man, was in his mid-thirties, slender, with black hair, glasses, and lightly tanned skin. Sweat pooled on his dress shirt, attesting to the summer heat. His partner, Larry Saunders, was well past middle-aged and quite heavyset. He shuffled forward in a tan suit with lapels straight out of a bad seventies TV show. Larry raised a tired hand and pounded on the door to the office.

"One moment, please," came a voice, muffled by the heavy wooden door.

Deadbolt after deadbolt was undone before the door finally opened. An elderly woman in a stiffly formal navy dress stood before them.

"May I help you?" she asked.

Frowning, Larry lifted a badge to eye level. "I'm Detective Saunders and this is my partner, Detective Morales."

"You must be here because of the incident."

"Yes, ma'am. Could we come in and ask you some questions?" Julian enthusiastically stepped forward.

"Of course. Right this way."

The woman led the two detectives into a neat sitting area.

"Could you tell us your full name and position here?" Larry groaned as he sat down, shifting his weight.

"Gloria Rutherford. I'm the office manager."

"When did you discover that one of the bodies was stolen?" Larry asked.

"This morning, just after eight o' clock. I saw muddy tracks going down the main walkway. I thought it must have been Herbert, but he is usually so careful about these things, a very thorough fellow. Tracking dirt about would be most unlike him."

"And who is Herbert, ma'am?" Julian interrupted.

"Herbert Wright is the night watchman and caretaker. He does a little bit of everything around here. I followed the tracks into the cemetery and saw a hole that certainly wasn't there when I left last night. Earth was strewn everywhere. I could tell right away it wasn't dug by a professional. When I got closer, I saw that a casket had been unearthed, and it was empty.

"I was perfectly shocked." An indignant look came over the old woman's face. "Why would anyone want to steal one of our patron's loved ones?"

"Do you mind if we take a look at the grave?" Larry leaned back in his chair, looking as bored as she was horrified. "We'll also need to talk to Herbert and any other night staff."

"Of course." Her composure recovered, Mrs. Rutherford smiled. "The burial plot is near the western wall. You can follow the tracks. I would be appreciative if you didn't make too much of a fuss in front of any grieving relatives. You understand." She stood up to dismiss them. "While you're out in the cemetery, I'll retrieve Herbert's contact information."

Larry stood and walked away without a word.

"Thank you, ma'am," Julian said, before running after his partner.

"What do think about the night caretaker?" Julian asked, out of breath.

"Not much. He's only an employee here. It wouldn't explain the others," Larry replied, rubbing at his aching back.

"Maybe the others aren't related. Maybe it's just a coincidence."

"Don't be thick."

When they arrived at the grave, Julian studied the tombstone.

"Fresh body, male like the rest," Julian observed as he read the marker. "See anything back there?" he shouted at Larry, who had circled behind the pile of dirt.

"Yeah," Larry replied wearily. "Another one of those star symbols."

Julian jogged to the back of the pile. A pentagram was sloppily drawn in dirt on the back of the tombstone, the Snatcher's signature.

"Okay," Larry gestured at his partner, "Grab some photographs of the place. I'm going to get the night watchman's home address and call in some patrol officers to close the scene."

When Julian finished photographing the scene, Larry was already waiting in the car.

"Where are we headed?" Julian asked as he slid in front of the wheel.

"Not far. Mountebank Street." Larry reclined in the passenger's seat with his eyes closed.

"Do you think there's some sort of cult behind all of these grave robberies? You know, with the pentagram and everything."

"No." One of Larry's eyes opened, gazing at his partner.

"Why not?" Julian scoffed. "Pentagrams, fresh bodies, all men. It practically screams cult."

"You really want this to be some kind of crazy hocus-pocus crap?"

"It's more exciting than drug deals gone bad."

Caught up in visions of hunting down cryptic cultists, Julian failed to notice his partner wincing. Julian hadn't been in the homicide division long, but he'd learned that Larry was a cautious man. For Julian, keen on righting the wrongs of the world, Larry's pace was stifling. He'd heard murmuring from other officers that Larry had gone off the deep end years ago after his partner was killed, but nobody would talk about it. Julian tried to keep that in mind when dealing with Larry, but the scent of a conspiracy was just too much. The Snatcher case had only landed on their desk after the murder at the St. Boniface Cemetery. Larry glanced over the files that were given to them by Commercial Crimes, but Julian was completely engrossed. The pentagram, the fact nobody had ever found any of the bodies. His imagination was running wild with insane theories, with which he irritated his partner.

At their destination, they found a stout man in front of the house pruning a hedge. Though the house was tiny, it was surrounded by lush greenery.

"Excuse me, sir. We're looking for Herbert Wright," Julian called out.

"You're looking at him," the man said, putting his hedge clippers down.

Larry moved up. "I'm Detective Saunders, and this is my partner, Detective Morales. We want to ask you a couple of questions about the break-in last night at the cemetery."

"Of course, detectives. Come in, come in." Herbert's eyes lit up. "I just found out about it myself. That Snatcher guy, right?"

The man was practically frothing at the mouth. It was so common it was almost a cliché: everyone loves a crime scene.

"Did you notice anything unusual last night?" Larry asked, his eyes scoping out the interior while Julian dutifully scribbled in his notepad.

"No, I was in the basement all night. We had a bit of a leak down there. No permanent damage, but a hell of a mess, I can tell you."

"It's a big job, digging up a corpse," Larry prodded. "Are you sure you didn't see or hear anything unusual?"

Herbert hesitated. "I did hear a commotion around three in the morning, like something was knocked over. I assumed it was raccoons. We have a raccoon problem."

"Do you normally make rounds of the graveyard during your shift?" Julian looked up from his pad.

"Normally, yes, but I was just so busy with the leak that I didn't have time. It's not like I ever find anything on my rounds. The worst I've ever seen is dumb kids trying to scare themselves, and they're harmless."

"Did you notice any mud or dirt on the ground when you left?" Larry asked.

"I usually leave around five in the morning when it's still dark. If there was any dirt tracked on the pathway, I must have missed it."

"That's it. We may have further questions for you later." Larry stood up.

"No problem, detectives." Herbert chuckled heartily. "If there's anything I can do to help, just let me know."

Julian thanked Herbert while Larry stormed back to the car.

"What do you think?" Julian laughed as he got into the car. "He isn't what I pictured. I was expecting some tall, sickly-looking guy wearing a robe, maybe with a stutter."

"Stop it with the cult bullshit. All it'll give you is a bad reputation," Larry said, reclining in the chair. "I think Wright's full of shit. His boss said he was thorough. You saw the dirt. It was all over the place."

"It was dark," Julian said.

"The whole front of the office would've been lit up by the streetlight. And what night watchman doesn't go outside when he hears a commotion, raccoons or no raccoons? Hell, even when it is raccoons, you try to scare them off."

"Do you think he did it?" Julian asked.

"I don't know yet. We can't connect him to the other grave robberies, and I still don't know what to make of the pentagrams. Our guy could have struck between 5:00 and 8:00 while the cemetery was unguarded."

Julian looked at him with excitement in his eyes.

Larry shook his head. "Don't talk about this cult nonsense to anyone else, you hear?"

"Yeah, whatever you say." All fun vanished from Julian's face.

Larry's hand shot out and dug into Julian's shoulder, shocking the younger detective.

"I mean it, Julian."

CHAPTER 5

Dorm life was strange, but Chris liked it. There was something fun about being surrounded by dozens of bustling people at all times - a far cry from living at home in the suburbs. Sure, Alice was loud, but the house was mostly dead. Luca lived across town. Cecil's work kept him out most nights. His irregular work hours were something that Chris and Alice had gotten accustomed to long ago. Alice had a long-running theory that he was a CIA field agent, toppling foreign governments or some nonsense. Chris was skeptical. She couldn't imagine her father being in any covert agency. He was too nice, too chatty, and too accident prone. The amount of times Luca had rushed them to the hospital because he'd fallen down a flight of stairs or gotten into a car accident was ridiculous. The upside to Cecil's frequent absence was that Chris adjusted to dorm life faster than some of her neighbors. At least she knew how to do laundry and fold shirts.

Chris's eyes were glued on her recently-minted student ID as she entered her room. She had waited two hours in line to get the thing, and she hated how her hair looked in it – much too flat. Cindy sat at her desk, leaning back and reading a trashy romance novel.

"Didn't you just start that this morning?" Chris asked when she noticed Cindy was already halfway through the book.

"Yeah, but I've read it before. I really need to check out the library. Did you get your ID?"

"It's terrible." Chris flipped the card onto the table.

"Whatever. Everyone looks like a serial killer on these kinds of things."

"I'm a serial killer, now? I thought my hair just looked bad."

"I – that's not what I meant." Cindy closed the book and stared at Chris, eyes wide, pleading.

"Just joking. I think I can see it, though. It's the soulless eyes, isn't it?

"You're weird. Where are you from, anyway?" Cindy asked.

"Here. I grew up about an hour away."

"Me, too!" Cindy squealed. "How cool is it that they paired up a couple of local girls in the same room?"

"Where do your parents live?"

"Oh. My parents died a couple years ago. Car accident."

"I'm really sorry," Chris said, eyes now firmly planted on the floor.

"It's okay." Cindy half smiled. "I have my big sister, Emily. Do you have any brothers or sisters?"

"Yeah. I'm a twin."

"Oh my God! Do you guys look the same? Do you wear the same clothes and trick people?"

"We're not identical," Chris said.

"That sucks."

"She's at MU, too," Chris said.

"What dorm?"

"She's staying off-campus. She said something about not wanting to be bothered by a bunch of frat boys."

"Her loss. More for us, right?" Cindy said with a wink.

There was a knock at the door. Chris opened it, revealing a young man with thinning, brown hair. He had a clipboard in one hand and a stack of posters in the other.

"I... I'm sorry if I'm interrupting you guys," he said. "I'm the RA, Norman Argyle." He reached out and shook Chris's hand. "You are, uh, Delacroix and Bell, right?"

"Chris and Cindy, yeah," Chris said.

"Sorry. That's what I meant. There's a floor meeting in ten minutes down in the lounge. Are you guys able to make it?"

"I will. Cindy?" Chris asked, turning back.

Cindy outstretched her hand and gave Norman a thumbs-up.

"Great." Norman let out a sigh, as if Chris and Cindy were the first to agree. "It shouldn't take long. I just want to get everyone acclimatized to the place. You know..."

"Like rules and stuff?" Chris asked.

"Exactly. Sometimes things get a little wild during the first couple of months." Norman smiled awkwardly, looking like someone who had never done anything wild in his entire life.

"Are you coming?" Cindy asked from across the room.

"I... yes. I'm the one holding the meeting. I think I said that," Norman said.

"Great," Cindy said.

Norman gave a stiff nod. He turned to leave, but stopped after taking a step. He reached for the doorframe and knocked again.

"Sorry. I don't want to be rude, but we had a noise complaint last night about your room. If you could try to keep it down...," Norman trailed off.

"I think that was me," Chris said, chuckling to distract from the blush that was growing on her cheeks.

"She had this crazy weird nightmare last night," Cindy added.

"Nothing like that has ever happened to me before. I'm sorry if it kept people up."

"We have a good campus psychologist available, if you want. Is this your first time away from home?"

"Yeah," Chris said.

"A lot of people have bad dreams their first time. I... I'm sure it's just nerves. If either of you ever need me for anything, my room's on the other side of the hall."

"Thanks."

Norman smiled as he closed the door, leaving Chris and Cindy alone. Cindy threw herself on her bed and started giggling.

"That's why I love coed dorms. He was so cute," Cindy said.

"You think so?" Chris hadn't thought he was much to look at.

"Do you have a boyfriend?" Cindy asked.

"No." Chris tapped on her underdeveloped chest. "I get confused for a boy more than I attract them."

"Whatever. Cute indie boys love the pixie look. Stick with me and we'll have a whole lot of fun this year."

"Whatever you say, Boss," Chris said, giving Cindy a mock salute.

The two of them strolled over to the lounge a few minutes later. The couches and chairs were all full, and they had to satisfy themselves with leaning on the wall near the entrance. It suited Chris fine because the room smelled like bleach with an undercurrent of vomit. At least the hallway only somewhat smelled of urine. Norman took the crowd through each and every rule of the dorm in excruciating detail. Even Cindy started yawning after the first half-an-hour. Chris admired his attention to detail – it reminded her of Luca – but her admiration could only carry her so far. When he began describing the routes used by garbage trucks, Chris nudged Cindy. She eyed the door. Cindy nodded. Chris waited for Norman to turn his back to them before grabbing Cindy's sleeve and running outside the door. The two ran all the way to the stairs and down to the street, laughing all the way down.

"Lunch?" Chris asked between breaths when they hit the street.

"I know just the place."

Cindy took Chris to a small campus pub called Sullivan's. It was a little past 1:00 p.m. when they arrived, but there was still a healthy amount of students hanging out in the booths and bar. A few of the lights in Sullivan's were burnt out, which left uneven light over the bar. It hid some of the grime. Cindy waved to the bartender as she brought Chris to a booth in the back where some of the larger shadows lingered.

"I bus tables here on weekends," Cindy said.

"Is it a popular place?" Chris asked.

"They 'forget' to card a lot, so it's a great freshman place. Do you drink beer? I'll order us some beer." Cindy glanced over her shoulder and raised two fingers.

The bartender pointed at her and nodded. Cindy didn't look a day over 18. Chris guessed she was serious about Sullivan's lax standards toward liquor laws.

"So? Tell me about it," Cindy asked.

"What?"

"The nightmare. It sounded really bad. You were rolling around, screaming until I woke you up."

"I don't know. It's hard to remember it all." Chris sighed. "I was strapped to a table and a guy cut into me."

"Like surgery?"

"Yeah, but there was more to it. There were these black claws that were attached to these horrible hands, and the guy who cut into me – he wore this porcelain mask like something you'd find in a horror movie."

"No wonder you were screaming."

"Can I tell you something?" Chris asked, putting on a fake smile as the bartender brought their drinks over.

"Sure, what?"

"It was really scary, but there was something familiar about it, like I'd seen it before. What's worse, parts of it felt... I don't know... right. Does that make sense?"

"Not really." Cindy laughed as she took a long drink of her beer. "But it was just a dream. You probably had some crossed wires or something. I read that sometimes you're having a few dreams at once without realizing it."

"That's probably it," Chris said hopefully.

"You excited about class tomorrow?" Cindy asked.

"I can't wait. It's a good schedule, too. All I have is Criminology and English tomorrow. That's not bad for Fridays."

"I think it's going to be a good year," Cindy said, smiling.

Chris smiled back. Everything was exactly how she pictured it would be, and soon she'd have her first real taste of academia. She looked into her perspiring glass of beer and smiled. Cindy was right – it was going to be a very good year.

CHAPTER 6

Chris's first class was Criminology, which was the course that she was most keen on taking. She stayed up all night when course registration opened up online to make sure she was first in line to sign up. Sitting in the auditorium, she wondered if that was necessary. There were only about thirty students scattered throughout the room. Chris sat about midway down, in the center of an aisle. She had gotten there twenty minutes early, a special feat for her since the class was at 8:30 a.m. and Chris was the definition of a late-riser. Chris had formed a station around what she considered the 'optimum seat'. She had her computer in front of her. Two text books sat at her right and she had a notebook with pencils, pens, and various tabs to her left. She wasn't planning on missing anything.

The professor barged through the door five minutes late. Her hair was wet, though there hadn't been rain in weeks. She clutched a messy bundle of papers in her hands, which she sloughed off onto the podium. The chattering around the room silenced. After a few minutes of double checking her notes, she began the class.

"A man's family is kidnapped," the professor said. "The kidnappers show up at the man's home. They tell the man to kill someone or they'll kill his family, and they'll be watching him so he can't go to the police. The man goes out and does the deed. He gets arrested the next day for murder. Is he guilty?"

Chris's hand shot up so fast, she felt her shoulder snap.

"Yes. Name?" the professor asked.

"Chris."

"What's your answer?"

"He can't be guilty because he didn't have a choice. The system can't expect him to kill himself or his family, so the guilty people are the kidnappers."

"Okay. No choice. Remember, I'm not asking if the kidnappers were guilty," the professor said. "Any other answers?"

A young man with curly brown hair raised his hand. He was the only one in the first row and all he had before him was a single sheet of paper.

"Yes. Name?"

"Michael Snow."

"Okay, Michael."

"He's guilty. The whole idea that he doesn't have choice is bullshit. God is clear about murdering innocent people, and His word is what our laws are based on."

"So you're saying he should have let his family die?" Chris shouted.

Michael turned around to address Chris directly.

"No, of course not. He should have saved his family from the kidnappers himself instead of murdering an innocent stranger."

"What if his solution to saving his family was murdering the kidnappers? Would he still be guilty?" the professor asked.

"It would be self-defense, because the kidnappers threatened his family. They aren't innocent," Michael said.

"Killing the other guy was self-defense," Chris blurted.

"But where would that get him?" Michael replied.

"You've both brought up some interesting points," the professor said. "The first question is what is needed to qualify as murder according to law. If it was just killing, we'd consider all soldiers to be murderers. The second question is how do we separate guilt from defenses. Can someone be guilty of a crime, but not be punished for it because they have a legitimate defense, and what could that defense be? You both suggested self-defense. Chris, can you claim self-defense over other people?"

"I don't know," Chris said, her breathing short.

"And Michael, what you're suggesting is vigilantism. What's the line the law makes between vigilante killing and self-defense?"

"Sometimes people have to do what's right, even if it's against the law," Michael said.

"Hollywood would agree with you." The professor raised her voice. "But our laws are not based on action movie logic. I'm going to ask you that question again at the end of the course, after you've learned a thing or two about criminal law. You'll be interested in how your perception changes over the year."

Chris scribbled that last bit in her notebook and circled it several times. She looked down at Michael. His scrap of paper hadn't been touched.

After class, Chris decided to call her father. He'd been pretty good about giving her some space, probably because of Luca, but Chris felt like hearing his voice. When he picked up, she could feel his boundless enthusiasm seeping through the phone.

"What's going on, Honey?" Cecil asked.

"Just finished my first class."

"That's great! How was it?"

"I really liked it. The professor is way smarter than my high school teachers. There was this one guy, though. He wouldn't stop challenging the professor all class."

"Oh yeah?"

"We got into a kind of fight at the beginning," Chris said. "I kind of felt like a jerk."

"Aggression can be good. You need to look at it differently," Cecil replied.

"Yeah?"

"Think of him like prey. You need to jump on him as soon as he exposes himself. Every time he says something stupid, you should cut right into him. Deflate his ego a bit."

"You think? I thought maybe I should just let him shoot his mouth off," Chris said.

"Trust me. Everyone else in the class is probably as annoyed as you. Take him down and you'll be a hero."

"I guess that makes sense. Thanks."

"You want to come home for dinner tonight?" Cecil asked.

"I don't know."

"Alice is coming. Please? I promise spaghetti."

"All right, Dad. Sure."

"Great. Come over at six."

At the end of the day, Chris jumped on the bus that led back out to the suburbs where she'd grown up. The whole day, her altercation with Michael had continued to repeat in her head. Was he justifying murder? Was it okay to kill people who didn't qualify as innocent? She had many questions, and a few snarky comebacks she wished she'd thought of earlier, but she had no interest in seeing him again. She hoped he'd drop the class, since he obviously didn't think he had anything to learn.

There was a bus stop close to the house and Chris couldn't help but feel off at the sight of the familiar yellow house on the hill. It felt weird going back so soon, even though it was just for dinner. The smell of slightly burned spaghetti sauce and garlic assaulted Chris's nose as soon as she got into the house. There was clinking in the kitchen. She stepped down a short set of stairs into the sunken family room, then up the other side, where the kitchen was. Cecil was manning the stove and jumped when Chris knocked on the table.

"Hey, Honey. You're early," he said. He grabbed her for a crushing hug, which she was forced to wiggle her way out of.

"It's six, Dad," Chris replied.

"Oh." Cecil squinted at the time on the oven clock. "I lost track of time. Sorry."

"Do you need help?"

"Don't worry about me. Can you text Alice and see what her ETA is?"

"Sure," Chris said.

She walked back to the family room and flopped down on the couch. She turned on the television and texted Alice. Chris frowned when Alice texted back. She hadn't even left. Chris didn't know what she expected. Alice was always late. At least now she couldn't make Chris late, too. A phone vibrated. Chris looked over and saw Cecil's phone face up on the table in front of her. There was a message from someone named Maxine. It said, *Need to see you, now*. Chris smiled. She'd never known her father to have a girlfriend.

"Dad, someone named Maxine is looking for you," Chris sang out, teasing him.

"Shit," Cecil shouted.

He ran out of the kitchen and snatched up his phone, fingers clumsily fumbling with the screen.

"I'm sure it's just a wrong number," he said.

"Whatever you say, Dad." Chris smirked, part of her proud that her father was spending time with women who weren't Luca.

Alice showed up an hour later. She strolled in and flung herself on the couch next to Chris.

"Dad still cooking?" Alice asked.

"Yeah," Chris replied. "Did you have classes today?"

"Chemistry and Chem Lab," Alice said.

"How were they?"

"Boring as shit. I've been doing way more advanced stuff for years. They were just going over molecular theory today. How can you even get into university without knowing that stuff? At least the facilities are better than the garage. How do you like wasting your life in the liberal arts?"

"I actually like not gutting animals," Chris said.

"It's called dissection and it's how you learn."

"You're so sick." Chris laughed. "I'm just glad I'm not going to run into any of your experiments in the fridge anymore."

"Cry baby."

"Shut up," Chris said, lightly tapping Alice on the cheek with the back of her hand.

"Have you 'saved the world' yet?" Alice said. She twirled a strand of her pink hair around her finger.

"I'm working on it."

Dinner was served with a side of questions. Cecil didn't let a single thing slip. Alice was visibly annoyed at each question, often audibly sighing. She only perked up when Cecil began asking questions about her experiments, much to Chris's dismay. Cecil always encouraged Alice's dissections. He'd even bought her a few scalpels when she turned sixteen. Chris smiled every time her father's phone buzzed. The mystery woman must be really anxious to get his attention. His face would contort as if someone had jabbed a pen against his ribs with each text. Alice didn't pick up on it as she stuffed her face with food. When Cecil was distracted by the phone, Chris posed the question of the kidnappers to her family.

"Call the police," Alice said immediately.

"He can't call the police. They're watching him," Chris said.

"That's what they said. I wouldn't trust them. They're just bluffing to keep you from doing what you should be doing."

"That's not the point of the question. What do you think, Dad?"

Cecil lowered his fork. He pressed his hand on his chin before smiling at his daughters.

"What you do is take one of the kidnappers. You force him to tell you where they're keeping your family, then you go rescue them," he said.

"That's not the point. The question is whether he's guilty of murder," Chris said.

"What do you mean by guilty?" Cecil said.

"That's what the professor said. Apparently, we're going to learn that."

"I don't think that's something you learn, dear, but good luck. It sounds like a fun class."

Chris was about to respond when the doorbell began sounding off repeatedly. It was like a petulant child was playing a prank. Cecil's face turned white. He didn't even have a chance to get up when the door flung open. In came a woman in her mid-twenties. She yawned upon entry. Her slicked back hair was light blonde and cropped at the nape of her neck. She wore a leather jacket over a white t-shirt and jeans. The woman glanced at the family sitting by the railing next to the sunken living room on the other end of the room. She walked to the couch and sat down. Chris noticed Alice straightening her posture, smiling slyly.

"Cecil!" the woman yelled.

Cecil practically jumped out of his seat. He ran down and tried to pull the woman out of her seat.

"You think you can just fucking screen my calls?" the woman said.

"It's not Thursday. I'm busy," Cecil replied.

"Aren't you going to introduce me?"

"No."

"Hey girlies," the woman yelled over at the twins. "You guys and me need to have a talk about Cecil, here. Have you ever heard of a Fiend –"

"This is Maxine," Cecil yelled over her. "She works with Luca and me. She's just coming over to remind me that we have a lot of work to do tonight."

"Yeah. He's giving me a raise," Maxine said.

"No I'm not," Cecil whispered.

"We can talk about it here, or you can get your ass down to Tartarus and get Fen to check the budget. I'm fine either way."

Cecil let out a groan that verged on a growl.

"I'm sorry, girls. I need to go to work. Stay as long as you want."

"It's all right," the twins said out of habit. Cecil getting called away to work was a regular occurrence growing up.

"Nice meeting you. I'm sure we'll chat soon," Maxine said, a grin stretched long on her face.

With that, Cecil managed to pull Maxine off the couch. He ushered her out, glancing back at Chris and Alice as he did so. When the door slammed shut, Chris turned to Alice.

"What was that about?" Chris asked.

"Who knows?" Alice said.

"Yeah, because you were too distracted by Maxine," Chris said.

"I'm only human."

"You don't think that was weird?" Chris asked.

"Lots of things are weird. I don't let it bother me."

CHAPTER 7

Chris had been certain that cracks would start to appear in Cindy's cheerful façade, but every morning she was greeted by the most oppressively happy person she had ever met. It was Monday, and they were going to the one class they shared, Symbolism and the Occult. Chris wasn't sure if she would stay in the class. She couldn't think of how the course would help her in the future, but a voice in the back of her head goaded her on to register. It turned out to be a popular class – she'd only gotten in after three other students dropped it.

"This is going to be so much fun," Cindy said.

"You know what they say: you haven't partied until you've partied Symbolism and the Occult-style," Chris quipped.

"Do they really say that?" Cindy had no ear for Chris's dry sense of humor.

"Just a joke."

"Oh. My sister, Emily, said the Symbolism and the Occult professor always invites students out to the museum after the first class. You're going, right?"

"Maybe. Let's see how the course goes first," Chris replied.

"Why'd you decide to take this course, anyway?" Cindy asked. "I know. You're really dark, right? I bet you were a Goth in high school."

"Sorry to disappoint, but I try to stay away from black and white colors," Chris said. "I don't know why I took the course. I guess I thought it would be fun."

"I'm totally right. You've got a dark side."

Cindy began making ghostly noises and wiggling her fingers at Chris until she was cut off by a man stepping in front of the podium at the head of class.

Professor Glenn Moore clearly took pride in his appearance. His perfectly tailored tweed jacket, paired with a checked collared shirt and slim tie, cultivated an image of intellectual authority. Chris was instantly mesmerized by the confident man. He looked young for a professor, but he was totally in command of the podium. Every movement, every glance, and every tiny smile caused Chris's stomach to flutter. There was no way she was missing that museum trip.

"Ghouls, goblins, and things that go bump in the night," Moore began. "No matter where you travel around the globe, every culture is obsessed with the supernatural. Over the course of human history, we have developed countless demons, devils and deities, each with its own story, symbols and significance. In the following weeks, we will be examining these stories and symbols, and I will try my hardest to convince you that what we're doing is significant."

Chris was captivated through the rest of his lecture. Her eyes felt dry from staring at him so intently. At the end of the class, Moore shouted over the backpacks being unzipped.

"Before you go, anyone who is interested may join me at the Gerstmann Museum at seven to examine their exhibit on Greco-Roman religion."

As students piled out the door, Cindy turned to Chris. "So, are you coming?"

"Definitely," Chris said, almost equaling Cindy's enthusiasm.

The Gerstmann Museum was an odd building. It was one of the few in Meridian that was built in the gothic style. The building was a collection of dark corners offset by the nearby red brick buildings for a striking effect. When Chris and Cindy entered the museum, a pleasant, elderly woman directed them to the west wing. Stepping into the correct room, Chris was struck by the sight of a giant lion, fixed in time through the art of taxidermy. A frozen howl was sculpted on its jaws, ready to swallow Chris whole. Beyond its sweeping mane was a bizarre deformity: the horned head of a goat rose from the lion's back. Looking further, Chris saw that the beast's tail wasn't a tail at all, but a snake firmly affixed to its haunches. Chris found the whole thing grossly fascinating.

She jumped when she felt a hand firmly rest on her shoulder.

"This is the Chimera," Professor Moore's voice echoed along the empty halls of the museum.

Chris gulped.

"They're fascinating, the minds that came up with these mythical Frankenstein's monsters." He took his hand away. "It looks like eight students showed up - better than usual." He flashed Chris a smile and, she could have sworn, a wink.

Chris stuck close to Cindy as they toured the museum. Professor Moore regaled them with stories of monsters and myths while they walked.

"Do you think any of these things ever existed, Professor?" Cindy asked.

A hot, red blush spread like wildfire over Chris's face and she pulled away slightly, hoping her charming professor wouldn't associate her with her naïve roommate. She instantly regretted the motion – why was she so wrapped up in what he thought?

"No." He chuckled, shaking his head. "You see, most of these creatures act as an explanation for the unknown." He gestured toward a painting depicting a woman in the grip of a muscular man in a Greek helmet. "For example, the story of Persephone was used by the ancient Greeks to explain the revolving seasons. I don't think that any real gods are going to be snatching you off to another world."

Cindy's shoulders sagged in disappointment.

"But some creatures seem like they were invented to scare people," Chris chimed in, hoping she wasn't making a fool of herself.

To her everlasting relief, Professor Moore smiled.

"That's absolutely right. Many mythological stories were used in the same way we tell ghost stories. Good observation. What's your name?"

"Chris," she responded weakly.

"I look forward to seeing you in class, Chris," he said to the awestruck girl.

After one of the most fascinating hours of Chris's young life, Professor Moore concluded the tour. The rest of the students quickly dispersed, and the professor wasn't far behind. Cindy and Chris stepped outside to find the evening dark and empty.

"I'm meeting my sister for some drinks in Gloucester. Do you want to come?" Cindy offered.

"No, thanks," Chris replied. "I think I'm going to turn in early."

Shoving her hands into her pockets, Chris headed for the dorms. Her eyes were down on the dry pavement as she walked, shuffling to the side and stepping through the crowd. She was replaying the evening in her mind, considering her words and the response she'd garnered from the professor. Moore was obviously a man of great knowledge and charm, and he had noticed her. Chris was so lost in reverie that she failed to notice she'd arrived at a red light, and slammed directly into the paused figure in front of her.

"I'm sorry," Chris said, cheeks blushing at her mistake. A sweat broke out over her forehead as she saw the recipient of her bump – Professor Glenn Moore.

"It's Chris, right?" he asked.

"Yes, sir," Chris said, automatically reverting to the most formal of language.

"Are you heading back to campus?"

"To the Old Dorm."

"I'm heading that direction. Would you like some company?"

"S-sure," Chris stuttered as the walking sign illuminated. She was half-excited at the chance to make a second impression, and half-terrified to undo the positive interactions from earlier by acting like a total idiot.

"Are you from Meridian?" Moore asked.

"Yeah... I didn't get too far, did I?" she said, aiming for self-deprecating and landing on self-effacing.

"There's nothing wrong with that," Moore insisted. "Not everyone gets to travel for school, though if you get the opportunity, I'd recommend seeing as much of the world as you are able. Travel can make such a difference in your perspective."

"I thought about applying to a school in Texas."

"I was thinking more of Scandinavia or France, but Texas is nice, too. At least they don't have our north eastern winters to contend with."

"Oh, yeah." Chris shook herself mentally. Of course Moore meant international travel. He was obviously very worldly.

"I'm just joking. The east coast isn't that bad. Have you been enjoying your classes so far?" Moore inquired.

"Yeah. They've been really interesting."

"That's good to hear. Some students don't like how academic everything is. They want things to be more hands-on."

"I definitely want to be hands-on. I figured this would just be the beginning."

"It might be. Sometimes I have students help me with my research. Would you be interested in that? I know it can seem a little silly, monsters and what not, but you might be surprised how deep an impact we can have in society."

"I'd love to help out. Anything you want." Chris realized by the burn in her cheeks that she was blushing, and hoped he couldn't tell in the dark.

"I'll keep you in mind next time something comes up." Moore sighed. "First year of university - I'm envious, actually. You learn so much about yourself when you first leave the nest. I've pretty much exhausted all there is to me. I wonder what you'll find." He smiled, baring his perfect teeth.

Chris blushed and returned her gaze to the road. The heavy topics seemed to recede into the night and rest of the walk mostly devolved into small talk. Professor Moore walked her up to the steps of the Old Dorm as if he were her date for the evening, making sure she got home safely. Chris pushed that thought as far from her mind as she could.

"Have a nice night," he said, waving. "If you ever need any advice or help adjusting to university, just come by my office. My door is always open."

CHAPTER 8

After a few weeks, Chris's life settled into a pleasant routine. Every time her professors spoke, she felt like they were whispering a secret just for her. Criminology was becoming tiresome, however. Michael in the first row seemed intent on challenging everything the professor said. Why couldn't he ever just listen?

When her last class was over for the day, Chris hurried to the campus food court. She hadn't seen Alice since their dinner with Cecil and she was keen to prepare notes about campus life. Chris arrived exactly when they were supposed to meet. Alice showed up nearly an hour later, to Chris's extreme irritation.

"Hey there, stranger," Alice said as she flung herself down on the seat opposite her sister. "I see you haven't flunked out yet."

"Very funny. How's life off-campus?"

"What's not to like?" Alice said as she tapped her fingers on the desk. "I can dress however I like and do whatever I want without everyone staring at me or calling me a freak. I'm not even the girl with the weirdest hair in my biology lab."

"Haven't you always done whatever you wanted?" Chris asked.

Alice rolled her eyes. "Please. Luca never let us get away with anything. I've decided to compensate by now doing everything."

"Aren't you so independent," Chris said. "How are the roommates?"

"Can't say. I've been too busy to do much socializing. They're planning on taking me out tonight, so we'll see."

"There's always more room in the dorms."

"Gross. You can enjoy being in a place with rules. I, for one, am glad to actually be free."

"I'm plenty free," Chris said.

"Can you drink in your room?"

"No."

"There you go," Alice grinned.

"Classes getting any better?"

"Maybe a little. You?"

"So far so good." Chris thought for a moment before smiling. "There's this one prof that's kind of cool."

"I bet." Alice giggled at the stars in Chris's eyes. "I call maid of honor."

"It's not like that." Chris scowled at a smiling Alice. "I just think he's a great professor."

"I remember the last time you had a boyfriend. You pulled his hair and threw him into a sandbox," Alice said.

"That doesn't count. I was six."

"What I'm saying is you need to get laid."

It was Chris's turn to smirk. "Is that what you're planning to do tonight? Troll the clubs?"

"More or less," Alice said, joining her sister's grin.

* * *

Hours later, Alice was trying to decide how little she was going to wear to the club. Her roommates had promised to get her in, and she wasn't going to waste the opportunity by being modest. She stepped into one of her more scandalous dresses. As she was adjusting her long, pink hair in the mirror, she heard the sound of glass breaking downstairs, followed by an ear-shattering scream. The whole house raced to the kitchen to investigate.

"Oh. My. God. Why is there a dead rat in the fridge?" Alice's roommate, Courtney, wailed.

"If I didn't keep it cold, it'd go bad before I got a chance to dig into it tomorrow," Alice said matter-of-factly.

"You're going to eat it?" Courtney asked.

"Of course I'm not going to eat it, dummy." Alice shook her head, unable to comprehend Courtney's confusion. "I'm going to dissect it."

Sam broke from the girls who rushed to console Courtney in the corner.

"New house rule: no dead animals. Is that okay with you?" Sam said.

Alice cocked her head like a confused spaniel. She could see that the other girls were serious about the rat issue, for whatever reason, and decided not to push her luck.

"Fine, whatever." Alice stomped upstairs to finish preening.

The ride to the club was noticeably awkward. Courtney refused to even look at Alice, forcing Sam to sit between them in the back seat while the other three girls from the house crowded into the front seat.

"Where are we going?" Alice asked, slapping the back of the driver's seat repeatedly.

"Room 42," Sam said, pulling Alice's hands away from the seat.

The last time Alice had tried to sneak into a club, she barely managed to glimpse the dance floor before being roughly ejected by the bouncers.

"You guys sure you can get me in?" Alice asked.

"Don't worry. We know the guy at the door." Sam smiled reassuringly.

After parking, the girls strode to the club with the confidence only possible in a pack. Alice enjoyed the brisk fall air on her skin, content in her skimpy choice of attire. A large line had formed outside, full of men and women in various states of undress, anxiously waiting to be let into the club. The housemates marched directly to the front of the line.

"Hey, Richard," Courtney flirted with the large man guarding the door.

"Oh, hey girls. Come on in," the man replied, nodding at them as they pranced into the club.

Alice basked in the envious glances from the line.

"I could get used to this," Alice whispered to Sam, who giggled as she wrapped her arm around the pink-haired girl's shoulders.

Inside, the group immediately scattered. In less than a minute, Alice was completely alone. The loud music, the lights, and the horde of writhing bodies overloaded her senses. Looking around, she didn't see anyone she knew, but she wasn't about to let that ruin her night. She weighed her options and decided to scope out the bar. As she approached the counter, the bartender poured her a drink.

"I didn't order this," she yelled over the music.

"That guy over there bought it for you." The bartender gestured at a young, attractive man nearby.

Alice grabbed the drink and nervously finished it in a gulp. Another immediately replaced it. She smiled at the young man, who waved back at her. He moved, sitting closer to her.

"Name's Ted," he shouted.

"Alice," she responded between sips of the second drink.

"Do you come here often?"

"No, I've never been at a club before," she admitted. "It's so loud!"

"Do you want to get out of here?" He placed his hand on her back and started rubbing in circles.

"No, I'm with a group and we should stick together," she responded, awkwardly pushing his hand away.

"I don't see anyone," he said, looking around. "You accepted those drinks, right? You wouldn't have done that if you weren't interested."

Alice felt a twinge of guilt, unaware of any nightclub etiquette.

"We could dance, maybe?" she offered, hoping to appease him.

"Come back to my place and we'll have some fun." He got bolder with his hands, creeping one up her thigh.

Alice jerked away from him. Etiquette be damned - she knew drinks weren't sex coupons. One of the bouncers noticed the situation, but before he could intervene Alice ran out of an employee exit into the adjoining alley.

"Come on. I'm just playing around," Ted said as he pursued her into the quiet alley.

"I'm not interested," she spat.

"It's all right." He grabbed her hand. "We don't have to tell your friends." He pulled her close.

Alice twisted in his arms, trying to escape.

He raised his hands, backing off. "See, I'm a nice guy. We won't do anything you don't want to, okay?"

Alice nodded, backing up against the wall. He advanced on her again.

"I just want to make you feel good," he said, pawing over her side, as his right leg moved between hers.

"Listen, asshole," she yelled, shoving him away, "Unless you can grow a pair of tits in the next five minutes, I'm not interested, so fuck off."

He looked at her like a hunter sizing up his prey. She stood with her hands on her hips, waiting for him to leave. Instead, he pushed Alice against the wall and ripped at her top, his left hand finding its way underneath her skirt. She spat at him as she struggled against his grip. Enraged by her resistance, he slapped her across the face. Alice's heart raced and time seemed to freeze as he continued to molest her. She felt like her head was wrapped in cotton. Snapping out of her trance, she swiftly kneed him in the groin.

"You whore," he whimpered as he doubled over, grasping at his crotch.

Alice grabbed the back of his head and pulled him roughly over to the wall. Without hesitation, she slammed his face into the filthy brick. He wailed and tried to free himself, but with each successive impact, he became less and less able to buck her off.

"I told you," *thump*, "I'm not," *thump*, "interested," *thump*, "so fuck," *thump*, "off," Alice shrieked in wretched fury.

When she let go of him, she was gasping for air and frozen in panic as she gaped at him. Ted collapsed on the ground, his face a mask of blood. With a few guilty glances back, Alice bolted down the end of the alley and into the neon-lit street.

* * *

Not far away, Luca walked briskly through the fall's chill to her car.

"I'm never letting Fen talk me into another blind date," Luca cursed under her breath as she opened her car door.

Her phone jangled to life. The ringtone was a profanity-laced rap song that Alice had programmed into it for herself. Luca had no idea how to change it back.

"It's late, Alice. What do you need?" Luca asked.

"Luca, you need to help me."

The young woman was hysterical, stopping Luca in her tracks.

"What happened?" she asked briskly.

"I think I just killed a guy," Alice said.

"You think, or you're sure? Take a moment before you answer."

"I don't know. He attacked me, and I hit him. Something came over me and I couldn't stop hitting him. Oh God, Luca, he stopped moving and I just ran," Alice said.

"Don't panic," Luca said slowly and deliberately. "Try to calm your breathing. You need to tell me exactly where you left him."

"I don't know. I was in, uh, Room 42 with my roommates, and I ran out an exit into an alleyway."

"Did anyone see you?" Luca spoke calmly.

There was a pause. "No. At least, I don't think so."

"I'll take care of it. Go home, clean yourself up, and don't tell anybody what happened. Okay?"

She could hear Alice trying to stop hyperventilating with little success.

"Okay," Alice whispered.

Nobody had entered the alleyway since Alice escaped. Ted had managed to pull himself up against the wall, but he was slipping in and out of consciousness. His face was drenched with blood and his left eye swollen shut. His weak, gurgling calls for help could not escape the alley. His good eye shot open at the sound of footsteps slowly making their way toward him. He looked up and saw a tall woman in a black suit kneeling in front of him.

"Who did this to you?" The woman asked.

'Alice' and 'pink hair' were the only words she understood from his garbled speech. Her face betrayed no emotion as she stared at him.

"That's too bad," she said coldly.

Ted watched as the woman stood up. She looked down at him and with a stiff, practiced kick to his head, Luca broke the young man's neck. She knelt down again and reached into his pocket, retrieving his wallet.

"Nobody messes with my girls," she explained to Ted's lifeless body.

CHAPTER 9

Detectives Saunders and Morales walked along the tacky, carpeted hallway of the faculty wing of Arcadia Hall at Meridian University. Julian knocked at a door covered in yellowing cartoons and newspaper clippings about witchcraft and demons.

"Come in," called a voice from behind the door.

In the office sat the characteristically well-groomed Professor Moore. Julian looked around in fascination, noticing that every spare inch in the office was occupied by potted greenery. Moore looked up from his work and followed the young detective's gaze.

"Do you like the plants? It's a hobby of mine," the professor explained.

"Mr. Moore, we..." Larry started.

"It's Doctor, actually," Moore interrupted.

"Dr. Moore." Larry frowned, "As we discussed on the phone, we have some questions for you concerning an investigation. We believe your expertise may be helpful."

"Of course, Detective. Anything I can do to be of service."

Larry gestured toward Julian, who retrieved a bundle of printed photos from his bag and placed them in front of the professor.

"What can you tell us about pentagrams like the ones in these photos?" Julian asked.

The professor studied the photographs intently for several seconds before looking back at the detectives.

"The pentagram is an ancient symbol, dating back as far as early Mesopotamian cultures."

Larry shot the fidgeting Julian an irritated look as the professor lectured them.

"Throughout history," Moore continued, "It has been used as a symbol in many different religions, sometimes as a benevolent sign, and other times harboring a darker tone. In the Americas, thanks in part to Hollywood, it is often associated with Satanism and neo-Pagan cults."

Julian perked up at the word cult, but his partner's stern gaze kept him quiet. His head was filled with romantic fantasies of the two detectives unraveling the strange and mysterious workings of a secret society devoted to some mad god. Talking to the professor had been his idea, though he knew Larry was hoping Moore would crush Julian's theories once and for all.

"Is there any significance in digging up the dead for any of these cults?" Larry asked dryly.

Julian tried to look casual, but his ears were ringing with excitement.

"As I said, the connection is primarily artificial. The pentagram is often adopted by misguided teenagers trying to frighten their parents or by new-age goddess worshippers, but not much else these days. I don't know of any cult that would fit in line with a serial grave robber." Moore's smile reached wide on his face. "You are asking me about the Snatcher case, correct?"

"Do you know of any pentagram-using cult that may be present in the city?" Larry asked, ignoring the professor's question.

"No, I don't. This is really the kind of thing you see only in movies. If your grave robber is leaving pentagrams at the scene of his crimes, I imagine he's more likely trying to scare you than to please some demonic prophet. I hope that's not a disappointment to you."

"We may have further questions for you at a later date," Larry declared as he marched out of the room.

"Thank you for your time, Dr. Moore," Julian said before racing off after his fleeing partner.

Julian met Larry in their car, which was illegally parked outside Arcadia Hall. Larry was reclining in the passenger seat, his lips stretched thin and wide, a silent sign of disapproval. His phone was balanced on the dash. Julian started the car and pulled away from the curb.

"Waste of time," Larry said.

"Don't be like that. It supports your theory that it isn't a cult," Julian replied.

"It *isn't* a cult. All that did was make us look like ten cent rookies, which I'm sure will get back to the precinct."

"Who cares?"

"You should," Larry said. He sighed. "I'm only looking out for you. My reputation's already shot. You could still have a career in this department."

"What are you talking about?"

"Looney Larry?" Larry asked. Glancing over at Julian's blank expression, he sighed again. "Never heard anybody call me that? I guess they don't talk about me much anymore. Things happened. I got... I got believing some stuff that wasn't real and I got real pushy about it. Just like how you're starting to be real pushy about this whole cult thing."

"I heard your partner died," Julian said, his voice low. "Does that have anything to do with it?"

"Yeah. It does. Drop the cult thing. Weird stuff doesn't happen in Meridian."

As Larry spoke, his phone lit up with a text. Larry quickly snatched the phone from the dash. Julian didn't see the message, but it was from someone named 'Lady Black'.

"Drop me off at the precinct," Larry said as he read the phone. Every bit of color had vanished from his face. "Something came up."

"Girlfriend?" Julian said with a laugh.

"Shut up, Julian, and hurry."

Julian had only known Larry the few months they'd been partners, but the idea of Larry having secret liaisons with a woman brought a smile to his lips. The older man wasn't even married, so why sneak around? As Julian drove, his mind kept going back to the pentagrams on the tombstones. They obviously meant something to someone. Commercial Crimes had thought it was just some kids at first, but the murder ruled out drunken tomfoolery. So far, none of the forensics had been able to point them to anything valuable. The shovels, left at each scene, were recently bought at different hardware stores in town, their price tags still affixed. None had usable fingerprints. The method of digging also varied from time to time, as if the Snatcher was deliberately altering his methods, or perhaps there were multiple Snatchers, working together.

This was the theory Julian favored, but he had nothing to back it up. And why would anyone steal so many bodies? Larry guessed it was an underground medical supply trade – something the older detective had seen crop up back in the eighties. Julian went back to the pentagrams. Scavengers don't go out of their way to put pentagrams on gravestones.

* * *

After Julian dropped him off, Larry got in his own car and drove to an abandoned factory in Westborough, a district of Meridian. He muttered curses under his breath the entire way, and his right hand shook as he shifted into park. Stepping out of his car, he felt a chill going down his spine. The building had been boarded up for the last five years. He hated meeting there. It was dark, it smelled, and he never knew if he'd walk back out in one piece. Rummaging through his trunk, Larry pulled out a flashlight. He swore when he turned it on: the batteries were dying, and only a dusky light emanated from its face. He crept into the factory, jumping every time a rat scuttled by or a shadow seemed to move.

"You're late," a voice said from an elevated walkway in front of the detective. A tall woman with short, black hair dressed in a suit stepped out of the shadows.

"I'm sorry," he said. Seeing her eyes narrow, he tried to calm himself, taking long, deliberate breaths. "So, Lady Black, what can I do for you?"

"See that the investigation of the body found behind Room 42 doesn't proceed." She remained expressionless, making the hairs on the back of Larry's head stand up.

"Why?" Larry asked, stepping forward in a bold breach of long-established etiquette.

"That's not how this works."

"I think – I'm sorry – I heard about that homicide. It was just a kid. Who did it?"

"What makes you think we know who the perpetrator was?" the woman said.

"I don't mean to overreach. It's just... can't Ramon or Stewart do this for you?"

The woman leaned against the railing. She stared at him for a full minute before making a sound.

"This is important, and you're the one we've chosen for this job. Do it, or there will be consequences."

"I'm sorry. I'll take care of it," Larry said.

"I thought so. Keep up the good work, detective. Your compensation is in the usual place." She turned and disappeared into the shadows.

Larry's shoulders sagged when she left. The woman, whom half of homicide knew as Lady Black, was someone Larry feared disappointing. The detectives who failed her never fared very well. He couldn't ask them about it though, because nobody who crossed Lady Black was ever seen again. Larry knew he needed to keep Julian out of it - the kid didn't need to be involved in something so dirty. Larry's curses grew louder and echoed off the abandoned machinery. He steeled himself and returned to the precinct that night to start the laborious process of covering up a murder.

CHAPTER 10

Chris tossed and turned for what seemed like the entire night. Her first university test was coming up and she'd been up the past two nights studying for it, despite Cindy's constant reassurances that it wouldn't be so bad. Chris didn't want the test to go 'okay'. She wanted to get the best possible mark. Perhaps it was a lingering bit of rivalry between her and Alice for the highest grades in the family? That thought entered Chris's head, but she dismissed it. She needed to be at the top of her class to make sure every future opportunity would be open to her when she figured out how to make a difference. Cecil had always told her to go "all out" when she wanted something. Chris took that advice to heart. At about 5:00 a.m., Chris finally drifted off to sleep, face down on her text book.

Chris woke up tired and cold, laying back in a worn recliner. The world seemed to spin around like she was suffering from motion sickness. The tacky posters on the walls advertising tutoring and non-academic events stoked the fires of memory – Arcadia Hall, a place she visited often during Professor Moore's office hours. What was she doing there?

The moonlight streaming through the window shone a pale green light. Chris stared at that light for a moment. She was dreaming. The light pulled at her memory, hinting at something long forgotten. Chris shook in her chair, yelling at nobody in particular as the dreamscape clouded her mind. A wave of nausea flowed into her stomach. She snapped her eyes shut and leaned back against the chair, willing herself to calm down. When she was sure she could keep the contents of her stomach from spewing forth, Chris sat up to take stock of her surroundings. It was definitely Arcadia Hall, and it was totally devoid of students or professors. The sound of her own breath filled her ears. She knew the calm wouldn't last, so she thought she had better try to get out of here.

She raced to the front door and yanked at the handle. It clanked uselessly, declining to open. Chris peered back, knots forming in her gut. The only other exit was through the basement level. Sighing, Chris began walking toward the stairwell, uncertain of what she was going to find.

The door to the stairwell opened far too easily. There were no windows, and the green glow didn't penetrate through the dark. Chris stepped forward and allowed the door to close behind her. She looked back – the front door was now a solid sheet of concrete, as if a door had never existed in the first place. There was nowhere to go but down, so Chris began descending the stairs. She calmed her breath and kept walking. She could hear her own footsteps clicking against the metal stairs, but something seemed off. She kept walking and listening, trying to determine what seemed wrong about the sound. She kept a steady pace, but her footsteps... they were strange.

She took a risk and slowed her step by just half a beat, and that's when she heard it: another step. There was a second set of footsteps clicking along those stairs, but they had been moving in perfect time with Chris to cover the sound. Chris's hands gripped onto the railing, sweaty palms twisting on the cold metal. The sound stopped suddenly, leaving nothing but dead air and the sounds of Chris's harried breathing.

A light tapping sound, grating and twisting, filled the void in Chris's head. The tapping grew louder, turning into the shrill screech of metal on metal. She kept moving downward, toward the hope of safety. Then she saw something: two large orbs, like eyes, giving off a faint, green glow from the darkness. They were right in front of her. One more step, and Chris would have collided with the monster in the dark. It had been there the whole time, waiting for her and watching. Chris remained very still as the eyes looked into her soul.

Shadows and green light flew up from the bottom of the stairs like some ungodly strobe light was malfunctioning below. It revealed the figure before her - it was a beast with a woman's body, but not a woman's face. Above the neck was a warped and blistered mass of flesh. It was twisted, like someone had pulled too hard on the skin on the left side of the face, dragging its features askew. But it's most distinguishing feature was its claws, long and black. They shone with a metallic hue, reflecting the sickly green light into Chris's eyes. Each finger was twice as long as a normal digit, and each one ended with a razor's edge. They tapped wildly upon the metal railing.

The Beast with the Black Metal Claws' eyes shone brightly, at home under the green light. They revealed little besides the anticipation of capturing the ultimate prize - Chris. It smiled as much as something that deranged could smile, baring yellow, crooked fangs wet with slobber. The Beast's twisted mouth moved as if to say something, but nothing intelligible came out, only husky wheezes and dust.

Chris bolted up the stairs. As she rounded the first corner, four huge scratches ripped into the wall, as if an invisible Beast were flailing around just inches from the fleeing girl. She ducked instinctually as another slash carved through the plaster halfway up the stairs. She saw a door in the wall beside her and identified it as her only chance. The Beast was below and the invisible claws were above, but this was here, right in front of her. She grasped the handle and yelped. In place of a round doorknob was a black metal hand with deep, inky claws, jutting out from the door. It wrapped around her hand in a ghastly handshake. As Chris ripped her hand free, the claws tore deep gashes into her flesh. Whimpering, Chris cradled her bleeding hand against her body. The claw in the door was reaching out for her, searching for her embrace. Chris retreated, avoiding the dripping, red-tipped claws.

She couldn't even catch her breath before the intensifying metallic screeching advanced up the hallway. Again, she realized she had only one option: the third floor. She stumbled up the stairs, blood and sweat dripping from her body as she scrambled. The door was open already, waiting for her. The edges of the frame bent inward. There were jagged pieces of metal dangling down as if the door was a huge metal mouth, ready to tear her limbs off with its rusty teeth. Chris turned back, fearful of the door, but she was met with the snarling face of the Beast with the Black Metal Claws. It reached out and shoved Chris with its black palm, sending her falling back into the gaping mouth of the door, falling into the blackness beyond.

She landed on the floor of a familiar hallway. At the very end, was Professor Moore's office. The light fixtures along the side of the room flickered and dimmed, letting off an electric hum. Chris fell to her knees as long shadows began creeping up the carpet, grasping out for her. She kicked her feet at the shadows and connected with one. Her foot landed with a dull thump upon the shadow and all the blood was sucked from the limb. She felt cold and numbness overtake her legs, like frostbite on a doomed mountaineer. She yanked her leg away from the shadows and felt pins and needles all over as the circulation returned. The lights at the end of the hall slowly went dark so that the shadows were all around her. Just as they overtook her prone form, the lights flickered again. But this time, they filled the hallway with a sickly green glow that made Chris retch.

Chris began carefully down the rows of cheap, wooden doors. She heard moans and scratches coming from behind the first two she passed. She didn't stop to investigate; she didn't dare. The third door creaked and shook as if something was pressing against it. Chris picked up her pace. The fourth door splintered visibly as if hit by a heavy object from the other side. Chris's heart pounded in her chest as she began to jog. The fifth door shattered open, a black metal claw scratched out, and dragged its eviscerating fingers over Chris's torso as she passed, but still she pressed on. She knew she had to get to Moore's office. Somehow, she knew she would find salvation there. It was just a little bit further. The next door broke open entirely. Through the door leapt the Beast with the Black Metal Claws. Its mock perversion of a face formed something similar to a smile as it hurried down the hall. Chris ran full sprint now, the heavy breaths and ghoulish clattering of the Beast propelling her forward.

Halfway down the hall, Chris's foot caught the side of the carpet. She yelped and toppled forward, finding herself on the ground once again. The door to her right broke open at the bottom and a second, identical Beast crawled out, grinning and clacking its claws with abandon. Chris rolled to the side, dodging its death-grip before climbing to her feet and continuing her sprint toward the salvation at the very end of the hall. Each door she passed buckled and broke open with the horrible sound of snapping wood. Each one contained a new Beast, which exploded out and joined the growing pack behind her. Four, five, six of them chased her, each reaching out, desperate to sink their claws into her weak flesh. Chris could feel the brush of air on her neck coming from their cleaving limbs. She was almost there.

The last door on the right blew open just as Chris reached it, knocking her backwards. The Beast within grabbed her wrists and pulled her close. Its breath stunk like fish. Chris trembled and turned her head from its twisted face. She tried to see the end of the hall, to focus on her target. She struggled to free herself from the claws of the Beast, but it held firm. Her eyes were reeling, glancing between the Beasts. They were standing, all with the same smile, watching her with the same eyes. They wouldn't let her see another moment of freedom. The Beast that had her in its grasp opened the door beside Moore's office and threw Chris in.

The door snapped shut. No light penetrated the room. Chris shook her shoulders, testing for the Beast's grip, but found none. It must have let go, she realized. But why? She felt along the wall for a light switch, and when she found one a steady stream of green light broke through the gloom. She wasn't in an office. It was the surgeon's room. The table in the middle of the room was conspicuously empty, as was the stool in the corner, but she wasn't alone. The surgeon stood readying his tools at the back of the room.

"Don't hurt me," Chris begged, as her hand reached behind her for a doorknob that no longer existed.

The surgeon didn't say anything. Instead, he walked forward with a skip in his step and extended his hand, offering her a scalpel.

"No." She pushed it away.

A grunt came from behind the mask as the surgeon shoved his hand forward again, silently insisting she take the scalpel. Chris mistook the shove for a forceful attack and tried to dodge, but he just kept gesturing at her with the infernal scalpel.

"Get back." She picked up the stool from the corner and flung it back and forth it in front of her as a warning.

The surgeon advanced on her, undeterred by the wild swinging of the stool. Chris reared back and slammed the metal stool into the man's mask with every bit of strength she could conjure. At last the surgeon retreated. He dropped the scalpel and felt frantically at his mask, trying to keep it in place, but it was too late. The impact had shattered the porcelain. Huge chunks of painted white glass fell to the floor, leaving his face exposed. When he looked up at Chris, the sight of him terrified her beyond all reason. It was the worst thing she had ever seen.

"Dad?" Chris asked, gaping at the familiar face before her.

The surgeon lunged forward, burying his scalpel into Chris's throat, all the while his exposed eyes, wide and twitching, bore into her own.

Chris awoke screaming and thrashing, desperate to escape her father's blade. She wasn't even aware of Cindy, crouching beside her and rapidly whispering comforting words. Dollops of sweat cascaded in streaks down her face. She pressed her hand against Cindy's and nodded to her, mouth agape as if permanently contorted. The image of the Beast with the Black Metal Claws was etched in Chris's mind. Tears intermingled with sweat as Chris tried to whisper the nightmare to Cindy, if only to prove that she wasn't crazy. She didn't know why that would work.

CHAPTER 11

Chris tried her best not to sleep the rest of the night. She went down to a corner store to pick up a case of energy drinks. The gruesome images from the nightmare constantly assaulted her vision. Every shadow was a possible threat, and every passerby was a potential monster. She rushed back to the relative safety of her room and settled in at her desk. The energy drinks kept her awake, for a time. By six o'clock, she was dozing off at her desk. It didn't help that she'd chosen to read a densely-packed book on the philosophies of Nietzsche. Reading about nihilism when the world seemed so confusing was strangely comforting.

When 8:00 a.m. rolled around, Chris stood from her desk. She wandered barefoot down the hallway until she got to Norman Argyle's room. Chris had hoped she wouldn't wake him. The kerfuffle that ensued behind the door after she knocked dashed those hopes. When a disheveled Norman opened the door, he flashed a smile and invited her in. Chris had never been in any other student's room, and was impressed by the plant life he'd managed to cultivate. There was vibrant greenery perched on every table and in every nook. She'd tried to have a cactus once, but it had died under mysterious circumstances. Chris suspected Alice.

"W-what can I do for you, Chris?" Norman asked, leading her to a tiny, patched up sofa in the corner of the room.

"I think you might get another noise complaint," Chris said, eyes firmly on her feet.

"Were you... uh, you had the nightmare before, right?"

"Yeah."

"Was it another one, or did something else happen?" Norman asked.

"I never had nightmares growing up. I don't even remember ever having dreams, really."

"Have you been eating well?"

"I... no. Not really," Chris said, remembering the skipped lunches and chocolate bar dinners.

"That might be it. Or maybe it's stress. Um, why don't I make you an appointment with a school psychiatrist? They're usually pretty booked up, so it might take some time for you to get in, but they could help."

"No, no." Chris raised her hands in adamant defense. "It was just a dream. I'm not crazy."

"You don't have to go to the psychiatrist. I-it was just a suggestion."

"What happens if I get more nightmares? Will I get kicked out of the dorms because of noise complaints?" Chris asked.

"I-I-I don't even know if there's going to be another one today. But no. If you're having medical issues, you can get a doctor's note."

"But I'd need to see a doctor?"

"L-let's not think too far ahead. Maybe you should call your parents? The nightmares could be homesickness."

"I hope you're right." Chris stood up. "I'm sorry for barging in here. I just wanted to tell you what's going on before any complaints."

"Anytime you, uh, want to talk, I'm a-available."

"Thanks."

Norman's door closed and Chris trudged back to her room. Was it just bad eating habits? Chris reached for her room's doorknob, but something was wrong. She recoiled from the cool metal handle. It felt like something had grabbed her hand, something large and sharp. Chris muttered to herself, promising she was awake as she once again reached for the knob. This time it felt warm to her. Inside, Chris grabbed her coat and cellphone before going downstairs and sitting down on the steps leading to the front door of the Old Dorm. She dialed Cecil's number by rote and was greeted by a long yawn.

"Hey, Honey. What's up?" Cecil said.

"I'm sorry if I woke you," Chris replied.

"Woke me? What time is it? I'm still at work, Dear."

"Why? Did something happen?"

"Nothing too bad. What's going on with you?"

"This is going to sound stupid. Like, I'm not five, but... I had this really bad dream last night."

"Really?" Cecil's voice immediately changed from sluggish tortoise to cocaine-laden hare. "What was it about?"

"It's not important."

"Was it about school?" Cecil pressed.

"Kind of." Chris sighed. "I'm sorry. I'm just feeling shaken up. It was so real, though."

"What do you mean?"

"Like, part of the dream I was running away from a monster. It had these big, black metal claws. I swear I could feel it every time it slashed me."

"Well -"

"And then I felt it again today. I keep seeing it every time I close my eyes and I thought I felt it grab my hand just a few minutes ago."

"That's some dream, Honey. Don't worry. It'll pass." Cecil's voice became distant and muffled.

Chris heard a struggle. Suddenly, Luca was on the line.

"Are you all right?" she asked.

"Yeah, Luca. I'm fine." Chris smiled to herself. Luca had always been so overprotective.

Another struggle with the phone ensued. This time, it was Cecil's voice that came back.

"Sorry about that," he said. "Do you want to tell me more about your dream?"

"No. It's all right."

"Just try to remember that it can't hurt you, okay? I remember back at your tenth birthday party, we'd hired a clown. I don't think you slept for weeks. But here we are, all these years later, and you haven't been eaten by a clown yet."

"I don't remember you being around then," Chris said, her smile dropping as she remembered the years her father was too busy with work to be there for them.

"Luca told me. Anyway, hopefully Alice won't tease you as much this time."

"I don't know, Dad. Maybe it was only shame that stopped me from being Coulrophobic."

"What's that?" Cecil asked.

"Fear of clowns."

"You're so smart." Cecil chuckled. "Do you want to come over for dinner?"

"That's all right. I'll talk to you later."

"All right. Don't worry about the dreams. They'll pass," Cecil said.

Chris hung up the phone. Norman was right: it felt good to talk with someone, especially her family. There was no reason to be afraid of a dream. Even so, Chris unconsciously rubbed her ribs where the Beast with the Black Metal Claws had slashed her in the nightmare.

Later that night, the dream was well out of Chris's head. Cindy invited her to a party her sister Emily was having. Chris had agonized over her outfit, ending up with a red dress shirt and a loosely worn tie with black pants. She immediately felt out of place when she arrived at Emily's. Every other party-goer was dressed down to an extent that made Chris look like she was wearing a tuxedo. Sweats, stains, and mismatched socks were the fashion of the day. Even Cindy, usually so prim, looked like she'd just gotten out of bed. Upon entry, Cindy grabbed Chris's arm and dragged her into the back, toward a woman who looked exactly like her, but with even more blonde hair.

"Emily!" Cindy let go of Chris's arm and hugged the woman.

"Hey, Cindy," Emily said, breaking the hug. She eyed Chris.

"Who's the cute boy?"

Cindy turned fire hydrant red. "This is my roommate Christine, and *she* isn't cute." She turned back to Chris. "That's not what I meant."

"Chris Delacroix." She shook Emily's hand.

"I'm so embarrassed," Emily said.

"Don't be. It happens a lot ever since I chopped all my hair off in ninth grade. The only person who gets upset is my dad."

"Are you French?" Emily asked.

"No?"

"Oh, sorry. Most people I know pronounce Delacroix like 'Roy' and not the French way. Are your parents French?"

"I've seen my dad try to order food at French restaurants. I can say 100% that we aren't French. I have no idea where we picked up the name."

"Cool. Anyway, there's beer in the kitchen."

"Nice to meet you," Chris said as she nudged Cindy to follow her.

The kitchen was packed full of people, and the beer supplies were running low. Chris saw one unopened can left. She reached her arm through a gap of chirping youths and returned with her prize. She was about to open it when she saw Cindy, sighing as she failed in her search around the kitchen. Chris handed her the can and the two left the kitchen. She stopped in her tracks as she entered the hallway.

"What is it?" Cindy asked.

Chris turned her back to the hallway. "It's that annoying guy from Criminology I was telling you about, Michael."

"Which one?"

Chris glanced over her shoulder.

"He's talking to Norman," Chris said.

"Let's go talk."

"No, Cindy. I really don't want to deal with him."

"We'll bitch about him later. It'll be fun."

"Fine." Chris sighed. She frowned all the way until her face turned and a pleasant smile fraudulently arose.

Cindy waved at the two.

"Norman," Cindy shouted over the crowd. "Who's your friend?"

"Uh, this is, I'm sorry. This is Michael," Norman said. "Michael, this is Cindy and..."

"Yeah, I know the other one," Michael said.

"Small world," Norman muttered.

"Do you really believe the shit you say in class?" Michael asked Chris.

"It's a party. I don't want to fight," Chris said.

"This girl actually, like, really believes that the police will help everyone and it's not each person's responsibility to do what's right."

"That's not true," Chris said. "Just because I don't think the police are evil doesn't mean I think people don't have responsibility."

"Oh yeah?" Michael replied.

"Did you guys hear about the Snatcher?" Cindy said. "He killed another person last night. Is that the kind of thing you talk about at Criminology?"

"C-can we not talk about the Snatcher?" Norman asked.

"There's another one," Michael said, ignoring Norman's plea. "The police aren't going to solve that. What do they care if someone is defiling holy ground?"

"Great talk," Chris said. "Nice seeing you, Norman." She grabbed Cindy's hand and yanked her away. Chris ensured that her shoulder collided with Michael's as she passed.

Chris dragged Cindy outside where dusk had finally given way to the blackness of night.

"I hate that guy."

"He seemed kind of like a conspiracy nut," Cindy said, sipping her beer.

"Maybe I should tell him I know who killed JFK?" Chris yawned, the adrenaline from the encounter with Michael leaving her body along with the last of her energy drink-fueled vigor. "I'm sure it's a great party, but I'm going to go."

"Are you sure?"

"I need sleep after last night. Next time, I swear I'll stay up all night with you."

"Okay. Fingers crossed no dreams," Cindy said.

Chris saw something glint out of the corner of her eye. She turned her head and looked out into the bushes across the street. There was something there. Chris placed her hand on Cindy's shoulder and squinted. Nothing. But she knew what she saw. It had to be. It was the claws of the Beast from her dreams. Her heart began racing as memories of the nightmares crashed upon her. The Beast wasn't real. She was just seeing things. The Beast wasn't real.

CHAPTER 12

Chris gazed at the restaurant wallpaper. It was an Italian motif, designed to transport budget-minded diners to the distant hills of the Mediterranean. It achieved that goal, or failed to, through repeated grape imagery and vaguely uplifting Latin phrases. She was there to have dinner with her father and Alice. Chris had tried to dodge the meeting, wanting to be left alone after her last nightmare. She'd read Cindy's book on dreams. It didn't help. It covered dreams about falling and wearing your underwear in public, but stopped short of being torn to shreds by monsters. She saw the snarling face of the Beast with the Black Metal Claws regularly, usually out of the corner of her eye or in reflections. When she'd first gotten to the restaurant and looked out the window, she'd almost jumped out of her seat. Outside, staring at her from across the darkened street, was the Beast. She was certain. A second look revealed nothing – nothing at all.

Chris hadn't been sleeping, subsisting on the barest of catnaps, but she couldn't escape it's influence. She was starting to wonder if the Beast could be real, a supernatural force that was stalking her. She considered asking Norman to help her see a psychiatrist, but she couldn't see how that would help. Either the Beast was real, and they'd think she was crazy, and she'd end up too doped up to do anything about it, or the Beast wasn't real, and she really was crazy, and she'd have to leave school. So there she was, just trying to cope with it alone.

Deep down, Chris was also nervous about seeing her father after her last nightmare. She knew it was ridiculous, but she couldn't quite shake the feeling of unease. She put her head on the table briefly, before remembering that she was still in public. Rising up, Chris ordered a black coffee and resigned herself to dinner.

Half an hour later, Chris was still alone at the restaurant. She was especially annoyed, since Alice had been the one to talk her into the dinner, but there was nothing she could do but down more and more coffee. Chris sighed when her father finally arrived.

"Hey, Honey. How's my little scholar?" Cecil beamed.

"Oh my God, Dad. Never say that again," Chris said. "Did you bring Alice?"

"No. I think she said something about being late. You look tired? Staying up all night studying?" Cecil asked.

"Yeah, something like that." Chris attempted a smile, but the corners of her mouth trembled so she dropped it.

"Are you having more nightmares?"

"No."

"Are you sure? It's all right if you are. They're just dreams."

"I'm sure, Dad."

Just then, Chris saw Alice bounding into the restaurant. She jumped on her father's back with a squeal, arm curling around his neck. Chris ducked to avoid the stares from the rest of the restaurant. After a brief wrestle, Cecil and Alice joined Chris in the booth.

"How's school been going?" Cecil asked.

"You know me, Dad. Calculus is my bitch," Alice said loudly.

Chris glared at her, looking around to see if people were staring again. Alice was grinning like a madman.

"Biology and chemistry, too. Was there every any doubt?" Alice poked Chris across the table.

"I don't have as many bitches as Alice, but I'm sure I'll develop a respectful partnership with my classes," Chris said. "There is one that's pretty fun. It's called Symbolism and the Occult."

Chris omitted the part where that particular class had gone from a minor elective to the most important class she took, and only partially because she hoped it would reveal answers to her terrible nightmares.

"You're into that kind of thing, huh?" Cecil laughed.

"It's because she has the hots for her prof, Dad," Alice interjected.

"Oh... Are your housemates treating you well, Alice?" Cecil changed the subject.

"They're a pain the ass," Alice snarled. "They won't even let me keep any experiments in the fridge."

"Why not?" Cecil asked with a bewildered look on his face.

"I don't know. I guess they're weird or something." Alice shrugged.

Chris smiled to herself as she counted the thing she loved most about university: not bumping into one of Alice's rodents when she reached into the fridge.

It was midnight by the time they left the restaurant. Cecil was smiling in a way he hadn't since his daughters left for university.

They said their goodbyes and Chris started home, cutting through the nearby Menos Park. She shivered in the late fall air, thrusting her hands into her pockets. Chris looked around the dark, deserted park and regretted her decision. The park was welcoming in the daylight, but it was a different story at night. The streetlamps along the main path were sparsely placed and many of them had burnt out. Fond memories of family Sundays in the park with Luca faded quickly as she crept along the path. Before long, she was enveloped by darkness so dense she could barely see five feet in front of her face. The sound of leaves rustling in the forest just off the narrow path and twigs crunching as she walked reminded her how alone she was.

After a few more minutes of steady walking, another thought occurred to Chris. What if she wasn't alone in this desolate place? For the first time, she was glad Luca had given her a can of Mace for her eighteenth birthday instead of something she actually wanted. She slipped a hand into her bag and groped as quietly as she could until she felt the cool comforting metal of the canister. She gripped it tightly, a talisman against the dark. It was hauntingly quiet, but as she approached an underpass beneath a bridge Chris became aware of muffled whimpers.

The underpass was covered in graffiti. It was difficult to see, but Chris could make out two figures locked in an embrace. A girl was pressed against the concrete wall, while a man seemed to be kissing her neck. Chris felt her shoulders slump. It was just a couple of college kids like her, taking their hormones out on each other. Chris looked around, wondering if she should look for another path back to school, but she couldn't find the courage to backtrack through the park. Instead she sped up, planning to get past the amorous couple as quickly as possible. As she got closer, she saw the girl slip to the ground like a ragdoll, head slamming into the concrete with a sickening crunch.

Chris stepped forward to help the fallen woman. Her good intentions disappeared as she finally got a look at the man. He was over six feet tall and naked except for ooze covering his body. The slime dripped black into the concrete ground. His absurdly long limbs hung at his side as he appeared to ponder over the woman. Chris gasped in shock as a flash of the Beast overtook her vision. She shook her head – he wasn't the Beast. The dreams weren't real, and this was a wholly different kind of monster. The man quickly turned his head, eyes fixed on her.

"Stand back, freak," she shouted, brandishing the can of Mace.

He paid her no heed and rushed toward her.

"Back off," she yelled, before spraying the man in the face.

He screamed and dropped to his knees, clawing at his eyes in pain. Dropping the Mace, Chris ran to the girl, who still lay face down on the ground.

"Hey, get up," Chris begged.

The girl didn't respond. She couldn't have. Her throat had been gnawed off. Where her neck once fixed her head to her body, now there was only blood and torn sinews. Chris nearly threw up when she saw the gaping hole. She heard a snap behind her. The man had regained his footing, and he was staring straight at her.

Chris tore out of the underpass, the man in full chase behind her. He lunged and she dodged, narrowly avoiding his grasp. Through the inky night she could see a distant row of lights. In her terror, she could think of nothing but reaching the glowing orbs. The path was narrow, with rocky hills to her left and a drainage ditch to her right. She ran as fast as her brittle legs could carry her, but he was faster.

Chris screamed when he grabbed her shoulder and tossed her into the ditch. She spun across the hard terrain, rocks and branches raking across her body until she finally crashed directly on her left arm in the shallow water of the ditch. The man barreled toward her, tripping and falling on his stomach a few feet from her landing place. For the first time, Chris got a clear look at him. His naked form was covered in hair and ooze, but most disturbing were his eyes. They were white. There were no irises, no pupils, no mercy.

It's not human, she thought. *It's not human. It's not human.*

As he crawled toward her, she could see a splintered bone protruding from his leg. He must have broken it in the fall. The man gurgled and groaned as he reached out one thin arm after another into the sludge, dragging himself ever closer to her. Chris tried to scramble backwards, but the more she struggled the deeper she sank into the thick mud. She couldn't feel anything in her left arm. She feared it, too, was broken.

Soon he was upon her. Chris kicked the man in the face as fast and as hard as she could, sending streams of blood into the air. She reared back and kicked him over and over again, until she heard a sickening crunch. His jaw snapped in two like dry wood and fell away from his face, leaving his tongue gaping and exposed, his drool flinging wildly into the night. He came at her again. Blood dripped from his face, boiling and disappearing as it hit the ground. The distinct smell of rotten meat filled the air, gagging Chris. Her next kick threw him back far enough to buy her some time. With her one good arm, she dragged herself to her feet.

Chris scrambled up the steep hill back to the path, before falling to her knees. She looked back at the creature. It managed to stand, but was betrayed by the broken leg. It plunged to the ground, the protruding bone tearing through even deeper flesh. Chris looked at the moon, silently begging for the sickly green light of her dreams.

Please, please let this be another nightmare.

To her utmost horror, the moon glowed clear and white. She wasn't going to wake up to safety. She would have to get there herself.

Chris pulled herself up on unsteady legs and ran. Her ears were battered by the screams of the monster she left behind. When she couldn't run anymore, she collapsed on the grass, heaving as she fought to catch her breath. Her arm was throbbing with pain. Gritting her teeth, she took off her jacket and rolled up her sleeve. Her arm was swollen and bruised, but it wasn't broken - small miracles.

Chris didn't remember getting home. Everything was in a fog. Someone on campus asked if she was all right, but all she could do was feebly mumble something and keep moving toward the Old Dorm. Her room was empty. Still in shock, Chris sat totally still on her bed. Did that just happen? She felt numb. It wasn't the Beast with the Black Metal Claws. It was something different, and it was no nightmare. Chris's fingers itched terribly and she kneaded them into her legs. It was real – those words repeated over and over again in her mind. She sat there for half an hour before Cindy stumbled in. She had been drinking. Chris could tell by the smile on her face, which was slightly askew. Cindy bounced over to Chris and started to hug her, but Chris's stiff movement and heavy breathing snapped her into sobriety.

"Are you okay?" Cindy demanded.

Chris's eyes stared vacantly in front her as she grasped her wounded limb. Cindy gave Chris a shake.

"I hurt my arm." It was all Chris could say.

Cindy carefully removed Chris's jacket and shirt.

"It's swelling a lot," Cindy said before she walked over to the fridge. When she returned, she was holding a cloth filled with ice cubes. "Hold this against it until the swelling goes down."

Chris nodded slowly, taking the makeshift icepack from her roommate.

"What happened?"

"I fell down on my way home." Chris's voice was detached, as if she was on some warm tropical shore far away.

"You're shaking like crazy," Cindy said quietly.

"I had a lot of coffee. With dinner, I mean. A lot of coffee."

"Let's get you under the covers, okay?"

"No," Chris said, surprising herself with the force of her words.

"I'm not tired, okay? I need to study."

Cindy looked unsure, but Chris forced herself to smile to show she was okay. It didn't look convincing, but Cindy accepted it and crawled into her own bed. Chris used her good arm to prop up her Psychology text book and flipped through the pages to a reading she remembered from last week. If she couldn't be well-rested, she could at least be well-informed.

The passage was about the limitations of human perception, how the things we see and hear and feel may be only a fraction of what's really there, or sometimes not there at all. It was related to mental illness. A person who sees things that aren't there, or that others can't see, isn't helped by being told there's nothing there. They perceive it, just as surely as others perceive their own bodies, or the weather. The writer was getting philosophical and wondering if there was any meaningful difference between reality and the perception of reality. If you feel it, he argued, then it is real. Chris read the passage over and over.

Were her dreams, which felt so real, crossing into reality somehow? Or was she really going crazy?

CHAPTER 13

Though it was five full days into November, Arcadia Hall was still covered in Halloween decorations. Cheap paper witches and ghosts hung from the ceilings, and jack o' lanterns lined the walls. Chris shuddered at the childish boogeymen. Their fixed, comical faces only acted as corners in which her mind's shadows could hide. She pushed through the tacky display to the faculty wing on the third floor. The long hallway with its stained carpeting sent chills down Chris's spine. She kept expecting to see the twisted face of the Beast with the Black Metal Claws with each door she passed. She hadn't slept the last night, hiding from her fears in wakefulness, but she wasn't safe in the real world either. She had to do something, and there was only one person she knew who could possibly begin to help.

Professor Moore's door flung open just as she was about to knock, throwing her off balance. Chris fell to the ground with a gasp, but it wasn't a monster that burst through the door. Instead, it was a stout man carrying a large plant.

"Sorry about that," he said.

"It was fun. Next time you can be the girl who gets knocked over and I'll be the guy with the Ficus plant." Chris tried to turn her embarrassment into a joke with little success.

"It's a fern." The man quickly turned away and shuffled down the hall, muttering to himself.

Chris saw the professor through the crack in the door. With a deep breath, she pushed the door ajar and knocked on the frame. Moore looked up from his papers and smiled, sending a wave of heat through her.

"What can I do for my favorite student?" Professor Moore asked.

Chris blushed and lost her words as she sat down. She tried to avoid his gaze, her fingers absentmindedly tapping on the arms of her chair. After a moment of silence that lasted far too long, she found the words to try to explain the situation.

"Professor, do you remember during the museum trip when my friend Cindy asked you if there were any real monsters?"

Moore put his hand on his chin in thought. "Cindy... Cindy...." His eyes lit up. "Oh, Emily's sister. It's so nice that she's taking the course. I'm sort of a mentor to her sister. She's one of my student researchers." He smiled widely.

"I have to ask you something important," she said, forcing the words out.

Moore arched his eyebrow in interest.

"Are there monsters out there? Real ones?"

To her utter embarrassment, he began to laugh.

"Monsters are invented by people. They don't exist in the real world," Moore said.

"I saw one yesterday," she blurted out.

"That's highly unlikely," Moore said. His voice was kind, but his words stung. "Historically, many monster sightings have turned out to be wild animals. Is that a possibility?"

"No," Chris cried, much louder than she'd meant to. "It was a man, but it wasn't a man. It came after me in the park. No animal is six feet tall, thin, and walks on two legs."

"I'm sure that you just had a bad dream, or perhaps you imagined it. I know midterms are a stressful time of year for students, and stress can lead to all sorts of issues," Moore suggested.

"No. I thought it might be a dream at first," Chris admitted, "But it was real. I saw it, I felt it, I could even smell it. I swear it's true."

Moore's disbelieving expression didn't change. Chris shuddered. His eyes seemed to pierce into the deepest recesses of her mind. After a long silence, he sighed.

"Tell me," Moore asked, "Besides the monster, how are you doing?"

"What are you talking about?" Chris asked.

"Exactly that," Moore pressed. "Are you enjoying your classes? Are you meeting new friends? How are you?"

"Please believe me," she pleaded. "It was really tall, with big teeth and white eyes." Her breathing became fast and erratic. "I saw it rip a girl's throat out before it started chasing me. It looked like a man at first, but it couldn't have been. I saw it break its leg and I kicked the jaw off its face, but it still kept coming, screaming at me with its horrible voice." The words spewed out of her mouth, uncontrolled and urgent. "It couldn't have been human. What kind of human is covered in black slime, or has blood that reeks like rotten meat?"

"Chris," Moore said slowly, "You're under a tremendous amount of stress. I want you to go to the campus health center and tell someone there what you're going through. Lack of sleep and intense stress can cause hallucinations in extreme cases."

Chris looked away, ashamed to look him in the eye. "Please," she said. "I don't want to be crazy."

"Don't be embarrassed," Moore said kindly. "This is something many students go though, although not always in this exact fashion. Just remember: you are smart, you are talented, and there's no such thing as monsters."

Chris nodded miserably.

"Good. Now go take care of yourself. Take a nap. And I'll see you in class."

There would be no help. Tears dropped from Chris's eyes as she shut Moore's door behind her. Stress was such a convenient explanation, but she couldn't accept it. She was doing well in her classes, she had a great new friend in Cindy, and a supportive family. Still, this was happening to her. There was something horrible going on. Chris openly sobbed when she realized that the horrible thing might be her own mind.

* * *

At the townhouse, Alice was having an equally emotionally exhausting afternoon.

"What did we tell you?" Courtney yelled at Alice. "Don't bring your dead things into the house. Why is that so hard for you?"

Alice brought herself mere inches from Courtney's face in an attempt at intimidation.

"I kept it in my room," Alice said matter-of-factly. "Why do you care what's in my room?"

"Get out of my face, bitch." Courtney pushed Alice back.

Alice let out a bestial growl, instinctually flexing out her fingers at her sides. First, she caught Courtney snooping around her room, and then the bitch had the nerve to start yelling at her. Alice pulled back her arm and slapped Courtney across the cheek.

The two girls stared at each other in silence until the faintest smile came over Courtney's face. Like a toddler trying to coax her parents to buy her a toy, Courtney burst into tears.

"Stop it. Don't be such a baby," Alice yelled over Courtney's indecipherable wails. "I said stop it." Alice grabbed her by the collar and shook lightly, as if she could snap her roommate out of her temper tantrum.

At that moment, the four other roommates, stirred by the commotion, rushed into the room and promptly misunderstood the situation. Alice screeched as two of the girls restrained her.

"Calm down, Alice," Sam demanded.

Alice let out a guttural cry, but realized that she'd been played.

"I'm sorry, Sam." Courtney sniffled and wiped crocodile tears from her eyes. "I saw Alice bring a dead animal into her room. When I tried to remind her about the rules, she started yelling and swearing. I tried to leave, but she attacked me."

"You lying bitch," Alice shouted.

Courtney reached out her arms and the other girls rushed in to hug her. Over their shoulders, she looked intently into Alice's eyes and smiled.

* * *

Chris and Alice met at the cafeteria a few hours later. Alice had insisted. For her part, Chris was too terrified and tired to put up any real resistance.

"I hate them," Alice blurted as she sat down opposite her sister at the cafeteria table.

"Nice to see you, too," Chris said. "What's wrong?"

"They don't care about me," Alice snapped. "That bitch Courtney snuck into my room and started trying to stir shit up." Alice contorted her face in disgust. "And then she starts crying and pretending that I'm the bad guy and all those other bitches always take her side."

"Why don't you move?" Chris suggested.

"I shouldn't have to move. She should." Alice reached over the table and took half of Chris's sandwich, shoving it into her mouth.

"Actually, maybe I should try to move out." Alice continued talking through her stuffed mouth. "What's wrong with you anyway? You're broodier than normal," Alice shoved her sister repeatedly in the shoulder.

"Nothing."

What could Chris say? That she was being tormented by monsters in her dreams, and now they were appearing in the real world as well? And she wasn't sure how real anything was anymore, and she was probably crazy? It was a little heavy for lunch.

"Nothing my ass. I hate when you pull the silent treatment. What the hell is wrong with you?"

"I haven't been sleeping," Chris said, "And, well, I think I'm going crazy."

"You and me both. I don't think I've had a good night's sleep in weeks." Alice again reached again for Chris's lunch. "You know what? I think we both need some sleep. Promise me you'll go to bed early tonight, okay?"

Chris nodded, still frowning. Alice didn't understand that sleep was one of the things that scared Chris the most.

"If something happens to me, could you... you'll be there, right?" Chris asked.

"What're you talking about? You better not be thinking of pulling some Unabomber shit," Alice said.

"No. Just...never mind."

Alice groaned. "You know I'm here for you. Dad and Luca are, too. Do you need something cheesy, like a hug?"

"No. Thanks, though."

"Sleep. Get sleep." Alice said as she finished Chris's lunch.

Chris trudged back to her room, her feet heavy, barely able to carry her through the door. She stood before her bed in the empty room and tried to convince herself to take a nap as Moore had suggested. She was so tired, but she didn't know if sleep would help at all.

Chris felt the faint but unmistakable tension of a second person in the room. It couldn't be Cindy – her roommate could never be this quiet. She spun around and saw someone watching her from behind the door. At first she doubted her eyes, assuming it was another figment of her imagination. She caught a glimpse of familiar blonde hair and tension melted from her shoulders. It was Cindy's sister, Emily.

"Hi, Emily. Cindy won't be back from class for another hour," Chris said.

"No," Emily said. "I'm not here for Cindy. I'm here for you."

"What?" Chris asked.

"If you really want to know what attacked you in the park," the blonde intoned, "Come to 58 Baker's Drive tonight at midnight. Don't tell anyone, including my sister and don't come unless you're serious. If you want a safe, peaceful night, just stay away, and I'll never mention this to you again."

Before Chris could form a response, Emily was gone. Chris knew she'd be at that meeting. Emily knew about the monster in the park. Only come if you're serious? Chris had never been more serious in her life.

CHAPTER 14

11:45 glowed brightly on Chris's phone when she left the dorm. The sound of the door closing didn't stir her loudly snoring roommate. Chris had to know if she was really going crazy, or worse, if there really were monsters in Meridian City.

It wasn't long before she found herself on the west side of campus, on Baker's Drive. Chris stopped in front of the skeletal frame of a building under construction. Bolted above the door was the number 58. It was the future home of a new dorm, and was full of gaping holes in the upper floors that were covered with ghostly plastic sheets, some of which had come loose and were waving in the wind. Taking a final glance back, Chris opened the heavy front door and stepped inside.

Whispers flowed through the building like wayward spirits. The floor was covered with sawdust, and Chris saw footprints in the dust, some leading up the stairs and others into the adjoining rooms down the hall. When she stepped forward, her foot met a bucket that was on the ground, sending a loud clank echoing around the building. She froze as the whispering halted.

"Hello?" Chris called, rubbing her still-injured arm, her fingers gripping into the bruised flesh.

Three figures emerged from the dark room on her right. They were shrouded in darkness, their unique features obscured. Chris felt a flash of fear – just what the hell had she gotten herself into? She squinted, trying to make out their faces, but she stopped when Emily pushed past them. At a signal from the blonde, the three figures faded into the recesses of the building.

"Come this way," Emily said, guiding Chris up the unfinished stairs.

"What's going on here?" Chris whispered urgently.

"I don't think I should be the one to explain this to you," Emily said firmly. "Just follow me."

They arrived on the second story and Emily knocked on one of the finished doors.

"Come in," a voice said.

When the door opened, Chris saw her favorite professor standing in the middle of the room, flanked by two young men. Relief and confusion washed over her.

"I'm glad you could join us, Chris," Moore said, flashing his usual wide grin.

"What is this? Who are these people?" Chris asked, trying hard to conceal the emotional upheaval she was undergoing.

Moore nodded at Emily to collect the men and leave the room.

"I'm afraid I have been lying to you, Chris." He put his hands on her shoulders. "I had hoped to shield you from the brutal reality we live in. You see, there are monsters in this world, hellish creatures that prey on the helpless. You saw one last night, but it was only one of many. They are more than mindless beasts – they are demons. Demons are worse than dangerous. They are purposeful and cunning as well. They menace the city, possibly even the country, hunting out innocents like you. I have brought together a group of students in order to stop these beasts once and for all."

"Why don't you go to the police?" Chris stood stiffly under his grasp, trying to piece together what he was saying.

"I tried that." He frowned. "But even with the proof I collected, they refused to help me. I believe the monsters have some kind of sway over the authorities, although I can't prove that theory."

"That thing that chased me," Chris stammered, "How could it control the police? It was just a rampaging beast. Couldn't you just film it and release the footage to the media? Show everybody the truth?"

"It's not that simple, Chris. You must have noticed how secretive we are here. There are good reasons for that. If people knew the danger with which they lived every day, there would be riots."

"This doesn't make any sense," Chris said. "How the hell is that even possible?"

"I know this doesn't make sense to you right now." Moore clasped her hands in his, an action that sent a wave of endorphins rushing through her system. "And I wish I could explain, but you need to see the truth, experience it. Don't allow me to overtake your opinions. Go with Emily and the others tonight and see for yourself."

Chris nodded, melting in his confident grasp. The danger she felt, the danger that haunted her dreams and now crept into her waking life, wasn't an intangible concept like the musings in her Psychology text. It was real, and Moore appeared to be in a position to challenge it. Why was he holding back?

"Okay. Come back in," Moore called out behind her.

The door opened and Emily reappeared.

"I would like you to take Chris with you tonight," Moore said.

"Are you sure?" Emily sounded uneasy.

"She needs to see for herself, just like you did," Moore replied with absolute finality.

Emily took Chris outside the room. They passed a few small groups of students as they made their way downstairs.

"Where are we going?" Chris asked as Emily ushered her back down the stairs.

"I'm going to show you something."

"What? I've already seen a monster."

"Just wait." Emily let out a loud whistle when they reached the bottom floor.

Chris tried to suppress her revulsion when Michael appeared from one of the side rooms. At least now she understood why someone like him would be at Emily's party.

"Chris, this is Michael."

"We've met," Chris said bitterly.

"I never thought I'd see someone like you here," Michael said. "I figured you were all talk."

"Shut up and get ready," Emily said, never breaking her stride.

"We've been following a demon for the past two weeks," Michael explained. "Today we're going to rid the world of its evil." His tone was peppy and light, as if he was outlining a Dungeons and Dragons game.

Outside, Chris found four more men sitting in a parked car. Emily nodded quickly to the foursome, and then pulled Chris to a second vehicle. Michael practically leapt into the front seat, leaving Chris alone with her thoughts in the back. Were they really going to see a demon? Did they take seven people knowing some wouldn't make it? She imagined Emily notifying her family of her demise. 'Mr. Delacroix, I'm sorry to tell you that your daughter has been eaten by a supernatural hell-beast. Please accept this shoebox of her remains and our deepest condolences.'

It was a long drive - nearly an hour. They were still in Meridian City, in some non-descript suburb Chris didn't recognize. Row after row of identical houses stretched out to the horizon, identifiable only by the colors of the doors and the particular blend of flowers in the garden.

"We're going to that one," Emily said, pointing to a house on the left.

Its front lawn was a sea of tacky ornaments. Chris saw the men from the other car sneak past an outcropping of pink flamingos.

"Go on ahead, Michael. I'll follow with Chris when you signal," Emily commanded.

Michael ducked out of the car and rushed after the others. When Emily was sure he couldn't hear them, she turned to Chris.

"How are you holding up?" Emily asked, appearing to be offering genuine concern.

Chris had no idea how to answer the question.

"You're not just messing with me, right? Is there actually a demon in there?" she asked. Chris smirked inadvertently at the ridiculousness of her own words.

Emily nodded gravely.

"How did you get involved with this?" Chris asked. "Is there a demon hunter class that I don't know about?"

"I used to be Professor Moore's teaching assistant," Emily explained. "He saw something in me, I guess. A drive to make the world a safer place. He told me the truth about the demons and gave me the chance to do something truly good. I know you're a freshman. He must think you're pretty special to initiate you so soon." Emily smiled encouragingly. "So don't be afraid. Whatever happens, you'll be on the right side."

"What about Michael?"

"The professor brought him on over the summer. He's an asshole and a zealot. He seems to think we're some kind of army of God. But he fights to protect the lives of innocent people, so at least some of his priorities are in the right place."

"What do you think?" Chris asked.

"He's a creep. I don't care where the demons come from. I only care about where they go – straight to Hell." Emily lost her train of thought when a light on the second story of the house flickered. "That's our cue. They've subdued the monster."

Chris was certain the whole neighborhood would wake up from the sound of her throbbing heart as the pair rushed to the back of the house. They found the door open and slunk inside. There were cat knickknacks everywhere: statues of cats, pictures of cats, ceramic cats, and a cat-shaped clock ticking menacingly on the wall, its eyes blinking back and forth.

"Quickly," Emily whispered from the stairs.

Approaching the second floor, Chris could hear a man yelling from a room at the end of the hall. It was Michael's voice, she recognized. Inside, five men surrounded a frail old man and held knives against his withered skin. The elderly man was dressed in threadbare, old pajamas. He shook against the ground, held down by his attackers. In his milky eyes were hot tears, which trailed down his worn skin and filled the wrinkles along the way. The fearful tears spread down past his chin onto the knife Michael pressed against his throat.

"What the hell is going on?" Chris cried, stepping forward in the vain hope that she could help the old man.

"It's okay." Emily wrapped a strong arm around Chris's chest, holding her in place. "This is what Professor Moore needed you to see. Don't let its appearance fool you. Don't you want to know the truth?"

Chris halted in her righteous indignation. She nodded her assent.

Emily released Chris and approached the crying old man. She grabbed his face, twisting it so he was forced to stare into her eyes.

"Show us what you really look like," she said.

His eyes gaped in terror at the young woman, and he started babbling, protesting his innocence. Emily struck him across the face.

"I said show us! Show us your true face, demon!"

Chris's breath grew dim, her lungs sticky. Two blisters bubbled up on the sides of the man's face. From these blisters popped brown, chitinous tendrils that reached above the man's forehead, each one capped by round, bulbous protrusions. The protrusions opened, revealing two goo-covered eyeballs staring at Chris.

"See?" Emily hissed. "They can look like us. They hide in plain sight and prey on the weak."

"Now you see the true face of the Devil," Michael said as he mercilessly buried his knife in the monster's throat.

The men held the creature down as it thrashed in some futile hope at regaining its stolen life. The tendrils retreated into the creature's face as it died, leaving nothing behind but the body of a decrepit old man, one nobody would ever know concealed a bloodthirsty monster. It was the most disgusting thing Chris had ever witnessed, but she felt something harden inside her. A drive that she had barely been aware of suddenly became steel coated. The monsters had to be stopped. She could stop them.

It was three in the morning when they got back to 58 Baker's Drive. In three hours Chris's entire life had changed. Her mind was spinning from the revelation that demons not only existed, but were masquerading as people. The thought made her sick. They could be everywhere, schools, hospitals, waiting for their chance tear out people's throats, just like that poor girl killed in Menos Park. Chris was under constant threat, and she hadn't even realized it. Professor Moore met them at the door.

"How did it go?" he asked, ushering the crowd inside.

"Mission accomplished," Michael replied.

"Excellent." The professor smiled in obvious relief. "And I see you all returned safely, thank God. Once we're done here I'll go back and take care of the body." He stretched out his arms, gesturing toward the whole room. "You did a wonderful job tonight. That demon won't kill again. You've saved dozens, maybe hundreds of lives. I wish I could give you a proper celebration, but, if you'll excuse me, I have to talk to our newest initiate."

The rest of the group filtered out, leaving only Chris and Emily with Professor Moore.

"Do you understand why we can't go to the media now, Chris?" he asked.

She nodded. She couldn't imagine what chaos would ensue if the whole world knew that there were demons prowling in plain sight.

"Why did you lie to me when I came to you this morning?" Chris asked.

"Truthfully, I was afraid. I had to think for a while whether you were ready or not to know the truth. I want you to help us stop these monsters from hurting any more people," Moore said solemnly. "But you need to understand what you're signing up for. I want to be clear: I'm asking you to risk your life to protect the lives of countless others. It will be dangerous, gruesome, and more than a little frightening. Can you do that for me?"

Chris looked at Emily. She thought of the monster that chased her into the ditch, the woman it had killed. She grasped at her injured arm, remembering the terror she felt as that creature tried to drag her down into the dead mud. She wouldn't be a victim.

"Yes," Chris declared. "I can do that."

CHAPTER 15

"Don't leave me behind this time, okay?" Alice insisted on the drive downtown. "I don't want some creep hitting on me again."

"Stop worrying, Alice," Sam said. "We won't let that kind of crap happen again."

The memory of her last night at the club was fresh in Alice's mind. It filled her with dread. She didn't expect to meet Ted there again – if Luca was to be believed, he would be in the hospital for quite some time. He apparently didn't remember anything, but Alice couldn't forget his face, twisted in anger and later covered in rage-rent blood. She shuddered and tried to put it out of her mind.

The walk from the parking garage was freezing, thanks to winter's swift approach, and Alice's skimpy outfit was not enough to protect her from the cold. Under assurances that she would be taken care of by the group, Alice had left her bag behind. This whole outing was supposed to be a peace offering, and a chance to start over for the roommates. She felt naked without her cellphone, but there was hardly any room for it on her outfit. She shivered and kept uncomfortably close to the other girls for warmth.

"I told you to bring a jacket," Sam said when Alice started to complain.

The group marched up to the bouncer and Alice watched once again in awe as he moved to let them in. When Courtney made it to the bouncer, she turned to face Alice.

"Not her, Richard. She's underage," Courtney said.

The rest of the girls looked back, giggling at her predicament. Alice tried to rush Courtney, but the bouncer stopped her.

"I'm sorry, but you can't come in."

Alice stepped back, her head spinning. She was cold, alone, and pissed off.

She looked around, trying to think of a way into the club. She'd love to see the looks on their faces if she got in without them. The fact that they could easily get her ejected again was far from her mind, which was preoccupied with revenge. The constant bursts of ice-cold wind were a strong motivator, too. She looked up at the club's sign, a buzzing beacon of hospitality, set against unfair faded red brick. There was a staff entrance in the adjoining alley, but the thought of going down that dark corridor filled her with fear. Peering across the street for a payphone, Alice thought she recognized someone. Actually, she was certain. In her usual madcap fashion, she sprinted across the road, shoving people out of her way and narrowly avoiding getting hit by a car. Alice ran up to the woman, who had stopped to watch the commotion, and grabbed her hand.

"Hey, do you remember me?" Alice asked, gasping for breath.

The blonde woman jerked her hand away from the girl.

"We met at my dad's place. Your name is... Marcie, Margot, no, that's not it." Alice's eyes lit up. "You're Maxine, right?"

"What are you talking about? Who are you?" Maxine cocked her eyebrow.

"My dad's name is Cecil Delacroix." Alice's teeth were chattering. "He said you two worked together for the government." The pink-haired girl's enthusiasm didn't fade as she bounced back and forth, partially in victory, and partially to keep hypothermia at bay.

"Sure, you're Cecil's kid. The government. What do you want?"

"My bitch roommates tricked me and left me out here in the cold while they got into Room 42." Alice pawed at Maxine's leather jacket. "Could you help me get into the club?"

"No, no, no, you don't want to go into that club." A grin came over Maxine's face, a sign Alice didn't know to fear. "That's where all the losers go. I'm on my way to a much better place. I'll get you in there if you come with me."

"I'm with you," Alice shouted, practically jumping as she latched onto Maxine's arm.

"What's your name, anyway?" Maxine asked.

"I'm Alice. Where are we going?" They were moving away from the nightclub crowds.

"Oh, you'll see. You know, you're lucky I ran out of cigarettes or I'd never be caught dead near any of those clubs."

As they proceeded down a darkened alleyway, Alice felt a little nervous and clutched Maxine's arm. She felt Maxine try to pull away, which only caused her to grip on tighter.

"Here we are," Maxine announced as they arrived in front of a row of abandoned storefronts.

"But there's nothing here," Alice muttered quietly. Was she being tricked again?

"Shut up and follow." Maxine opened the door to an old deli. The sign was so rusty it was impossible to make out more than a few letters.

They stepped inside, and Alice couldn't believe her eyes. She saw a long line of people who were clearly dressed for a nightclub. The walls were draped with velvety, purple curtains, and only dim sunken fixtures running along the floor provided any light. More importantly to the frozen girl, the room was heated. Alice basked in the warmth as Maxine dragged her forward. There was a single door leading into the curtain with a bouncer guarding the way. He was dressed in a worn, black suit a size too small for his bulging muscles and had a headset connected to his ear. The sight of Maxine marching toward him tightened his face with fear. Maxine didn't make small talk with the man. She just ignored him, relying on him to react to her. The bouncer jumped out of the way as Maxine walked past him into the club with Alice in tow. Alice reveled in the power her new friend seemed to exercise.

Loud bass pounded through the walls as Alice studied her surroundings. She was in a narrow, unlit hallway with black, concrete walls. The floor was metal grating, which clanked as they walked. At the end of the hall was a small walkway leading to another velvet curtain guarded by another black-suited bouncer. A neon sign above his head read 'Bronze'. To the right of the curtain was a long staircase leading down.

"Why does it say bronze?" Alice asked her savior.

"The place is divided up into several zones." Maxine rolled her eyes. "You need a card to access to each. The deeper you go, the more exclusive it is."

"What kind of card do you have?" Alice was awestruck.

"I don't need a card. I go wherever I want."

A huge grin spread across Alice's face. She followed Maxine who was barreling down the stairs. Soon they came to another platform, which had another curtain, guarded by another bouncer. The word 'Silver' was written above it. Maxine yanked Alice down yet another set of stairs. The words 'Gold' were written above the curtain. Just like at the entrance, the bouncer jumped out of Maxine's way. When Alice stepped through the curtain, the din of music overwhelmed her, and she was blinded by the indigo, purple and pink lights that covered every surface. When her eyes adjusted, Alice saw something she could have never imagined.

There was a huge, sunken dance floor in the center of the room with raised platforms all around. The gleaming platforms held tables and chairs for people to recover between dances. A circular hole in the ceiling led upwards, presumably through the less exclusive areas. Along the walls were five separate bars, so you never had to travel far for a drink. Music boomed out of giant speakers suspended from the ceiling and bombshell waitresses patrolled the floor with trays of colorful shots. Alice was dizzy from the sights as Maxine dragged her to a table.

She wasn't looking at the post-modern décor or stunning lights. She was dead focused on the club's patrons, bottlenecked on the dance floor.

"So, do you like it?" Maxine asked.

"These people," Alice gasped. "They're...they're..."

"Demons," Maxine interrupted the bewildered girl, a wolfish grin enveloping her face.

The room was filled with creatures beyond Alice's comprehension. Some looked human except for curled horns, or tails. Others were larger than life, with huge frames and hulking muscles. Some had tentacles running down their backs, and others were covered in boney spikes. There was no end to the variation. Alice tried to catch her breath. The creatures didn't seem to be interested in hurting her. Actually, they just seemed to be trying to have fun. Most of them were on the dance floor, messily grinding against each other, guzzling colored drinks and losing themselves in the music.

"Surprise," Maxine said, smile wide and sly.

After a moment of silence, Alice turned to her.

"This is amazing," the pink-haired girl shouted over the loud music.

"What?" Maxine said, shaking her head as her smile dropped to an annoyed frown.

"Come on, let's dance!" Alice grabbed Maxine's hand roughly, pulling her down to the dance floor.

A look of joy came over Alice's face as she danced. She made no effort to distance herself from the demons while she moved. In fact, Alice tried her hardest to get close to them. She wondered how each of them worked. The horns seemed easy enough to explain. They were probably just bone growths, but the independently moving tentacles? What kind of nervous system would be required for something like that? Alice's mind was lost in the delight of a secret world.

After about an hour of dancing, an exhausted Maxine pulled herself from the crowd, with Alice hot on her heels. The blonde was gasping for air, unaccustomed to sustained exercise. Alice tried to pull Maxine back, but she pushed her off. Alice settled for sitting at a side table with her.

"What's that?" Alice asked, pointing at the enclosed loft that overlooked the gold area. The entrance was guarded by yet another bouncer.

"That's Elysium." Maxine tried to catch her breath. "A little piece of heaven at the bottom of Hell," she recited.

"What kind of card do you need to get in there?"

"Purple, royalty only. Also, the boss here has a fetish or some shit for purple. The place was mostly black until he took over."

"Can we go up?" Alice squealed.

She was already on her way when Maxine grabbed her and flung her onto a chair.

"No. There's nothing up there worth seeing."

Alice looked briefly disappointed before leaning forward, placing her head between her hands, and resting her elbows on the table to look into Maxine's eyes.

"So, what does a girl have to do to get a drink around here?"

Maxine laughed in spite of herself. Alice watched her closely as she got up and went over to the closest bar.

Hours later, the two women stumbled back into the street. Alice wanted to stay, but was dissuaded when Maxine pointed out that the club was closing. Maxine immediately lit up a cigarette when they hit the early morning air.

"Can you call me a cab?" Alice gestured at her outfit, emphasizing its lack of pockets.

"Hail one back on the main road." Maxine paused. "Do I need to tell you that this place is a secret?"

Alice shook her head.

"So you understand what I will do to you if I find out that you started spouting shit about demons, right?"

Alice nodded, smiling to herself.

"Then it's time for you to go," she said, shoving the girl down the alley.

"Thanks for everything, Max."

"Don't thank me. I'm not your friend."

"Then see you later, stranger."

Alice skipped down the alleyway, now immune to the despotic cold. The world had just gotten much more interesting.

CHAPTER 16

"What the hell is going on?" Julian shouted as he stormed through the police station, shadowed by a junior officer who was failing to keep up.

"He just showed up and confessed."

"Who is he?"

"Suspect is Norman Argyle, age twenty-one..."

Julian stopped short, forcing the beleaguered officer to shoot past him and circle back. "Does Larry know?" he asked through gritted teeth.

"Detective Saunders?"

Julian stared at the officer, searing him with the anger that had been welling up since he heard through the grapevine an arrest had been made in the Snatcher case. The officer glanced at a clock on the wall.

"Yes, sir. He got here about half an hour ago."

His suspicions confirmed, Julian slammed his palm against the wall. "This is my case, damn it. Why wasn't I contacted immediately?"

"We wanted to make sure that he wasn't just doing it for attention."

"That's not your job. It's mine. Where is he?"

"This way," the officer replied.

Larry was leaning against the wall outside the interrogation room.

"Why didn't you call me?" Julian demanded.

"Calm down," Larry said. "I haven't been here long either. Did they fill you in on the details?"

"Just his name, and that he stumbled in around midnight shouting that he was the Snatcher. What do you make of this?" Julian said, swallowing his frustration. It wasn't supposed to be like this. He was supposed to solve the case. It had taken too much of his life to be solved by a stroke of chance.

"Nothing yet. We're going to go in and confirm that he's the Snatcher."

Norman sat with his head bowed. His lips moved constantly from the moment he'd arrived, though he had barely uttered a word. Larry eased himself into a chair across from the suspect, while Julian leaned over the table, half for the intimidating effect and half out of frustration. Julian noticed dirt lining the inside of Norman's fingernails. Larry's expression betrayed no emotion, no thoughts at all. Julian had once commented on his partner's ambivalent expression as an interrogation technique. Larry said he'd picked it up from someone he dealt with, someone who rankled him. Try as he might, Julian had failed to coax any more details from the senior detective.

"Mr. Argyle, I'm Detective Saunders and this is my partner, Detective Morales. We understand you have something to tell us."

Norman looked up for the first time since the detectives had entered the room. He stared at Julian as he replied to Larry.

"I-I-I did it."

"Did what?" Julian asked.

"The, uh – I'm the Snatcher."

"Tell us in detail how you did it," Larry asked.

Norman continued staring at the ground.

"The... first time I unearthed the dead, it was at the Fairhaven Baptist Cemetery on the east side of town. I salvaged from the grave the fresh body of Michael Taylor."

Julian slapped the metal table, attempting to shake Argyle's nerves.

"That's public knowledge. It doesn't prove anything," Julian said.

"Please continue, Mr. Argyle," Larry said.

"Y-yeah, sure."

"You seem nervous," Larry said.

"No. I-I'm not. After unearthing the body, I used the disrupted earth to form a p-p-pentagram upon the grave. I repeated this each time."

Julian grimaced. The pentagram wasn't public record. The detectives put their suspect through his paces, asking him to list every step he'd taken, the details of every grave, over and over, trying to root out any inconsistencies. His story was flawless: he knew every name, every site, and every idiosyncrasy. But Norman, alleged grave robber and murderer, couldn't even look Julian in the eye. He had a hard time envisioning this kid as a killer.

"Why did you dig up those bodies?" Larry asked.

"I couldn't let them go to waste," Norman said as he began shaking. He rubbed his neck, massaging beads of sweat into his skin.

"What do you mean, waste?" Julian asked.

"If they stayed in the ground much longer, they'd start to decay, and then they'd be no use."

"Go on, Mr. Argyle. What did you do with the bodies?" Larry asked.

"I sacrificed the b-bodies to Baphomet." Norman paused to catch his breath, which had become rapid and uneven. "I will be rewarded for my faith when I die."

"You mean the bodies you uncovered." Julian placed both hands on the table, frowning deeply.

Norman sat up straight and flung his neck as far back as it would go. He slowly nodded his head.

"Why just men?" Julian asked.

"Baphomet only desires the strong."

"Are you part of some devil-worshipping group, Mr. Argyle?" Julian asked.

"No. He only speaks to me."

"What about the West Blair Cemetery?" Julian asked.

"I-I already described my trips there."

"It was the only place you robbed twice. Why was it targeted again? There were plenty of cemeteries that you could have hit instead of that one."

For the first time since the interview began, Norman paused to think. "I went there twice because it had less security than the others. It, it was getting harder to sneak into the cemeteries."

Sensing weakness, Julian pushed further. "Why did you decide to turn yourself in, Mr. Argyle?"

"It was... was too hard to sneak into cemeteries now. Security has been beefed up."

"That's a reason to stop committing crimes, not a reason to confess to them. Why did you decide to incriminate yourself?" Julian stared Norman down. He tried to look as hard and unmoving as possible. "Was it out of guilt? Or did you want the attention, the notoriety? Because I have to say, as attention-seekers go, you're looking pretty weak to me."

"My Lord said my time was over. I-I didn't need another reason."

"Where are the bodies, Mr. Argyle?" Larry asked.

"I disposed of them at sea."

"Where?" Larry asked.

"I d-d-don't remember."

"I bet," Julian said.

Norman refused to say another word. The two detectives left him to stare at the ceiling in solitude.

"I don't buy it," Julian said after they left the room. "He couldn't give us a single good reason why he was turning himself in."

"He had details nobody else could have. The guy's obviously crazy. Don't look for sense in his motives."

"Come on, Larry. The guy couldn't even look at me. There is no way he did that alone. He's an accomplice at best, if you ask me."

"His story checked out. We're going to charge him,' Larry said.

"We should be careful. We don't have any evidence that he did it except for his word."

"I'll check with the higher ups, but don't expect this to go much further."

"What are you talking about?" Julian asked.

"This is too high profile. They aren't going to let you dredge up the cult angle, especially with me involved."

"Why?"

"I told you before. I'm an embarrassment to the department. Sorry your cult idea didn't pan out the way you wanted. At least you got a bit of a show at the end."

"I'm going to look into him, see if there's any reason to believe he's making it up."

"Sure. Just bring everything to me first. I'll deal with the rest." Larry took out his phone and began texting, something Julian rarely saw his partner do.

"Who are you texting?" Julian asked.

"Nobody. I'm going to deal with some red tape. Get some rest."

Larry walked off. Julian stayed behind, taking one last look at Norman Argyle through the window in the door. His story was too fantastical, yet convenient at the same time. Baphomet? It sounded like something out of a cheap novel, and he didn't buy it for one moment. Norman wasn't alone. There was something more going on. Julian sighed. He felt tired, more so than he had for a long time.

The Meridian Fiend

CHAPTER 17

Sleep was the enemy, coffee the friend. Chris's initiation into Moore's group of demon hunters had made her braver during the daylight hours, but at night she was still overwhelmed by fear. The last nightmare had thrown everything she believed into chaos. Whether she walked across campus or sat in the cafeteria, she had flashbacks to the surgeon's room, her father's eyes, and his scalpel in her neck. She couldn't face the dream world. But days without rest were taking their toll. Studying at her desk, Chris was prepared for the creeping, overwhelming need to sleep. A large table fan blew at her. It stood next to the open window, so Chris was perpetually hit in the face with the stimulating cool air. A hot pot of coffee rested within grasping distance, ready to fill her with a fresh jolt of caffeine as needed. Finally, loud music blared through her headphones. But sleep was inevitable. It reached out and pressed its warm fingers over her eyelids, guiding them closed. It felt so good. Chris struggled against the temptation, but her thoughts were fading. Her body was heavy with desire, for sleep, sweet sleep. Chris fluttered her eyes a few times, trying to fight off that most primal of biological needs, but a second wave of exhaustion ended her resistance, and she succumbed to the thing she feared most.

The air smelled stale, as if Chris was an insect, stuck in box by a demented child for show and tell. It was hard to breath and even harder to think. As darkness subsumed her, then bafflingly receded, Chris found herself splayed out on unforgiving asphalt in the middle of an abandoned, residential subdivision. Her initial confusion made way for despair as she became aware of the sickly, green glow from the moon. She had failed. The nightmare world prevailed once again.

"Goddamn it," she cried as she rushed to her feet, looking around for any sign of the Beast with the Black Metal Claws.

She jumped when the door of a nearby house opened. Cloaked in the shadows was a smiling, middle-aged man in a polo shirt, grasping a bag of garbage.

"What're you doing out at this time of night?" the man asked.

"I don't know." Chris was trembling. "I don't want to be here."

"Do you want to use my phone?" the man offered kindly.

The man stepped off his doorstep and was bathed in the green light from the moon. Chris barely stifled a scream as the normal-looking man disappeared into the night. In his place was a heaving, naked creature with black ooze bursting from every pore, like the monster from the park. It laid its eyes on her and began advancing slowly. Doors creaked and ordinary-looking people exited their houses. They walked in ho-hum strides off their porches. Then the moonlight hit them and they vanished, immediately replaced by oozing creatures, identical to the one that attacked her in the park. They twitched and bobbed. Steady steps on fantastically long legs sent them forward, all utterly focused on one thing: Chris. Hordes of those creatures lumbered toward her like something from one of Alice's zombie movies.

Only one house was not spewing oozing monsters. It rested at the end of the street, between two giant trees that seemed to go forever into the dark night. Could it be refuge? Chris ran for it, keenly aware of the grimy beasts giving chase all around her. One of the pursuing creatures managed to get a grip on her and sent her falling to the ground. It landed on top of her, munching and gnawing its crooked teeth in her face. She shoved it off and crawled past the legs of four more monsters before she was able to struggle back to her feet. Another creature reached out for her, but, with a heavy shove, she sent it back, toppling several of them in the process. More and more creatures converged on all sides, and through sheer numbers began pressing her to the ground, suffocating her. In the frenzy to consume the tiny figure the beasts began to throw each other down, claw and tear at each other's throats in mindless jealousy.

The creatures absorbed the air around Chris, leaving her no choice but to crawl over the slimy bodies of the fallen. They grabbed at her as she passed, seeking her smooth, hairless flesh. She became coated in the slime from their bodies and slipped through their grasping hands. One managed to grip her jacket and jerked her backwards. Chris quickly fumbled with the jacket buttons before slipping out of it, discarding it for the creatures to devour.

Once clear of the fiendish clump, Chris forced her legs to lift her once again and carry her toward the one safe-looking house. When her feet touched the grass of her supposed-sanctuary, the earth burst open, sending her sprawling forward. Out of the earth came huge, pink flamingos, tethered to the ground. The birds squawked and reared their heads toward Chris, focusing their dead, plastic eyes on the terrified girl. Without warning, they swung their pendulous necks toward Chris. One of the creature's razor sharp beaks connected with her arm, cutting through the thin fabric of her shirt with ease and drawing blood. Chris screamed as she scrambled past the birds, darting from side to side to avoid their flailing beaks. When Chris managed to scamper through the door, leaving the horrible groans of the creatures and the squawking birds behind, everything went dark. The green glow streaming through the windows dimmed until there was nothing.

The house was completely silent except for a mechanical clicking sound. Chris crept forward in search of its source. When she entered the kitchen, she noticed that she was surrounded by the same cat-themed knickknacks that she had seen in the demon's house. They all pleasantly stared at her, their fixed expressions of joy and mischief unchanged in the nightmare. Looking up at the wall, Chris saw the culprit of the infernal mechanical clicks: it was a cat-shaped clock, whose eyes were moving side to side in time with the second hand. Each time the eyes moved they released a small 'click'. Chris didn't know why, but she knew the sound mattered. It was driving something. It had to be. She reached out to pull the clock from the wall, to tear the batteries free and stop the mechanism, but something stayed her hand.

"Chris?" a voice shot out like a light in the dark.

Chris saw a figure move into the kitchen from a room in the back. The voice was warm and familiar: Cindy.

"What are you doing here?" Cindy asked.

"I don't know." It was the only response Chris had, though she silently begged for another.

Behind her, Chris sensed a change. The darkness wasn't quite so intense. She turned and saw that the clock, the one with the rotating eyes, had changed. From the white orbs at the center of the face were two burning beams of green light. The eyes were emitting strong beams and spraying them across the room as they moved, second by second. One second, half the room would be infected with the green, leaving the other side in blackness. The next second would reverse the order. Chris looked around in horror as the once-peaceful cat decorations took on sinister appearances when the green light touched them. Playful expressions turned to howls of fury, and bright eyes darkened and glared. Then, when the light inevitably moved on, the toys returned to their harmless state. The truth was beneath the darkness, totally concealed. Chris began to shake.

"Are you all right?" Cindy asked, clearly not aware of what was going on. The young blonde stepped further into the room to comfort her agitated roommate.

"Stay back," Chris yelled as Cindy stepped into the green light emanating from the cat clock.

Cindy disappeared from Chris's vision, immediately replaced by the Beast with the Black Metal Claws. Its twisted face smiled as it advanced on her. The next second, when the green light shifted to the other side of the room, Cindy was back. Her concerned face revealed her ignorance to the transformation. The next second, she was the Beast, snarling and sharpening its claws against one another with a slick sound. Chris stepped back until she felt the unyielding push of the countertop in the small of her back. She reached behind her and felt along the cool laminate for something, anything she could use to defend herself. Her fingers soon ran against a rectangular shape that felt of polished wood – a knife block. Chris wrapped her hands around a filet knife and whipped the weapon out.

"Get back, Cindy," Chris screamed as she flung the knife back and forth in front of her.

Cindy stopped, her eyes bulging in fear, but every other second the Beast made large steps forward. With a shout, Chris lunged forward and shoved the knife up between the Beast's ribs. The two of them fell to the ground and Chris wrenched the knife out of the wound. She stabbed the Beast over and over again. There was resistance at first – the Beast's bones and sinews fought the invasion of the knife, but Chris pressed on in a frenzy. She ripped the knife from the demon's flesh and felt blood fly into her face, invade her eyes, her mouth. It had to die. Chris stabbed until her arms ached, never pausing, never risking a breath. Tears flowed as she no longer saw the Beast's twisted face, but the empty, murdered face of her friend. But she didn't stop stabbing. Blood spattered backwards, falling from the plunging knife, coating Chris's face, body, and hands. When her arm ached too much to keep thrusting the knife, Chris fell to the ground beside Cindy's leaking body. She sobbed uncontrollably as she tried to pull herself back onto her feet. Then pitch black enveloped her. She screamed and flailed the knife, searching for invisible creatures.

A blinding, green light burst through the darkness, causing Chris to shield her eyes. When she regained her vision, there were dozens of Beasts in front of her, each of their twisted faces smiling in exactly the same way. She stabbed the nearest Beast, but the others descended upon the poor girl, their claws sinking into her weak flesh as they ripped through her until there was nothing left.

Chris woke up screaming, her eyes darting around the dorm room, still seeing imagined monsters everywhere. When the real Cindy tried to console her, as she had in the past, Chris reared back and struck her, terrified that at any second she could become a sick and twisted monster. Cindy backed off and raised her hands.

"Cindy?" Chris said, breathing ragged. "I'm sorry. I didn't mean to."

"Something happened," Cindy said, rubbing the side of her jaw.

"What?" Chris asked.

"It's Norman."

CHAPTER 18

It had been a few days since Chris's last nightmare, and she was starting to crack up. She had managed to keep sleep at bay, but she knew it wouldn't be long before she lost the battle once again. She sat alone at the cafeteria, waiting for Alice for their regular Friday lunch. As usual, Alice was late. She bounded in twenty minutes after Chris got there.

"Wow, you look terrible. Not doing so great, huh?" Alice asked.

"I've had a really rough week. My RA turned out to be the Snatcher," Chris said, her eyes bloodshot.

"Holy shit, that was your RA? Did you know him?" Alice asked.

"A bit. He was always nice to me. I can't picture him as a murderer."

"You never really know people."

"I guess you're right." That was almost the theme in Chris's life these days, she thought dejectedly. You can't know who's a demon. You can't know who's a murderer. She was grateful at least Professor Moore and Emily were there to show her a clear path to the good side, but it was still so goddamn hard.

"I know exactly how to make you feel better," Alice declared. "I'm going to take you clubbing tonight."

"I don't have a fake ID, so I can't go clubbing," Chris explained, hoping that would derail any plans Alice had.

"That's the best part. I know how to get into this club without ID." Chris opened her mouth, but Alice cut her off. "I don't care if you don't want to go, or if you have plans, or if you have the damn flu, you're coming with me tonight, and we're going to have fun."

"You know you can't force people to have fun, right?"

Alice stared, waiting for a better answer.

"Fine, fine," Chris conceded. Arguing with Alice was futile. Besides, if she was in a nightclub, she wouldn't be able to sleep. In her own weird way, Alice might actually be helping.

"Trust me," Alice declared. "This is a night you will never forget."

The cab dropped them off in the middle of the nightclub district. Alice was dressed skimpily, as was becoming her trademark. Chris was dressed in the same clothes she wore to lunch and had no intention of dancing, something Alice had been pestering her about ever since they left.

"Enough with the secret, which one are we going to?" Chris asked as they began walking down the street.

"Nope, still a secret. It's the most amazing place ever. And I don't know its name."

Chris's anxiety level soared higher the farther they walked from the other clubs. She shouldn't have worried about demons or dreams at all. Alice was going to get them murdered, in an alley probably. That seemed about right. After walking through a particularly dark alley that further convinced Chris of their impending doom, Alice stopped suddenly in front of an abandoned deli.

"Ta-da," Alice shouted, flinging her hands toward the door.

"Your secret is an abandoned building," Chris fumed. "You aren't great at surprises."

"Go on in," Alice said, helping her sister through the door with a friendly shove.

Chris was shocked to find the actual makings of a nightclub inside.

"See?" Alice beamed. She skipped past the line of people to the bouncer.

"Back of the line," he said, looking her up and down.

Chris quickly turned and started to leave before Alice dragged her back.

"No, you're letting us in right now." Alice smiled sweetly.

The bouncer frowned, shaking his head. Alice's expression changed from sweet to sadistic.

"I would really hate to see what would happen to you if you didn't let us in. After all, we're friends of Maxine."

"Maxine doesn't have any friends."

"I was really hoping you'd say that. You see, I'm a little bored today and I can't wait to see what Maxine does to you when I tell her you wouldn't let me in. Maybe she'll be nice and you'll only spend the rest of your life in a wheelchair." Alice paused for effect before reaching into her purse and pulling out her phone. "What's your name, anyway?"

Beads of sweat dripped down the side of the bouncer's face.

"Ray," he replied, his voice shaky.

"Thank you, Ray," Alice said coldly as she started dialing the phone.

"Wait," he shouted. "Go on in."

Alice squealed with delight and dragged Chris through the dark curtains.

"What is this place?" Chris asked, looking around the dark corridor.

"It's the best nightclub ever," Alice said. She pointed to the sign above the door. "You see the word 'Bronze' there? Each part of the club needs a different card in order to get into, but we shouldn't have a problem as long as we keep namedropping Maxine."

"That woman who works with Dad?" Chris asked.

"She showed me this place, and, best of all, the bouncers are terrified of her, so we don't need clearance."

Alice held tight to Chris's hand as they ran down to the bottom of the club. Standing in front of them was another bouncer in front of the gold area.

"Watch this," Alice said as she leisurely strolled up to the young man.

"Card please," he said authoritatively, reaching out his hand.

"I think it would be in your best interest if you remember who I am," Alice said, placing her hands on her hips. His eyes bulged in realization when he remembered the last time he had seen this girl.

"Please, come in," he said, moving quickly out of the way.

Chris couldn't help but smile. She was actually starting to enjoy this. It was nice to be away from her life for a bit, especially with how complicated it was getting. She also liked being around her twin. It reminded her of a time where things were a lot easier.

The music was deafening when they entered the gold area. All Chris could see were beams of blue and indigo bouncing across the room. Alice wrapped her hands over her sister's eyes.

"No peeking," Alice yelled, dragging Chris to a table on a nearby platforms. When they were safely seated, she released her twin and waited for Chris's eyes to adjust to the club.

Chris looked down into the abyss and saw her nightmares gleaming back at her. Monsters were everywhere. Horn and claw flashed in the indigo lights and shook to the blaring music. The creatures were grinding their beastly flesh together, a Satanic display of animal lust. Was this where they met, where they bred? Did they agitate each other with gruesome tales of their last kills, or was this where they came to celebrate a particularly bloody week? Alice was shining as every drop of color left Chris's face.

"Alice," Chris choked out. "We have to get out of here now."

Alice flicked her on forehead.

"What are you talking about?"

Chris tried to move her lips, to explain to her boneheaded sister about the danger she had placed them in, but she was paralyzed with fear. Demons were all around her, grinding, crushing, pulsing.

"Isn't this place amazing?" Alice said. "Do you see those people down there? They're demons. Can you believe it? Demons!"

Chris scrambled to her feet and began hyperventilating. Alice caught her and shoved her back down. Chris was sweating, desperation gripping her like a straightjacket.

"What is wrong with you?" Alice asked as she watched Chris implode.

"I don't know if you realize this, Alice," Chris managed to speak, slowly and deliberately. "But demons kill people, and we're the only humans in sight. We have to get out of here right now, before they see us."

"Do any of these guys look like they're getting ready to kill people?" Alice shook her head with a grin, as if Chris was speaking utter nonsense.

Chris looked at the demonic shapes on the dance floor below, silhouetted in flashing purple and indigo, and frantically nodded her head.

"Fine, we can go." Alice made a guttural cry of frustration.

Chris leapt out of her seat and stepped head first into an immovable figure in a black suit.

"What are you doing here?" asked a familiar, disappointed voice.

"Luca?"

CHAPTER 19

Luca stood with her hands on her hips, her stony face twitching with anger.

"We're just leaving," Chris stuttered out, looking back at Alice.

Alice offered no support. She appeared to have died on the spot.

"You two are coming with me," Luca said, clearly unsatisfied with Chris's response.

Neither girl moved. Neither thought they could.

"Now," Luca shouted. She grabbed Alice by the scruff of the neck. Chris stood frozen and helpless until a strong push from Luca propelled her toward the stairs. Luca herded the two young women to the entrance of Elysium, the shrouded overlook above the dance floor.

"Is there a problem, Ms. Russo?" the bouncer asked, his body becoming more erect as she approached.

"These two are in a lot of trouble, and so is whoever let them in here. Find out who's stationed at the doors, or you're the one the one who will pay for it."

The bouncer gulped and immediately busied himself speaking to someone on his headset. Chris considered making a run for it, but Luca shoved her through the door. It didn't matter. Chris could never outrun Luca, and she knew it.

Inside, there was a crowd of demons standing around a bar, and more spread out on couches around the room. When the door closed, all Chris could hear of the club surrounding them were the faintest beats of bass. The room was garishly colored, with purple and indigo blurring her senses and making the demonic forms seem even more horrific. Maxine was lounging in a corner with a bottle of wine, her feet on top of a table. She scowled when she saw Alice and raised her hands in a mock clap, ridiculing the girls. Luca glared at the blonde accusingly. Maxine simply gave her the middle finger and grinned.

"Out, now!" Luca yelled.

With a few gestures, more black-suited men ushered all of the demons out of the overlook without a word. If she had been less terrified, Chris might have marveled at the control Luca obviously possessed over the creatures, or at least most of them. Maxine didn't acknowledge the order and bouncers gave her a wide berth. She obviously wasn't somebody you messed with, but she frightened Chris the least out of everything she'd seen that night. At least Maxine was human – or was she? Chris remembered the frail, old man Michael had killed. If Maxine was human, she wasn't doing a good job of pretending to be innocent. Taking her time, Maxine eventually followed the crowd out.

The back wall had huge windows overlooking the gold area of the club. A long, black leather couch ran the length of the wall, flanked by a semi-circle of chairs. Sitting cross-legged on the couch, eyes wide with shock, was Cecil Delacroix.

"Dad? You, too?" Chris looked at her father, tears in her eyes.

He let out a loud sigh and leaned back into the couch.

"Down, now," Luca barked, pushing the girls into chairs facing their father. The Delacroix family stared at each other for an eternity, until finally Cecil spoke.

"How did you get in here?"

"It doesn't matter how they got in, Cecil," Luca said. "This never would have happened if you had talked to them when I told you to."

Cecil bent forward, placing his elbows on his knees and cupping his face in his hands.

"I suppose I owe you two an explanation," he began.

"Damn right you do," Luca added.

"Okay, let's start this simple," he said, rubbing his eyes. "Let's forget how you got here. What do you know about this place?"

"Just that it's a demon club and you need cards to get into different areas," Alice said.

Luca gestured at Cecil to continue talking.

"This place is called Tartarus," he said. "Like you said, Alice, it's a demon club, but more importantly, it acts as a kind of community center for the demon population in Meridian City. Demons come here to have fun and be themselves in public. They also come here to air grievances and deal with problems." He gestured around the room. "This we call Elysium. It acts as the command center for Tartarus."

Chris wondered if this was what her dreams had been telling her – her father's mask represented this secret life, where he apparently allowed man-eating beasts to 'have fun and be themselves'. She could hardly contain her disgust and raising anger. Had he known her dreams were premonitions when he'd acted so reassuring on the phone? Was it really possible that he'd knowingly betray her?

"Dad, are you telling us that you're in league with demons?" Chris finally found the courage to speak.

"No, I am not doing this. This is just not happening," he declared, flinging himself onto his side and pulling his feet onto the couch.

Luca shoved his feet to the floor and hauled him back to a seated position.

"This is a long time coming. You have to do it now," she whispered.

"Fine," he hissed before returning his eyes to his children. He gestured for them to get up. "Come up here. I want you to look out the window."

The two girls slowly rose from their chairs and peered down at the dance floor.

"What do you see?" Cecil said.

"Demons and some humans," Alice said.

"The human-looking ones are probably demons, too," Chris corrected her bitterly.

Cecil guided them back to their seats.

"You're right, Chris. There aren't any humans in this club," he said.

Chris couldn't see why he wasn't concerned about that fact.

"That's why it's so dangerous. We have to get out of here before they turn on us, Dad. Don't you see how crazy it is for us to be here?"

Cecil winced and looked at Luca. She nodded.

"I don't think you're getting it." He made a wide gesture around the room. "There are no humans in this club, anywhere."

Chris's blood froze as she finally understood his meaning.

"No," Chris shouted.

"What?" Alice asked, bewildered.

"You idiot, he's saying that we're monsters!"

"Demons," Cecil corrected the girl. "We're all demons."

"You're lying. This is some kind of sick joke," Chris cried.

Alice had an uncharacteristically somber look on her face, which she was cradling in her hands, but she didn't say anything.

"I think I would know if I were some kind of monster," Chris insisted. "What are you really hiding from me?"

"Enough of this," Luca said, frustrated. "Show them."

Cecil's eyes pleaded with Luca, but her stern gaze held firm. Letting out another sigh, he stood up and removed his button-down shirt. Standing in just his undershirt, he extended his right arm. The twins looked in amazement and horror as his skin started peeling back from the tips of his fingers. From beneath the flesh emerged long, slender claws made of solid, black metal. Soon there was nothing recognizable as skin on his entire arm. There was only inky, black steel, bending and popping where joints should be, from the tips of his claws to his shoulder. He twisted his shining wrist and pointed at a terrified Chris.

"Now, unless you want a DNA test, I think we can safely say that I am not lying to you," he said.

"That arm," Alice shouted. "I've seen that kind of claw in my nightmares."

Chris gaped at her sister. Were their nightmares genetic?

Cecil sat down, skin reforming along the length of his arm. In seconds it was back to normal, as if nothing had happened.

"That's pretty normal. I would expect some part of your demon side to make it into the dreams," he said.

"You gave me these nightmares. Why?" Chris stood up before being pushed back down by Luca.

"No, I didn't cause your nightmares, Honey." Cecil smiled adoringly at his girls. "Those kinds of dreams start up when demons get to a certain age and start being able to manifest."

"Manifest?" Alice asked.

"All demons are born totally human-like. When they mature, demons start to be able to manifest their demonic traits, like I just did with my arm. Demons like us can transform their arms into metal and sprout really cool claws. If you're having the dreams now, you'll both be able to manifest soon."

"You may not have had such a hard time with the dreams if *someone*," Luca glared at Cecil, "Had told you all this when you were younger like I told him to."

"Dad, I have a question," Alice said meekly after a prolonged silence.

"Sure, Honey, what is it?"

"I'm guessing you don't actually work for the government."

"Yeah... that wasn't the best cover story," Cecil said.

"Then what do you really do?" Chris asked, even though she was terrified of the answer.

"What do I do?" He grinned, pointing at himself. "I'm the Overlord."

CHAPTER 20

Chris stared out the window of the car, her eyes fixed on the passing streetlights. Her mind was still trying to get around her father's announcement. She looked over at Luca, who was driving the car. Her face bore no emotion, which was typical. Chris now wondered if it was because she was a demon.

"What are you?" Chris asked the older woman.

"You already know what I am," Luca replied.

"Luca," Chris asked quietly, "Have you ever killed anyone?"

"Yes," Luca replied quickly.

"How many?"

"I don't know." Luca kept her gaze fixed on the road.

"Like, one or two?" Chris asked with bated breath.

"I'm not having this conversation with you right now. Maybe when you've calmed down a little bit."

"When did you find out you were a demon?" Alice piped up from the back seat, leaning over the console.

"I've always known, and put your seatbelt on," Luca responded.

Alice fiddled briefly with her seatbelt before leaning forward between the front seats again.

"I always thought you and Dad worked for the CIA or something. You know, with all the 'partner' talk and your gun."

A subdued smile slowly crept across Luca's face.

"The government story never made sense. What kind of government employee is out at all hours of the night?" Luca shook her head, "But we couldn't change it after the first dozen times he used it. That's your dad; he never thinks things through."

"So..." Alice continued, "What do you actually do? Max told me Elysium was the most exclusive part of the club."

Luca cringed at Alice's casual mention of Maxine. "I do security, keep everybody safe, and I help your father."

"And what is an Overlord?" Chris broached hesitantly.

"Major cities and regions are assigned Overlords. They organize the individual communities and make sure everything stays secret," Luca said.

Chris's eyes darted far from the imposing woman with the inescapable truth. A secret world of monsters, just like Moore had warned – it went much deeper than Chris ever would have imagined.

"We'll talk more about it later," Luca stated to nobody in particular.

* * *

Cecil lay draped over his couch in Elysium, one arm flung dramatically over his eyes. He had turned off all the lights and closed the curtains, wrapping himself in darkness. He felt sick, like he'd lost something valuable that night. The look on Chris's face throughout the ordeal was burned into his mind. The sudden surge of music told him someone was coming inside the overlook. He edged his arm away from his head to peer at the intruder: Fenris Holt, head administrator of Tartarus. Fen was in her late thirties, but her makeup was expertly applied to make her look as young as the barmaids she supervised. She wore a white button-down shirt, a pencil skirt, and a bow-tie. The fabric of her skirt stretched uncomfortably across her hips and rippled with every step, which, of course, was her intent. Her glasses did nothing for her 20/20 vision, but she got a kick out of taking them off and shaking out her blonde hair for a sultry effect. Onyx horns poked through the suspiciously flawless skin on her forehead.

"Where are they?" Her shrill voice rang out. "You told me that I could meet them when you fessed up."

"Luca took them home." Cecil rolled his eyes at her pouting face. "Next time they're here, I'll introduce you. I promise."

Fen clapped with glee before flinging herself onto a chair.

"So, how'd it go?" she asked.

"It could have gone better," Cecil said as he pulled himself to a seated position. "I should have dealt with this years ago. Luca's been after me to do it since they turned sixteen."

"You should have told them way before that. If you do it when they're little, they don't even know to be shocked."

"Yeah, well, I know that now." Cecil glowered at her unsympathetic response.

"I'm sure they'll come around." Fen smiled reassuringly. "I mean, it's a lot to take in all at once." She stood and made her way to the bar.

"Alice wasn't too freaked out, but I'm not sure Chris will ever speak to me again," Cecil admitted.

He could hear the clanking of bottles and ice as Fen busied herself behind the counter. She returned with two drinks, handing one of them to Cecil.

"I'm worried, Fen. I've done some terrible things in my life, but I've never felt so worried. I don't know what I would do if I ever... lost Chris."

"You're her dad. She'll come around."

* * *

Alice looked at Chris, who was staring out the window as if in a trance. It was a lot to take in, and Alice had many questions. She glanced down at her fingers, which itched perpetually ever since she was little. Was it because there were huge claws under the surface, ready to come out? Would they show up on an x-ray? Could the molecular structure of her extremities actually be manipulated at will and, if so, was there a way to harness that power in a lab? Was she going to kill people? These were all important, but Alice had a more pressing thought.

"Hey, Luca?" Alice asked. "Why are we just learning about this now? Is that normal?"

"It's not normal at all. You have your father to thank for that. I told him to tell you years ago, but would he listen? Of course not, because that would spoil his fun. He used to go gallivanting around every day, just doing whatever he pleased, while I took care of you. Then, when he realized how much he was missing, he couldn't deal with a tough conversation. So, here we are."

"But why not tell us to begin with?"

"We didn't have a normal childhood. He wanted different for you."

The car pulled up in front of Alice's townhouse. As Alice got out of the car, Luca rolled down the window.

"I'll get you a card for Tartarus. Until then, don't try to trick your way in, and stay far away from Maxine. She's a terrible person."

* * *

Chris watched Alice walk away until her bright pink hair disappeared into the dark house. The car pulled out, and Chris realized that she was trapped with a murderer.

"It's going to be okay, Chris," Luca said. "Better that you find out now, and not when you manifest for the first time."

"I'm a monster."

"Don't say that. Demons in this town are just trying to get by, like everybody else."

"Maybe you're wrong," Chris said. "You said that I should have manifested a long time ago. Maybe it isn't going to happen?"

"It doesn't work like that," Luca said firmly. "Demons have a small chance of manifesting around the age of sixteen. It gets increasingly likely as you get older, and all demons manifest before they reach twenty-three. There's no way to tell when you'll start to get the dreams. I was twenty when I first manifested, and your father was seventeen."

"Why should I believe anything you have to say?" Chris snapped, keeping her head turned toward the window. "Apparently, you've been lying to me my entire life. You guys didn't think it was important to let us know that we're monsters? Maybe a 'hey girls, don't forget that we're a bunch of murderers' pep talk before sending us off to university."

"There's a lot of things I would have done differently."

"And the nightmares. Nobody even tried to prepare us for them. Do you have any idea how horrible they are?"

"Of course I do. Every demon goes through them. You're strong. You'll be fine."

"I haven't been fine," Chris spat.

"You're angry. I'll come over tomorrow after you've had some rest and we can talk."

"So you can lie to me some more?"

Luca sighed. "Call me when you're ready."

The two sat in awkward silence until they arrived at the old dorm. As Chris leaned out of the car, Luca grabbed her arm.

"You're going to be fine." She patted the young girl's hand. "I'll get you a card to get in Tartarus, too."

Chris ran inside without looking back.

Cindy was lying on her bed with headphones in her ears. She jumped up at the sight of Chris coming through the door.

"Where have you been?" Cindy asked.

"I was just at the library, learning some things," Chris said, her jaw clamped so tight that it came out more as a mumble.

"Did something bad happen?" Even the earnest Cindy saw through Chris's lame excuse.

Chris shook her head, but was unable to put on a fake smile.

"I have been freaking out," Cindy said. "Emily told me she was finally going to let me into her secret club. Maybe, if they like me, I can put in a good word for you." She shot Chris an exaggerated wink. "I bet that would make you feel better, right?"

Chris didn't respond. She tossed herself into her bed and stared up at the ceiling as Cindy replaced her headphones. Her life was a lie. Peaceful childhood days were clothed in sheep's skin as butchers looked on, clasping their hands and licking their lips. Everything was always leading to the slaughterhouse, but nobody had warned her. To hell with them then, Chris thought, sneering. If the people she trusted most had kept the truth from her, she'd have to get it from someone else. She couldn't think of anyone more qualified than a professor of the occult, who'd risked so much to show her what was behind the curtain. But that wouldn't work.

Chris groaned and rubbed her eyes. She was the enemy, or at least she would be when the dreams took the last of her sanity away. Was she still human until then? Could she confront the Beast with the Black Metal Claws and emerge normal? That demon that attacked her in the park was an empty, vicious shell, and if Luca and her father could betray her trust, maybe they were empty too, in their own way. Would that happen to her? Chris fell asleep that night feeling like darkness was creeping up from every corner.

CHAPTER 21

The days after Chris's trip to Tartarus had been hell. It took many false starts before she called her father, but she had questions about her 'situation' and very few sources of information.

"Hey, Honey," Cecil said in a saccharine voice that now got under Chris's skin.

"Have you ever killed anyone?" Chris asked out of the gate.

"You must have so many questions. I'm really sorry how the other day went."

Chris's eye twitched at his evasion. She looked at the window in her room without saying anything for a time, gazing at her reflection, unconsciously rubbing her arm.

"What am I?" Chris asked.

"You're a demon."

"Is there are cure?"

"It's not a disease, Dear. You're a different species from humans."

"What else have you been lying to me about? Are there angels, goblins, and leprechauns, too?"

"Not that I've ever heard. I think people just confused demons for those things."

"How many monsters are there?" Chris asked.

"A lot. We don't really do censuses too often, but we float between one and three percent of the population. You've probably met a bunch of demons without even realizing it. Actually, do you remember Rebecca from across the street when you were growing up? I deal with her father sometimes. She's a demon, too."

"Have you ever killed anyone?" Chris asked, her guts seizing.

"Don't be worried about killing people. If you don't want to, you won't."

"Dad, I'm asking about you."

"I'm sorry, Honey, I have to go. There's a big emergency here at work. Why don't you give Luca a call?"

Chris heard the phone disconnect. Her father hadn't meant to tell her the truth, but it had been perfectly clear. He was probably waiting until she was so crazy from the dreams she wouldn't challenge him anymore. She wouldn't let him drag her into his bloody trap. Chris turned her eyes from her reflection. She only knew one place left to go.

At the end of the day, Chris entered the construction site at 52 Baker's Drive. The air was cold, but Chris didn't feel it. The walk went by in a blur. Inside, she saw Emily and Michael talking near the stairwell.

"Did you actually invite Cindy to come tonight?" Chris asked, approaching Emily with crossed arms.

"I thought it was time. She's been asking a lot of questions about where I've been," Emily replied.

"Cindy doesn't need to know about this kind of stuff."

"I'm not forcing you to tell your sister. Cindy needs to know the truth about what's out there, and I'm going to tell her."

"I'm sorry," Chris stammered, as she realized she had become her father, willing to lie to Cindy to protect her feelings when there were real threats out there. Chris braced herself against the wall and almost threw up on the spot.

Emily looked at Michael. They both snickered.

"Don't worry about it, Chris. I was pretty freaked out, too, after the first time. But it gets easier. You'll see that we're doing what's right," Michael said, patting her on the shoulder.

Chris jumped at the sound of a commotion coming from behind her. A large group of figures entered through the eastern exit, chatting loudly.

"How many of us are there?" Chris asked, surprised by the number of men.

"I would say we're up to twenty-six, twenty-seven when Cindy shows up," Emily said after a moment of thought.

It wasn't long before Cindy nervously poked her head through the door. Emily smiled softly and waved her over.

"Oh my God," Cindy exclaimed with her usual exuberance. She skipped over toward her roommate. "I didn't know you were already a member, Chris."

"Yeah, sorry I couldn't tell you," Chris replied.

Cindy hugged her. The physical contact felt good. It helped bolster Chris for the night to come. Emily nodded to Michael before taking Cindy's hand.

"I need to take you upstairs now, okay?" Emily said protectively.

Chris and Michael stayed behind as Emily took Cindy up to see Professor Moore.

"Do you believe in God, Chris?" Michael asked when he was sure Emily was no longer in earshot.

"My family isn't religious," Chris said. The understatement of the century, she thought.

"I'm trying to get my head around why you're here." Michael asked, seeming genuinely confused.

"I'm here to help people. You're here because of God?"

"We *are* killing demons. The professor opened my eyes. We're going to stop this plague."

"Do they have to be stopped?" Chris asked.

"What kind of question is that?"

"Are you sure they're all murderers? How much do you actually know about demons?"

"I know enough. You haven't seen what they can do yet. I'll admit the last one we killed was on the weak side. You should have seen the one before that. He could have orphaned a lot of kids."

"How many people did he kill?" Chris asked, more firmly than before.

"I don't like your tone."

"I don't like how you're not telling me anything," Chris spat.

"You want to see someone die? Is that it?" Michael asked.

"I want proof that these demons are all evil."

"Then we'll show you." Michael scowled. "We're on scouting duty tonight. Maybe if you're lucky, you'll get to see what you want. I pray to God we don't though."

Looking past Michael, Chris saw Emily holding Cindy's hand as they came down the stairs. Cindy had a blank expression on her face, unusually lost in thought. Chris felt a twinge of sadness for her normally joyful roommate. This was a heavy burden, one she wished Cindy didn't have to bear. She was just a gentle soul. Emily took Michael to discuss the strategy for the night, leaving

Chris to take care of Cindy. Chris reached into her messenger bag for the personalized thermos Alice bought her for their birthday. It was filled with the coffee that was slowly replacing the blood in her veins.It was shaping up to be a long night.

"Is it true?" Cindy asked.

"I'm sorry," Chris said.

Emily and Michael finished their discussion and made their way back to the initiates.

"All right," Emily announced. "It's time to head out."

They drove to a residential area near the port on the east side of the city. The homes there were old, prefabricated houses. They were made after the Second World War as low-income housing for veterans. Emily pointed at a single story house on the right. There was light flickering through a window, undulating unpredictably on the grass of the front yard with a harsh bluish-white light.

"That's the place," Emily said, pulling the car up to the curb.

Chris looked over and saw a man in his thirties sitting in front of a television set eating cereal.

"How sure is the professor?" Chris whispered.

"We wouldn't be out here if there wasn't a good reason to suspect him," Michael shot back.

"What if he moves?" Cindy said loudly, looking up expectantly at the group.

"We'll find another window," Emily said. "Now keep your voice down."

After an hour and a half, the stakeout seemed like a bust. Chris struggled to keep her eyes open. She lifted her thermos to her lips and took another belt of coffee. She looked over at Cindy, who was nuzzled up to Emily, sleeping soundly. Emily herself was staring out the window in a daze. Michael was the only one who seemed completely alert. His unblinking gaze was fixed on the man, who was laughing hysterically at the television. Chris felt a sudden rush of energy when she saw the man pick up his phone. He threw his arms in the air and yelled into the receiver. Emily nudged Cindy, jolting her awake.

"Duck," Michael said, throwing his arm over Chris and forcing her head down.

The man stormed outside in a fit and got into his car.

"Okay, Em," Michael said softly. "Follow him, but keep your distance."

Emily sat up in the car and started the engine. They drove far behind the man's car, keeping their headlights off. Eventually, the man stopped in front of an old, brick house and ran inside.

"Park here," Michael said, pointing to the side of the street about a block away.

As soon as the car came to a stop, Michael bolted out and ran across the street, keeping his head low. The others hesitated briefly before following him. They stopped in the bushes to the side of the house. The front door stood wide open. They heard shouts echoing from inside, but no discernable words. It sounded like at least two people were arguing about something, and they were both furious. A gunshot rang out.

The foursome jumped when the man left the house. He was covered in blood. The red liquid looked black in the moonlight and coated his forearms and hands. The shining, viscous liquid reminded Chris of the black metal claws she'd seen on her father and in her dreams. There it was, just like Michael promised. They spent one night watching a demon and got to be witness to a murder. Professor Moore wasn't playing around in the dark – he knew exactly what dangers they were confronting. The blood-soaked man reached his car in a panic and tried desperately to open the door. The searing screech of tearing metal filled the air. Chris saw that the man's hand had been replaced by a fearsome talon, like something from a bird of prey. The man shook his hand frantically for a few seconds before he was able to return it to human form and opened the door to the car. He jumped inside and sped away before any of the demon hunters could react. Just like that, he disappeared into the night.

Chris and her friends raced back to their car, with Emily again taking the wheel. She steered them back to campus, passing wailing police cars along the way. Chris unconsciously ducked every time one of the police cars passed, the sirens and flashing lights filling her with dread.

"Did you see his hand?" Cindy squealed.

"Its hand," Michael corrected her. "Don't treat it as if it were human."

Chris looked out the window at the passing streetlights. She wasn't human either, or she wouldn't be soon. She reached into her jacket pocket for her thermos, hoping the coffee would focus her mind.

"Shit," she yelled.

"What?" Emily yelled back.

"My thermos. It's not in my pocket." Chris wracked her brain, trying to remember the last time she saw it. "It must have dropped out of my bag. We have to go back," she said, clutching at the driver's seat.

"We can't." Emily frowned. "Didn't you see the police? One of the neighbors must have heard the gunshot."

"What if they find it?" Chris asked, trembling. "It has my name on it. My stupid sister had it engraved."

"Don't worry. Nobody's going to connect you to any of this?" Emily calmly reassured her.

When they got back to the construction site, Professor Moore was there to greet them.

"So, was my suspicion correct?" he asked.

"Yes, Professor," Emily responded.

"Good. Now we can start planning." The suave professor stooped beside Chris. "How was your second time out? Are you okay?" he inquired, tussling her short hair.

"Yes, Professor," Chris said.

"You look rattled," he pressed. "I really want you to be honest with me if you're struggling here. I know you have a heavy burden, and I want to help you carry it. And if this is too much for you, well, you have only to say."

"Are you going to kill him?" Chris asked.

"We don't have a choice."

"Have you ever tried talking to the demons?"

"I tried talking to one. He wasn't communicative. They like their secrets, and they want to keep being able to kill people without punishment."

"Are they all like that?"

"Every single one. I'm sorry to bring you into a world of killers, Christine, but I need your help."

"What if a demon gave themselves up? What if they wanted to help?"

"That's an interesting question. Truthfully, it hasn't come up. If it weren't for the certain fact they would be lying, I'd jump at the chance. Imagine what we could learn from them."

"Learn?"

"I'm sorry. That's the academic in me. Of course we couldn't accept a demon into our midst or show mercy. They'd kill us or corrupt us. That's all they do." He squeezed her shoulder in reassurance, and left her to collect her thoughts. To Cindy, he turned and offered a careful smile. "And you, Dear, do you understand what we're up against?"

Cindy nodded. "Yes, sir, and I'm happy to help."

"Good girl. Chris, could you take Cindy back to the dorms? I have some things to discuss with Michael and Emily."

Chris gestured for Cindy to follow her.

"I'm sorry you had to get involved in this," Chris said, mimicking the words Emily had said to her when she first joined.

"Yeah," Cindy said as she shuffled along. "Maybe we shouldn't kill him. I mean, we don't know why he did it. Maybe he had a good reason?"

"There's no good reason for murder, Cindy," Chris said, shoving her hands into her coat pockets as she tried to extinguish her own lingering doubts.

Cindy didn't respond. How could she? Chris thought. Murder wasn't something one rolled underneath the rug and pretended like it didn't exist. The monster from the park murdered; the man with the talon murdered; Luca murdered. Would she kill people someday? Did she even have a choice? Chris felt more confused than ever.

When she got back, she called her father. She asked him directly if he'd ever killed anyone. He said no. Then he laughed uneasily for minutes. Chris knew not to believe him. She knew she shouldn't. But she had to try. It was her only hope.

CHAPTER 22

Alice lounged on her bed, her eyes transfixed on her computer. Pictures of horrifying creatures were prominently displayed on the screen. Demons. It was a massive head-trip for the pink-haired girl. She'd thrown herself into learning as much about her heritage as possible. It wasn't easy, though. Although she offered to talk things through, Luca actually had limited patience for the billions of questions Alice lobbed at her. The internet wasn't exactly helpful, either. Luca had told her that Meridian City had the third largest demon population per-capita in the eastern United States, and that there were a few thousand of them milling about, doing who-knows-what. At times, while she sat in the cafeteria at school, watching throngs of students putter by, Alice found herself wondering exactly how many of them there were, hidden in the crowd. Back in her room, she scoffed at the website, which claimed to detail ways to summon demons from the fiery pits of hell. She reached out for her phone and called her father, a new line of questions forming in her head.

"Hey, Honey," Cecil answered in his usual way. "What's up?"

"What's the deal with hell?" Alice asked.

"Like fire and brimstone and... oh, I get what you're asking. There's no such thing, as far as I know."

"So, demons don't, like, pop out of hell portals or something?" Alice asked.

"You know, I'm starting to regret getting you hooked on horror movies."

"Whatever. Where do demons come from, then?"

"First off – don't trust movies and TV. Demons aren't spirits or ghosts or anything crazy. We're just born like everybody else. The only catch is that, being a different species, we can't crossbreed with humans."

"That means... mom would've been..."

"Yeah. The type of demon, meaning the manifestation, is passed down on the mother's side," Cecil said.

"And how does manifestation work? I saw your claws. Are they under the skin all the time, or does something trigger them? And how does your skin grow back?"

"I'm not really the best person to answer that." Cecil laughed. "As long as it works, I'm happy."

Alice's next thought was disrupted when she heard her roommate Sam yell up the stairs for her. She quickly said goodbye to her father and went downstairs.

Alice paused after she crossed the threshold into the living room. All of her roommates were sitting on the couches, apparently waiting for her.

"We have to talk," Sam said, frowning deeply as she gestured for Alice to sit. "The girls and I have been talking, and we feel it would be best for everyone if you moved out. Of course, we'll give you a couple weeks to find a new place."

"You're kicking me out? What gives you the right? Is it because of this bitch?" Alice spat back, nodding her head to Courtney, who wept unpersuasively on the couch at the attack.

"I'm sorry, Alice," Sam replied. "Your constant attacks on Courtney are only part of the problem."

Alice crossed her arms, unconvinced.

"There's the dead animals, which we've talked about."

"That only happened twice," Alice insisted.

"Please let me finish," Sam said. "You've also been keeping the house awake with your night terrors."

Alice clenched her jaw at the mention of her nightmares. They had been getting more intense recently, and she'd woken up screaming more than once.

"It just isn't working out. I hope you understand," Courtney added.

"You know what?" Alice said. "*You're* not working out. Fuck you."

Alice stormed out the door, locking shoulders with Courtney as she turned. Her heart was racing and her mind went to dark images of her now-former roommates being skewered in her dreams.

Alice ran as fast as she could down the street, passing block after block. Tears stung her eyes and the cool morning air burnt her skin. Why was she crying? Alice tried to keep calm, but frustration and regret over how she handled that situation swirled in her mind. She wandered aimlessly for hours. Her attention was brought to the sky when she felt something cold fall on her cheek. Looking up, she saw snowflakes wafting from above.

Alice cursed under her breath as she shivered. She thought of calling Luca to pick her up, but she couldn't bring herself to do it. Instead, she kept running, eventually finding herself in front of her father's house. There was a motorcycle parked outside, but Cecil's car was nowhere to be seen. Alice was shaking, too cold to think, too cold to notice that the door was ajar when she approached the house.

"Dad?" Alice called through chattering teeth as she walked through the front door. She saw someone laying on the couch, smoking a cigarette, but it wasn't her father.

"Maxine? What are you doing here?" she asked.

Maxine glanced at her and sighed.

"Your dad told me a while ago that I couldn't ever come here again, so I break in occasionally to rearrange things, smoke around the house. You know, do things that piss him off." She took a better look at Alice, who was practically blue. "What's wrong with you? Do you even own a coat? I would think that Daddy Dear would buy his poor little runt something to keep her warm."

Alice burst into tears. She stayed in the doorway, giving Maxine a pleading look. The blonde rolled her eyes.

"I'll listen to what happened to you, but, if I do, you owe me, okay?" Maxine generously offered.

Alice nodded.

"Fine, sit your ass down and get talking."

On the couch, Alice fidgeted, uncomfortably tapping her fingers on her knees. Maxine broke the silence with an annoyed groan.

"I said I would listen. I never said I would ask questions, so you'd better start talking, or I'm out of here."

"Are you a demon, too?" Alice asked, trying to slow her breathing.

"No, I'm just an innocent schoolboy that got lost on his way to the candy store."

"I was kicked out of my apartment today." Alice blushed.

"Really? That's it?" Maxine started laughing.

"They said that my nightmares kept them awake at night. I know I shouldn't care what they think. It's just... the dreams. They're too much. I'm not sleeping, and now I'm falling apart about what some stupid bitches think of me." Alice grabbed at her knees, her knuckles turning white as she focused.

Maxine put out her cigarette on the table, marched over to Alice, and slapped her across the face.

"What the hell's wrong with you?" Maxine barked.

A stunned Alice stared blankly up at her. Maxine brought her hand back and struck the girl again.

"Don't be so weak," she said.

A flush of anger replaced the tears on Alice's face.

"I've held up my end of the bargain," Maxine said, rubbing her hand and falling back on the couch.

"You didn't do anything," Alice roared.

"What did you expect? Did you want me to kiss it better? Get over yourself, Runt. Everyone goes through the dreams, and you don't see anyone else crying about it." Maxine carefully ignored how traumatic the dreams tended to be.

Alice lunged at her. A smile broke out across Maxine's face as she punched Alice in the stomach with inhuman strength, sending her onto the floor, gasping for air. Maxine kicked her onto her back before placing her booted foot over her throat and applying pressure.

"There's a reason that people are afraid of me, Runt." She smiled, watching Alice's face turn red. "Maybe you need a lesson. Free of charge, of course."

Alice's arms beat impotently against Maxine's powerful leg. Anger and fear danced through her veins. Life was slowly leaving the young women when Maxine removed her foot and sat down again, leaving Alice sputtering, trying to catch her breath on the floor. Alice reared her head toward Maxine with the intent to glare, but she realized she wasn't upset anymore.

"I assume you're here because you don't have anywhere else to go? Am I right?" Maxine asked as she prodded Alice in the side with her boot. "I could call in my favor now, but I think I'll give you a choice this time."

Alice rubbed at her throat as she gave Maxine a confused look.

"You could move in here, back with your dad. I'm sure he'd love it, but I don't think you want that. I mean, who would? The thought of having to relive your childhood? Ugh, makes me sick," Maxine explained, a superior smirk fixed on her face. "So here's the deal. I have some room in my apartment, and I think I could deal with your face on a regular basis. Of course, you'd have to pay me whatever rent you pay now, as well as do all of the cooking and cleaning."

It was Alice's turn to laugh. "You broke into my dad's house and beat me up. In what world would I want to live with someone like you?"

Maxine held two fingers in front of her face. "Two reasons: first, I don't care if you scream at night. Actually, I think I prefer it." She chuckled. "Second, bitch all you want, but I can tell you're having fun."

Alice's heart was pumping wildly. She looked into Maxine's bright, blue eyes and realized she was right. All the pain she had been holding onto since she left the townhouse was now a distant memory.

"Deal."

Alice held onto her new landlord for dear life as they flew through Meridian on Maxine's motorcycle. Alice had never been on a motorcycle before. She liked the cool winter air and specks of snow hitting her on the face, and the warmth of the body in front of her. They eventually pulled up in front of a historic townhouse downtown.

"This place is broken up into three apartments," Maxine explained as she brought the bike into an adjoining garage. "There's a decrepit blind woman on the bottom floor, some foreigners on the second floor, and I'm on top, exactly where I belong."

The wooden steps groaned as they made their way up to the third floor apartment. The repugnant smell of rotting food hit Alice's nose when the door opened. There were piles of garbage littering the floor and beer bottles covering most surfaces.

"Okay, house slave, time to get to work. I want this place to shine by the time I get back," Maxine sang as she headed back out the door.

* * *

Maxine practically skipped into Tartarus. The bouncers wisely didn't trust a happy Maxine and cleared the way as she approached. Climbing the steps of Elysium, she nearly giggled. The room was mostly empty. There were a couple of patrons at the bar chatting loudly, and Fen buzzed around, taking inventory.

She strutted toward Cecil, who was sitting, as usual, cross-legged on the couch at the back of the room. Luca was standing nearby and gave her a dirty look as she approached, but Cecil smiled pleasantly. He was so weak. This was so easy. Maxine bent backwards over the chair in front of him, looking at him with her face upside down.

"Guess who's bunking with a little Delacroix now?" she crowed, unable to contain her joy as a dark look came over his face.

CHAPTER 23

Chris gasped as the loud crackle of static wrenched her eyelids open. She wasn't in her bed anymore. Instead, she was propped up on a couch in front of a small television set, the source of the blaring static. The television itself was shedding a faint green light, coating over her like venom. So, she was in the dream world again. Chris leaned back into the chair and closed her eyes, trying to settle her stomach despite this unliveable hell. At least, she considered, she knew what she was really up against. The longer she fought off the Beast within, the longer she could retain her humanity. At least, that's how she hoped things worked. If she lost herself here, she would lose herself just as surely in reality, and she wasn't ready to let that happen. Wiping away the stubborn tears that appeared in spite of her resistance, Chris opened her eyes and took stock of her surroundings.

She was in a small room. Aside from the sofa and the television, there were picture frames everywhere, all of them black and empty. A quick glance out the window confirmed what Chris had feared: parked across the street was Emily's car, which meant she was in the killer's lair. Without a second thought, she raced to the front door. She didn't bother testing the knob. She rammed her shoulder into the wood with all her might, but the door refused to budge. It was jammed shut. They were always jammed shut.

Chris peered out of the windows beside the door into Emily's car. She saw three figures sitting, waiting – Emily, Cindy, and Michael. She wondered if she could call them to her to help her in this fight. Some backup sure sounded appealing. Chris banged on the window and called out to them, begging them to come to her aid. They didn't move, not a single flutter. She squinted her eyes and stared as hard she could through the green light. Around Emily's neck was a thin, black line. The same mark was just visible on Cindy and Michael as well, like they all had tiny strings wrapped around their necks. But they weren't strings, Chris realized. The people in the car weren't people at all. They were mannequins, with plastic painted eyes and empty smiles. There would be no help from those puppets. Chris flipped her back toward the door, eyes searching the flickering dark for the Beast with the Black Metal Claws - her perpetual tormentor. There was nothing but silence in the long, dark hallway.

In her dream-addled state, Chris began a cautious march toward the end. Along the walls were more empty picture frames, black emptiness surrounded by gleaming gold. The messy light from the television projected large hulking shadows, twitching to life on the opposite walls. From beyond the darkness-encrusted frames, something was stirring.

Chris jumped when a shadow shot recklessly into the frame next to her, nearly knocking the picture off the wall with a heavy thump. She stared as the shadow transformed within the frame from a fuzzy blackness to demonic face. Its features almost looked human, except for the black eyes and the curled horns enveloping its forehead. The creature slammed its horned head into the glass of the frame, like it was trying to escape. The glass held, at least for now. Chris turned from the caged monster and continued walking, hoping that monster would stay trapped.

The next picture frame she passed formed a demon, too, and the next. Soon every frame behind Chris was occupied by frenzied creatures, adorned with so many fangs and claws, and each one was crashing against the glass. The cacophony of clangs and clashes filled the hall and began to disorient the girl, but Chris kept moving forward. As the sound of horns against frames grew louder and louder, she found it harder to focus on finding her way out. Were any of the frames broken? Had any monsters escaped? Chris couldn't tell. She struggled to hear anything over the din of the frames and, for a brief moment, thought she caught a breath on the back of her neck. She turned around, certain a monster was just behind her.

Nothing. Just the same, green hallways with the same gallery of flesh-eaters clamoring for freedom. Now that they had her attention, every monster boasted their biggest smiles. As hollow snap, and every last demon broke through their frames. The nearest monster's arm broke through the canvas and glass in a bloody mess and pulled the rest of its body out. Writhing tentacles wriggled from its back, each one covered in brown slime, snaking down the corridor, searching for something to smother the life out of. Another photo was ripped open by a bird-like talon, grasping for the frame. The next disturbed picture frame fell to the ground with a crash and a tiny, soaking wet man leapt out of it. He cricked his head to the side and smiled at her, bearing huge shark teeth.

More and more demons were piling up on the floor. Chris turned and ran. With every step she took, the corridor seemed to get longer, stretching out to oblivion, the end now invisible through the darkness. She ran for what seemed like hours, glancing behind frantically at the growing horde of demons chasing her, reaching for her flesh, perpetually only a few strides behind. A tentacle wrapped around Chris's neck and jerked her backwards. Chris gasped, her airflow constricted. She fell backwards, landing flat on her back and heard a sickening crunch in her left shoulder. The demons swarmed around her. One tore a strip of flesh from her torso like a slab of meat and grinned as blood arced through the air and coated the faces and arms of the creatures above her. Chris tried to scream, but she couldn't breathe. The tentacle was still wrapped firmly around her neck, allowing her just enough air to stay conscious, but not enough to struggle. Her head was pounding from the lack of circulation, and her face was turning purple. Chris gathered all her strength and twisted her neck downward as far as she could until the tentacle was aligned with her mouth. She bit down as hard as she could and tore into the demon. Blood oozed into her mouth as her teeth ripped deeper into the appendage. The monster screeched and recoiled, finally freeing Chris's throat.

Chris gulped in the sweetest air she had ever tasted, and then pulled herself to her feet. She couldn't allow these demons to take her. An attempt to sprint in her exhausted condition failed and she fell forward, landing on her hands and knees. The monsters were mere feet behind her, but nothing happened. Still gasping for air, she craned her neck around. They were all gone. There were no demons behind her, but in their place were scores and scores of mirrors reflecting an ever-brightening green glow from the ceiling. Each mirror returned a smiling image of herself. Chris whipped around in a circle, trying to spot a single variation in the grinning facsimile from the mirrors, but they were identical. She was sure it was some kind of trick. She tore the fabric from the bottom of her shirt and wrapped her hand in it. If the mirrors represented her demon side, then she would have to destroy them.

Chris stepped up to the biggest mirror and reared back, prepared to smash the glass. Before she could take a swing, a crack appeared at the corner of the frame. It was small at first, but it grew quickly. Dozens more cracks sprouted from it and raced up the mirror and to the edges of the frame. Chris looked around – cracks were spontaneously generating in every mirror in the room. Just in time, she realized what was coming and hit the floor with her arms wrapped around her head. The mirrors shattered all at once, as if on cue. Broken glass soared through the room like a choreographed dance of destruction, then shattered on the ground. Chris felt it slice into her arms and back as she huddled on the floor, but her neck and face were protected. When she was sure the glass shower was over, she stood up. Shards slid off her back and crinkled to the floor.

Inside the broken frames remained the smiling image of Chris. Only now, she realized, it wasn't an image. They were real. The doppelgangers slid out of their frames and advanced on her, the original. Chris tried to back away, but the smiling copies herded her easily into the center of the hall. She was surrounded by her own smiling face, but she was sure the intention wasn't friendly. Before she could make a move, Chris felt the earth shift beneath her as the floor opened up, and she fell into the abyss.

Chris woke up on a cold, concrete floor. Around her were knickknacks and old, rusted appliances. A window near the ceiling let her know that she was in the basement, and the green light that streamed in told her she was still locked in a nightmare.

"Stay back!" came a shout from the other end of the room.

Flipping over, Chris saw Michael and Cindy standing with knives drawn. Behind them, a musty scarecrow in the shape of Professor Moore sat with his legs crossed, a wide smile fixed on his face as if he were an idol.

"It's all right," Chris said, dusting herself off. "It's just me."

"I said get back, monster," Michael yelled, advancing on the confused girl and swinging his dagger, narrowly missing her.

"Please leave us alone," Cindy cried.

Chris stumbled back as Michael continued his assault. She reached over to a large mirror covered by a dusty, yellowed sheet. Grasping the mirror tightly, she launched it at Michael. He screeched as the mirror shattered over his face, leaving four deep cuts as if someone had scraped a heavy claw against it. Holding his scarred face, Michael retreated back to the Moore scarecrow.

Something on the floor caught Chris's attention. In each of the thousands of jagged mirror shards on the ground was a twisted, blood-shot eye gazing up at her. A large, black metal claw burst through the largest shard on the ground and grasped onto a nearby cabinet. Chris felt like she was outside of her body, unable to move even an inch as the Beast with the Black Metal Claws dragged itself up from the hell within the mirror shards.

The Beast smiled its twisted smile. It knew that Chris couldn't move, and it wanted her to watch as it destroyed her friends.

The wounded Michael didn't even have time to scream before the Beast's claws sawed through his neck. His severed head sprayed the room with blood as it tumbled to the ground. The Beast kicked it at Cindy. She covered her face, falling quickly as the Beast's claws traced through her stomach like a saw blade through an orange. While Cindy sputtered out her last breaths on the floor, the Beast bounded over to the Moore scarecrow and peeled it like an onion, revealing a second scarecrow beneath the surface. The surgeon now sat in Moore's place, cross-legged at the back of the room. His porcelain mask was back in place.

The Beast approached the frozen Chris and grinned, bearing its fangs at her. It bent over and, with its right hand, picked up a shard of glass from the floor. Against her will, Chris's body jerked down, mirroring the Beast, picking up a similar-sized shard with her left hand. The Beast's laugh echoed through the basement as it brought the shard to its throat.

"I'll kill you for this," Chris whispered as her body betrayed her and placed the shard next to her pulsing jugular. "You're the one who's going to disappear. Not me."

The Beast laughed harder before it slowly dragged the glass through its own throat, forcing Chris to do the same, screaming all the way.

CHAPTER 24

Julian sat in the waiting area of a psychologist's office surrounded by decade-old magazines and hushed conversation. He frowned at the sight of the receptionist lazily reading a tabloid magazine. A large picture of Norman Argyle was plastered across the cover. The headline screamed 'Snatcher Hangs Self in Police Custody'.

"Come this way, Detective Morales," the receptionist called after about ten minutes.

His gaze lingered on the tabloid magazine.

Dr. Silvia Matthews sat behind a large, wooden desk in the center of the room. The doctor was a woman in her mid-forties who wore a no-nonsense grey suit and a warm expression.

"How can I help you?" she asked.

"As I mentioned on the phone, I'm here to ask you some questions about Norman Argyle," he explained, taking a seat in front of her desk.

"I read that the police let him commit suicide in his cell."

Julian cringed at the thinly veiled accusation. Norman's death in custody was huge embarrassment to the Meridian City Police Department.

"Am I correct that you saw Mr. Argyle as a patient up to six months ago?" he asked.

"Norman was a particularly memorable client."

"How so, Doctor?"

She hesitated, tapping a pen against the side of her desk. "Norman was a very troubled man. He was paranoid to an extent that few un-medicated patients are, and was afflicted by a perpetual savior complex."

"Is that so?" Julian kept his gaze steady.

"He had vivid sexual fantasies revolving around saving women."

"Did he ever mention anything about the occult, specifically the name Baphomet?"

"No. He never referenced anything supernatural, but during his last appointment I got the impression that someone was influencing him. If he was under the belief that he was being contacted by some sort of spirit or demon, I have no doubt that he would listen. He wouldn't be the first to create some sort of higher being to obey in order to absolve guilt from especially heinous crimes."

"Why did you stop seeing Mr. Argyle as a patient, Dr. Matthews?"

"I recommended that he get medication to help with his condition, as I had many times in the past. However, this time he became violent, screaming that he had found a purpose and he didn't need medication. He then stormed out. I never saw him again."

"In your professional opinion, was he a threat to anybody or himself?"

"No. He had fantasies, but he was a timid, easily influenced personality. That last outburst was extremely out of character for him. I didn't think he was a danger to anyone, which is why I never contacted the police."

Julian stood up. "Thank you for your time."

Larry was reclining in the passenger seat when Julian got back to his car.

"Find anything interesting?" Larry asked.

"For someone so fanatical, I would have expected his psychiatrist to have at least heard the name Baphomet from him. She thought that someone may have been controlling him."

"Doesn't mean anything. The guy was crazy and I wouldn't put any faith in anything he said. I think he made the whole devil worship thing up. He was clearly a delusional kid."

"How can we be sure he wasn't making the whole thing up, then?" Julian struggled to keep the annoyance from his face. He was tired of Larry's constant attempts to stifle him.

"It's possible, but he knew too much about the case to not be involved somehow. I seriously doubt that there's some underground cult running around digging up bodies for God-knows-what."

"I think Norman got in deep with the wrong people and they brainwashed him into confessing," Julian said. "There's more to this than we're seeing."

"There isn't anything weird going on here, Julian," Larry bellowed, grabbing Julian by the shoulder. "There's just one sad, crazy kid. Do you understand me?"

Julian was caught off guard by his usually laidback partner.

"This isn't finished," Julian said.

"It is for us. We've been assigned a new case." Larry tossed Julian a file folder that was packed with gory images of a murdered man.

Julian looked at the pictures intensely, trying not to let his frustrations spill over or taint his impressions of the new case.

"What did this to him?" Julian wondered aloud. The man in the photos had lacerations all over his chest and neck. They were ragged and deep, not like any gunshot wound Julian had seen before. "It looks like he was attacked by some sort of wild animal," he added.

"Pit bull, I suspect," Larry explained. "The victim, Jacobs, fired at his attacker." Larry took out a picture of the wall at the crime scene and pointed at it. "The positioning of the bullet shows that Jacobs was firing at a person, not some animal. There's a local gang that uses pit bulls as part of their loan shark operation. They starve 'em, beat 'em, then turn 'em on poor fools who can't make their payments. My money says this was a final collection."

"No cult this time, huh?" Julian asked. "If there was, would you even let me investigate?"

"What are you getting at?"

"That you have been holding me back. Norman didn't kill those guys, or, if he did, he wasn't alone. But we're going to let this kid take all the blame. One half-hearted look at his dorm and a trip to his psychiatrist's office isn't enough."

"Do you actually buy his story about the demon?" Larry asked.

"It's worth looking into. I don't think we'll find a demon or anything, but I'm betting there are some people who would kill for the fantasy of Baphomet. Why is the department covering this up?"

Larry sighed. "I told you they call me 'Loony Larry', right?"

"Yeah."

"There's some really messed up shit out there, Kid, and I didn't want you to get involved. Do you know how many cop deaths we've had over the last twenty years? More than Boston. More than New York, even, and there's only one thing we can do about it. Don't ask questions, Julian. It ain't easy, but sometimes it's better to just accept things the way they are."

"That's not how you make things right," Julian said, holding back barbs on his tongue.

"No, that's how you stay alive."

CHAPTER 25

Luca woke up at 4:59am, as she did every day. She stretched a muscular arm out from the blankets in time to stop the 5:00am alarm she set every night. She kicked the sheets from her naked form and commenced her morning exercises - sit-ups off the edge of the bed.

The room reflected Luca's Spartan sensibilities. There were no books, knickknacks, or gadgets. Next to the bed was the only other piece of furniture, a small night stand. It held her cell phone, gun, and a framed picture of herself with Chris and Alice. The girls were eleven in the picture, ecstatic over their first and only trip to Disney World. They were grabbing Luca's arms, trying to pull her toward every ride at once. Uncharacteristically, Luca was laughing. Every day, when she saw the picture, Luca remembered how happy they'd all been that weekend: the girls, beguiled by a fantasy land; her, soaking in their joy; and Cecil behind the camera, playful and proud. Today, Luca was determined to restore their makeshift family. She had invited the girls to visit Tartarus at 10:30 that evening. Chris had promised to come, and Alice had promised to force Chris to come. It was going to be a good day.

Her sit-ups finished, Luca strode silently to the bathroom to complete the next step of her morning routine. She moved with military precision, carrying out each step exactly the same way and in the same order every day. Luca loved order. It proved she was in control. The bathroom mirror reflected scars mapping her body, evidence of her own weakness. Her picture reminded her of joy, but her reflection reminded her of pain. It was good to keep both in mind.

Back in the bedroom, Luca opened an ironing board and prepped her suit. She ironed every piece daily, and years of practice ensured a perfect turnout. Luca had chosen the black suit as a uniform several years ago to cover for her lack of fashion sense. When she was promoted to head of security, she decided her staff should dress the same way to present a united front. Later, when Cecil became Overlord and promoted her again to head of special operations, she simply merged the department with security and imposed the uniform on her special agents as well. Luca affixed her shoulder holster over her crisp, white shirt and left the apartment. It was precisely 6:30am when she pulled into Cecil's driveway, giving her plenty of time to read the news before he woke up.

Luca had just finished catching up on current events when Cecil lurched into the kitchen, disheveled and swearing. That was one way mornings were different without the girls: Cecil didn't have to watch his mouth. He still made breakfast, though, and he still did it as haphazardly as possible.

"Morning, Luca," he said, covering his mouth as he yawned. "What're you thinking for today? I might still have some eggs left."

"No, you don't. You used the last of them yesterday."

"Waffles it is, then." Cecil stood on the tips of his toes to check the cupboard.

"Coffee first," Luca said, holding her mug up in the air.

With slightly burned waffles on the table, Cecil consented to talking about work.

"What's on the agenda today?" he asked.

"The girls are coming tonight," Luca reminded him. "Before that, Sergei wants to talk to you about Theodore Langley's disappearance. He'll be in early."

"I don't think I can take four hours looking at pictures of his grandchildren," Cecil said, sipping his coffee.

"Yuki's concerned about some proposed logging legislation that may affect the West Blair forest, but it's not urgent," Luca added.

"Come on, Luca. Stop teasing. Did we get one?"

Luca's special ops team had been on the hunt the night before, trying to solve the rash of demon disappearances that had cropped up in the past year. After months of dead ends, Tartarus had gotten a complaint from a demon who said a strange car had been parked outside his home for hours with four people inside, watching him. The complainant, Jim Bowers, was known to be a bit of a crank, but a tip was a tip and Luca sent two men to scope it out. When the team pulled onto Bower's street, the car sped away, squealing its tires in haste. They didn't get the license plate, but they got something better: a young man who had been creeping through the bushes for a closer look when his friends fled the scene. Luca had gotten the call at 3:00am.

"He's being detained in Tartarus now, ready for you to question him," she said.

"It's been too long since I've had a chance to interrogate anyone," Cecil said with enthusiasm seldom mustered in the morning.

"The Ghoul problem is starting to be an issue," Luca said.

"Yeah, yeah, we'll deal with it."

When they arrived at Tartarus, a man in a black suit was waiting at the entrance. Luca inspected his uniform while Cecil breezed inside.

"Straighten your tie, Finney," Luca barked. The man jumped to correct his dress and nearly choked himself in the process.

"Report," Luca demanded.

"We have the suspect in the holding cells, ma'am. We've made sure to keep him sleep deprived for easier interrogation as per the Overlord's standing orders," Finney replied without hesitation.

"Good. We'll go over the duty roster at noon," she said.

Luca strode inside to find Cecil. She headed for Elysium, but found his usual perch on the couch suspiciously empty. Behind her, a tiny old man approached.

"Good morning, Luca dear. Is Cecil available?"

"Of course, Sergei," Luca assured him. "I'll bring him up for you." Looking around, she spotted Fen and a black-haired girl mopping up blood. She tried the girl, hoping to avoid a conversation with her pushy friend.

"What happened here?"

"A small fight, Ms. Russo. No fatalities," the girl stuttered.

"Where is the Overlord?" Luca asked.

The girl was shaking. Luca walked away, not interested in questioning the terrified creature any further.

Fen was sitting at the bar going through a substantial amount of paperwork.

"Fen, where's Cecil?" Luca asked with a sigh.

"He said he'd be in the holding cells," she cooed. "You really should have asked me first. Nadine is useless." Without warning, Fen reached out and grabbed Luca's head, running her fingers through the cropped, black hair. "You really need to do something about this, Luca. Just once let me take you to my stylist."

"This is exactly why I didn't ask you first," Luca exclaimed. She broke free of Fen's surprisingly strong grasp and descended into Tartarus' restricted areas.

Below the cylindrical nightclub, Tartarus was a maze of stark, grey corridors and unlabeled doors. Every hallway was exactly the same as the last, purposely designed to confuse unauthorized visitors. Tartarus was more than a community center for the demons of Meridian: it was city hall, a research facility, a secret intelligence unit, law enforcement headquarters, a public relations firm, and a fortress dug into one sunken lair. There were bunkers in case of attack, and an impressive armory that Luca personally took inventory of every two weeks since a particularly frightening combination of bomb-making supplies had disappeared.

Luca continued until she reached a stairwell heading down. It led to the holding cells, and Cecil's interrogation room.

"How do I look?" Cecil stepped out of the room in a surgical outfit, holding a bag of tools, and making a small twirl.

"Work first, Cecil, then fun." Luca shook her head. "Sergei's waiting for you upstairs."

"Shouldn't this take priority?" he pleaded. "Sergei's here about a disappearance. Our suspect might be involved in the disappearances. If I do this first, maybe I can give Sergei some good news."

"Get changed."

Cecil pouted, flouncing out of the room to retrieve his clothes.

Luca frowned. It was going to be a long day, but at least she'd get to see the kids.

CHAPTER 26

Snow fell softly outside the dorm, hypnotizing Chris with its easygoing whirls and specks. She was proud that she had managed to stay awake for two days straight, subsisting on minute-long catnaps interspersed throughout the day. The Beast with the Black Metal Claws was at bay – for now. She sat over her Psychology textbook, feverishly imagining that the winning strategy to fighting her own mind might be lurking inside, if only she could tease it out. The sleep deprivation was toying with her mind, but she was hardly aware of it. She felt like she had ascended to a higher plane of existence, one where everything was just about to become crystal clear. Her head lowered itself down onto the book and consciousness finally slipped away.

"I'm awake!" Chris shouted as her eyes flung open.

Her neck was stiff, and she couldn't move her head. Tears flowed freely from her eyes when she realized why. Her safe, warm room was a in a far off place. She was somewhere far more sinister: a dark room, where she was strapped to a silver metal table. Each of her limbs was held down by leather restraints, and a large band travelled across her forehead, keeping her head pinned. Behind her was the sickly smooth sound of metal being sharpened. Beast or surgeon, she wondered. Or did it matter? Either way, she had to find a way off this table. Her eyes searched the room, straining in their sockets. It was a fully equipped operating room. The light above her reminded her of a dentist's office. There were metal carts covered in sinister instruments clearly designed for rending and ravaging flesh. Around the edge of the room were massive window panes and behind them, row upon row of human faces, watching her, observing. Their eyes were her own.

Chris wasn't focusing on them, or the brown stains of dried blood covering every surface in the room. Chris's trembling eyes were squarely focused on the occupant of the stool in the corner: the Beast with the Black Metal Claws. It didn't acknowledge her presence, its own gaze focused on the ground like a scolded child. Gone was the maniacal glee it displayed in her last dream. Gently held in its deadly claws was a porcelain mask.

"Could you hand me the mask, Sweetie? Daddy needs it for work," a voice came from behind Chris's head.

The Beast raised the mask, but couldn't bear to look at the surgeon.

"Thank you, Dear." A hand reached over Chris's face to retrieve the mask.

Chris tried to remain calm, to think of a way off the table. The surgeon stepped into her view and waltzed over to the wall.

"Watch this," he said as he flipped a light switch.

Everything went dark briefly before a second set of lights turned on, filling the room with the sickly, green glow.

Chris screamed and thrashed as much as she could against the straps.

"I love that light," the surgeon said with a giggle. "It really freaks them out."

The surgeon dashed back to the table and turned to the carts of torture instruments. One by one he picked them up and examined them, rolling them over his hands, balancing them, testing them. He took a circular blade with jagged edges and rolled it over Chris's stomach as if he were picking out an outfit for her. The Beast with the Black Metal Claws leapt to its feet and howled in anguish.

"It's all right, Honey," the surgeon said, glancing over at the Beast. "It's just a game. It's all a game."

The Beast shook wildly, trembling in fear of the man. It lowered the volume of its howls, but it didn't stop.

"Please let me go," Chris whispered.

"Quiet." The surgeon pounded on the table next to her, before kneeling in front of the Beast, grasping its eviscerating appendages in his soft hands. "Please be quiet, Sweetheart. It'll just take a second."

The Beast's wails calmed and the surgeon walked back over to Chris.

"I don't have time for this," he said under his breath while he picked up a scalpel with a shaky hand. "What do you know?" he asked loudly.

"I don't know anything," Chris declared.

"We'll see about that," he said as he used the scalpel to cut away the fabric of her top, leaving her bare chest exposed. "Last chance."

"Fuck you," Chris yelled.

The surgeon didn't say anything else. Instead he lowered his scalpel into her chest, the flesh yielding as blood oozed and spurted from the wound. The pain was excruciating. Chris's screams and thrashing caused the Beast to renew its own protestations.

"Shut up, Chris," the surgeon shouted at the Beast, accidentally shoving the scalpel far into Chris's chest.

Chris's vision blurred and the searing pain dulled.

"Fuck! Look at what you made me do," the surgeon admonished the Beast as Chris's eyelids fell dead.

"Awake," Chris shouted, her head shooting up from her book. "Goddamn it!" She buried her head in her hands. Somehow she was getting more helpless in the dreams.

A series of loud knocks at her door startled her out of her dismay.

"Come in," she called.

"Hey, Stranger." Alice snaked her head past the door.

"Alice? I thought we were meeting downtown later?"

Alice waltzed into the room and closed Chris's book.

"Hey!" Chris whined.

"No time for work now. We're going early so we can have fun before you get mad at Dad again."

"I'm not going to get mad at Dad. I just don't want to go to a demon club."

"I'm not taking no for an answer," Alice said with her hands on her hips. "Plus, I already compromised. I was going to come grab you almost two hours ago."

Alice rummaged through Chris's closet, pointedly ignoring her sister's glare, and threw a black pea coat at Chris.

"Fine, I'll call a cab," Chris said. It was impossible to say no to Alice unless you wanted to be pestered until she lost interest – and she never lost interest.

A few minutes later, they were outside, waiting for the taxi to pick them up.

"How have you been holding up about, well, you know?" Chris asked.

"Fine, I guess. I don't know if it's really hit me yet. I've been trying to figure out what it really means. Luca's already sick of me asking questions."

"Dad barely answers mine," Chris said. "What about the dreams? You've been having them too, right?"

"Yeah." Alice laughed uneasily. "They aren't fun, are they? I had this one last night where these huge rats had pinned me on a tray, and started ripping me open." Alice took a deep breath. "Shit. I swear I could feel the blade sink into me." She shuddered. "Luca says they're important to get us acclimatized to manifesting, but it's not fair."

"It's horrible." Chris started tearing up. "I can't sleep, and when I do, I'm chased around by monsters all night. And I'm even starting to feel like one."

"Um, Chris? You are a monster."

A dark look overtook Chris's face.

"Don't be like that," Alice said, punching Chris on the arm. "Just because you're a monster doesn't mean you're a bad person. The dreams will pass. You just have to stick it out. We're monsters together, okay?"

"Maybe you're right." Chris smiled weakly.

"Of course I'm right. I'm always right," Alice said.

"You're not filling me with confidence anymore." Chris laughed for the first time in a while.

When they arrived at Tartarus, it was still before 8:30pm. It was probably the first time Alice had been early for anything.

"I know you got all freaked out last time, but you have to admit that Tartarus is a pretty awesome club," Alice said.

"I wouldn't know. I don't go to clubs."

"Well, it's pretty good compared to the other one I've been in."

Chris couldn't stop herself from laughing at Alice's confidence. When they arrived at the storefront, Chris paused, looking at the sizeable line.

"Don't worry," Alice said, nudging her. "Luca said all we had to do is flash the cards she gave us."

Chris eyed the purple card Luca had foisted upon her a few days earlier. Emblazoned on it was a hopelessly out of date picture from before she cut off all her hair. Luca didn't take many pictures.

"No," The bouncer said as they approached. "You two aren't getting in here. I don't care if you're actually friends with Maxine or not. Last time I let you two in I got into a lot of trouble."

Chris stepped back, but Alice was unfazed.

"Oh, don't be like that. Look here," Alice said, pulling out the purple card.

"Delacroix?" the man read out the name on the card, his eyes flipping between the young brown-haired girl on Alice's card and the pink-haired trickster before him. He went white. "Go right in. I'm sorry for the inconvenience."

"I'm thinking we should get a drink before going up to Elysium," Alice suggested on their way down to the gold area of the club.

Chris nodded frantically, her eyes darting all around. Her earlier ease with her sister was fast evaporating. The forms of manifesting demons hanging around hit her with the cold truth of the insane world in which she lived. They looked so ridiculous in club clothes, bopping to the music, like they were normal people, like there weren't horns and claws and tails jutting obscenely from their bodies. Alice said being a demon didn't make her bad. Looking around, it was easy to be lulled into that viewpoint. The demons seemed so happy, so almost harmless.

Maybe, Chris reasoned, maybe she could hold onto her humanity. Maybe she'd escape the dreams intact. She recalled the demon who tried to kill her in the park. Was it possible that he was an aberration? Then she remembered Luca's candid admission of murder. But it didn't have to be that way. It was still possible her father hadn't killed anyone. Sure, he was cagey on the subject, but maybe he just hated talking about work. Or better still, was ashamed of the killing Luca had done. Luca was the one with the gun, not him. If her father, the so-called Overlord, didn't kill, maybe she had a chance.

Alice flashed her card at the bouncer in front of the curtain, flitting past him without stopping.

"Aren't you afraid of these monsters?" Chris asked.

"No. They should be afraid of me," Alice boasted, her response drowned out by the strains of dance music.

They ordered drinks from one of the bars and plopped down at a table; Chris steadfastly refused to dance.

"Oh my God." A shrill voice pierced through the noise. "Cecil said you were coming tonight."

Chris turned to see who was shrieking at her. It was a woman in her late thirties. She had long, blonde hair and was dressed in some sort of sexy secretary outfit that looked like a Halloween costume. Chris shuddered when she noticed small horns breaking through the woman's forehead.

"You have to come with me," Fen cried, pulling the girls toward Elysium. "I have heard so much about you two," Fen gushed as they entered the overlook. "Has your dad said anything about me?"

Chris and Alice looked at each other and shook their heads, earning a pout from their host. Her sullen mood lasted but a moment.

"I'm Fen, as in Fenris. You know, the wolf," she said, making chomping motions with her mouth.

The girls exchanged confused glances.

"I work with your dad." Fen sighed.

"What do you do here, Fen?" Alice asked.

"Well, your dad's the Overlord, so he's in charge of the whole show. Luca's in charge of the security force and special operations, and I'm the head administrator, in charge of the day-to-day running of Tartarus."

"What's the security force?" Chris asked.

Fen leaned in to squeeze Chris's shoulder. "They protect the club, mostly. Special operations do the more fun stuff, like investigations. Most people can't tell the difference between them, though." She thought for a second. "Basically, if they're wearing a black suit, they're Luca's guys."

"Where's Dad, anyway?" Alice chimed in, taking a sip of her drink.

Fen gave herself a smack on the forehead. "Oh, of course! I'll take you guys to him.

"This is the entrance to the restricted areas," Fen explained, pointing at the heavy door on the side of Elysium. "We aren't just a club, you know. All of our more serious functions take place back here."

When she opened the door, two men in black suits stepped out of the way at the sight of her.

"You guys at university?" Fen asked, as they walked.

The two nodded in unison.

"Demons around the city have been going missing at a lot over the past year, so, you know, watch out for that."

Chris felt a pang of guilt at hearing about the disappearances. It had to be Moore's group. So the demons kept track of each other and noticed if one went missing. Was it because they cared for each other? Fen seemed nice. The longer she spent in Tartarus, the more normal everything seemed. Every passing demon with horns out, made the horns seem a little less strange. Maybe Professor Moore didn't know what he was talking about. Maybe her father was telling the truth.

* * *

In the prep room near the holding cells, Luca was trying her best to get Cecil back to work.

"I need to do that more often," Cecil said through a surgical mask, a euphoric look in his eyes. He ran his fingers down his protective coat, enjoying the way the blood oozed out of the fabric.

"What did you find out from the boy?" Luca asked.

"Not too much, but there's no doubt he was involved. The kid was practically brainwashed, and wouldn't tell me anything about his group."

"So, it was a waste of time." Luca sighed.

"That's a weird way of looking at it," Cecil said, unhappy at Luca's disparagement of his cherished hobby. "He did let slip the names of the two other demons he was watching, so we can send some security over."

Cecil was cut off when Fen flung open the door. His heart dropped when he saw his daughters cover their mouths in disgust. He frantically reached out for a towel to cover himself, but it was too late. Despite Luca's prodding, he hadn't even begun to get changed, and was covered with the congealing blood spatter of his toy.

* * *

Her father, the surgeon. Visions of her nightmares filled Chris's head. So it wasn't just a twisted vision her subconscious had conjured up. It was the literal truth. Immense fear and sadness overwhelmed the girl and she bolted out of the room.

"Chris!" Cecil called out frantically.

"Stay here. I'll get her," Luca said, racing after the girl.

"Hey, Dad," Alice said quietly, stepping in front of the confused Fen.

"Hey, Kiddo. How's the new apartment?" Cecil asked sadly.

* * *

"Stop, Chris," Luca yelled. She chased the terrified girl through the restricted areas.

"Stay away from me," Chris yelled, fury bursting past her lips. She was not nearly as fast as Luca. The older woman caught up to her easily and wrapped her arms around the girl, holding her in place.

"Just come back and we'll talk about it," Luca pleaded.

"What's there to talk about? Dad's a monster just like everyone around here. You're all liars!"

"Let's go back and he'll explain."

"I thought he was different. He was supposed to be different," Chris sobbed. "I can't look the other way for him, or for you. He's just another monster."

Chris beat her hands impotently on the older woman, her face covered in hysterical tears.

"Chris, please, calm down and listen to me."

"Why do you care? You're not my mom. I don't know who you are. You're just some stranger, just another monster."

Luca dropped her.

"Do you want to talk about your mom? Fine, we'll talk about your mom." Luca was incensed. "Do you even remember what her face looked like?"

Chris sobbed.

"Do you?" Luca demanded.

Chris shook her head, unable to look Luca in the eye.

"Of course you don't. I'm the one who raised you kids when your dad was too busy chasing her around. I fed you. I taught you to hunt. I took you to school."

Chris scrambled for the door, unwilling to hear another word.

"You should be grateful I'm not your mom," Luca shouted to her fleeing back.

Chris hastily disappeared.

The only sound that could be heard was the furious beating of Luca's heart. She slumped down to the ground, her back against the wall. She was fighting back tears.

"Come back," she said quietly.

CHAPTER 27

Alice tiptoed through the door to Maxine's room, careful not to make any sudden noises. Maxine snored, somehow occupying the entire king-size bed. Alice carefully collected stray dishes and slunk back to the main room. Since she had moved in, most of the apartment had been saved from Maxine's messy nature. The leather couches were free from clothes and spilled beer, and the table had been uncovered for the first time in years. Alice carried the dishes to the kitchen. Sighing heavily, she dropped the plates into the sink and started scrubbing. When she was finished, she bagged the garbage and started downstairs to the dumpster. When she got back to the apartment, she checked the clock on the stove: it was one o'clock.

"Nope, time to get up," she said. She stomped into Maxine's room with a smile.

"Max, you awake?" she whispered, waiting for an answer with a hand cupped around her ear. When none came, Alice shrugged and jumped roughly into the bed.

"Holy fucking shit!" Maxine sprang up, head flitting around in every direction. When she spotted Alice, her eyes narrowed and her lips curled into a sneer.

"It's time to get up," Alice said sweetly.

"What did I tell you about waking me up?" Maxine asked.

"You said you'd kill me," Alice said matter-of-factly.

"And yet here we are."

"You say you'll kill me a lot," Alice said, never losing her grin.

"Don't tempt me, little girl." Maxine waved a finger at Alice before rolling out of bed.

Alice pretended not to look when the sheets fell away from Maxine's barely clothed form.

"Anyway, it's past one and we have a busy day in front of us," Alice said, watching the blonde dress.

Maxine let out a frustrated groan. "Busy?"

Alice pretended to pull out a notepad and mimed flipping through the pages, a gesture she had picked up from the blonde.

"My dad's coming over to have dinner with us at five. So we only have three and a half hours of video games before we have to get ready."

"You're never going to beat me, you know." Maxine smiled.

Landlady and house slave sat in front of the television and lost themselves until it was close to five. After losing yet another brawl, Alice groaned and threw down her controller.

"Fine, you win," Alice said. "Hey, aren't you supposed to be taking care of dinner tonight?"

Maxine threw up her hands in victory. "Don't worry. I've got it covered," she said, pulling out her phone. "Get me a beer."

"I thought you'd be pissed off that Dad was coming. Don't you hate him? You're always bitching about him." Alice skipped to the kitchen and returned, beer in hand.

"No, I don't fucking hate him. I just like making sure he knows his place. Hell, if I hated him, I wouldn't have made him Overlord."

"What?"

"It's a long story. Plenty of drama. Not interesting."

Alice shrugged. At this point she knew when Maxine wasn't going to elaborate, and she really didn't see the point in provoking the impossibly strong woman. Not just yet, anyway.

Alice jumped at a knock at the door. "Shit, he's here. Get up," she shouted.

Maxine responded by raising her middle finger over the back of the couch.

"Whatever." Alice ran to the door.

She found her father there, dressed as always in slacks and a loose button down shirt. He raised a box of beer with a smile.

"Hey, Dad. Come on in." She took the beer from him and placed it in the fridge.

Cecil looked around at the sparkling clean apartment.

"This isn't exactly how I expected your apartment to look, Maxine," he said.

Maxine started an insult, but Alice interrupted.

"You should have seen the crap I had to clean up when I moved in. I'm surprised she didn't have bugs."

"Fuck you both," Maxine shouted from across the room.

Cecil let out a laugh, apparently surprised that Alice had the guts to interrupt the sadistic blonde. Alice stood in the kitchen, confused. Until now she had thought they were enemies, and that she was brokering some sort of uneasy peace with this dinner.

"Hey, Runt," Maxine said, turning her head to the kitchen. "I said I was going to take care of dinner, and I just did. You're going to need to pick it up at the pizza place on the corner."

Alice pouted as she went to the closet to grab her coat and boots.

* * *

As soon as she left, Cecil turned to Maxine.

"Okay, Maxine. What the hell are you doing?"

"I don't know what you're talking about." She leaned back, losing her grin.

"Why is my daughter living here?"

"I don't know, Cutter. Maybe I like the idea that your precious little kid is at my beck and call." Maxine felt unsure of herself, but tried to maintain a cool attitude. She was unused to feeling unsure.

Cecil sat back, a smile crossing his lips.

"Good. I'd rather her here than with the random people she was with before. Besides, I don't think there's a safer place in the city. It's like living in the eye of the storm."

"Fuck you." Maxine stood up and started for the kitchen. She opened the fridge, reached past a dead rat that was sealed in a plastic bag, and grabbed a beer. "You drinking?" she asked.

Cecil nodded.

"Get it yourself, Fuckwad."

* * *

Alice got back to find her father and Maxine drinking on the couch. She stared suspiciously as she placed the pizza on the kitchen table. Nobody moved. Alice quickly gave up and moved the pizza to the couch.

"That's my girl," Cecil said as he grabbed a slice.

Alice jumped onto the couch between the two of them.

"So, Cutter, Little Pink here told me that your other kid ran away from you," Maxine said, smiling when Cecil took a sharp breath. "I'm just saying, it must feel pretty awful to have your daughter think you're a monster. I know I'd just want to kill myself."

Alice noticed her father was uncharacteristically silent. "She'll come around," she interjected on his behalf. "You know her. She's always been stubborn. I remember in fourth grade when everyone had to change desks at the end of the term. She refused. It wasn't like it was a special desk, but she got it in her head that she was being loyal to the desk. She fought for weeks to keep her old desk until the teacher just switched it out before class one morning."

"Yeah," Cecil said, his voice raised, an indication of some regained footing. "She's just a little freaked out right now. She'll come back. We just need to give her a little space."

Alice practically had to duck under the glare Maxine shot in her direction.

"Whatever happened to that boyfriend of yours, Maxine?" Cecil asked. "What was his name? Mike? Matt? No, that wasn't it."

"Mark," Maxine said. "Had to let him go. He couldn't take my intensity."

"I don't think there's a lot of people who can put up with the bruises that come from being attached to you." Cecil laughed.

Maxine tried to stutter out a reply before throwing her half-full beer can at his head.

After a few hours of conversational sparring, Cecil got up from the couch.

"I think it's time for me to get back home. Some of us have to work in the morning." Maxine flipped him off. "Can't wait for Thursday, huh?" He turned to Alice. "Let me know if you hear anything from Chris, okay?"

Alice nodded.

"Love you," he said, kissing the girl on the forehead before walking out the door.

"Fuck. I thought he'd never leave." Maxine got up from the couch.

"Who's Mark?" Alice asked, rushing up behind the blonde.

"Just the most recent addition to my long list of exes." Her voice fell slightly as she spoke. "How the hell did he know about him? I have to be more careful."

"Don't be weak," Alice teased, punching Maxine hard in the side while trying unsuccessfully to imitate the tall blonde's voice. "Don't worry. I'll be your wingman."

The sad look left Maxine's face. She laughed at the thought. When her laughter subsided, she smiled sadistically.

"Did you just punch me?" Maxine asked, cracking her knuckles.

Alice laughed as she ran away, to enjoy being the prey, the pursued, until Maxine inevitably caught her.

CHAPTER 28

Chris sat alone in Criminology. Michael had invited her to sit with him ever since she'd joined up with Moore, but she steadfastly refused. Even when he was on her side, Michael was insufferable. Criminology was quickly becoming Chris's least favorite class. When she'd started, she'd expected to gain a clear understanding of the law, which she assumed was based on justice, on right and wrong. Things had changed. Not only was the class revealing obvious weaknesses in the legal system, but her life was, too. How can anyone have faith in policy or procedure when demons are allowed to exist? When monsters like her father could drag people to their secret clubs and murder them with impunity?

Chris hadn't spoken to her father since that night in Tartarus. On her way home from school, she often had to stop herself from habitually dialing him. He'd try to explain himself, and Chris knew she might listen. He used to be her hero – someone who fought the good fight with his government job. Now he was a monster. Worse, he was someone she might become if she gave in to the darkness in her dreams.

The Criminology professor had begun her lecture early. Though exhausted by the nightmares and fed up with the subject matter, Chris continued diligently taking notes, only this time with snarky commentary.

"Our country is subject to the rule of law," the professor said. "The same laws that govern you and me, govern everyone in our society."

"That's bullshit," Michael said.

The professor gave a protracted sigh. "Yes, Michael? You have a question?"

"You can write as many laws as you want, but, if nobody enforces them, then we've got nothing."

"Corruption may be too complex an angle right now," the professor said.

Chris raised her hand.

"Yes, Chris," the professor said.

"But it's true," Chris said. "People get away with murder all the time, and the police don't care. They don't care about due process. Norman Argyle hanged himself in police custody, and I haven't heard anything about any investigation into what happened."

"There're probably reviewing it internally," the professor said.

"That's the problem," Chris continued. "How can we claim our country is governed by the rule of law when the people supposedly responsible for enforcing laws keep everything secret? I'm tired of secrets. They might as well be paid off."

"That's certainly an interesting perspective, but I don't think we can condemn all police because of the suicide of a multiple murderer."

"But what about the monsters out there?" Chris asked.

"Excuse me?"

"The real monsters. The people killing and hurting other people while the police don't do anything?" Chris continued.

"I think we've moved into conspiracy theory," the professor said. "We can continue this after class if you want to take advantage of my office hours."

Chris got back to her dorm after an infuriating conversation with her professor. It was hard to argue that the police were incompetent or corrupt when *she'd* look crazy for mentioning a secret world of demons.

"What are you doing after exams?" Cindy asked, as Chris threw herself on her bed.

"I don't know. I won't be going back home this year." Chris didn't know how to explain that she might never go home again. She couldn't risk being corrupted by her family.

"Do you want to spend the holiday with me and Emily? We're doing it at her townhouse this year."

Before Chris could respond, there was a knock. Chris answered the door. She found a police officer looking down at her.

"Excuse me. I'm looking for Christine Delacroix."

"I'm Christine Delacroix."

"Could you come with me to the station, please? We have some questions for you relating to the murder of Devon Jacobs."

"Of course, Officer," she stuttered. Chris grabbed her coat and followed him outside, leaving a confused and distressed Cindy behind.

The ride to the police station was quiet. Chris's mind spun out of control. She tried to mimic Luca, keep her face as emotionless as possible, but it was impossible to hide the panic in her eyes. She tried to distract herself by staring out the window, hoping that the officer wouldn't notice how terrified she was.

"What's going on?" she asked quietly from the back seat.

"I don't know, ma'am. I was just told to pick you up for questioning."

Chris was led through the large, wooden doors of the police station. She saw a bustling sea of activity in Meridian City's busiest precinct. She wondered if any of them were being paid off by her father to leave him alone. The officer brought her through several concrete corridors, depositing her in a room at the end of a hall. The room had a small, wooden desk pushed up against the wall with two worn chairs on either end. Shaking, she sat down, noting that the padding on the chair had been almost completely worn down. Chris deduced Devon Jacobs must have been the man who was murdered by the demon she and the rest had scouted. It was outside his house that she had dropped her thermos. She silently cursed Alice for having it personalized. Damn her thoughtfulness. She was screwed.

Chris sat there for over an hour until the door finally opened. It was plenty of time for her to convince herself she was going to be fine and then fall apart again, so she was a nervous wreck. A man came in carrying a brown box. He dropped it on the table and sat down in the other chair. Chris tried to sit as straight as she could, hoping her perfect posture would help sell her story. The man ignored her for a few minutes while he browsed through a file. He was a good-looking man in his mid-thirties with slicked-back black hair. Chris pretended that she was the detective and sized him up to take her mind off her nerves.

"I'm sorry to bring you out here in such style, but we're very busy," the detective finally said. "I'm Detective Morales." He tapped his pen absentmindedly against the desk. "Do you know a man named Devon Jacobs?"

Chris shook her head quickly. "No. Well, the officer who picked me up said that you wanted to question me about his murder."

"Have you ever been to Steven's Lane?"

She shook her head again. He reached down into the box he had brought with him, retrieving a plastic evidence bag. Chris's heart seized when she recognized the silver thermos.

"Do you recognize this?"

"That's my thermos."

"We found this in the bushes outside the victim's house. Are you sure that you've never been to Steven's Lane?"

"I lost it over a month ago at a study group meeting in the library. I left it behind." Her breathing became erratic. "Maybe even two months."

Detective Morales stared at her. Chris's heart beat wildly in her chest. She was certain he saw completely through her. After a moment of silence, he closed the file in front of him and collected the thermos.

"I thought as much," he said, shocking Chris. "Thank you for your time. I'll have an officer take you back to campus."

Chris tried not to let her relief show.

* * *

Getting back to his office, Julian threw the case file onto his desk.

"Just get back from questioning the girl?" Larry asked from across the room.

"I don't think she had anything to do with it."

"Why not?" Larry asked.

"First, I think she wet her pants just being in the room with me. I don't think someone like that is going to be hacking someone to pieces or feeding someone to an animal. Second, she looked like a small boy. I don't think that someone Devon Jacobs' size would have a hard time overpowering her. There's no way he would have needed to pull a gun on someone like that.

"If she's a witness, she's too scared to talk. Let's try to build the case a bit first before coming back to her. She may be more responsive if we know who to protect her from. I think our time would be better spent looking at your loan shark connection."

"On that note, we're going to talk to some of my contacts down on the east side," Larry said.

"No can do." Julian shook his head, blushing. "A friend of mine set me up on a blind date."

"Good. You need to get out more. If you spend all your time working, you won't have anything when the job gets hard. And this shit?" Larry waved his hand at the files on the gruesome murder they were investigating. "This is the easy part."

* * *

It was evening when Chris arrived at Arcadia Hall. She hadn't really expected Professor Moore to be there so late, but sure enough he was at his desk grading papers. She stepped softly into the room and waited for him to look up. If he was surprised when she did, he gave no sign.

"Sit down, Chris."

Chris sat down and began to speak, slowly and clearly.

"The police questioned me today about Devon Jacobs. I saw the demon kill him. I dropped a thermos at the crime scene."

Moore slowly removed his glasses and gave Chris the same kind of stare as the detective had earlier.

"Why didn't you tell me about all this before, Chris?"

"I didn't want you to be angry, and... I didn't know if I could trust you."

"Do you trust me now?"

"You're the only one who's tried to tell me the truth."

"That's good. I want us to be honest with each other. It's the only way a mission like ours can ever succeed. Did the police seem suspicious when you talked to them?"

"No, not at all. They let me go right away."

"That's good. But I have to tell you, I'm feeling a little suspicious now. If the police hardly questioned you, why did you feel compelled to come see me?"

"I..." Chris felt her voice become trapped in her throat and struggled to free it. "I'm afraid of becoming a monster."

"We all have a little bit of monstrousness in us, I think," Moore said pensively. "We need it to survive the brutality of the world we live in. But as long as you're afraid, I'd say you have nothing to be afraid of." He laughed gently. "It shows how passionate you are about doing the right thing. And I want you to remember, no matter what you see out there, no matter how much it may disgust you, that's okay as long as you see it for what it is: a grim necessity."

"What makes us different from the demons?" Chris asked.

"What do you mean?"

"We're going to kill. The group's killed before. How are we different from them?"

"Ah, I see." Moore placed his hand on her shoulder. "We're killing to protect people. It's awful work, I know, but, if we don't, many more will suffer. It may seem trite, but someone has to be willing to take in some darkness to stop it from spreading even further. That's our sacrifice, and our burden."

Chris nodded. She believed him.

CHAPTER 29

Snow squeaked hollowly under Luca's feet as she attempted to force concern for Chris out of her head. The cold had never bothered her. In fact, she had always preferred it, but it did little to soothe her now. When she arrived at her destination, she found a cheesy-looking sign welcoming her to Vivaldi's Old World Italian Restaurant. She immediately wanted to leave.

Luca resented Fen's constant attempts to butt into her love life, but had to admit that her bed would be perpetually fallow without the frequent blind dates. When she walked through the door, the sickly sweet smell of tomato invaded her nostrils. The tables all had red and white checkered tablecloths and solitary candles. She rolled her eyes at the clichéd decor. Dozens of couples sat around the tables having romantic dinners. Clearly, Fen had picked a popular place. The perky young hostess piped up.

"Welcome to Vivaldi's. Do you have a reservation?"

"Yeah, one second," Luca said, reaching into her pocket. She was flustered, forgetting the name the reservation was under. She quickly searched through her email. "The reservation is under Morales."

The girl crossed a name off the reservation book before taking her to a table in the back.

Luca's phone rang.

"Hello?" Luca answered it while she took her seat.

"How's it going?" It was Fen.

Luca's eye twitched in annoyance. "He hasn't even gotten here yet." She paused for a moment. "And don't call during the date."

Luca hung up, not waiting for Fen to respond.

She crossed her arms and stared out the window. Her gaze fell on a happy family walking down the street. There was a father marching ahead, while a mother ushered two small boys along behind him. They seemed so happy. The sight filled her with anxiety, to the point that she barely noticed when the waitress came by to go through the wine list. Luca, who had no taste for wine, pointed at the cheapest thing on the menu. She glanced over her shoulder toward the door where a slim man was coming out of the cold. Noticing the hostess pointing toward her table, Luca braced herself.

"You must be Luca," the man said. "I'm Julian."

She shook his hand as he sat down.

"How long have you known Marylyn?" he asked.

"I don't know anyone named Marylyn," Luca said bluntly. "She must be friends with the person who set me up."

"Oh yeah, that must be it," Julian said nervously.

They sat in an awkward silence. Luca crossed her arms and looked at the ceiling, while Julian's gaze was entirely focused on the menu. When the waitress returned with Luca's wine, Julian finally put the menu down. Luca ordered the pizza with the fewest toppings, while Julian ended up with some unpronounceable dish.

"I'm sorry I'm not more talkative," he said, adjusting his glasses. "I haven't actually been on a date in years. I'm usually too busy with work."

Luca looked at the man for the first time since he sat down. He was attractive enough, and she could use the distraction.

"At least this is the first blind date you've been sent on," she offered. "I don't even know what number I'm on now."

"Your friend certainly sounds persistent."

"You don't even know the half of it," she said, taking a deep drink of her wine.

There was another pause before Luca decided to try to make small talk.

"What do you do?"

"I'm with the Meridian City Police Department. I'm a homicide detective, actually." He swelled with incorruptible pride.

Luca looked at him as if he were joking and started to laugh.

"What's so funny?" Julian asked, scratching the back of his head.

"Nothing," Luca said. "Just an interesting coincidence."

They chatted pleasantly through dinner. For the most part, conversation was about how all-consuming they both found their jobs. Luca dodged most of Julian's questions, but he didn't seem to mind. Luca had to admit that she didn't necessarily hate this one. He was good-looking, polite, and he didn't push for answers she didn't want to give.

Upon leaving the restaurant, Luca pulled Julian into a nearby alcove. He rubbed the back of his head, a simple smile plastered on his face.

"I had a good time tonight. Maybe we should do this again sometime," he said awkwardly.

"I'm not looking for any kind of relationship," Luca said.

Julian's smile fell as he braced himself for what she was about to say next. He'd been more relaxed in her company than he'd felt in months, and he'd been hoping to recreate the experience. He tried to decipher what she was thinking, but her expressionless face was impossible for the detective to read.

"You seem like an okay guy, so I'll take the risk," Luca said. "I don't want to go on dates, or go to expensive dinners or anything like that. I work pretty much all day, every day, just like you. What I want is occasional sex and nothing more. If you can do that, I'll take you to my place tonight and we can talk about doing this on a regular basis. If you can't, then I'm gone. Does that sound agreeable?"

He looked like a deer in the headlights. After a couple of seconds, Julian nodded.

When they reached the apartment, Julian looked around the living room while Luca hung up her coat.

"Did you just move in?"

"No, I've been here ten years."

He was shocked. There was a lone chair in front of a television, and nothing else. He'd been through more carefully decorated drug dens.

"I see you're going for the simple aesthetic," he said. "Do you have any roommates?"

Luca kissed him roughly. "Shut up and follow me."

"Yes, ma'am."

When they got to the bedroom, Luca tossed him like a toy onto the bed.

"Wait while I get changed," she said.

She pulled off her blazer, neatly folding it on a chair before turning to her belt. Julian watched from the bed, heart pounding with excitement.

"Why do you have a gun?" Julian asked, noticing her shoulder holster.

"I work in security. Don't worry, Detective. It's registered."

She was lying. In the back of his mind, Julian knew, but the sight of her pants dropping to the ground pushed further questions far away. He turned to the side table to take off his glasses, where he noticed Luca's Disney World picture.

"Are these your kids?" he asked, taking hold of the frame.

Her glare prompted him to carefully put the picture frame back down.

"No more questions," Luca ordered. "Take your clothes off."

* * *

It was midnight, and Larry was skulking through the police department toward his office. The Snatcher case was solved as far as most were concerned, but he had promised Julian he would look over the evidence, and as much as he pretended he was just doing the kid a favor, he knew something wasn't right about the whole thing. Larry had made a plea to reopen the case, but his superiors weren't interested. Of course, he kept Julian's name away from this. It was one thing for 'Loony Larry' to have suspicions, but dragging his young partner's name into it would ruin the kid's career for sure.

There had been enough media hostility surrounding the case since Norman Argyle's jailhouse suicide. Nobody wanted to invite any more scrutiny. Julian was right, though. Things didn't add up. Larry wasn't willing to make any bold assertions until he had some real evidence to back it up, a lesson he had learned the hard way. He could never admit it to Julian, but the pentagrams did make Larry suspect a paranormal connection, but there was no cult at work. Norman may have been some delusional kid, but when Larry looked at him, all he saw was a puppet. The whole thing reeked of demons to him, particularly the stagnant smell of a woman he only knew as Lady Black.

Larry shuddered at the thought of the evil woman who had killed his old partner years ago. He could still see her as clearly as if she was standing right in front of him, with her perfect black suit and her powerful Italian pistol. Her cold face had haunted his dreams for years. Homicide was in her pocket. There was no point making inquiries with other detectives. He had burned his bridges long ago, and nobody else believed that the thugs that held them in check were actually demons. Brutal, murderous monsters, sure – they all knew they were being paid off by figurative devils. But actual fang-and-claw demons was a bridge too far. Larry gritted his teeth at his own cowardice, vowing that he'd find out the truth behind the Snatcher case before it was too late. He knew he had to hurry. It was winter now. The ground was cold and hard, not suitable for digging. He had no doubt that the arrival of spring would be met with another series of grave robberies. He hoped to be ready by then.

CHAPTER 30

"What are you doing today?" Alice asked Maxine, who was rummaging through the fridge.

"I have very specific plans that cannot be changed," Maxine replied, carrying a mountain of food and booze to the couch.

"But it's Christmas. Aren't you going to see your family?"

"No. I don't like people, including my family." Maxine stopped in her tracks. "Especially my family."

Alice went to grab her coat from the closet while Maxine arranged her snacks around the television.

"You can come with me to Dad's if you like," Alice offered.

"That is the absolute last thing I want to do. I am going to sit here all day and watch Christmas specials while getting as drunk as I possibly can, as fast as I possibly can. It's tradition."

"Do you want me to bring you back some turkey?"

"Of course I fucking want turkey. What kind of stupid question is that?"

* * *

Exhausted and paranoid, Chris hadn't scored on her Christmas exams the way that she would have liked. When she handed in her Criminology final, knowing it was a B at best, a realization came over her – she didn't care. Chris had come to college to make a difference, but the only real change she could make was with Moore. Classes had begun to grate against her skin as professors preached about a world Chris knew didn't exist, a world without monsters. Her future had never seemed so opaque.

"Chris, are you ready?" Cindy's shrill voice shouted at her from the door, interrupting her thoughts.

"Sure, let's go," Chris declared.

"Emily's new place is amazing. I can't wait to show you around."

"Does she have any roommates?"

"She asked me to move in with her, but I don't want to leave you here alone."

"You should go. Don't worry about me," Chris said, patting Cindy on the shoulder before fishing out her pants from a crumpled pile of clothes on the floor. "Who knows how long I'll be around anyway."

"You're not going to flunk out," Cindy said adamantly. "And we can coordinate classes next semester so we can help each other."

"All right," Chris capitulated, too tired to explain that her grades were not the problem.

"Oh my God!" Cindy's squeal was like a drill in Chris's head. "I've got a fantastic idea. Why don't we both move in with Emily?"

"I guess, if I were listing reasons, not being invited would be at the top."

"But you'd do it if you were invited?"

"I don't know. I don't want to keep someone else awake with my night terrors."

"Emily won't care," Cindy said without a thought. "Come on. It'll be so much fun."

"Fine," Chris agreed. "If Emily says it's all right, then I'll move out. But, you actually have to check with her."

Chris hoped Emily would refuse. She didn't need someone else to wake up with her dreams. At the same time, Chris had never felt so alone. It used to be an oddity if she went two days without calling her father. Now, it had been over a month. As if on cue, her phone buzzed. She looked down. It was her father. She didn't answer.

* * *

Not too far away, Luca had just picked up Alice.

"Heard anything from Chris?" Alice asked as she put her seatbelt on.

"No." Luca sighed. It wasn't for lack of trying.

"I stopped by her place a little while ago, but she wasn't really interested in talking. I think she's still mad at Dad."

Luca grimaced. She knew she was the one who had pushed Chris away, not Cecil. The guilt was killing her. She should never have mentioned the girls' mother.

"Did you get me anything?" Alice squeaked.

"I guess you're just going to have to wait and see," Luca replied.

"Do you think Chris will show up?"

"No. Your dad's holding out hope, but I wouldn't expect some Christmas miracle. She… she probably just needs more time." Luca paused. "I forgot to mention. Your father invited Fen to come to dinner."

Alice nodded rhythmically, turning on the radio. "I asked Maxine if she wanted to come, but she's just going to get drunk alone."

"Good. Let her be alone. I don't want to have to deal with her when I'm not working."

"Will you get mad at me if I ask a question?" Alice asked.

"No." Luca sighed. She had gotten sick of Alice's incessant questions a long time ago, but she tried not to let it show.

"Dad mentioned he wasn't the only Overlord. How many are there?"

"I don't know the exact number. There's one for every major city in the U.S., and a few smaller ones. Other countries have different systems."

"Is anyone in charge of everything?"

"We have a lot of autonomy, but officially we're subservient to the Overseer's office in Washington, DC. They approve our budgets and distribute funding, as well as hand down policy. They don't want to be bothered most of the time, but if we really screw up, we'll hear about it."

The smell of turkey hit Alice in the gut when she walked into her dad's house. Fen was already there, sitting in one of the kitchen chairs with a glass of wine and watching Cecil cook.

"Hey, Alice," Fen shouted with an exaggerated wave.

"Have you heard from Chris?" Cecil asked.

"Sorry, Dad. I called her earlier today, but she didn't answer."

He tried to give her a faint smile, but couldn't quite manage it.

"Calm down, Cecil," Luca said. "And stop calling her. It's only going to make things worse."

He sighed heavily and returned to the food.

"How'd exams go?" Fen interjected, trying to get the subject off Cecil's wayward daughter.

"Aced them, no problem," Alice said, smiling. She took a look at Fen quizzically. "Where are your horns?"

Fen's forehead was perfectly smooth, betraying no sign of her trademark onyx horns.

"It takes energy to keep them out. I only do it in the club because it adds to my allure," Fen said, framing her face with her hands.

"It takes effort?" Alice crooked her head.

"Any manifestation of demonic traits requires energy," Fen said as if she was reciting something from a biology textbook. "The reason you see it all over the club is because people are trying to show off."

Alice rubbed her head. She had assumed the opposite, that demons had to work hard to conceal their manifestations.

Out of habit, Alice started setting the kitchen table, making sure to follow her father's instructions to set an extra place for Chris in case she decided to show up.

"Cecil, stop calling her," she heard Luca snap in the kitchen.

"I just want to make sure she knows that she's welcome here."

"She knows, Cecil. She's the one that doesn't want to come. Pushing her too hard is a mistake," Luca insisted.

"Oh, are we talking about mistakes now? How about we discuss your little homicide detective?"

"We are not having this conversation, Cecil," Luca shouted.

"No. I think it's the perfect time," Cecil responded in kind, pouring his frustrations and agony out in wild and furious shouts. "You're the one always talking about loose ends, but here you are putting us all in danger."

Alice thought it would be best if she stayed out of the kitchen for a while. Looking over, she saw Fen sneaking into the living room, clearly having the same thought.

"Why'd you come to dinner?" Alice asked over the shouts coming from the kitchen.

"What, you aren't happy that I'm here?" Fen asked, pouting.

"I didn't mean that. Do you have any family?"

Fen chuckled before taking another sip of wine. "My parents and brother live in Canada. That's where I'm from. I usually go up for the holidays, but the storm yesterday grounded my plane, so here I am.

"Thank God you found out about being a demon or I wouldn't have been able to come. Your dad didn't want to cross his personal and business life until he told you guys. I know, stupid, right?"

"I wish he'd said something earlier. It's hard to get my head around everything," Alice said.

"I can only imagine. It's so weird to keep it a secret. When I was a little girl, I got really annoyed when my friend's dad said my dad didn't really have fangs, that I was just playing pretend. My parents had to sit me down and explain about humans, not the other way around." Fen giggled.

Cecil and Luca's fight collapsed in emotional exhaustion, and dinner was served. The party of four gathered around the table and loaded their plates. The room filled with the satisfied silence of a good meal until Alice decided to break the spell.

"Dad, isn't it weird that we're celebrating Christmas, since we're demons and all?"

"What do you want us to do?" Cecil laughed and shrugged his shoulders. "Growing up, you knew we weren't religious, but we still celebrated Christmas. It's a fun tradition, nice for family, you know – all the good stuff."

"But aren't we, you know, unholy?" Alice asked, squirming in her seat.

"You know I don't believe in God," Cecil said pensively. "But even if there is one, I don't think we know anything about him. That includes what he considers holy and unholy."

Alice was unsatisfied with the answer, though she wasn't quite sure why.

"I believe in God," Fen piped in. "My family is Lutheran. Being demons has never stopped us from practicing. As far as I'm concerned, Jesus died for my sins, too."

"But we're demons," Alice said.

"What's written in holy books is very different from reality. We're just a species that generally has higher-than-average aggression," Luca said. "Religion has nothing to do with it."

"Demons aren't like what you see on TV," Cecil said in between bites of his food. "Take Fen, for example. She's a Succubus, which in movies means that she wants to suck out the souls of men by having sex with them."

Fen turned toward Alice and winked.

"But," Cecil continued, "The only real truth to that myth is that Succubi often have high sex drives."

"Yeah, and not all Succubi are dynamos like me," Fen said. "There's one girl at the club, Nadine. She's a Succubus too, but she couldn't be more of a timid little prude."

"So, you're a Succubus," Alice said, looking down at her food.

"What am I?"

"Didn't I already tell you?" Cecil asked. "I must have."

Alice shook her head.

"Oh, sorry. You've been asking so many questions that I just assumed I mentioned it. We're Fiends, characterized by our claws and our enjoyment of cutting into things."

"I didn't know Fiends were a type of demon," Alice said.

It was a word that she came across a lot in her research, but it was used as a synonym for villain or evil being. Alice fumed at the holes in her studies.

"Some demons have really weird names," Cecil said. "Sure, there are Succubi, like Fen, or Devils, like Maxine, but a lot of us are stuck with stuff like Fiend or Azure."

Alice nodded while she stuffed her face with turkey.

Cecil spent the rest of the meal glancing over toward the empty seat at the table. When everyone's plate was empty and Luca started to clear the table, he reached beneath his chair.

"Luca and I got something for you, Kiddo," he said, pulling out a sloppily wrapped box.

Alice's eyes shone brightly as she took the package. Ripping through the wrapping paper without care, she revealed a set of surgical tools.

"Those look like yours," Fen said to Cecil. She was hovering over Alice's shoulder, trying to get a better look.

"Yep, they're the same kind. I thought you'd get some use out of them, Ms. Future Surgeon," Cecil said, tousling his daughter's hair.

She hugged him before looking up. "Hey Dad, can I take some turkey home?"

* * *

The townhouse Emily was renting felt safe to Chris. It's dark, wood panelled walls, and sparse decorations reminded her more of a log cabin than a two-story house in the city. Maybe it was the silence.

"We haven't gone out for the professor in a while," Chris said when she got settled on the cheap couch in front of the television set.

"He thought it would be best if we took a break during exams. After all, almost all of us are students," Emily explained. "Don't worry. We're going to start up strong after Christmas."

Chris was glad to hear it. She didn't know how much time she had left.

"What's the plan? Are we making turkey?" Chris asked, smelling at the air.

"Nah, we're just going to order some Chinese food," Emily said.

Chris nodded. It wasn't very Christmassy, but maybe it was better that way. She'd rather not be reminded of what she was missing.

"That works, too."

Cindy got up from the couch when the doorbell rang. Chinese food was nigh.

"Night terrors, huh?" Emily asked a surprised Chris when Cindy was out of earshot. "Have you been to the doctor?"

"Yeah," Chris lied. "She said they were a hormonal thing and they'd pass soon."

"That's good. I'd really hate to have to say no to Cindy at Christmas, especially when she's so excited."

"I don't want to be any trouble. If you want, I can tell Cindy it's a bad idea."

"Don't be so down." Emily softly punched Chris on the shoulder. "It'd be a lot easier for me if I don't have to look for another roommate. And, if you stay here, we don't have to watch our mouths when it comes to the professor."

"Then I'm in," Chris said. At least she wouldn't be alone.

Cindy returned with the food, laying it out on the table in front of the couches.

"Hey, Cindy, I asked Chris and she agreed. We're all going to be roommates," Emily said happily.

Chris almost regretted her decision when Cindy's squeal of glee hit her ears. It took almost five minutes to escape the hug. While she attempted to free herself, Chris heard her phone vibrating on the table.

"Your phone has been busy all night. Is anything going on?" Emily asked.

Chris checked her messages. There were twenty eight missed calls: one from Alice, one from Luca, and twenty six from her dad.

"No," she told Emily. "Nothing important."

* * *

It was close to midnight when Alice said goodbye to her family and arrived back at Maxine's apartment.

"I'm home," Alice yelled as she walked in. "I have turkey," she added, raising a plastic bag full of leftovers and shaking it back and forth.

The television was blaring and there was a huge collection of garbage piled up around it. As she got closer, Alice could see Maxine's head pressed into the back of the couch. From the plethora of discarded candy wrappers, it looked like she had been there awhile.

"Hey, Max," Alice said, pushing the bag of food onto Maxine's face.

"Merry Christmas," the blonde slurred before vomiting on the floor. "No more booze," she added when her stomach had finished emptying itself.

Alice put the bag of leftovers down and helped Maxine to her feet. "Okay, time for sleep." She managed to get a stumbling Maxine into her bed.

The drunken blonde fell asleep the second she hit the mattress. When Alice returned to the living room, she surveyed the damage, knowing she was the one who had to deal with the mess.

CHAPTER 31

The weeks after moving in with Emily had been a blur for Chris, who still spent most nights sleepless and scared. Fortunately, Emily slept like a stone.

"Are we going to meet at the construction site tonight?" Chris asked, walking down from her new room.

"No, it's too cold for that now," Emily replied from the kitchen while she washed the evening's dishes. "Professor Moore is coordinating between some of the older members and we're organizing everyone on a smaller level. Tonight's going to be big.

"Edgar Warrington, that demon we were watching before Christmas, is the target tonight. Nine of us are going. We shouldn't need that many if everything goes right, though. I know you probably want to participate more, but can I ask you a favor?"

"What is it?" Chris asked.

"I want you to look after Cindy, and make sure that nothing happens to her. That means you two will be staying back, mostly. Do you think you can do that?"

"Of course," Chris assured her.

"We're heading out in an hour." Emily patted her on the shoulder.

Unbidden, the image of her father dressed as a surgeon, dripping with blood, crashed into Chris's mind. It happened whenever she let her guard down, this vision of the past and her potential future. Chris scratched at her hand, remembering the black claws of her dreams. Was it really only a matter of time before she ended up as twisted as her father?

When they arrived on campus, there were several idling cars parked in a row. A group of men stood a few feet away, chatting and smoking.

"Wait here," Emily instructed as she went to speak with the men.

Michael and Cindy emerged from another car to join the group. Emily was pointing at several of the men, obviously issuing orders, while Michael and Cindy joined Chris in Emily's car.

"Hey," Michael said.

"What were you two doing?" Chris gave him a fake smile.

"We were meeting Professor Moore at his office," Cindy said, jumping into the car next to Michael.

"Emily said you aren't going in," Michael said. "That's good. There'll be a lot of blood, I'm guessing."

"Blood doesn't bother me," Chris snapped back.

"We're not planning on giving the guy a paper cut," Michael said. "Emily can take it, but, trust me, you girls don't want to be out there. Don't worry. There's a lot more to do than just kill. You can help with any wounded."

"Have you ever hunted?" Chris asked, looking his thin frame up and down.

"Hunting? Like animals?" he asked.

"Yeah."

"No."

"Well, I have been hunting. A family friend taught me and my sister how to use a gun when we were ten. I think I can handle blood."

"That's different," Michael said. "You have no idea what it's like to kill something that looks and acts like a person. Do you want to kill one of these things?"

"No... I don't know," Chris said, eyes lowered on the ground. She wanted to pull her own weight, but the thought of killing someone made her want to retch. It was actually nice to have a non-lethal way to help the professor, but that didn't stop her from wanting to slap the condescension off Michael's face.

Emily returned to the car and leaned in to address the group.

"We're going to be the surveillance car, so we're parking in front of the building. When we confirm he's asleep, we'll signal the others to move in."

They parked in the same place as last time, watching Edgar Warrington through the window of his house. He was watching television in the dark again. He reminded Chris of her father. They were both killers, even if they looked nice and friendly on the outside.

"I brought some energy drinks so you guys would be a little more alert this time." Michael rummaged through his bag.

"Be quiet," Emily whispered.

He rolled his eyes and tossed around the silver cans. An hour later, their quarry stood up and turned off the television before he disappeared inside the house.

"We'll give it half an hour, then I'll check around the house for windows," Michael said, leaning forward.

"I can do that," Chris said.

"It's an important job. If he gets wind of us, we're screwed," Michael said.

"I'm a lot smaller than you and a hell of a lot quicker, unless those energy drinks do something for your shuffling."

"She can do it. It's just a quick scouting mission," Emily said, interrupting Michael's assuredly barbed comeback. "Give the house a quick check for entrance points and run back. We'll stay here with Cindy."

Chris nodded her agreement as she eyed Michael.

Chris's head swam with possibilities of what the creature would do if it caught her as she slowly exited the car. Why had she volunteered for this? Oh right, because she was stupid.

"Keep your head down," Emily reminded her.

Chris ran across the street, keeping as low to the ground as possible. She slinked along the side of the house. A light flipped on, flowing through a window next door. Her heart nearly stopped, and she flung herself flat on the ground, black coat on white snow. Peering up, she could see a middle-aged man in a bathrobe digging around in the fridge next door, oblivious to her. She scrambled to her feet, and slunk to the back of the house, where she saw two windows.

"Smart, Chris, really smart," she whispered to herself.

She crept carefully beneath one before raising her head up to peek inside. The blinds were down, but she could make out a bathroom. She snuck to the other window. This one didn't have blinds. Looking in, she could see Edgar Warrington in bed, sleeping soundly. Chris dashed back to the car, circling the other side of the house to avoid the neighbor's light.

"Is he asleep?" Emily whispered.

"Yeah, in a bedroom in the back of the house."

"Okay, one second." Emily's fingers blurred across her phone as she texted. "Are there any doors in the back?"

"No, just two windows."

Emily returned to her phone. Moments later, Chris saw shadows moving ahead. A group of men was approaching the house.

"We're going in." Emily gestured to Michael. "Chris, you and Cindy stay here. I'll text you when it's safe." She handed Chris a butcher's knife. "Just in case."

Michael and Emily left the car to join the group converging on the house.

"What's going to happen?" Cindy asked.

"They're going to kill the monster."

"Are you sure that we're doing the right thing?"

"What do you think?" Chris asked.

"I don't know. Are demons all bad? Everyone only talks about killing them."

"I know how you feel," Chris said. "I wasn't sure either, but we saw that demon kill someone last time."

"I didn't see anything," Cindy said, "Just blood. We don't know what happened."

Chris didn't respond. Part of her wondered if Cindy was right, but then again, that part also wanted to forgive her father and get very far away from demon hunters. That was the selfish part of her mind, willing to accept lies and platitudes if it meant getting her easy life back. She longed to give into it.

Chris felt a prick on her hand. Looking down, she saw that she was unconsciously cradling the knife. Its blade felt like an extension of herself, and it wanted blood. Chris threw the weapon on the ground, desperate to get away from those kinds of thoughts. So that was her life. On the one hand, pretend violence didn't exist. On the other, tear her enemies apart. She was in the middle for now, but she knew how precarious the balance would be. From the house, they heard a large crash and several small bangs, followed by an extended silence.

"I need to see it," Chris said, willing herself out of the car. "I need to know what's happening in there. Stay here and keep your eyes open. I'll be back as soon as I can."

Chris wasn't sure why she felt so compelled to witness Michael and Emily's work. A tiny voice down in the bowels of her heart whispered to her, willing her to see the blood. Her fingers itched terribly, and she jammed them into her pockets as she walked, an image of the knife entering her mind. Chris silenced the whisper. She was going to see what needed to be done.

The knob had been removed from the door. A groan creaked through the house. Chris shuddered, but pushed through to the bedroom. There was a man sitting on a chair outside of the bedroom, a knife hanging limply from his hand. Several of the other men were milling through the house, and someone was gagging in the bathroom. Chris could feel moisture in the air. It clung to her skin like paint. She took a deep breath and slowly opened the bedroom door. Laying near the door was one of the men of their group, his head caved in, blood spilling all over the floor. On the other side of the door was another man lying on his back, his throat crushed. Their lives were terrible sacrifices. Edgar Warrington was stuck with a knife in his throat near the bed. He was covered in stab wounds, with blood seeping through his shirt, permeating everything around him. Chris choked on the heavy smell of iron, covering her mouth at the gruesome scene.

Michael sat on the edge of the bed, rubbing his hands, a sadistic smile covering his face.

"Where's Cindy?" Emily asked.

"I... I had to see it," Chris said.

"There." Emily gestured at the body. She frowned. "Okay guys, we have to leave now."

"What about the bodies?" Chris asked.

"The professor takes care of the mess," Emily reminded her as she strolled back to the car, texting the entire time.

Chris approached Michael, who was sitting motionless on the bed.

"Are you okay?" Chris asked.

His head jerked up like he was jolted out of bed. Pulling his knife free from the demon's neck and wiping it off on the sheet, he left Chris alone in the room.

She knelt in front of the body, staring at the creature's dead eyes. All she could see was her own corpse.

The Meridian Fiend

CHAPTER 32

"Runt! I need to kill somebody or fuck somebody today. I'll let you choose, because, if it doesn't happen, I'm taking it out on you," Maxine proclaimed as she left her bedroom for the first time that day.

There was no answer.

"Where the hell are you?" Maxine asked dejectedly.

She marched to Alice's room and shoved open the door, but all she found was an empty bed. Maxine checked the rest of the apartment before realizing she was searching for a friend.

"Fuck this," she declared, and switched on the television.

After half-starting three trashy reality shows, she turned the TV off and flung the remote across the room. She stared at the ceiling, irritated at everything around her, before an epiphany struck. She rushed to her bedroom to dig through her sheets. Moments later, Maxine pulled her phone from a tangle of blankets with a victorious shout.

She immediately texted Alice.

'Where the hell are you?'

'Out with friends,' blinked the phone.

Maxine frowned, feeling more alone than she had in a long time. She stared at the phone, not sure exactly how to respond. She cycled through a series of threats in her mind, ranging from mild beatings to full out disembowelment. She smiled, imagining the look on Alice's face as she beat her friends' faces in. She was sure that if she did that, Alice wouldn't abandon her again anytime soon.

'When are you coming back?' Maxine texted.

It was mere minutes before Alice responded, but it seemed like an eternity. Maxine had gotten up and started pacing back and forth, her eyes still fixed on the phone, occasionally shaking it in frustration. Eventually, the vague word 'later' popped up.

"Fuck you," she shouted impotently.

Maxine stomped to the kitchen in a huff and grabbed a beer, ignoring Alice's most recent experiment congealing in the fridge. She went back to the couch to do the thing she hated more than anything: waiting.

* * *

An hour later, Alice strolled through the door, arms laden with shopping bags. Maxine was near the door, leaning against the wall with a beer in her hand.

"Why do you waste so much time on nobodies?" Maxine asked. "If you don't want to be here, then maybe you should just fucking leave. Start packing and get the hell out."

"Hello to you too, Sunshine," Alice said, a sly smile crossing her lips. "Do you like my hair?"

Maxine looked at the girl's head, noting with surprise that Alice's fading pink hair was now restored and styled short and spiky. She nodded slowly, unsure where this was going.

"Good. I'll start making lunch," Alice said, pushing the stunned blonde out of her way.

"What are you doing?" Maxine asked, peering her head into the kitchen.

"Nothing big, just sandwiches," Alice responded, bent over in the fridge.

"I told you to get out. Why are you still here?" Maxine tried in vain to sound authoritative over the shaking in her voice.

"You say stuff like that a lot," Alice said. "It's your best quality. You always say and do whatever you want. But I know you don't really want me gone. If I left, who would make you lunch?"

"Fuck, you're weird." Maxine shook her head in surprise. Alice wasn't like anyone she had ever met.

Later that night, Maxine declared that she was going to reward Alice's loyalty with some drunken debauchery. They went to Tartarus, the only club Maxine cared to visit.

"You haven't had a boyfriend over since I met you," Maxine said. "So tonight, I'm going to make it my mission to get you laid."

"I don't want a boyfriend, Max."

"Why would I get you a boyfriend? I'm just picking you up someone to fuck. No need to thank me. Stay here. I'm going to troll around."

Maxine disappeared into the crowd. Watching her sway across the room, Alice saw Maxine chatting up a group of guys. Alice's eyes never surveyed the group, remaining firm on Maxine. She couldn't help but be mesmerized by the confidence Maxine had. Luca had always called Alice headstrong, but Maxine took it to another level. She laughed when Maxine began making over-the-top lewd gestures at the group as if pantomime was necessary to explain what she wanted.

Maxine pulled one boy from the pack. His hair looked like it was made of fish bones that cascaded and curled around his neck. Maxine ran her hands up and down his body as she presented him to Alice. The boy squirmed under her scrutiny. It was the nicest thing Maxine had ever done for another person, and the last thing Alice wanted.

"His name's Stephen." Maxine smirked. "You two start getting it together while I see if I can find someone for myself."

Stephen sat down as Maxine wandered away.

"Your friend said you were looking for a one night stand," he opened.

Alice brought her glass to her lips and finished off her drink in a single gulp.

"I'm sure you're nice and all, but I'm not really interested," she said, shying her gaze away.

"That's a relief. Your friend scares the hell out of me. Did you know she threatened to break my arm?"

"Yeah, that sounds like her." Alice laughed with stars in her eyes. She offered him her hand. "I'm Alice."

"Nice to meet you, Alice." He shook her hand and grinned.

Their small talk was interrupted when Maxine came back without having found another suitable victim.

"Are you two still here? Get a room already," she said, wrapping her hands around Stephen's shoulders, kneading into them.

"He's just leaving, Max," Alice said coldly.

Maxine tightened her grip on the boy's shoulders until Alice's glare persuaded her to lift her hands, allowing Stephen to escape.

"Okay, he's not your type. I get it. Don't worry. There are a ton of boys here, and it's still pretty early."

Alice shook her head again.

"Why are you so damn shy about sex?" Maxine demanded.

"What's wrong with you?"

"I'm gay, Max."

"What?" Maxine said, stopping in her tracks only for an instant before a steely glare replaced wide-eyes. "Whatever, we'll find you some girls then. It's a bit harder, but I'm sure there's a Succubus around here that bats for the right team."

"I don't want a Succubus."

"What do you want, then?"

"I..." Alice looked down at the ground as she tapped her fingers on the table.

"This is what I mean about being weird. You know, I'm starting to feel insulted, Runt. I take you all the way out here to get you some, and you don't know what you want?"

Alice's heart was racing. Her eyes slowly crept up until they met Maxine's.

"I want you."

"Oh, Christ." Maxine's hand ran through her hair. "Get that thought out of your head, quick, because it isn't going to happen."

"I'm sorry." Alice felt as hard as Luca, her face paralyzed, heart slowing down to a crawl.

"It's not that I don't dance with girls sometimes. Like, I don't care about that, but..."

"I understand." Alice got up from the table. "It was a stupid thought. I'm going to get some air. Be back in a few minutes."

The cold air burned Alice's skin as she got out of the club. She was sweating harder than she ever remembered. Why was she so stupid? Of course Maxine didn't want her. She cursed the tears that began traitorously dripping down her cheeks. There was nothing to be upset about, Alice tried to reason. It was just a foolish dream to begin with. Alice jolted into reality when someone's hand slammed hard against her shoulder. She turned and saw Maxine.

"You look terrible," Maxine said.

"I'm fine," Alice said, quickly trying to compose herself.

"I don't want to talk about this shit," Maxine said.

"Yeah, I know."

"Let's get out of here."

Alice was still sobbing when they got to the bike. Maxine knew she wasn't capable of comforting her. It was something she simply couldn't do. The words couldn't even form on her lips, despite a few honest efforts. But, as they sped through the night, Maxine was filled with overwhelming guilt, a feeling she was unaccustomed to and did not enjoy. She pulled off the highway and into the parking lot of a convenience store.

"Stay here," she commanded.

When Maxine returned, she thrust a bag into Alice's hands.

"Hold this. I know something that's going to cheer you up." With a roar, the motorcycle came back to life and darted out of the lot.

Maxine brought Alice to the townhouse that had briefly been her home. She dismounted, adjusting her leather jacket as she helped her confused companion off the motorcycle. When Alice opened the bag from the convenience store, she found several cartons of eggs. She looked up at Maxine, who lit a cigarette and smiled. Alice beamed back at her, face full of mischievous delight. They ran through the yard, tossing egg after egg at the offending dwelling. When every last gooey projectile had been smashed, Alice doubled over, gulping for air. Maxine walked over to the panting girl and put her arm around her shoulder.

"Want me to kill them?" she offered casually. "I can break their necks, or burn the house down. I have some explosives I stole from Tartarus that I've got nothing to do with. Whatever you want."

"No, no, that's okay," Alice insisted. "They can't hurt me. Thanks for the offer, though."

"Fine. Watch this." Maxine turned to a nearby telephone pole, flicking her cigarette into the snow.

She held out her hand to the transformer while Alice looked on in confusion. Maxine grunted, her face narrowing in concentration. A loud crackle and boom filled the air as a bolt of electricity arched between Maxine's hand and the transformer, spraying hundreds of sparks into the sky. Alice gaped in awe as every light on the street went out with a satisfying pop.

"Holy shit," she whispered, barely able to contain her excitement.

"You can shoot electricity from your hands?"

"Just one of the many reasons I'm better than everyone else."

Alice grabbed Maxine's hand and studied it intensely. "How does it work?"

"What? I don't know. Some shit about electrons."

"Well, yeah, that's a good starting point. Can all Devils do that?"

"Nope. It's super rare. Most Devils have to live with just the crazy metabolism." Maxine explained. "Now, I'm tired and pissed off. Since I'm not getting any tonight – thanks to you by the way – I think we need to get so drunk tomorrow kicks us straight in the face."

"I'm with you." Alice said.

CHAPTER 33

The early morning at Tartarus unfolded the same as always. Luca's security officers performed thorough inspections of club facilities, and cleaned up any blood and teeth that may have found their way to the dance floor after a fight the night before. A few bartenders and hostesses came in early to deal with bar stocks. Cecil sat at his usual perch in Elysium, reading the news on his phone, barely propped up by the coffee in his hand.

Past the club and into Tartarus's restricted areas, things were much quieter. Luca spent a few hours each day at the gym facilities. This day, she'd chosen to do a morning jog on the treadmill, never being fond of running in front of strangers. The exercise helped her forget the on-going demon disappearances, which were becoming problematic, and the fact she hadn't seen Chris in far too long. After about an hour-and-a-half of running on the treadmill, the door to the gym opened and Fen came in. She was dressed prim and proper and ready for work, a sure sign that the only muscle she intended to exercise was her tongue.

"Have a minute?" Fen asked.

"Will you leave if I say no?" Luca replied.

"I need advice."

"No."

"I didn't even ask what it was."

"I'm not helping you seduce Cecil," Luca said. "I know you're spending all tomorrow going over the budget with him."

"You're no fun!" Fen's shoulders dropped. She crossed her arms and squinted through her glass frames. "Didn't I hook you up?"

"And I'm very grateful," Luca said without an ounce of feeling in her voice.

"How's it going with the boy-toy anyway?"

"He's very energetic, and he's available on-call," Luca said. "You picked a good one, finally."

"Those are the best ones." Fen sighed. "I need someone else to play matchmaker with now. Does Alice have a boyfriend? I know this cute Hekaton that would be just perfect for her."

"Alice is gay."

"Really? I never would have figured. When did she come out?" Fen asked.

"Officially, two years ago, but I've known since she was ten. There's only so many posters of women's volleyball players you can put up in your room before someone gets suspicious."

"How did Cecil take it?" Fen asked.

"He doesn't care, though he was blindsided when she came out. He doesn't pay enough attention."

"What about Chris? Is she, you know, that way?"

"No. And I don't want to talk about Chris."

"She still mad?" Fen asked.

Luca didn't respond, but her breathing loudened over the sound of her sneakers hitting the treadmill belt.

"I get it," Fen said. "You're scared, but it'll be fine. It's a lot to take in. When she's ready, she'll come back."

"What if she doesn't?" Luca asked.

"You're her mom. She won't forget that."

"I'm not her mother. You know that. The bitch screwed off the day the twins were born."

"Semantics. I remember when you were taking them hunting for the first time. The day before, you spent hours agonizing over every detail. We must have spent three hours in the armory trying to pick out rifles for them. I wish I could have met them when they were young. They sounded so cute."

Luca smiled. "I messed up with one of rifles. The recoil was too much for Chris. I had to give her my sidearm."

"See. She'll remember that."

"I wish I could help her. The dreams are so terrible. I just want to grab her and tell her it's okay, but now she won't return my calls." Luca groaned and stopped the treadmill. "I'm going back to work."

"Oh, right. That's why I came here. How's the investigation of the recent disappearances going? I saw a lot of man hours being allocated for it in your report." Fen asked.

"I've got 24 hours surveillance on two potential targets. That pig Warrington disappeared. We're checking into that now. Kent's brother, Ralph, was also a potential target, but the dumb Skull Head won't accept any help."

"Are we close to getting the culprit?"

"We're waiting for them to move. When they do, we'll have more."

"Okay, I'll give you some more leeway in the budget," Fen said as she left Luca to get showered and changed.

Hours later, Fen was in her office, sipping coffee to maintain her focus on her reports, but her mind kept wandering. She kicked her desk in frustration.

"Need to focus," she said under her breath. Her phone screeched to life, as demanding as ever. It was a number she didn't recognize.

"Hello?"

"I need to meet with you for lunch," came a frantic voice. It was Maxine.

"I don't know. I've got a lot of work to do."

"Please."

Maxine never asked politely for anything. Actually, Maxine never asked for anything at all. She demanded plenty, but never asked. Fen was intrigued.

"I can meet you at Cuthbert's on Queen in half an hour." She immediately heard the phone disconnect.

"Nadine," Fen shouted. Her nervous assistant rushed in, head bowed.

"I'm going out for lunch. If anyone important comes looking for me, call my number immediately." Fen was halfway out the door when she turned back. "To clarify, when I say anyone important, I mean Cecil, and only Cecil."

Although Cuthbert's, Fen's choice for lunch, was trendy and crowded, she had no problem securing a somewhat private booth in the back of the café. She was a regular, and not above flashing her assets. She didn't have to wait long before Maxine stormed into the restaurant, all leather and bluster. The Devil slammed herself into the booth, and then cried out in pain when her back touched the seat.

"What's going on, Maxine?" Fen asked.

"I have a fucking problem," Maxine said. She remained bent forward.

"I figured that out already. Why'd you call me?" Fen watched Maxine's eyes dart to the side. "Don't you normally complain to Cecil?"

"I can't talk to him about this. It's about Alice."

"No, Maxine." Fen's eyes bulged out. She brought her voice down to a whisper. "Please tell me you didn't kill Alice. She's so nice and friendly and Cecil's going to try to kill you and then you'll kill him and I'll be alone forever." Fen started hyperventilating.

"Keep quiet," Maxine snapped, grabbing Fen's shoulders from across the table. "I didn't kill Alice. It's worse than that."

"Worse?" Fen asked, cocking her head to the side. She saw Maxine blush for the first time ever.

"I may have gotten a little too drunk last night and, well, nailed her."

"You had sex with her?" Fen whispered frantically. Maxine didn't respond. Fen's expression froze as she adjusted to the reality of the situation. "Was she any good?"

It was Maxine's turn to freeze as she tried to stutter out a response. "Why does that matter?"

"Why are you so embarrassed?"

"Aside from the fact that she's Cecil's kid, how about the fact she's only eighteen?"

"Oh, that's no big deal," Fen giggled. "How old are you anyway, twenty-four?"

"Twenty-six," Maxine snapped back.

"Hah, that's not so bad," Fen waved dismissively.

Maxine tried to sit back and brood, but as soon as her back touched the seat, she leapt forward with a yelp.

"What the hell happened to your back, anyway? Aren't you supposed to be the big, scary Devil?" Fen was enjoying the upper hand she thought she had.

"You want to see what's wrong with my fucking back? Take a look."

Maxine turned to lift the back of her shirt. Her back was covered in bloody bandages. She tenderly pulled one aside, revealing long cuts in rows of four.

"The Cutter's claws popped in the middle of it." She quickly lowered her shirt before anyone else saw. "My bed's a fucking mess."

"What are you going to do?" Fen's smile didn't drop.

"I don't know. That's why you're here. If you haven't noticed, I'm fucking panicking."

"If I managed to bed a Delacroix, I wouldn't let him go."

Maxine groaned, prompting a shrug from the older blonde.

"What's the big deal? Explain that you were drunk and plead with her not to tell her dad." Fen winked. "That is, unless you fancy another trip to machete junction."

* * *

Alice was perched on the couch when Maxine got back to the apartment. She had her hands splayed out in front on her face. They were made of solid, black metal. She was so transfixed by her new toys, she barely registered Maxine's presence.

"Did you clean the sheets?" Maxine yelled.

Alice gazed blankly at her.

"You're buying me new fucking sheets, Cutter." Maxine procured a beer and sat cautiously on the couch.

"Anything you say." Alice offered a dreamy smile. "I had an amazing time last night. My claws are amazing. You're amazing. That was amazing."

"Great. We can't ever do that again."

The smile on Alice's face fell. "What did I do? Is it because I'm..."

"No, it's because I work with your dad," Maxine interrupted sharply. "That's a pretty big conflict of interest, Runt."

Alice felt a knot form in her stomach. Ribbons of skin floated from her elbows, wrapping her arms in flesh, until she was vulnerable like a human again. She nodded her silent assent to Maxine, who mercifully retreated to her bedroom. Alone, Alice struggled to return to the status quo even though she knew things would never be the same. She was a demon, and she was in love. Those things don't go away.

CHAPTER 34

Cindy burst into Chris's room, as she often did. They no longer shared a 16 square foot space, but that didn't mean Cindy had respect for concepts like privacy and knocking. Cindy tiptoed across Chris's room to envelop her in a comforting hug. Chris was grateful for Cindy's affection, which kept her from feeling totally disconnected.

"It's just been me and Emily since Mom and Dad died. I've always had lots of friends, but I'm really glad you're here," Cindy said, tightening her grip.

"Where did that come from?" Chris asked, caught off guard by the personal nature of the comment.

"I know you've been having family troubles."

Chris bit her lip. She wouldn't let herself get emotional. She toyed for a moment with telling Cindy the truth, that she would soon become lost to her demonic nature. Would Cindy make a pact not to let her turn? She almost laughed at the thought. One, this wasn't a cheesy zombie movie, and two, Cindy was still sympathizing with the demons. She'd try to be Chris's friend no matter what, and Chris couldn't even trust herself not to kill the poor girl. The thought filled her with revulsion, but she couldn't promise herself nothing would change when the manifestation took over.

Chris sighed. "You worry too much. I'm fine."

"It's just important that you know I'm here for you. It's you and me together, okay?"

Chris remembered the last time someone had said those words: Alice, her estranged twin. She felt sick again.

"Everyone's going to be here in about an hour, so if you want to shower, you should do it now," Cindy said.

Chris smiled as Cindy left, and then cried for a few minutes when she was gone. In the shower, she tried to scrub her bad memories away with the thin layer of grime covering her skin. Emily was throwing a party for everyone fighting for the cause. These were good people – even Michael – who were willing to risk their lives to save others. They got no recognition, no rewards, but they still fought for what was right.

Chris chose dark, fitted jeans and a red button-down shirt, which did little to accentuate her androgynous figure. She briefly considered looking for more feminine clothes, but dismissed the idea immediately. If she was going to impress the professor, she had to project confidence, and she never felt like herself in a skirt. She reached back in her closet for a tie. Her hand connected with something smooth and hard - a picture frame. Chris cringed at the image inside. It was her high school graduation. Her father stood with his arm around her, looking as proud as he could be. Chris shoved the frame to the back of the closet and covered it with clothes, cursing her weakness for keeping it at all.

Within an hour, the party was at full swing. Voices echoed around the room, though Chris couldn't make out a single conversation. Michael seemed utterly surrounded by his own clique, four or five other men, who might as well be the same person for how identically they dressed. Emily padded around the room, trying to elicit small talk with everyone. Chris had her eyes on a bigger prize. In the corner, Cindy was in deep conversation with Professor Moore.

"How long have you known about the monsters, Professor?" Cindy asked.

"I've known for a couple of years now, although I didn't officially start forming this group until the end of the summer. Before then, it was just Emily, me and a few others."

Cindy looked at the man with hesitation.

"Have you found your work fulfilling?" he asked expectantly.

She started to talk, but was quickly cut off.

"Of course she does, Professor. We all do," Chris said as she walked to the couch, shooting Cindy a warning look.

"There's my favorite student," he exclaimed happily. "I haven't seen you since exams. Have you been feeling all right?"

"I'm getting better," Chris said, words falling fast from her mouth.

"You're worried about killing," Moore stated plainly.

"It's not that, but... I'm sorry," Chris said, refusing to let the professor know that images of violence had been creeping into her waking hours as well as her dreams. Her fingers felt like they had a mind of their own, like they were in control.

"Don't be. I had a feeling you wouldn't be up to handling the dirty deed."

"Do you think we're making a difference?" Chris asked, wanting desperately to confess the horrible truth about herself and get it over with.

"I'm certain of it. I've known about demons for quite some time now, and I've never seen them as worried as they are now."

"Worried?" Chris asked. "What do you mean?"

"They're a little more onto us. Things are getting dangerous. They wouldn't be on edge if we weren't making a difference."

Chris nodded, remembering Fen talking about disappearances like it was a growing problem.

"Are you still worried demons might not be evil?" Moore asked.

"I just want to believe that some demons could be good."

Moore smiled a sad smile and tapped her on the side of the arm.

"I wish I still thought like you. Trust me. The horrors that lay in the demon world do not believe in anything good, as I have had the misfortune to see for myself."

"It's just... never mind," Chris said.

"What's on your mind?"

"Edgar Warrington, and demons like him. They must have day jobs, right? Families, too. Are demons all sociopaths? Do they only kill humans, or do they kill each other as well?"

"Those are fantastic questions. I've been working on my own research for some time, asking just that. I might have to pick your brain a bit later. From what I can tell, demons don't have any kind of morality. They'll kill their own, or humans the same way we'd step on an ant. They seem to be able to pretend to be human enough during the day, but I don't believe they have emotions the same way we do."

"Oh... and what about children?"

"Children?"

"There must be demon children. Do they all have no emotion, or do they lose their emotion as they grow up?"

"I don't know, Christine. But, if you stay with me, we can try to find out those answers together."

Chris nodded as a wave of nausea spread through her. She still had emotions – anger, fear, sadness. They all fought to claim her heart. She wondered briefly if the Beast with the Black Metal Claws would sever them entirely in time.

CHAPTER 35

"Are you still seeing that girl?" Larry asked when the two detectives got back from a new homicide scene.

"Yeah, but I'm not really 'seeing her'," Julian said. "We just have sex a couple of times a week."

"I'd say you hit the jackpot, Buddy. You get all the perks of having a girl without all the problems." Larry laughed. "Have you checked her out yet?"

"No, I don't want to know any more about her. It's more mysterious this way."

"Don't be stupid. She's not going to be sexier when we bring her in for being a drug mule."

"It feels nice to let go of control every once in a while," Julian said with a smile as he gestured toward all the clutter surrounding the stubby detective's desk.

Larry's phone started vibrating. Julian glanced at it. There was a text from the woman Lady Black that only said '4:00'.

"Well, I've got some work to do, so I'll see you later," Larry said as he hastily grabbed his coat.

"Meeting a lady friend?" Julian teased.

"Shut up, Julian," he responded, glaring at his partner as he rushed out of the office, leaving a laughing Julian behind.

Julian could feel his phone vibrating in his pocket. Grabbing it, he saw a text from Luca: '7:00'. It was going to be a good night.

Hours later, Julian lay naked in Luca's bed with his arms resting behind his head.

"I really needed that," he said.

She ignored him as she got dress.

"I feel useless at work," he confided. "I wanted to be a cop to help people, protect them and keep the bad guys at bay." He sighed. "It seems like half of our investigations end in confessions that don't make any sense. Something's going on. My partner won't talk to me about it. He just says to *roll with it*, which, you know, doesn't fill me with confidence. I feel like the only one on the force who's not either lazy or corrupt, and I'm not even sure what's worse."

"You don't know who I am," Luca said, turning toward him as she buttoned her shirt. "Just because I have sex with you doesn't mean you should trust me."

"But the fact that you point that out makes me trust you more," he said, playfully grabbing her by the hips and hugging her tightly.

She shooed his hands away, but not before he managed to provoke a small, uncharacteristic giggle. He leaned back on the bed, sighing deeply.

"It's sick that this random sex is the best thing going on in my life right now," he said. "I feel like a failure, like a boy playing detective."

"Not much good is happening with me, either. You see that girl there," she said, pointing at one of the kids in her picture. "I've lost all contact with her. She ran away a couple of months ago. It's my fault for chasing her off." She sat on the bed beside Julian, who was getting concerned. "I could find her, no problem - I put a GPS tracker on her phone - but what's the point if she doesn't want to see me?"

Julian sat up to hold her, but as soon as his comforting arms touched her body she straightened her back and pulled away.

"Forget it," she said, regaining her composure and cursing herself for doing exactly what she promised Cecil she wouldn't do – get attached. "Put your clothes on, and I'll take you home."

"My partner is going to pick me up on Elm." Julian grabbed his phone and started texting.

"I'll walk you that far, at least. I wouldn't want the poor, defenseless detective to get mugged."

She was trying to joke with him, to pretend like she hadn't revealed holes in her armor.

"You know I have a gun, too, right?"

She gave him a condescending smile.

"That thing could hardly be considered a gun." She pulled her gun out of her holster. "This is the Beretta M93R - Italian made, three round burst, or single shot, maximum stopping power at close range."

"Should I be worried about what you do?" Julian asked.

She replaced the gun in her holster and glared at him until he backed down.

"Whatever," he said, averting his gaze. "Me and my toy will be just fine, but you're free to come along."

They tried to make small talk as they cut through the alleys toward Elm Street. Just before they reached the main road, a loud, banging noise drew Julian's attention to a nearby dumpster. A naked man stumbled out of the darkness into their path.

"Sir, are you okay?" Julian asked, noticing that the man was covered in some kind of lubricant.

"Son of a bitch," Luca cursed.

Julian looked back at her and ducked as she pulled out her gun. She fired three shots into the man, who collapsed onto his back.

"What the hell are you doing?" Julian yelled.

"Get out of my way, Julian," she said, shoving him to the ground as she approached the injured man.

Julian's jaw dropped when he saw the man rise to his feet, despite the three holes in his chest. Luca kicked the man, sending it back down, and fired two bullets into its head. She turned back to Julian and gestured toward the man's body. The detective stared in awe as the body started rapidly dissolving. The blood was boiling and the smell of rotten meat saturated the air. He'd been wrong – whatever that thing was, it wasn't human.

"Stay down, Julian," came a voice from the end of the alley.

He looked up and saw Larry running toward him, reaching for his gun.

"Don't worry, Larry. Whatever it was, it's dead now," Julian said.

Larry pointed his gun at Luca.

"I said stay down."

Luca watched the older detective with a cold, detached gaze.

"Stay away from Julian. He doesn't need your shit," Larry yelled, his jangled nerves made obvious by the tiny tremors in his hands.

Luca raised her hands over her head, the gun dangling around her index finger. Larry's eyes turned to Julian for a split second to make sure that he wasn't hurt. Taking advantage of his lapse in concentration, Luca gripped her gun and pointed it at the aging detective.

"I don't need the boy," she said.

"Julian, over here," Larry said, urging Julian over to him with a wave of his left hand.

Julian scrambled across the alley, slipping briefly in the goo that the creature had left behind.

"Go on, detective. You have what you came for. I think it's time for you to get out of here," Luca said, lowering her weapon.

"What kind of trick is this?" Larry asked, keeping his gun firmly aimed at the woman.

"Think of it as a gift. You still have a job to do," she said as she turned away, knowing that he didn't have the guts to pull the trigger.

Larry pulled a stunned Julian back to his car.

"What the fuck was that?" Julian yelled.

"That was Lady Black." Larry's hands were still shaking as he tried to calm down. "She's the mouthpiece for a criminal organization that funnels a lot of money into the police department." Larry's voice was unsteady with fear. "My partner and I tried to investigate her eight years ago. She slaughtered him, and nobody cared.

"She's not human, Julian. She's some sort of monster. I know how it sounds, but you've got to listen to me. I saw her rip my partner to pieces in front of me. But when I told the truth about what happened, I just sounded crazy. Loony Larry. Let his partner die and lost his mind." He let out a heavy sigh. "She's got the whole goddamn homicide department in her pocket. I hoped that she wouldn't target you as long as I did everything she wanted, but obviously I was wrong."

Julian sat back, unable to take in everything he had seen.

"Why didn't you shoot her, then?" the younger detective asked.

"It wouldn't do any good. Someone else would just replace her. This has been going on for decades at least."

"What about that thing she killed?" Julian's head was spinning.

"What thing?" Larry asked. He had arrived too late to see the dissolved creature. "Just promise me you'll stay away from her."

Julian cursed as he rested his head on the dashboard.

CHAPTER 36

"Vampires are stupid," Alice stated when she got home from the movies. "How is anyone supposed to be scared of them? They need to make up their minds whether they want to eat people or bone them." She started unsheathing her black, metal claws, the skin on her hands peeling back as her fingers elongated into points. "Now, if they had these babies, maybe I'd be afraid of them," she said with pride.

"You're the one who wanted to go out with your friends. The way I see it, this is all your fault," Maxine said from the couch.

"I thought they'd want to see something a little less lame." Alice groaned as she flopped on the couch. She placed her clawed hand onto Maxine's leg, making the blonde tense up.

"Don't you have work to do?" Maxine asked, her eyes fixed on Alice's predatory claws.

"Sure, I could do some biology readings, but wouldn't you rather hang out with your favorite roommate?" she said, pushing her obsidian hand further up Maxine's leg, a greedy smile spreading on her face.

Maxine could smell alcohol on Alice's breath. Clearly, she and her friends had done more than just watch a bad movie. She kept her eyes locked on the girl's claws, her eye twitching as she remembered what they had done to her back.

"Come on, Max. Don't you want to play?" the young woman said innocently as she started nuzzling Maxine's neck.

"What did I say about this never happening again? Was I not fucking clear?"

"What if I pretended I was a sexy vampire?" Alice offered as she bit Maxine's neck.

"Now you're going to get it," Maxine said, pushing the girl off and cracking her knuckles.

The next day, Fen was waiting in Cuthbert's after receiving another frantic phone call. She smiled brightly as she flagged Maxine down.

"Are we girlfriends now?" Fen asked. "Because, if we are, I need to talk to you about your hair. I know slicking it back is easy, but you're never going to get a boyfriend if you don't put some effort into it." Fen's eyes were alight with possibilities. "While we're at it, have you thought about makeup? I've got some emergency supplies in my purse. If you come to the bathroom with me, we can really make you shine."

Maxine slammed her fist against the table in an attempt to stop the overexcited woman.

"Shut up," Maxine said a little too loudly, provoking stares from nearby patrons. She lowered her voice. "I'm not your friend. I just don't have anyone else to talk to."

"Fine, tell me what's actually wrong," Fen asked, her bright smile gleaming in the light.

"It happened again."

"Yeah, I figured."

"Great. Now are you going to help me or not?"

"Details first," Fen said, bending her hand dismissively. "Were you drunk again?"

"No, I wasn't drunk." Maxine blushed, looking away. "She's very pushy."

"That's your excuse?" Fen put her hand over her mouth, trying to contain her laughter. "I've seen you use your Devil-enhanced muscles to crush Luca like she was a newborn baby, but little Alice forced herself on you?"

"No, I... it's really hard to say no to her," Maxine stuttered out.

"Come on. You wanted it, didn't you?" Fen asked.

"It needs to stop."

"Why does it need to stop?"

Maxine was taken aback, stuttering a bit before regaining control. "I thought you were the one who was afraid of what might happen between me and Cecil?"

"Maybe it's not that bad. I mean, you two mess with each other a lot."

Maxine groaned, burying her head in her arms on the table.

"There's a big difference between pissing someone off and sleeping with their kid. You see that, right?" Maxine asked.

"Why don't you just try it out on a trial basis?" Fen suggested. "For all you know, everything will fall apart as soon as the initial thrill wears off. If it doesn't work out, then he'll never have to know. If it does work out, then..." She paused, her eyes rolled back in thought. "Then how about Alice and I explain it to him while you're really far away?"

"That's not bad," Maxine said as she sat up straight. "We don't even know if anything will happen. Maybe it'll all blow over and I'll have been worrying about nothing. Why bother Cecil with the details now when it could fizzle out in a couple of days?"

"I think it's so sweet that you care so much about Cecil's feelings," Fen crooned. "If you weren't trying so hard to get into Alice's pants, I might feel threatened."

"I don't care about his feelings. I just don't want to have to kill him. He's one of the only people that I don't actively hate."

"That's practically a declaration of love, coming from you." Fen pretended to pout and fluttered her eyelashes. "Since I'm here, does that mean you don't actively hate me, too? Or am I your backup in case this jailbait situation falls through?"

Maxine bit her lip and narrowed her eyes. She wasn't used to being teased, especially by a floozy like Fen.

"Are you all covered in claw marks again?" Fen reached across the table and pulled at Maxine's shirt.

"No, I'm not letting my guard down around the fucking Cutter again," she said as she unconsciously rubbed at her back.

"Probably a good idea. After all, there's only so much money you can take from the budget for new sheets. Luca's pissed about that, by the way."

"Fuck her. But don't tell her why I needed the sheets."

As much as it pained Maxine to admit it, talking with Fen had made her far more confident about the situation. When she got home, the door to Alice's room was closed.

"Runt? You in there?" she asked, pounding on the door.

There was no answer, but Maxine could hear shuffling behind the door. Trying the doorknob, she found it was locked.

"Open this door right now, or it's coming down," she yelled.

Once again, there was no response. Pursing her lips, she kicked the doorknob off in one swift motion.

"You're fixing the fucking door," she said, pointing at Alice, who was huddled in her bed. Maxine's expression went from anger to confusion when she saw Alice's suitcase out and her room devoid of any of her posters or personal effects. "What are you doing in here?"

"I'm going to call Dad and move back in with him until I find a new apartment," Alice said, her eyes red.

"Why?" Maxine's heart dropped.

Alice didn't respond, marching with her bags out into the main room.

"I asked you a question," Maxine yelled, in pursuit.

Alice turned, her bags in her hands. "You said we could never do it again, and it happened again last night. Then you left as soon as you woke up. I think it's clear I can't stay here anymore."

Maxine groaned as she sat on the arm of the couch, keeping her eyes on the emotional girl.

"What if... what if we just keep going on like normal and see what happens?" She couldn't believe she was suggesting this.

Alice dropped her bags and put her hands on her hips. All the nervousness, all the meekness, disappeared from her face. In its place was an enormous smirk.

"So, what you're saying is that you want to be my girlfriend?" Alice asked confidently.

Maxine was caught off guard by the abrupt switch in the girl's demeanor, for the first time recognizing Cecil in the young woman.

"I asked you a question," Alice repeated.

The stunned blonde nodded slowly. "Did you plan this?"

Alice jumped over the back of the couch. She brought her arms around Maxine and whispered in her ear.

"Nobody gives me nearly enough credit."

Maxine started to laugh as Alice's lips found hers.

CHAPTER 37

Chris sat in thought in Emily's car. She still had so many questions and nowhere to get answers. Professor Moore would never lie to her, but he was as much of an outsider to the demon world as she was. She probably knew more about it than he did. Her father... well, she couldn't believe a word he said. Luca, too. Did they both totally lack emotion, or was that a theory on the part of the professor? Luca never showed emotion, so maybe he was right. Her father, on the other hand, always went over the top. Maybe he was overcompensating for the feelings he didn't have. She missed how excited he would get at every holiday, even going so far as to concoct a Columbus Day song, which he, Chris and Alice would sing over and over again every year, much to Luca's annoyance. Holidays were always so exciting at her house, so happy. No. Chris shook her head. She couldn't let those thoughts in.

Whatever the reasons, Chris had managed to push the shame and fear of her secret out of her mind, at least for the night. She sat in the passenger seat of Emily's car, tapping her hands against her jeans to some imaginary beat, while Cindy slumbered peacefully in the back seat.

"Just scouting again tonight?" Chris asked.

"Michael has the details, but it should be a pretty quiet night," Emily responded.

Chris nodded her head along with the beat her hands were making against her legs.

"Why are you so excited today?" Emily asked suspiciously.

"Excited?"

"You're beating your legs like a drum."

"Oh." Chris stopped. "I didn't notice." Her hands were always sneaking around, doing things behind her back. They were getting harder to keep still. At least they were still human.

Emily looked back at the sleeping Cindy, and then turned to Chris.

"Cindy isn't convinced we're doing the right thing. I'm hoping tonight will convince her. You're on board, right?"

"Of course," Chris said, hands wringing in her lap. "We're helping people."

"I'm glad we're on the same page. Nobody's above the law. I don't care if they have their reasons," Emily said, obviously rebutting Cindy's points without even hearing them.

Snow fell fast and heavy when they arrived on campus, making visibility difficult. Michael pounded at the driver's side window as soon as they parked. Emily rolled down the window.

"We've got a kill tonight," he said.

"Why wasn't I told about this?" Emily asked.

"Calm down," Michael said. "I just got the word five minutes ago. The professor insists."

"Same address?" Emily asked.

"No, you're still doing the scouting mission alone. The kill is another demon, one the professor thinks is about to strike."

"Fine. You guys go ahead to the kill." Emily said.

Michael nodded and turned to go, but Chris reached over Emily to stop him.

"I'll come with you," Chris said.

"I don't think you should," Emily sputtered.

"I have to. It'll be all right. I'll stay safe," Chris assured Emily before disappearing with Michael into the darkness.

Like the last time with Edgar Warrington, she was drawn to the carnage. She needed to see if the demon was a mindless beast like the one that attacked her in the park. She had to be certain she'd made the right decision.

"Where are we going?" Chris asked as she climbed into the front seat of a pickup truck. She didn't recognize the driver.

"I don't know. We're going to follow Michael up there."

"How many are with us tonight?"

"We're at fifteen." He paused. "I'm Dave, by the way."

They drove to a heavily wooded area on the outskirts of the city. The trees were cut by a dirt road with a mailbox stationed at the end. The numbers 742 were barely visible through the blizzard. Michael and the other men in his car rushed up the path. Chris took off her seatbelt and tried to get out, but Dave stopped her with an arm across her chest.

"They're checking the place out. We're not going in yet."

Chris nodded.

After nearly half an hour of waiting, she saw movement coming up the driveway. Michael tapped on Dave's window.

"He's spooked. He must have noticed something. It doesn't look like he'll be going to sleep," Michael

"We going back?" Dave asked.

"No, the professor needs this done tonight. There are a lot of lives at stake. We'll break in from the front and back simultaneously and overwhelm him. You guys are going through the back. Move when you get the signal."

Chris almost had a second thought as the gravity of the danger she was putting herself in came home to roost, but she pushed it back down with ease. Her instincts drove her forward. Her fingers, hidden deep in her pockets, were thirsty for a scarlet drink. But it wasn't just her burgeoning bloodlust. Every chance she got to see a demon was an opportunity to figure out her place in the world. Was she doomed to be a monster, or could she be saved?

Chris and Dave jumped out of the truck and dashed down the driveway. The snow and ice beat back against Chris's small frame. But she persisted, against the elements and a solitary voice, whispering, begging her to stop. Her gaze was focused on the light coming from a distant cabin, which pierced through the starless night and seared into Chris's vision. It was bright white. This was all very, very real. Rounding the back of the cabin, through the trees, they met a group of six men huddled around an imposing snow bank. Chris took a knife offered by a man she didn't know, and joined the men in the huddle.

"When we get the text, we run in," a man said.

"No guns?" Chris asked.

"The professor doesn't like guns. Too much noise."

"We're out in the middle of nowhere. Who's going to come running?" Chris asked.

"We don't know if there're more demons out in these woods," Dave responded.

"What if the door's locked?" Chris asked.

"Jay already picked the lock. We're all set," a man said. "Now be quiet."

She huddled with the men, hoping that the pounding of her heart would stop. After a few minutes, one of the men's phones lit up. There was a text from Michael that said 'go'. All of the men stood up quickly, and, along with Chris, rushed into the house.

When she got to the front room, there was an enormous, burly-looking man with his hand around a vigilante's throat. There was no flesh on the upper half of his face, only a solid black skull with eyeless sockets. His human-looking jaw snapped shut as he flung the intruder to the ground. That was the face of the demon – twisted and awful. There was nothing in his eyes, no fear, no anger, no sadness. It was another mindless beast intent on cleaving through flesh. The sight chilled Chris's blood, and she shoved her back against the wall. Her knife was clutched in her hands and pressed up against her chest. Panic surged through her. She went to step forward, but the demon threw one of the vigilantes at her. The boy's body struck her sideways, knocking the wind out of her lungs. Chris's head banged against the wooden wall and the room blurred as she tried to regain her senses.

Two vigilantes were slumped on the floor, stunned. The rest of Michael's group were circling their prey, slashing at it when they could. Dave lunged, stabbing the creature and sending a spray of blood across the room. It grabbed Dave and hurled him against the wall, causing it to quake.

Move, move, move, Chris willed herself, but her feet just wouldn't comply. Her fingers wanted to get in the fight, but her mind was desperate to flee. The blood flowing from the skull-faced creature was beginning to coat the floor and make everything slick. The other vigilantes tore and stabbed where they could until its flesh was more red than anything else, but still it lived. Chris tried again to jump in and fight for the cause, but she couldn't. She hated her cowardice, but, every time its horrible face turned toward her, her entire body trembled. Killing it might lead her to salvation, but that chance was slipping away as it came closer to death with no intervention from her. Michael rushed behind it and stabbed it in the back repeatedly. The creature tried to turn, but fell to its side. Another man jumped on the creature's back. It bucked in vain as he managed to slit its throat.

Chris gazed at the monster, sputtering blood all over the floor as it fell, dead. It was all over, and she hadn't even raised her knife. So much for saving the world.

"Is everyone all right?" Michael asked.

"I'm going to be feeling this for a month," Dave replied.

"You're telling me," said another man.

"Great job, guys," Michael began. "We sent him back to Satan."

Somewhere in the room, a phone began to ring. The men checked their phones, but none had calls. Then one of them knelt by the monster, who now looked too much like a man for Chris's comfort. He reached into the creature's pocket and removed a ringing phone. As if on cue, light streamed through the large glass window in the front of the cabin, highlighting the youths and blinding Chris. She could hear the hum of an engine and the sounds of rubber compressing snow. A car was coming down the driveway.

"Fuck," Dave shouted.

Michael rushed over to the other side of the front door.

"There's no time to escape. We'll take care of whatever comes in," he declared, as they all moved into hiding spots around the room.

Chris remained still, leaned up against a post in front of the door, locked in terror's embrace.

A car door slammed shut and the sound of carefully placed footsteps crumpling snow filled the air. Whoever was coming toward the door was doing so cautiously. Michael waved Chris over to him, but she hadn't recovered the use of her legs. She was standing opposite the door, directly in the line of vision of whoever was approaching the house. Even in her frightened state, Chris knew she was about to die, killed by one of her own kind as she failed to rebel against her nature. It seemed poetic. Even the Prince of Denmark didn't get as tragic an ending. The door burst open with a bang when a powerful leg collided with the weak wood. Chris yelped at the sound and turned her head, barely willing herself to look at the intruder.

"Chris?"

Luca, gun raised, filled the doorway.

One of the men took advantage of Luca's hesitation and slashed her across the hand, forcing her to drop her weapon. The gun slid across the floor, landing mere feet from Chris. Luca turned to the man who cut her, wrenched the knife out of his hand, and shoved it up through his chin and into his brain. Chris cried out in horror. A man on the other side of the room ran up and stabbed Luca in the side. Pulling the knife from the dead man's head, she slashed her new attacker across the throat, sending him to the floor, gasping for life that was soon gone. Two more men rushed her and slashed across her chest and back. She dropped the knife. Blood seeped freely through her white dress shirt.

Luca dodged another knife blow, then slammed her fist into a man's face. She stepped back momentarily to assess the situation. She hunched her shoulders and clenched all her muscles, a look of immense concentration on her face. The back of her jacket ripped along the seams and fell away. From the center of her spine sprang four brown, sinewy tentacles. One shot toward Michael, who narrowly escaped her grasp by jumping through the large window in the front of the room. Another tentacle grabbed a nearby man by the throat and crushed the life out of him in seconds. Luca cried out in pain as a man made it past her flailing appendages and stabbed her in the stomach. She knocked him onto the ground and stomped on his face until his neck snapped.

Two of the tentacles grabbed Dave by the arms and stretched him out in front of Luca. He screamed as his bones twisted in their sockets, until the sinews broke and both arms twisted free of his torso. Luca let his corpse fall and tossed the limbs to the ground. Chris winced when the spatter painted her red. Luca was swaying back and forth, unsteady on her feet, but she was still able to catch a fleeing man by the ankle and drag him across the floor. He clawed at the ground, trying to pull away, but fell dead when Luca buried a knife in the back of his head. Chris covered her eyes and cowered against the wall, hoping that everything would just go away, that she'd wake up back in her bed, before the world went insane, back when Luca was responsible for kissing her cuts better and not the carnage before her.

When all the screaming stopped, Chris opened her eyes. Luca was struggling to stand. Her shirt no longer showed any hint of white. It was saturated with blood, and too much of it was her own. Her tentacles receded back into her body while she teetered from side to side. Luca tried to take a step forward, but fell back instead, banging her head against the wall. The only sound in the room was

Luca's labored breathing as she sat there, staring at Chris. Her eyes stared deep into Chris's soul, and Chris had to struggle not to look away. Michael peeked his head into the cabin. Luca was barely conscious, but she still saw him lurking in the window. Luca's hand shot out, feebly grasping for her gun, but it was out of her reach. Seeing the monster more or less subdued, Michael climbed inside and strode toward Chris. Something desperate awoke in Chris. It was more than fear; more than anger; more than sadness. It set her in motion for the first time since the slaughter began, and she scrambled to grab the gun. Luca's pistol felt heavy in her hands, but she knew how to use it – Luca had taught her. She looked at Luca then Michael. Compatriots, they both nodded.

Of the fifteen people who had entered the building, only Chris and Michael remained. There were bodies everywhere and the room was thick with the smell of gore. Chris raised the gun, pointing it at Luca. She was supposed to save people from monsters. Wasn't she? Luca's pained wheezing didn't masquerade the danger she posed. Luca didn't beg for her life. All she did was stare at Chris with her deep, green eyes. Her mouth was flat, expressionless. Her brow unfurled. No hint of emotion was readily apparent on her face. But Chris saw something powerful in her eyes. Looking away, Chris refused look at them any longer. She pressed down on the trigger, hand shaking wildly. Flashes of demons filled her head: the creature from the park, who had chased her with mindless, murderous intent; Edgar Warrington, who killed with his detestable talons; her father, in blood-soaked surgeon's garb; the Beast with the Black Metal Claws, its twisted smile goading her on; and Luca, who'd read her to sleep every night when she was little.

Chris finally understood what she saw in Luca's eyes – love. The professor was wrong, about the emotionlessness of demons, and maybe everything. Even if he was right, Chris couldn't follow him. Maybe it was her demon side winning out? She didn't care. All it took was a single look from the woman that raised her and Chris's certainty came crashing down. Chris fluttered her eyes, as if waking from a long nightmare, and turned the gun on Michael.

"Leave," she said.

Michael stared blankly at her.

"Get the fuck out," she shrieked, firing the gun into the floor in front of him.

Michael ran for his life.

Chris dropped the gun on the floor. She yanked her phone from her pocket and called Cecil.

"Dad, Luca's seriously hurt. Get out to 742 on Route 44. I don't know how long she has left."

She looked at Luca, the vicious, efficient killer bleeding on the floor. Chris ran to her and tried to apply pressure to her wounds, but there were too many. She could feel Luca's heart rate slowing.

"It's going to be okay," Chris said, more afraid now than when her own life was in jeopardy.

Luca looked up at her.

"I love you," Luca whispered. She closed her eyes and went limp in Chris's arms.

CHAPTER 38

When Cecil burst into the cabin, he saw his lost daughter trying to revive his unconscious partner amidst the wet trappings of a massacre. An ambulance was out of the question. He threw both women in the back seat of his car and raced to the nearest hospital. Chris feebly pressed her hands against Luca's wounds in an attempt to stay the blood that gushed maddeningly out. By the time Cecil tore into the ambulance bay, her arms were painted red. She only let go when Cecil wrenched Luca from her grasp and sprinted inside. Chris entered the hospital in time to see Luca spirited away on a stretcher, bound for emergency surgery. She looked at her father. He looked back. Neither spoke. All they could do was wait.

* * *

Cecil paced endlessly back and forth, as if his heart would seize the moment his legs ceased. Chris sat like a statue in the hospital waiting room. Guilt was a powerful paralytic, and hospitals unnerved her at the best of times. There was something about the smell that made her stomach turn in a sea of sterile blue and white. She remembered all the times she'd been worried about her father after he'd 'fallen down the stairs'. How did she ever believe that? Her life was such a lie. Behind her eyes played a highlight reel of the past few hours. They had been the worst of her life, and the night wasn't over yet.

Hours later, a nurse with a clipboard approached Cecil. Chris watched in fear, trying to overhear the hushed conversation. Cecil placed his head in his hands and relaxed his shoulders, whether out of despair or relief, it was impossible to say. Chris rose in a sanguine haze from her seat and went to him, prepared for the worst. He turned to address her for the first time that night. She expected cross words, harsh tones, and tears. Instead, she received a hearty thumbs up and bountiful smile from her father. Chris gasped audibly as a sea of relief crashed over her tiny form.

The nurse led them to Luca's room. Chris paused. She didn't deserve to see the shattered woman. Luca was trapped in a hive of bandages and tubes amidst the gentle, disturbing buzz of machinery. Folded neatly into the bed, she looked so small. Chris hardly recognized the broken woman before her as the pillar of strength she knew. Cecil sat beside the bed and gently stroked the woman's hand. There was no sign that Luca was aware of his presence.

"She's going to be okay," he whispered, passing Chris a sly smile. "Have to say, I was worried for a second. I'm not used to seeing her lose that much blood." He gazed at Luca for a few moments before turning to his daughter. "Let's head home."

Chris nodded. Her eyes fluttered as her attention was pulled from Luca, the victim of her stupidity. She'd been in shock for hours, unable to fully feel. Now that Luca was safe, reality hit her like a bat to the gut.

As they drove home, Chris could barely look at her father as flashes of the surgeon from her dreams blinded her to the man beside her. He was rhythmically tapping on the wheel with one hand and steering with the other. Chris could still smell Luca's blood from the back seat. How much blood was he used to seeing Luca lose? She should have asked. It was too late now. Chris longed for punishment. Maybe she belonged on a table, being ripped apart.

"I'm probably going to have to clean the back seat before the next time I take you two to soccer practice, huh?" Cecil joked.

"Do you think Luca will be all right?"

"Don't worry about Luca. She's great. I'm more worried about the car cleaner's bill."

"I'm sorry."

"Don't worry about it, Honey. I wish you'd call more, but I just need to get used to the fact you're on your own now."

It was surreal. There she was, covered in blood, in a bloody car, with the demon Overlord and he was joking like she was a pre-teen. She was cracking under the weight of her own guilt. He was now talking about a chocolate cake he tried to make that turned out as hard as a rock. She smiled at him in time with the highs and lows of the conversation. A habit, she realized. He was still lying, trying to pretend like they weren't knee deep in Luca's blood. Chris had to hand it to him: she almost believed that things were normal, if only for a moment.

They arrived at the house far too quickly. It had been only a few months since she had moved out, so ready for her adult life to begin. Now she wasn't so naïve. Chris entered the house first, but she could feel Cecil on her heels, his breath on her neck. She felt his arms curl around her shoulders as he brought her in for a hug.

"I missed you, Dear," he said, face wracked with what Chris thought might be genuine emotion – she wasn't sure. "Are you hungry? I've got some left-over Chinese food in the fridge, or I can make you a casserole?"

"A casserole? It's the middle of the night."

"How about a sandwich?"

"No, thanks, Dad."

"That's too bad. I'm going face first into the chow mein. Are you tired? I'm exhausted. Are you tired?"

"Yes."

"Great. Well, not great, but I'm sure you'll feel better after some sleep," Cecil announced brightly. "I haven't changed your room one bit. You still have a few bits of clothes that were in the wash when you left."

"Don't you want to talk about where I've been?" Chris asked.

"We can do that later, Honey. I'm just happy you're home. You are home, right?"

"I've made my decision."

"That's what I wanted to hear."

Chris found it surreal to be in her old room. It almost felt like she'd never left, that there were no demons, her father wasn't a monster and Luca wasn't steps from death. The metallic stench of dried blood blistered the illusion. Chris was filled with pangs of revulsion. She rushed to the bathroom, peeling off her stained clothes and discarding them behind her. She stepped into the shower and cranked the handle to the hottest setting, scrubbing the scorching water into her skin until her entire body was red and raw. Only when the water circling the drain turned from pink to crystal clear did she finally feel clean.

CHAPTER 39

Chris didn't entertain trying to stave off sleep that night. Her entire body was aching and her mind was broken from living through a real nightmare. The second her body fell on her old bed's familiar springs, she was out.

She awoke in bondage, a disturbingly familiar experience for the traumatized girl. Her legs were free, but a quick glance downwards confirmed that her arms were restrained in a white straightjacket. She was leaning against the padded wall of a holding room, totally enclosed with a door on one end and a tiny barred window at the top of the other. Chris laughed to herself until her lungs begged for a coughing fit. The nuthouse? It seemed almost fitting. Moonlight streaming through the window shone green light upon the room, as if Chris needed any further proof that she was once again locked in a nightmare. Kicking her legs out and wedging her useless upper body against the wall, she managed to pull herself up to her feet. As she did so, the green light dimmed. Something stooped in front of her window, blocking it out. She turned around and saw the twisted smile of the Beast with the Black Metal Claws taunting her in her cage.

"I'm going to get you," it croaked in a garbled, twin voice that modulated from baritone to soprano concurrently.

Chris recoiled in shock. The Beast had never spoken coherent words, and its awful voice tore through her heart like a hungry buzzard.

"So soon now," the Beast said, shakily craning its neck up toward the moon.

Chris wasn't listening. She was kicking at the door to the cell with everything she had. To her amazement, the heavy padded door gave way and she stumbled through it, leaving the laughing Beast behind her.

Chris found herself in the bleached, white hallways of the hospital. Behind her, she heard the door to her cell snap shut. To her left was a blank wall, but the corridor stretched on to the right. The corridor was lined with closed doors, with no hint as to what lay behind each one. At the very end of the hall Chris thought she could see a reception desk. Chris rushed down the hall, hoping to find an exit, or at least a way out of the straight jacket. If the Beast with Black Metal

Claws caught up to her, she sure as hell wanted her arms free. As she passed a door, an arm shot out and grabbed her. It gripped the shoulder of her straight jacket and tossed her with ease into a waiting wheelchair. Looking up, she gasped at the bloodied and bruised form of Luca. Even more shocking then her battered appearance was her choice of garb: Luca wore hospital scrubs in place of her usual suit. The scrubs were sea foam green, but they were rapidly changing color. Blood leaked steadily from Luca's back, chest, and especially her stomach.

"What are you doing out of your room?" Luca asked, shaking her head.

The blood on Luca's scrubs spilled down across Chris's shoulders, sinking into the white fabric of the straightjacket.

"I'm so sorry," Chris pleaded. "I didn't mean for this to happen."

"Is that so?" Luca replied coldly. "Let me check your chart." From behind the wheelchair she produced a brown clipboard bearing a single sheet of paper. Luca ran her finger down the page. "It says here that you're a selfish little girl who only cares about herself." Luca never took her eyes from the paper. "It says you'll never regret what you did enough to make up for it. Ah yes, and that you must be prepped for surgery. He's waiting for you, you know."

Luca ignored Chris's brittle screams and wheeled her back into the corridor. All the way down the hall, Chris saw the doors on either side snap open. There were faint sounds coming from each one, forming a macabre symphony of screams and metal scrapings. As they approached the first room, a few sounds came into painful clarity. It was Luca's voice, pleading for mercy. Chris turned to look and saw another Luca, this one with her gut split open and held gaping by four metal hooks. A masked doctor stood over her and reached into her abdomen, playing with the goo inside. The nurse Luca didn't seem to notice. She just kept wheeling.

In the next room, another Luca was strapped to a hospital bed. There, another doctor was driving a vacillating saw through the deep, red muscles of her thigh, severing it from the body. He'd been working for a while – it was the only limb that Luca had left. Still the nurse Luca walked on, oblivious or uncaring. Every room was the same. They all featured Luca, tortured, or sometimes dead.

The figure standing over her was always a doctor, but Chris knew the truth. It was all her fault. She wanted to avert her eyes from the sight of yet another gruesome Luca scene, but guilt kept her attention. She couldn't look away, and so she absorbed the sight of Luca's powerful body being torn to shreds, destroyed, and discarded over and over again. When they reached the reception desk, Chris was exhausted. She hardly cared what happened to her anymore, if only the torture of Luca would stop. From behind the desk, she heard a faint tapping sound. The Beast with the Black Metal Claws emerged, beaming its twisted smile. It leapt forward, brandishing its claws at Chris. The nurse Luca stepped between Chris and the Beast in an oddly protective motion.

"No," she said sternly to the monster. "It's not time yet." She waved her finger at the Beast, scolding it like a child.

The Beast roared and glared at Chris with murder in its eyes.

Luca rolled Chris through a set of double doors to an operating room. The Beast followed them, but kept its distance. Once inside, Luca removed Chris's straightjacket. Chris vaguely considered trying to escape, but she knew she could never overpower Luca. With all the guilt she felt, she barely wanted to, anyway. Luca deftly lifted Chris from the chair and deposited her on an operating table. Though Chris had gone limp and wasn't resisting, Luca still secured her to the table with leather straps. When Chris was fully bound, Luca walked over to the wall and busied herself with an IV.

"What anesthetic would you like to use on the patient, Doctor?" Luca asked, turning to the surgeon, who appeared over Chris's shoulder.

"Anesthetic? And ruin the fun?" The surgeon laughed and he pressed the porcelain mask on his face against Chris's forehead.

"Doctor," Luca said disapprovingly.

"Spoilsport," he whined. "Give me the green mixture. No, wait," he outstretched his arm. "The black one."

Luca nodded and returned with an IV bag full of a shimmering black liquid. She reached down for Chris's hand and rubbed an alcohol swab across the front. While Luca prepped Chris, the surgeon took a series of long, plastic tubes and pressed them against Chris's mouth. She clamped it shut. The surgeon beat her across the face with his spare hand. A gasp was all he needed and he shoved the tubes in Chris's mouth. Once in, they seemed to have a mind of their own, and they snaked down her esophagus, choking the girl. Her eyes went wide. At the same time, Luca brought the IV needle to Chris's hand and inserted it.

Chris's eyes pleaded with her tormentors. The black shining liquid disappeared in her veins, burning and spreading like a virus through her body. The tubes prevented Chris from making a noise, but she stared, eyes bulging in horror as the skin on her hands began to peel back, revealing solid pieces of black metal.

The Beast walked up and leaned down next to her face.

"Soon," it whispered.

CHAPTER 40

Chris woke up screaming. She clutched her hands to her mouth, checking for medical torture devices. She found none and confirmed that her hands were still flesh. Looking down, she saw her childhood bed. For a second she was confused. How much had been a dream? Was it possible that none of the past five months had happened at all? She swung her legs out of bed and brushed her feet against the clothes she had left on the floor the previous night. They were covered in dried blood. So much for that bit of false hope.

Chris checked the time. It was one in the afternoon. She felt a heavy weight on her back, pushing her downstairs. Cecil was on the phone in the kitchen. Deep, black circles ringed his eyes. He was still in his bloodstained clothes from the day before. When he noticed her, his face transformed into the most impossibly bright air she could imagine. Along with his change of appearance, he hung up the phone without saying goodbye to whoever was on the other side.

"Hey, Honey. Are you sure you don't want to sleep some more?"

"Did you sleep at all last night?"

"I've been a little busy. Don't worry. I had a nap earlier."

"Who were you talking to?"

"Oh, nobody. Just something for work."

"At Tartarus," Chris stated.

Chris saw his smile struggle to remain up. He froze, seemingly unable to think of an answer that would extradite him from having to talk about demon affairs.

"Yeah... Tartarus," he said after a time. "Don't be mad."

"I'm not mad," Chris said, grateful that he actually admitted what he was doing. It wasn't much, but it was the most he'd ever copped to.

"What's going on?"

"I'll take care of it. Do you have classes to go to? I can drive you to school, if you like."

"I can afford to miss a few days."

"How was your first term?" Cecil asked.

"Fine. Are you going to work today?"

"Not this afternoon. I've got a couple of errands to deal with. They'll probably take me until the evening. After that, I haven't decided yet. Depends how I feel."

"What errands?" Chris asked.

"Nothing important."

"Please, I'm asking you: where are you going today?"

Chris saw his body tense.

"You can't keep lying to me. I need to know."

"The guy in the cabin," Cecil began, a frown now plastered on his face. "His brother is somebody important. I need to break the news to him in person. That's where I'm going today."

"I want to go with you," Chris said, breathlessly.

"That's not a good idea. Tell you what: I'll do my errands, and you can relax around here. Then, later tonight, you can meet with Alice for some supper."

"No. You're not brushing me off. I made the decision to come back, and you're going to show me the truth about the demon world."

"Well, first thing is there isn't really a *demon world*," Cecil said.

"Most people just live like we do." He sighed. "The only reason I have to make that clear is because, where we're going today, the demons are definitely in their own little world. Think of it like Chinatown, only for a really awful group of guys and bad food."

Chris huddled in the passenger seat of Cecil's car. She could feel his discomfort. She wondered if he could feel hers. She'd seen demons from the eyes of Professor Moore and other outsiders. The demons she'd seen were violent monsters. Did it even matter? Chris knew where she stood now. If demons were the same kind of mindless monsters as the creature from the park, then she'd have to live with that. There was no going back to Professor Moore after what she did to Michael. She prayed her father would show her something that could vindicate her choice.

"We're going to see Kent in the Burrows," Cecil said. "He's big. He's violent, and he hates women, so this might not go over well."

"And it was his brother?" Chris asked.

"That's right. I forgot to add that he's going to be very angry."

"Will he be sad, too?"

"What do you mean?

"Can demons feel sad?"

"I don't... yes, demons can feel sad, like I was sad when you were gone. We're not really different than anyone else except for a few predispositions, like our higher than average aggression, and it's a personal choice how far to indulge that. Did you think demons were sociopaths?"

"I wasn't sure."

Cecil laughed. "Just because Luca's tough doesn't mean we're all robots. You should know better."

"I'd know better if you'd taught me."

Cecil didn't respond for a whole two minutes. To the two of them, that brief lull in the conversation felt like an eternity.

"About Kent," Cecil said, finally. "I don't want you to talk, but, if you have to, choose your words very carefully, and do not use the word monster under any circumstances. Demons don't like the word monster, and Kent's a bully who will take any excuse."

They arrived in a seaside neighborhood on the outskirts of Meridian situated high atop a cliff. Chris looked down to see a seven story drop to the ocean below. Mere steps from the edge was a row of run-down houses with the windows boarded up. Cecil parked in front of the house closest to the edge and led Chris to the front step.

"Remember what I told you," Cecil stressed.

A giant of a man opened the door. His massive, muscular frame filled the entrance. He had to turn to the side in order to push through the door, lest he take a piece of the frame with him. Though it was winter, sweat dripped longingly over his muscles. He frowned deeply at the sight of Cecil, and his face began to drip fluid. Chris gasped audibly as that dripping turned into a full melt. The skin from his upper face dripped away to reveal a black skull with gaping, empty eye-sockets. It was the same manifestation Chris had seen on the man in the cabin.

"What are you doing in the Burrows, Cutter?" the man asked.

"I'm here to see Kent," Cecil replied calmly.

"You can deal with me. Kent doesn't need to waste his time on puny things like you," the man bellowed.

"I don't usually deal with lackeys, Garfield, but maybe I can make an exception for you." Cecil sidled up to the man and slid a finger down his slick pectoral muscles. "You know, I think you'd make the most interesting sounds when I get you on my table."

Garfield jerked back, grudgingly allowing Cecil and Chris through the door. Chris's stomach churned upon seeing her father threaten someone, but she did feel safer.

The interior of the house had been completely gutted. There was no furniture, or decorations, or even floors. It was a shell built around a dark pit tunneling into the earth.

"Take off your coat. It's going to get very hot," Cecil said quietly.

Together, they descended into the ground, with the hulking Garfield bringing up the rear. Cecil had something of a skip to his step, and Chris had a hard time keeping up. The tunnel was carved directly into the earth, with no support beams or scaffolding. Chris felt her heels sink slightly into the dirt with every step. The tunnel had clearly been there for a long time, polished smooth by constant traffic. It was silent and dark. The only source of light came from wooden torches staked into the walls, and they were few and far apart. As they got deeper into the earth, Chris perceived faint voices in the distance. The further they walked, the stronger the voices became. There could be hundreds of people down here, Chris realized. The row houses were just a cover for an underground colony of demons.

"Are we going to hell?" Chris whispered, glancing back at the man behind her.

"What is it with you girls and hell?" Cecil laughed. "No. These guys are Skull Heads. At least, that's what we call them. The actual name of the demon type has some Asian sound to it that nobody can pronounce, including most of them."

"And?"

"They like to dig and they like it hot."

Chris couldn't help but chuckle at her own stupidity. It wasn't hard to be romantic as they delved into the bowels of the cliff, fires flickering in front of them, and sweaty monsters around every turn.

When they passed the first of many forks in the tunnel, Chris was almost knocked over by the blast of heat. Eventually, Cecil turned down a secondary tunnel, then another, then another. With each turn the air grew hotter until Chris's clothes were soaked with sweat from the heat. She lost track of how many twists and turns they had taken. She was totally overwhelmed by the oppressive atmosphere of the pit. Finally, Cecil arrived at a door. He stepped through without knocking.

"Cutter," a deep, guttural voice rang.

The room was filled with enormous skull-men sitting on battered couches. There were hollows dug into the dirt wall filled with carefully tended fires. The center of the room was occupied by a single, enormous fire pit, adding to the already incredible heat. A large, naked woman was hanging upside down, wrapped in leather bonds, trapped in a steel cage. Chris gasped at the sight of her. Skull Heads surrounded the cage, taunting their prisoner. It was barbaric. She wanted to rush in and save the woman. Cecil seemed to notice her reaction. He placed his hand on her shoulder.

"Nobody likes this," he whispered.

She didn't believe him.

The largest man in the room, standing at nearly seven feet tall, stood up from one of the couches. Unlike the other skull-men, he had two large, straight horns of bone protruding from his forehead.

"Did you bring this boy for Kent to toughen up?" the man asked in a deep baritone.

"Hey there, Kent," Cecil said calmly. "This is my daughter, Christine."

A smaller Skull Head slipped behind Chris and grabbed her rear, eliciting a gasp from the girl. Chris, still fuming over the caged woman, turned and shoved him backwards. Then she balled up her fist and punched him on the chin. His eyes burned with rage at the insult. He growled and thrust his hand forward, striking Chris directly in the abdomen, sending her wheezing as the air from her lungs was knocked from her mouth. His other fist reared back. Chris winced, anticipating the impact, but it never came. She opened her eyes. Cecil's razor-sharp black claw had circled around her attacker's neck and was lightly pressed against his jugular. His other black claw hooked into the collar of the Skull Head's shirt and ripped it open. The claw came to a rest over his ripped stomach; it ran in tiny circles, leaving bright red scratches.

"Apologize, Cullen," Cecil whispered into the man's ear before biting it lightly.

The man glanced over at Kent, who was watching the entire event in silent interest. Cullen let out a low rumble, his throat becoming red and cut as his windpipe vibrated against Cecil's claw.

"Don't be like that." Cecil giggled. "Tell you what: beg her for forgiveness, or I'll start thinking about more permanent disfigurements." The claw circling Cullen's stomach dipped down, leaving a red streak as it ducked under the man's belt.

"Wait," Cullen said. "I'm sorry."

"You can do better than that." Cecil's eviscerating fingers continued lower.

"Please. Please don't. I'm sorry, little Cutter. Please don't."

"It's all right, Dad," Chris said.

Cecil smiled and retracted his claw from the man's crotch. Cullen breathed a deep sigh of relief. His entire body was trembling. Cecil let go of his throat. Cullen roared as soon as he was free. Chris glanced over at her father, who was laughing as if nothing serious had happened. Cullen's body weight was shifting in his direction, like he was about to launch a new attack. He didn't get that chance. Chris didn't let him. Her leg swung back, foot striking him directly in the crotch. He fell to his knees and sputtered the kind of misogyny Chris had never heard in person.

"Time to talk alone, Kent," Cecil said, patting Chris on her shoulder.

Chris's heart was beating rapidly. That was the second demon she'd disabled with a kick. She followed that kick up with a sequel to his ribs. The bastard deserved it.

"Leave us," Kent ordered.

The Skull Heads filtered out quickly, leaving a cloud of dust in their wake, and dragging a nearly passed out Cullen with them. Cecil kept his hand on Chris's shoulder, signalling her to stay.

"What are you doing here, Cutter?" Kent asked, sitting down.

Cecil took a seat opposite Kent and motioned for Chris to do the same.

"Don't you enjoy my pretty face?" Cecil asked, brushing his own cheek with one of his claws. "I'm here to talk about your brother, Ralph. We found him murdered early this morning in his cabin."

Kent leapt to his feet with a deafening roar. He stormed over to the naked woman and violently shook her cage, slamming her against the bars.

As she watched the caged woman scream, Chris remembered that this brutality was exactly what she'd been trying to stop. Kent dropped the cage to pace back and forth, threatening to kill Cecil and Chris where they sat. Terrified, Chris turned to her father, who sat, patiently waiting for Kent to finish his tirade. Finally, Kent returned to the couch, waving his hand at Cecil to continue.

"We learned he was being watched by a vigilante group. He refused a security detail, but he called us last night for help," Cecil said, leaning back. "When Luca arrived on scene, he was already dead."

"Who did it?" Kent roared. "The Burrows will see to it that they all burn."

"They're already dead, and, I can assure you, they suffered," Cecil said.

Kent fell back on his couch. Chris watched the skin from the side of his head begin to bubble and pull until she was looking at a very human face. Kent's eyes weren't hidden anymore. They were red, and blood shot. His chest was expanding and contracting at an alarming rate.

"Did he go out with a fight?" Kent asked in a voice too small for his stature.

"He did. The only reason they had a chance is because it was more than a dozen on one."

"That idiot. He should have..." Kent pressed his hand over his face. "You need to leave. This is a time for grief, and women have no place watching men grieve."

"I'll be in touch," Cecil said as he turned to leave.

"Thank you for telling me, Cutter. Kent will not forget this."

Chris followed her father out the door, grateful to be leaving this horrible place. Kent was a monster, that was certain. But she could feel his pain from losing his brother. There was something human about that, even if it was only a glimmer.

"Do we need a guide?" she whispered.

Cecil tapped his finger on his temple. “Never come to the Burrows without memorizing the layout.”

CHAPTER 41

Cecil was noticeably quiet upon their return to the car. He was smirking, but Chris could see the wheels in his head turning underneath the false front, trying to figure out a way to spin what she'd just seen, no doubt. His mouth opened and closed, and he clicked his tongue as if he was going to say something. But he was never able to finish the thought – or not willing. Chris decided she'd need to take over the conversation, or she'd be left in the dark forever.

"Why do they call you Cutter?" she asked.

"It's a nickname they give demons like us, Fiends. We tend to cut things with our claws. It's kind of an insult, but it's not wrong."

"Is that why you almost killed that guy in there?" Chris asked.

"I wasn't going to kill him," Cecil professed. "It's just a game. These macho types are so easy to play with."

"Is this all a game to you? Am I a game to you?"

"That's... that's not what I meant. I just like to get under people's skin. Think of it as a stage persona. Luca says I'm too dramatic, but she doesn't have a sense of humor. Besides, with people like Kent, you have to show your dominance somehow, and I'm never going to beat him at arm wrestling."

"Does it hurt?" Chris asked.

"What?"

"Becoming a demon."

"Nobody becomes a demon. We're both demons and always have been. If you're talking about manifesting, no – it doesn't hurt. You know, we don't have to talk about this, if you don't want to."

Chris gave him a half smile. Part of her begged to recede back into the pleasant world of black and whites. That part of her was only a whisper now.

"Why didn't you tell me that I was a monster?"

"Demon," Cecil corrected. "Don't call demons monsters. They find it dehumanizing."

"Really, Dad? You know what irony is, right?"

"Luca does most of the ironing."

Chris groaned. "Please, answer my question. Why am I only finding about all of this now?"

"Okay. Okay, okay, okay." Cecil took what was perhaps the world's largest breath. "Do you promise not to run away?"

"I'm not going anywhere, Dad."

"Okay. Demons... well, we are... it's about choice."

"Choice?"

"Yeah, choice. Most demons are just regular guys, who go to work, raise families, and watch television."

"I'm betting Kent is a ball at the company barbeque," Chris said, rolling her eyes.

"Kent is different. Some demons and demon communities ostracize themselves from society. It's really rare, and it's mostly Skull Heads. Still, Kent owns three major Meridian construction companies, and most of his time is spent either managing them or yelling at me."

"And this relates to choice, how?"

"As I said, most demons are regular people. Those in the Overlord system aren't."

"The Overlord system?"

"It's our governing body. Overlords manage individual areas across the country. You see, demons, even the normal ones, can be a little violent, and part of our responsibility is making sure we stay secret. We also have to collect dues, and deal with general troubles and feuds. Sometimes, some of the people in the Overlord system have to do, well, bad things, to maintain order and protect the community as a whole."

"Have you ever killed anyone?" Chris asked.

"You see, the thing about choice is that I didn't get one. Luca and I were forced into the Overlord system when we were kids, so we've had to do some interesting things. I wanted it to be different with you guys. I wanted to give you a choice. You're a demon. You can be violent. You can work in the Overlord system. Or you can work in a coffee shop, quiet and peaceful. I don't care what you do. I just wanted you to have the choice."

"So, why didn't you tell me?" Chris yelled. "Yes, thank you Dad for not raising me as a murderer, but why didn't you tell me about being a demon? It's not a choice if you're missing half the information."

"I always thought I'd tell you when you were old enough to understand, but I was worried." Cecil said.

"Worried about what?"

"That you'd get mad and run away."

In the resulting silence both parties couldn't look at each other. Chris's face was red, and she felt so hot she was certain she was still in the Burrows. She wanted to yell at him some more, but she didn't. Only one question really mattered.

"Dad?"

"Yes, Honey?" Cecil asked in a singsong voice as if the last few minutes were a distant dream.

"Have you ever killed anyone?"

"I..."

"Before you answer," Chris said, interrupting him, "Let me tell you something. I'm mad, but I'm not going to run away. I need to know about demons, but I also need to know you're going to tell me the truth. I can handle anything you say, just don't lie to me."

She watched Cecil tense, flexing every muscle in his face, before releasing them along with a deep sigh.

"I've killed a lot of people."

Chris nodded, lips pursed.

"I enjoy killing people," Cecil added.

"So, you're a monster."

Cecil cringed. "I don't hunt for people to kill. It's only in the line of duty. Think of it like when soldiers kill people."

"It's nothing like that, and you know it," Chris snapped back.

"I just wanted for you to have a normal life like families on TV."

"But that's not real."

"I guess not," Cecil said.

"I want to see what you do – what you really do," Chris said.

"It's boring, trust me. My old job was much better."

"Can I tag along for a little bit? There's a lot I want to learn."

"Well, sure, Honey. You can be my little assistant." Cecil's peppy persona reared its head back into the conversation. "Oh, wait. I don't want you to miss class. Maybe you can come to Tartarus some nights. I can give you the grand tour. We missed our chance last time."

"I'll drop my classes for the term. This is more important," Chris said, breathing elevated.

"Are you sure? You were so excited for college."

"I can go back in the fall. Right now, I need to know who I am, and you're the only one left who can help me."

"I'm sorry," Cecil said.

"About what, specifically?" Chris asked.

"I'm not a very good dad. I should have been around more when you were young, and I should have told you. Can you forgive me?"

"Let's just see what happens."

CHAPTER 42

As it turned out, dinner with Alice wasn't simply a suggestion to get rid of Chris. Cecil had already arranged it while she was sleeping. Chris was relieved to get away from her father after their heady conversation earlier, but she was equally afraid to face Alice after running away. Her father would evade; Alice would attack. The walk downtown left her feeling numb. She looked up at the restaurant Cecil had chosen. It was a trendy-looking sushi restaurant, bustling with servers dressed in matching black pants and shirts. The hostess smiled brightly when she entered and asked if she had a reservation.

"Delacroix," Chris said quietly.

The woman led her to a table nestled in a corner. The restaurant was dimly lit, and Chris could see sushi chefs in an open kitchen preparing food.

Alice, of course, was late.

Twenty minutes after having first entered the restaurant, Chris saw Alice stomp through the doors. She did not look happy. Chris braced herself for the worst.

"Fucking bitch," Alice said loudly, provoking stares from other patrons. "I can't believe you have the balls to show up now."

"Well, I can see charm school finally paid off. Mr. Beauregard is sure to fill up your dance card at the debutante ball." Chris tried to lighten the mood.

"I'm not even going to try to talk to you if this is how you're going to be," Alice whispered through gritted teeth.

"What do you want from me, Alice?" Chris asked.

I want to know why my sister disappeared; I want to know where she's been; and I want to know she's fucking sorry."

"I'm sorry, Alice. Okay?" Chris sighed. "I've just been dealing with a lot of stuff."

"Oh, that's okay then," Alice scoffed. "Chris has to deal with stuff, so of course she can ignore her family. She's not being selfish."

"I needed time alone to figure things out," Chris said, crossing her arms.

"With a bunch of demon killers?"

"How much did Dad tell you?"

"Everything he knows, which isn't a lot. I can't believe you got pissed off at dad because a little blood, then hooked up with some guys who almost killed Luca."

"A little blood? He's a murderer."

"He's our dad. You should have talked to him."

"It's not that simple. I wanted to learn about demons."

"I asked Dad. Nobody got sent to the hospital," Alice said.

"And you believed him?" Chris shook her head. "He kept this from us our whole lives."

"I trust Dad. Even if I didn't, there's Luca, Maxine, everyone else in Tartarus. I'd bet they all know more than your douchebag friends."

Chris laughed at herself. "Next time I'll ask you before I resort to vigilantism."

"Whatever. You drank the Kool-Aid. I can't blame the cultist when the cult leader is the one brainwashing people."

"It wasn't a cult, and I wasn't brainwashed. I'm the one who made the choice to help them."

"Then what changed? Help me understand, because I can't really get my head around your journey to crazy town."

"I couldn't kill Luca," Chris said definitively.

"That's it?"

"That's enough. I don't know if she's evil, or really exactly what she's done in her life. I don't even know if I'm evil, or what evil is anymore. But that doesn't matter. Luca's family, and you don't shoot family down in a cabin in the woods."

"Good to know. Does that mean you wouldn't shoot me in the face either?"

"Well, you? That's a whole other question. Sometimes you get really pushy."

"Be careful. I'll get Maxine to beat you up, and trust me, she's way stronger than you are."

"Maxine's that woman who works with Dad, right?"

"Yeah, she's my roommate."

"Wait, how long have you been living with her?" Chris asked, shocked at Alice's living arrangements.

"It's been months now. Remember that time you stormed off and decided to cut all contact? I was going to tell you then."

"Did you even think before moving in with some strange woman?"

"She's not a stranger anymore." Alice smiled.

"What if she was crazy?"

Alice lost control in a fit of laughter. "Oh, she's definitely crazy, but she's my kind of crazy. Besides, she's only tried to kill me a couple of times." Alice's smile faded. "I need to tell you something, and you can't tell Dad, okay?"

"What is it?"

"No, you have to promise not to tell Dad first," Alice insisted.

"I promise," Chris said, increasingly worried. She wasn't sure their family could handle many more big revelations.

"I'm seeing someone."

"Really?" It was Chris's turn to start laughing. "You're worried that Dad will find out about your girlfriend? What's wrong with her?" Chris buried her face in her hands as she laughed. She couldn't believe her sister was so worried about a girlfriend.

"What's her name?" Chris teased.

"Remember my roommate, Maxine?" Alice said quietly.

Chris nodded.

"Well, it's her."

"Really? What does Maxine even do at Tartarus?"

"Dad makes her work on Thursdays. She told me she's a Devil, which makes her superior somehow," Alice explained.

"I'm so sick of not knowing these things. What does that even mean?" Chris asked.

"Apparently, it means she has the power to sit on her ass and play video games all day. Or maybe she's squandering her gifts. I don't know. She doesn't really like talking about herself. Anyway, apparently, she's supposed to be the Overlord, but she was too lazy to do it, so she pawned it off on Dad. Don't ask." Alice swelled with pride. "Did you know that she can shoot electricity out of her hands?"

"Is this thing with her serious?" Chris asked.

"She's really fun to be around and she accepts me for who I am. Oh, and she's great in bed," Alice said with stars in her eyes.

"For future reference, I don't need to know about that last part."

"Yeah? Then you're not allowed to talk about your feelings." Alice stuck her tongue out.

"Don't you mind being a demon?" Chris asked.

"What did I just say about your feelings?" Alice asked.

"I wasn't listening."

"I bet. It took some time to get used to, but I've come to terms with it," Alice said. "My claws are pretty cool." She raised her left hand and made a fake swiping motion toward Chris.

"You mean you've already manifested?"

Alice nodded, smiling. "They came in while I was having sex. It was amazing."

Chris rolled her eyes.

"The best part is that the dreams stop. I haven't slept so well in nearly a year."

"Must be nice," Chris said, dropping her head. "But have you, you know, changed? Do you still feel like yourself?"

"I feel fucking amazing. Why are you so afraid of demons?"

"They kill people, Alice."

"People kill people, too." Alice shrugged.

"Those people are called murderers, Alice, and they go to jail. Demons just go about their lives, unpunished. How can you be so blasé? How do you live with being something like that?"

"Chris," Alice lowered her voice, "We're demons. We have to live with it." She sat back in the chair and crossed her arms. "Nobody's forcing you to go out and kill people. Who cares what other demons do?"

"It makes me feel dirty."

"I'm not planning on killing anyone, and I know you aren't going to kill anyone. Isn't that enough? Can't you live with yourself if you aren't doing anything wrong?"

"What about Dad?" Chris asked.

"What about him?"

"He told me he's killed people – that he actually likes doing it."

"Uh huh."

"Is that all you have to say?"

"Do you want to go to the police?" Alice asked. "I think there's a station a few blocks from here. We can explain the whole thing to them, and send Dad away for the rest of his life."

"Hi, Officer. There's this guy. He's our dad, and he's in charge of a bunch of demons. Anyway, he kills people. Could you please arrest him? No, I don't have evidence," Chris said in a high pitch. "Yeah, I bet that would go over great."

"Dad does what Dad does. You haven't been around, and I'm guessing your little cult doesn't know much, but Dad does good work."

"I'm sure he's an artist with a knife."

"Not that. He keeps demons safe."

"Safe from who? They're demons."

"From assholes like your friends; from each other; and from the rest of the world."

"That doesn't excuse murder."

"It doesn't have to be an excuse. You know that. If you didn't, you'd have killed Luca, so stop wasting my time with your damn feelings."

"Bitch." Chris smiled.

Chris felt good to be home, even if a dark shadow was forever cast upon its foundations. *It doesn't have to be an excuse.* Sometimes Alice was more in-tune with her than she ever thought possible. In that instant, something very strange happened. For a solitary moment, Chris felt like she could accept being a demon. It passed, but the sheer fact the moment existed gave Chris something to think about.

CHAPTER 43

Chris woke up before Cecil, not an uncommon occurrence, but now she wondered if he often slept late because he was up all night at Tartarus. She still wasn't sleeping well, and the dreams were coming more frequently. Alice's had stopped. She seemed all right, like the act of manifestation hadn't changed her. Maybe she'd be fine too.

About an hour later, Cecil slowly stomped downstairs. He went directly into the kitchen and began to make breakfast.

"Luca's awake," Cecil said. "I stopped by and saw her yesterday, while you were with Alice."

"Thank God," Chris said. "I was worried."

"Don't be. Luca's as tough as they come." Cecil sighed. "So, I'm supposed to ask you a few questions."

"About where I've been?" Chris asked.

"Yeah. How big is the group?"

"I'm not sure, at least a few dozen. I wasn't really in the inner circle. Did the group do a lot of damage?"

"Don't worry about that. I've got it covered. Are they killing their victims?"

"I saw them kill three demons, including Kent's brother."

"Damn. I was hoping they were keeping them hostage or something. Where are they taking the bodies?"

"I don't know."

"Okay. Who's in charge? Tell me the names and addresses of everyone you know who's involved." Cecil rubbed his hands together, a hint of menace tipping his lips.

Chris froze. She stuttered for a time before falling silent. Emily, Cindy, and Professor Moore – they weren't evil. She couldn't toss them to someone she was certain had murder on his mind. It wouldn't be fair.

"Can we do this later?" Chris asked.

"It's kind of important."

"Please, Dad?"

"Yeah, you're right." Cecil chuckled uneasily. "We can deal with this in a day or so."

"In a few days... yeah." Chris had no idea how she was going to get out of this, but it edged foremost in her thoughts.

The ride to Tartarus was awkward. Neither wanted to be there, but both were forcing themselves through the discomfort. Cecil chatted about television. Chris stayed mostly quiet. The previous day had been a serious head trip for the girl. Cecil took her through the various levels of Tartarus, providing inoffensive anecdotes. Chris kept her eyes on the busy employees. Tartarus was closed during the morning and afternoon, but there was still a commotion. Demons in black suits ran around doing who knows what. Other demons were dealing with inventory and cleanup after an assuredly messy night. Chris called them demons, but, to any outsider, they'd be called people. Not one of the people they passed was manifesting. Her father explained that nobody bothered during the day. It took too much energy, and there was nobody there to impress. After going through bronze, silver, and gold areas of the club, Cecil took her into Elysium.

Cecil didn't linger there long. He directed her to a side door, and into the grey corridors of Tartarus' restricted areas. Security officers in black suits parted as he walked though. He pointed down a hallway about three doors in.

"If you go down that way, you'll hit a security checkpoint," Cecil said. "After that is the staff area. There's another entrance behind bar 3, if you're looking to get back here without stopping by Elysium."

"Um, good to know," Chris said.

He pulled her through the maze of corridors until they were face to face with the only door that stood out from the rest. There was a pink heart on it. Behind the door was a receptionist room that was full of boxes.

"This is Fen's office. It's technically mine, but she needs it more," Cecil said as he pushed through a door in the back of the receptionist's room and into Fen's office proper. Nobody was behind the desk.

"Could you check back in Elysium for Fen?" Cecil said as he grabbed a printed document off the table and started flipping through it.

"Yeah, sure."

Chris returned to Elysium, but couldn't find the bubbling blonde.

"Excuse me," she said to the young woman squatting behind the bar. "I'm looking for Fen."

"She went back there." The woman pointed back to the restricted areas.

Chris clumsily thanked the girl before heading back to the door. The guards stepped forward to block the way.

"You aren't authorized to be back here," one of the guards said.

"I was just in there."

"You were accompanied by the Overlord. We can't let you in unless you have clearance or you're with someone with clearance."

Chris reached for her phone and dialed her father's number.

"Hi, Dad. Can you tell these guards that I'm allowed in the back?"

She handed the phone to the man and watched his face turn pale. He handed the phone back to her and quickly moved out of the way, mumbling an apology. Chris crossed back into the restricted area. After three turns, she was completely lost in the maze. The tiny thrill she'd gotten from getting inside was superseded by the fear of being lost. How she could have been so cavalier? She was alone and unprotected in the control center for the entire demon operation of Meridian. Eventually, she gave up trying to find that lone heart door. She opened a door at random, hoping to find someone who could point her in the right direction. The room was dark, but she could hear faint noises coming from the corner.

"Hello," she called, fumbling for a switch. When the lights came on, Chris screeched at the sight in front of her.

In the corner, strapped to a table, was a large, naked creature dripping black ooze into trays placed around the table. It was agitated, shaking against its restraints. One of its legs had been amputated, and worse, it was missing its lower jaw. Chris recognized it immediately: it was the same demon that attacked her in Menos Park. Chris turned and ran face first into her father.

"Where have you been?" he asked.

"What the hell is going on here?" Chris yelled. "Are you running experiments on other demons? What kind of sick place is this?"

"I'll explain." Cecil sighed. He pushed his terrified daughter back into the room. "That thing over there isn't a demon."

"Bullshit," Chris spat, crossing her arms and eyeing the exit.

"This thing is called a Ghoul. Do you remember the Snatcher crime spree last year?"

"What does that have to do with you?" Chris asked. "Do you dig people up, too?"

"Don't be silly. I'm not the Snatcher. He's the one making the Ghouls," Cecil continued to lecture. "What he's been doing is taking human corpses, fresh usually so the muscles are still good, then grinding up demons into a thick paste and covering the body with them, along with a couple of chemicals." He sounded calm and collected despite the horrific details he was recounting.

"After a fun mutation, the creature gets up. They're more or less mindless killing machines that ooze this paste in large quantities, and dissolve entirely when they die." Cecil moved over to the creature and lifted up one of the pans on the floor. "We found this one trying to crawl its way out of a park several weeks ago. Luca decided to bring it here to study. Usually, we just kill them. They're too dangerous to allow them to roam freely. They'll eat anything, human, demon, or animal. Hunting them down has kept me and Maxine busy most Thursdays for months. Lucky for us, the corpses melt away pretty quickly, because, you know, Maxine would never clean up."

Chris backed up slowly until she found herself pressed against the wall.

"It's not a demon," she said pathetically. So much of her perception of demons was based upon the Ghoul, and it was a lie. Everything was a lie and she was the liar.

"We've been after the Snatcher for a while now," Cecil continued. "There haven't been any grave robberies recently, but we keep running into these things around town."

Chris wasn't listening. She just kept staring at the writhing creature on the slab.

"I know it's creepy looking, Honey, but don't worry," Cecil said, trying to cheer her up. "The Ghoul's all tied up. It can't hurt you."

"But it already did. It chased me through the park," she said breathlessly. "It tried to kill me. I'm the one who broke off its jaw."

"Great job."

He raised his hand, hoping for a high five. Chris obliged him. She didn't know why.

* * *

The rest of the day at Tartarus was uneventful. It was a Monday, and few patrons bothered to come down to the club. The lack of action, coupled with her early rise, led to Chris nodding off in Elysium. She was immediately transported into another nightmare. It was different than before. She didn't feel the overwhelming urge to run, or the clawing guilt in her insides. When she fell into the dream world, she found herself in a small, featureless room. From the ceiling hung one solitary light bulb beaming out a green glow, which was reflected in the mirrors that covered the walls.

Chris turned to examine all the mirrors, trying to see if there was anything special about them. They reflected each other, tossing light back and forth like an endless game of catch, with Chris helpless in the middle. The infinite reflections growing smaller and smaller, spiralling into infinity, were dizzying, but Chris couldn't look away. There was nowhere else to look. Eventually, in the corner of one of the mirrors, Chris saw a hint of black. She approached the mirror and knelt before it. She saw the Beast with the Black Metal Claws climbing from mirror to mirror within the reflection, beginning with the deepest image. It was fast and agile, as Chris had come to expect. Soon it had arrived at the very nearest reflection. It was only the fragile glass that separated it from its quarry. It raised its claws as if to tear Chris's face from her skull. She flinched, throwing her arms up to protect herself, but nothing sliced her skin. Instead, the Beast tapped on the glass, tap, tap, tap.

"What do you want?" Chris screamed, covering her ears from the ever-loudening tapping.

The Beast pressed its face against the glass, further distorting its already twisted visage.

"You," it said with its garbled voice. "You, you, you, you, you, you, you," it repeated over and over.

It beat its head against the mirror until the glass shattered and fell away, and the Beast crawled into Chris's world.

The Beast dropped onto the floor, taking its time as it felt Chris's heartbeat speed up with fear. It shook like a dog, dislodging the tiny shards of glass from the mirror, locking eyes with the terrified girl.

It charged forward. Chris ducked and dodged to the right. The Beast roared as its claws met with hard glass instead of supple flesh. While it was distracted, Chris rifled through the broken glass to find a shard big enough to use as a weapon. She lifted one triumphantly seconds before another eviscerating slash forced her to dodge. The glass dug into her palm and blood dripped down onto her wrist, but she hardly noticed. She brandished the shard like a dagger and menaced the Beast.

"Leave me alone," Chris shouted.

"Leave me alone, me, me, me," the Beast parroted.

She slashed the Beast across the chest with the shard, drawing blood, and provoking a pained scream from the Beast. It grasped its chest in shock and glared at Chris in blind fury. Chris slashed a second time, but the Beast wouldn't fall for that again. It avoided her strike easily and stepped just to the side. It was no great task for the Beast to snatch her by the collar with one clawed hand, and stab her in the ribs with the other.

Chris didn't scream. She barely even felt any pain. She just saw her vision go red with rage when she realized what the Beast had done. She raised her arm, still clutching the shard of glass, and buried it in the Beast's chest.

"Go away," Chris said.

"Away, away, away, away," the Beast squelched through gritted fangs.

Chris pushed forward. She was able to knock the Beast off its feet but she was still entangled in its grasp. She fell, too, and landed on top of it. The shard dug deeper into her palm. Blood from the Beast's wounds mingled with her own blood, and poured all over the white floor, forever staining it. She pulled the glass shard out of the Beast's chest and plunged it back in over and over again, screaming indiscernible obscenities. Blood poured from the Beast's mouth, but its twisted smile never dimmed. Chris hated the sight of that smile. She was determined to erase it from the Beast's face.

Chris moved her left hand over the Beast's throat. She glanced up at the remaining mirrors in the room. Reflected back at her was the image of herself splayed out on her back with the Beast on top, clutching her throat, with its right set of claws buried in her chest. Shocked, her gaze fell down. The Beast's face contorted and untwisted, like whoever was yanking it to the side suddenly let go. All the features fell back into their natural place. Its hair grew out, and teeth dulled. Within seconds, Chris was gaping down at herself. The doppelganger bolted to life and grabbed her in a tight embrace. Chris felt her body grow numb and melt into the other Chris. She cried and struggled for her life, but nothing could stop the assimilation.

Then there was nothingness. The Beast was gone, and so was Chris. Neither would ever return. In their place stood something different, something neither Beast, nor human. Looking up at one of the mirrors it both smiled and cried at the same time. Its face looked like Chris, as did its torso and legs. But its arms were covered in black metal and ended with long razor-sharp digits.

It looked into the bloody mirror shard and a smile crept across its lips.

CHAPTER 44

Julian had buried himself entirely in his work since he'd witnessed Luca shooting down the creature in the alley. He didn't eat and he stopped taking time for himself. At first he thought he could solve the insecurity Larry's revelations had awakened through dedicated policing, but everywhere he turned his efforts to investigate the truth were blocked. If Larry was to be believed, half the department took money from Luca and her gang to look the other way on a massive criminal operation in the city, one that killed with impunity. The channels he had always trusted, police, the courts, the law, were now cut off from him. Larry tried to ease Julian's growing depression, but he wouldn't step out of line. He was too afraid of Luca.

Julian took out his phone and checked his messages - there were none. He had texted Luca nearly a dozen times since the last time he saw her, but she never responded. He knew he should leave her alone. Grappling with the existence of monsters was enough, but whatever she was mixed up in was terrifying, and she appeared to be high in the organization. Despite Larry's grave warnings to stay away from her, Luca ruled Julian's thoughts. The time he'd spent with her over the past months was the happiest he could remember. His work was humiliatingly restricted, but when he was with Luca, he could forget all of that and relax. He thought he offered her the same relief; she had started to open up to him about her problems. But what was he thinking? She was a criminal, and a brutal one at that. So why did he know that, if she texted, he would drop anything to run to her apartment and leap back into her bed?

"No," Julian muttered when a very stupid idea sprang to mind. "I can't believe I'm doing this." He bolted out of the office.

Julian parked on Elm Street, cursing under his breath while walking to Luca's apartment building. He stopped at her door, turning away and muttering. Moments later, he turned back to knock. No one answered. He went to leave, making it halfway down the corridor before stopping.

"Son of a bitch," he said as he returned to the door.

Julian pulled out some tools and started picking the lock. It had been a long time, and he fumbled miserably for several seconds before he heard the tell-tale click.

"Hello?" Julian called as he gazed into Luca's shadow-cloaked abode. There was no response.

Hesitantly, he moved through the apartment, looking for any trace of his ex-lover. It was hard to tell if the apartment had been abandoned. There was no food in the cupboards, or plates, or silverware. Strangely, there was chocolate in the fridge - a lot of chocolate. Every shelf and drawer was full of chocolate snacks, but aside from the candy there was nothing edible in the entire kitchen. Confused, he headed for the bedroom. The bed was meticulously made and there didn't seem to be anything out of place. Checking the closet, he found several identical black suits and little else. Everything was just as he remembered it, Spartan and precise. He sat on the bed, wondering what he was doing there. Something was out of place, he realized. The picture, Luca's only picture, was gone. She wasn't coming back.

* * *

On the other side of town, Larry Saunders was performing similarly clandestine actions. He had exhausted himself trying to find something new from the existing Snatcher evidence at the station, and now he was desperate enough to make another visit to Norman Argyle's empty dorm room. His run in with Lady Black had scared him off of the case at first. He was certain that she was watching him, biding her time before she finished him off. However she was involved in the Snatcher case, whatever sick purpose she had for all those dead men, she would not permit him to meddle without being appropriately punished. He knew what that meant. He'd seen what her tentacles could do. The paranoia was eventually overcome by the guilt he felt over letting her control his life again, letting her prevent him from doing his job. Norman's room was still closed off by the police. Unlike Julian, Larry had no knowledge of lock-picking. However, he did have a hammer. With a bang, he removed the doorknob. A student poked his head into the hall at the noise, but retreated quickly when Larry flashed his badge.

Norman's room was empty. The furniture and personal effects had been removed by the police. There were heavy scuff marks on the hardwood floor in the bedroom where the dresser used to be. Larry swore to himself when he noticed the distinct lack of scuffing throughout the rest of the room. He'd spent so long avoiding looking at crime scenes with a critical eye out of fear of Lady Black that he missed something terribly obvious. It wasn't the police removal of the furniture that caused the marks. Norman must have moved the dresser back and forth over and over to leave such a deep impression. Larry knelt down and knocked on the floorboards. He was rewarded with a hollow 'thunk'. The old detective kicked himself. He should have found this the last time. Using the back of his hammer, he pulled up the loose floorboard. There, staring up from the dark cavity, was a stack of plain envelopes held together with a rubber band.

"Goddamnit," Larry whispered to himself.

Larry sat down on the floor and looked through the letters. They were written in a strange shorthand that he couldn't decipher. The only thing that stood out to him was the signature. The letters were from an H.W. It wasn't exactly what Larry expected. He was hoping to find some further connection to Lady Black, maybe even discover her identity, but he supposed that would be too easy. He would have to decipher the letters, and then maybe he would get the break he needed to free himself from her shadow, and discover the truth. It almost made him feel like a real detective again, like he'd been before he came to know the horrors that controlled his world like demented puppeteers. He bundled up the letters under his arm. It was an exciting break, one that he felt compelled to share.

* * *

Julian sat devastated in his car. All he'd ever wanted was to be a good cop, and now that was impossible if he didn't want to be killed by monsters. And if he couldn't be a good cop, then he needed refuge, comfort from his worries, something he could only find in Luca. Luca, who was the reason he couldn't do his job, the source of his stress, and the only one capable of soothing him. He felt himself sinking into self-pity when his phone began to ring.

"Hello?" he asked, praying it was her.

"Julian." It was Larry. "I was looking through the evidence for the Snatcher case and I found something big. It's still early, but it could change everything."

"The Snatcher? I thought we were burying that one like all the others?"

"Don't tell anyone. I think Lady Black's involved. She may have slipped up. If anyone else finds out, you might be in danger, so stay away from dark corridors."

"Meet me at the office. I'll help," Julian said.

"No. I got a text from Black earlier today. I have to meet her in an hour."

"Where?" Julian asked.

"Don't worry about it. I'll deal with her. You just stay safe."

Larry hung up.

Julian pulled up to the station just in time to see Larry's car drive off. Julian kept far behind and saw Larry pull into a lot of an abandoned factory near the port. He parked out of sight across the street and waited. He couldn't quite see the entrance, but after twenty minutes Larry's car emerged and sped away. This was his chance – Julian darted outside and ran full sprint into the factory.

Rusted machinery sat fermenting in the open air. He shouted Luca's name as he moved past broken machinery. Two forms appeared on a platform above his head. Julian's heart started beating quickly when he saw a black-haired woman, but his excitement was short-lived. She was too scrawny and too young to be Luca. Julian found himself staring at her nonetheless. Something niggled at the back of his mind. He studied her for a moment before it dawned on him: he recognized her. It was that girl he questioned about the Devon Jacobs case. She had a notepad and stood behind the other figure, a middle-aged man. She was avoiding eye contact.

"Hey there," Cecil said, flashing the detective an unnervingly bright smile. Unlike the indifferent Lady Black, he seemed disturbingly interested in the detective. "I couldn't help but notice you yelling someone's name. How did you come by that information?"

"Where's Luca?" Julian asked.

"And you are?" Cecil replied.

"Detective Julian Morales. I'm with homicide."

"Ah, so you're the famous Julian. That's sweet. What are you after?"

"I'm looking for Luca."

"You aren't going to be seeing her for a little while at least." Cecil sighed. "The problem now is that I'm probably supposed to kill you."

Julian slowly reached for his gun.

"Oh, don't be like that," Cecil chided. "If I was actually going to kill you, I'd have jumped down there and cut your head off without giving you a second to think." He looked back at Chris. "Is Detective Morales one of ours?"

She flipped through the notepad and shook her head.

"I'm not sure if you're stupid or a desperate romantic. Maybe it's both." He started laughing. "You've clearly got guts. How would you like to be on the payroll?"

Julian frowned. Sleeping with Luca was one thing; he wasn't actively hurting anybody but himself. But to actually take dirty money, impede investigations, get his hands dirty - that was inconceivable. He tried to speak, but something held his tongue.

"Think it over, okay?" Cecil stopped and turned toward Julian, his smile dropping. "Also, we'll kill you and everyone you've ever cared about if you interfere with us in any way." Cecil chuckled before disappearing in the dark, Chris trailing behind him.

Julian cursed at himself as he pulled into his car. He was a homicide detective, not some money-hungry corrupt cop. He wanted to see Luca again, but would his desire cost him his soul? When he got in, he heard a tapping on his window. Looking up he saw Larry's scowling face. Julian rolled down the window.

"I'm not so old I don't notice my own partner tailing me," Larry said.

"I want to know what's going on. All of it."

"No, you don't. I'm trying to protect you."

"Bullshit. Exactly how much money does it take to own a homicide detective? You talk about being against them, but you still take their money, don't you?"

"It's not that simple."

"Sure it is. They break the law, and you cover up their murders," Julian shouted.

"Yes, it's a terrible way to live, and I don't want you to be stuck doing the same. This is a choice between life and death for me, but you can still stay clean. These are monsters – real ones. Your search for demons with the Snatcher wasn't wrong, but you have to back off. These guys will kill you, and I can't let that happen. You can be honest. Let me do the dirty work, and we'll figure this out."

"Who was the man?" Julian asked.

"I don't know, and that scares me. What did you say to him?"

"Nothing. He offered me a job."

"Did you accept? Larry asked.

"No."

"Keep it that way. Once you're in, the only way out is a bullet."

"You can't keep me in the dark." Julian said. "I can handle it."

"No. Not yet. Give me some time."

Larry didn't wait for another question. He left. Julian raised the window and yelled out in the car, beating his hands against the steering wheel.

CHAPTER 45

Chris was struggling to stay awake, waiting for Cecil to finish his Overlord duties for the day. She hadn't had a nightmare recently, but getting back into a sleep routine was difficult. Every time she closed her eyes, she still expected to wind up trapped in the green dimension. She had been shadowing her father, learning about the demon operation. Cecil's new policy of transparency had revealed, to her surprise, how bureaucratic his job really was. It was far from the murder parade she had envisioned. There had only been a few frightening situations. One was the day they had extorted cops, especially because one of them had interrogated her before. The rest all involved Maxine, and Chris got the impression the blonde Devil was something of a special case.

Cecil was nearly finished with the last of the people who had lined up to yell at him that day. A large portion of his job was taking abuse from demon representatives around the city bothered by by-laws and parking committees, and trying to work out compromises with them. Chris was regularly amazed with his patience.

"Hey, Kiddo." Cecil walked over to her when he was finished. "It's Thursday, so I have to make Maxine work."

"I'll just grab my bag," she slurred.

"No, you need to get some rest." He pushed her back down. "I'll take care of Maxine alone tonight."

Cecil wasn't risking taking Chris out with Maxine ever again. He'd been using Chris as a personal assistant both to teach her about demons and to keep an eye on her, but he still wanted to keep her away from dangerous situations. Their last outing had shown that being in a car with Maxine qualified as a dangerous situation.

"There's a spare bedroom in the back." He looked down at her and smiled. "I'll get Fen to show you."

Fen rushed over to guide the girl into the grey corridors.

"We do have a spare, but I'm going to let you sleep in my room tonight, since I live here. Much more comfortable." Fen winked.

Chris followed Fen to her bedroom in a haze. When Fen flung open her door, Chris had to shield her eyes from the bright pink that covered every surface, but soon found herself entranced by the large, fluffy bed. Fen looked on with a smile as the young woman crawled into bed and immediately fell into a peaceful sleep.

* * *

Not long after, Maxine stormed into Elysium in a huff.

"Having a good night?" Cecil asked.

"That's the fucking problem. I was having a great night, but now, for some reason, I'm here."

He just smiled.

"Fine, what are we doing today?"

"Well, you killed two people last time we went to deal with Kent's problems, so I'm thinking a Ghoul hunt would have a lower body count."

"It's not my fault." Maxine laughed as she pantomimed a heart attack. "One of those things touched me, so I thought I'd see how many I had to kill until someone apologized."

"That's the definition of your fault, Maxine. I'm still dealing with the fallout."

"Where's your loser kid?" Maxine looked around the room. "Is she following us again like the lost little puppy she is?"

"No, it's just us tonight."

"How long is she sticking around anyway?"

"She's just helping out until Luca gets back."

"Good. I don't like the way she looks at me."

Cecil parked outside of Stanford Park. It was the largest park in the city, taking up a huge section of the upper west side. Adjacent to the university, it was a popular spot for runners during the day. At night, it was mostly empty. Meridian had been plagued by a large increase in sexual assaults in recent years, and Stanford Park had a particularly bad reputation. It was also one of the biggest Ghoul hotspots in the city.

"Why the hell are we going to Stanford? Menos Park is much better. It has a playground," Maxine joked.

"You don't really seem like a playground person," Cecil said. "Unless it involves stealing from children."

She faked a fit of laughter before smacking him on the back of the head.

"Okay, you check to the north and I'll take the south," he suggested.

"Perfect. You know I always like to be on top."

"Please don't kill anyone." Cecil groaned as they parted.

Maxine offered no response other than sticking her middle finger up over her shoulder.

* * *

When Cecil was well out of sight, Maxine slumped. She didn't want to be out here. The only solace she had was imagining the look on Alice's face. She had left the girl in heavy bondage awaiting her return. In a way, it might be better to extend the evening, just to make her wait a bit more.

"This place is a fucking dump," Maxine said quietly, noticing that most of the lights were burnt out. "Any fucking things out there?" she yelled, cupping her hands in front of her mouth.

She heard a sound coming from behind her. Turning around, she saw a man in a heavy coat approaching her. He pulled out a knife.

"Oh no, a big scary man. What am I going to do?" Maxine said, faking a swoon.

"Money," the man demanded.

"How much you got?" she asked in return.

"No, your money. All of it, now."

Maxine's eyes lit up. She beckoned him to come forward.

"Don't be a pussy," she taunted.

The man darted forward, swinging the knife in an arc toward her chest. Maxine stepped back, effortlessly evading the man's slash.

"Boring." She yawned.

The man thrust the knife at her stomach. Maxine grabbed his hand and twisted, breaking his wrist. She kicked the knife away and grabbed his face with her other hand, spitting in it, and tossed him onto a nearby bench. He scrambled to his feet and tried to throw a punch with his good hand. Maxine easily caught it and snapped that wrist as well. She kicked him hard in the stomach, knocking the wind out of him. Taking advantage of the opportunity, Maxine jumped on top of him. She pinned his arms to the ground with her legs and rained blows on his face until he was an unmoving mess of blood on the ground. Smiling, she stood up.

"You still with us?" she asked, kicking the man hard in the ribs.

He gasped in pain.

"Be thankful that someone specifically told me not to kill tonight, or you'd be having a much worse day."

The man groaned as he spit out some of his teeth.

"Good boy," Maxine said, tapping him on the cheek. Leaving him behind, she continued along the path, looking for Ghouls.

* * *

Cecil sat on the bench near the bathrooms, tapping his hands to an imaginary beat. They had been searching for two hours, and he was ready to call it a night. Just as he finished texting Maxine to come back, he heard a groan echoing behind him. Turning his head, he heard shuffling from the bathrooms.

"About time," he said, mid-yawn.

Cecil reached into his jacket pocket and pulled out three scalpels, which he held tightly in his right hand. Inside the bathroom, he saw a Ghoul pawing pathetically at its own dripping reflection in the mirror. As he approached, the creature turned and bellowed at him. Cecil threw one of the scalpels at the thing, hitting it in the chest. It screamed out in pain and reached for the piece of metal lodged in its torso. Cecil frowned and threw another scalpel into the creature's eye, sending it flailing around the bathroom.

"I've really got to practice more," he said as he held out the last scalpel. He closed his eyes, took a deep breath, then sent the last scalpel directly into the creature's windpipe.

"Yes," he exclaimed, clutching his fist in victory. It felt great to be in the field, which he could do whenever he wanted as long as Luca was away.

"Where the fuck have you been?" Maxine asked upon his return to the car.

"Found a Ghoul," he said calmly. "You?"

"Nah, just some stupid mugger."

He glanced at her with weary eyes.

"No, I didn't kill him." She smirked, watching his disbelieving frown. "I did beat the living shit out of him, but he's still alive," she clarified.

"That's the most I could have hoped for," Cecil said.

They drove in silence. Maxine watched the horizon, hoping the sun would stay down for a while yet.

"How's Alice?" Cecil asked, yawning.

"She's your good kid. Why worry about her? How's the bad one? Still fucking useless?"

"I think she's doing better," Cecil said.

"Jesus, you're oblivious."

"It's a balancing act. I have to show her just enough to get her acclimatized to some of the less savory things without overwhelming her, but not so little that she'll be upset at me hiding things from her."

"The problem is that you're a psychopath," Maxine said. "Even the big bads throw up at what you get up to."

"That's very comforting. Thank you."

"The way I see it, she'll either puss out or end up twice as sick as you."

"I don't know which I'd prefer," Cecil said, trying to smile.

"I think you do."

"I just wanted her to have a normal life," Cecil said.

"Where's the fun in that? Normal is boring. Besides, she lost any chance of being normal the second she was born. Sick parents have sick kids. I should know. I was the same," Maxine said, her lips pursed and gaze lost out the window.

"Now that's a scary thought."

CHAPTER 46

Chris was fidgeting endlessly on the drive to Emily's townhouse. She promised herself she'd be in and out before anybody saw her, nice and easy.

"I'm surprised you waited this long to pick up your stuff," Cecil said.

"It's just a really uncomfortable situation," she said, evading his glance.

"Uncomfortable because..." he prompted.

"Why do you think, Dad?"

"Oh yeah. Did you call in advance?" he asked.

"I'm hoping nobody is home."

"Yeah, that makes sense."

"Right up here." Chris pointed at the townhouse. "I'll be right back." Her heart was beating wildly.

Chris quietly opened the door and stepped inside. Nobody was there. Everything was calm. She moved carefully upstairs to her room, grabbed a bag, and started filling it with her things. Her hands trembled as she threw everything she could find into two suitcases.

"Oh my God," Cindy's voice rang behind her. "Chris, you're back."

Chris tried to focus on filling her bags.

"Where have you been?" Cindy asked as she bounded into the room.

"I had a lot of thinking to do," Chris said. Adrenaline flooded her system in ways that made her hands shake harder.

"Why are you packing your bags?" Cindy prodded at Chris, attempting to make eye contact with the shaking girl.

"I have to go," Chris said, voice low and gruff, trying to finish her task before Emily noticed the commotion.

"Please look at me, Chris," Cindy begged.

"I'm sorry, Cindy." Chris quickly finished shoving what she could into the bags. "But I can't stay here. Please understand."

Chris pushed past the young blonde and started downstairs, desperate to leave this chapter of her life behind, but it wasn't to be; Emily stormed into the living room.

"Where the hell have you been?" Emily said.

Chris felt her blood run cold. She was filled with an overwhelming urge to run. She could hear Cindy rush into the room.

"What the hell happened?" Emily asked quietly. "Michael said that you helped a monster escape after it killed everyone in the team." Emily snatched Chris's arm, holding her in place.

"I'm sorry."

"That's not an answer," Emily growled. "Where have you been and did you really help a monster escape?"

"Leave her alone, Em," Cindy interjected. "I'm sure she had a good reason for leaving."

"Don't be so stupid, Cindy," Emily said, turning toward her sister. "She didn't just disappear. She disappeared with a monster, and now she's back, safe and sound. That means she can't be a victim or a hostage like we thought. Don't you understand the stakes here?"

Chris tried to yank her arm from Emily's grip, but the older girl held firm.

"You're not leaving until you give me some answers," Emily shouted.

"I don't think the professor knows what he's doing," Chris said.

Emily slapped her, sending her glasses flying to the floor.

"I thought you understood," Emily yelled.

Chris looked back at her with clenched teeth. Emily slapped her again.

"They're monsters, Chris. You've seen them kill people. Why the hell would you protect some horrible creature?"

Chris opened her mouth, but Emily slapped her in the face again.

"That thing killed thirteen of my friends. They were good people, they wanted to help, and now they're all dead. Why'd you help it? You were supposed to be on our side," Emily screamed.

Chris wished desperately for an answer she could give that would explain her betrayal, but there was none.

"Stop it, Emily," Cindy cried. She tried to pull Emily away from Chris, but the older girl threw her to the ground before turning back and pushing Chris into the wall.

"We showed you. They aren't human. Just because they look like us doesn't make them humans. They all deserve to be put down. Didn't you understand? Wasn't it clear?" She hit Chris in the face again.

Something in Chris snapped. She used to see bravery and nobility in Emily for being so willing to sacrifice her life for a good cause, but that was over now. Today she had come in hoping to avoid a confrontation. She'd still seen Emily as simply misguided, like she had been. Now Chris saw something very disgusting, twisting underneath Emily's bloodshot eyes.

Emily reared back to deliver another strike, but Chris caught her hand and shoved her back.

"What do you know about demons?" Chris shrieked. "They're not the ones stalking around in the bushes and murdering people while they sleep." She was shaking. "Last I heard, that's what you do. You and your friends are nothing but a group of cowards who murder people in their sleep, just because you're scared."

Emily screamed and rammed Chris against the wall.

"You're with them," she yelled. "They've brainwashed you somehow."

Chris gasped in pain at the blonde's assault, but repelled her by bringing her knee up and striking the blonde.

"You don't know anything, Emily. You're blinded by what the professor has told you and what you can see from the windows of your car. Things are more complicated than that."

"No, they all need to be wiped out before they kill everyone." Emily spat back at Chris.

"That's so easy, isn't it? That's really what I've learned since I've been away. The whole time I thought I was making the hard decision to do the right thing, even though it was dirty, but now I know it was the easy way out, because it gave me a black and white answer. But there's no such thing, don't you get it? There's no such thing as black and white."

"What the hell are you talking about?" Emily wailed. "You're defending murderers."

"Stop it," Cindy yelled, but nobody listened.

Chris pushed Emily against the wall, pinning her there.

"Stop this, Emily," Chris shouted, slamming her hand against the wall above Emily's head.

Chris's hand hit the wall with a piercing crunch. For a moment, it was as if the only sounds in the room were convulsing hearts. Chris pulled her hand back in disbelief, dislodging part of the wall in the process. When she looked at it, she saw five razor sharp fingers made of solid, black metal. Deep inside she felt the tiniest twinge of satisfaction and, even deeper, something she didn't understand at all.

Emily cowered in fear.

"Do you see this?" Chris waved her claw in the air. "If you want to kill demons, then you can start with me."

Emily couldn't bear to look at her.

"I saved that demon in the cabin because her life was worth more to me than your damn crusade." Chris pointed her claw at Emily. "You talk about monsters and judgment, but you don't know anything. You're the monsters. You're the ones who are killing people."

Emily shook her head violently.

"I'm here right now, and this thing," Chris raised her claw in front of her face, "Could kill you without any problem, but I'm not going to kill you. I could have given your name to people who are very interested in who's been killing all their friends, but I didn't. I protected you and, somehow, I'm the monster. You wouldn't show me the same mercy." Chris turned back to Cindy. "I'm sorry, Cindy. I didn't mean for any of this to happen."

Cecil was checking his email on his phone when Chris raced out of the house. She reached the car. Her claw tore through the metal frame. Hearing the wrenching sound of metal against metal, Cecil reached over and opened the door. Chris jumped inside and slammed the door, tearing five new slices into the upholstery in the process.

"We need to get out of here, now," Chris insisted, her breathing ragged and uncontrollable.

"Are you okay?" Cecil asked.

"Drive," she yelled back.

"Breathe, breathe," he repeated rhythmically as they pulled out of the driveway.

"Just take me home," she begged. Tears were freely pouring down her cheeks. "How the hell do I get rid of this?" Chris waved her black hand in front of her face.

Cecil's eyes lit up with pride. "Just stop thinking about it. You have to work to keep it out, remember. Ignore it and it will return to normal."

Chris sat back limply. Despite her speech to Emily, she was still deeply uncomfortable with her demon heritage. Now, with this beastly claw, she couldn't even pretend to be a normal person. All she knew for sure was stalking people in the night wasn't the answer to any of her problems. It was another few minutes before skin started pulling itself back up her arm.

CHAPTER 47

Cecil gave Chris the night off. He didn't want to know what happened in that house, and it was easier to avoid the issue if Chris wasn't around. He decided to visit Luca before heading home early.

"Excited to get out of here?" he asked when he entered Luca's room.

"Don't you have work to do?" Luca responded.

"Nothing's going on." He tapped his hands on his legs, trying to contain his excitement. After making sure there were no nurses around, he leaned in to whisper to Luca. "Chris manifested for the first time today."

The information was enough to get Luca's attention. She looked over at Cecil and smiled uncharacteristically.

"What happened?"

Cecil looked around again. "I don't know the details, but she got into a fight with her old roommates, and she was good to go when she stormed out. I'm not looking forward to getting the mechanic's bill from where she tried to get back in the car, I can tell you that."

"Wait, did her roommates see her claws?"

"I'm not sure."

"Find out. If they know, they'll need to be contained."

Cecil nodded slowly, cursing under his breath.

"So, how's the food here?" He asked, trying to change the subject.

"It's too bland, makes me sick." She sulked.

"Oh, if you're sick, you might not want this," he said as he pulled out a bar of chocolate from his pocket.

She snatched it from his hand and hastily tore open the wrapper, moaning when she bit into the soft chocolate.

"Thank you," she said, pausing from her meal.

He chuckled as he tapped her on the leg.

Cecil groaned when he got home. He sat in the car for nearly half an hour, desperate to think of a way out of the frank conversation he needed to have with Chris, but failed to come up with a compelling enough excuse, even for him. When he gathered the nerve, he entered the house and shouted her name, but there was no answer. Cecil was gripped in panic. She might have run off again. What the hell was he thinking, leaving her alone in a state like that? He couldn't find her on the first floor, so he rushed to her bedroom. Please, please let her be there.

"Chris?" He pounded on her door. He heard a groan coming from inside. "I'm coming in."

Chris was laying in bed with her back propped up against the headboard, her eyes completely glazed over. She was clutching a nearly empty bottle of vodka in her hands.

"Hi, Dad," she slurred out.

"What are you doing?" Cecil asked.

"I don't want to be a monster," she whimpered.

"You're not a monster," Cecil said, raising his voice. "I don't know how many times I have to say that." He snatched the vodka away from her.

"Please give it back," Chris whined.

"No. I'm sorry you had a bad day, but I'd be a way shittier dad if I let you drink your emotions away."

"Shittier dad. That's funny."

"I know I've made some mistakes," Cecil was careful to modulate his voice. "But I still love you, and I can't let you harm yourself."

"I don't want to have claws."

"I know, Honey, but they're not going to go away. Maybe you could try talking to Alice. She's doing well. She might have some good advice for you."

"Alice is so perfect, isn't she?" Chris snapped, spraying a cloud of poisonous vapor as she did. "You just think that because you don't know she's sleeping with that blonde psychopath."

Cecil froze. "What did you say?"

"Nothing." Even in her drunken haze, Chris knew she'd gone way too far.

Cecil's heart was beating faster and faster.

"No, not nothing," he said between his teeth. "What are you talking about?"

Chris started to messily cry.

"Look at me," Cecil said. He knelt down and gently cupped her face. "Are you talking about Maxine?"

Chris nodded through her sobs.

"Son of a bitch," Cecil said. He rushed out of the room. Pausing in the doorframe, he looked back at Chris, who was pathetically reaching for the bottle he had put on the nightstand.

"You're coming with me." He pulled her to her feet.

Chris keeled over and threw up on the floor. Cecil bit his lip. He looked down at his daughter, who was panting on top of her own mess.

"We'll deal with that later."

He led her to his car and belted her into the back seat. She sat there, vaguely aware of what was going on.

"I can't believe she would do this just to get to me," Cecil said to the barely conscious girl as he tore out of the driveway.

When they arrived at Maxine's apartment, Cecil opened the glove box and pulled out a revolver. Chris had passed out on the way there. He stood, tapping at his leg, looking back and forth between the car and the apartment building, weighing rage and parental concern. Groaning, he picked Chris up and carried her up the three flights of stairs to Maxine's door.

"Thank God you're so thin," he muttered, propping Chris up in the hallway. "Stay here." He pointed at her.

Cecil breathed in deeply and broke the doorknob off with a single kick, a trick Luca had taught him long ago.

"What the fuck?" Maxine ran half-naked into the living room, glowering when she saw Cecil standing in her broken doorway.

"What the hell are you doing here?"

"I assume that Alice is back there?" Cecil gestured to Maxine's bedroom with the revolver.

"Oh, fuck," she said at the sight of the weapon. She'd worked with Cecil long enough to know he hated using guns – they were no fun. If he had one, he meant business. She raised her hand in front of her, preparing to unleash a deadly bolt of electricity. "Stay back there, Cutter. You don't want this to get messy." She looked down and saw the skin on his other hand peel back.

"This is too much," Cecil yelled. "I don't care what you do to me, but you better as hell leave my girls out of it."

"It's not like that," Maxine shouted back.

"What's going on?" Alice asked, tearing out of Maxine's room.

"Get over here, Alice," Cecil ordered.

"No," Alice responded, placing her hands on her hips. "Both of you need to sit down, and we'll talk this out."

Cecil looked between Maxine and his daughter.

"Please," Alice pleaded.

"Fine." Cecil's skin wrapped back around his metal claw, and he lowered the gun.

Alice glared at Chris through the door as she prepared to host a peace conference.

"I'm sorry you had to find out like this, Dad," Alice said.

"Why did you target her?" he asked Maxine, tapping his hand loudly on the table.

"I said it wasn't like that." Maxine sighed heavily. "All right, when I let her stay with me, I was trying to screw with you, but," her eyes darted to the side. "Things have changed since then."

"This is so screwed up." He continued tapping on the table. "Alice?"

She nodded at him and placed her hand on Maxine's.

He looked into her wide eyes and winced. "All right."

"That's it?" Maxine asked, flinging her hands into the air.

"That's it for now." He glared at her, taking a deep breath before relaxing his shoulders and releasing the tension that had been gripping him since Chris's revelation. It was clear he could do nothing to change the situation. The only person he could say no to less than Maxine was Alice.

"Alice, could you see to your drunk sister in the hallway? I have to have a private chat with Maxine."

Alice hesitated.

"I'm not going to try to kill her. I promise."

As soon as Alice left, Cecil stared at Maxine. Normally, if he had treated her like this, she'd have broken an arm, but some unfamiliar feeling was keeping her passive in the chair.

"You're sure about this?" he asked.

She didn't respond.

"You aren't doing this to screw with me?"

"I don't have to tell you anything," she said, crossing her arms. "What right do you have to order me around?"

"Please, Maxine. It's late; I'm tired; and I need to know that you aren't going to hurt my daughter." He looked at her with deep concern.

"It's not about you, Cutter," she said. "And for your information, the little Cutter likes it when I hurt her. Are you happy now, or do you want me to sign some stupid fucking waiver?"

"Next thing I know, Chris will be engaged to Kent." Cecil shook his head.

* * *

Alice stomped toward Chris, who was barely conscious. Her fists were clenched, shaking with adrenaline and frustrated betrayal. Alice knelt down and whispered.

"I can't believe you told him."

Chris tried to shake her head.

"If that had gone any differently, somebody would have died. It probably would have been Dad. And it's all because of you."

Chris started to cry. "Don't be mad, please," she begged.

The tears only made Alice angrier. She was the one who'd been attacked and she was sick of being diplomatic.

"There's something wrong with you."

CHAPTER 48

Chris vowed never to drink again as the first rays of the sun hit her in the eyes. She tried to gather her memories of the previous night. The pain she caused Alice burrowed into her skull worse than the sound of the abominable knocking on her door. She didn't say anything, so her father let himself in. One partially opened eye was vaguely aware of him collecting her discarded clothes from the previous day before ducking back out. Chris felt like a child, minus the hangover. It was a long time before she was capable of willing herself down the stairs.

"How're you feeling?" Cecil asked from the kitchen as soon as her foot hit the first floor.

"Not great."

"I'm sorry." Cecil walked over and gave her a mug full of coffee. "I know yesterday was hard on you, but look on the bright side – no more nightmares."

"Yeah..."

"Cheer up. Luca's getting out the hospital today."

"I thought it was tomorrow," Chris said. She wasn't ready to face Luca yet.

"It was, and then she threw her phone at one of the nurses for asking if she needed help going to the bathroom."

"That sounds like her." Chris chuckled, then groaned as it made the vein in her head throb harder.

"I think if she knew that was all it was going to take, she'd have done it the second she woke up." Cecil glanced over at the clock on the microwave. "We should probably head out for the hospital soon. We're going to pick up Alice on the way."

"How about you drop me off at Alice's and pick us both up on the way back?"

"Need to apologize?"

"I'm not sure anything I can say will be good enough."

Cecil wrapped his arm around her shoulder and brought her head close to his chest.

"Don't worry," he said. "She can only yell so much before her voice gives out."

"Gee, thanks, Dad."

Chris took a shower before leaving. After, she stood naked and dripping in front of the bathroom mirror. She focused on her hands and felt the skin begin to peel back, revealing a set of elongated black metal claws. Focusing as hard as she could, the black metal continued creeping up her arm until it hit her shoulder, but she couldn't get it any further. The mirror was a mix of pink and glinting black. That was her now. Chris tapped her claws on the sink, marvelling at the sensation. It was dulled, like she was wearing gloves, yet, paradoxically, she could feel more in her fingers than ever before. The texture of the porcelain leapt out as if it were shards of broken glass. Chris felt the exact temperature variation in every inch. Her concentration lapsed, and the black metal retreated down as far as her elbow, ribbons of flesh wrapping the deadly substance. Chris tapped at her upper arm after the black metal disappeared. It was as squishy as ever. The metal wasn't under her skin, but rather disappeared entirely when covered by flesh.

Chris de-manifested. Her fingers returned to normal. She looked up in the mirror and noticed she was smiling. Her heart was beating quickly as if she'd just dropped out of a steady jog, and a few beads of sweat fell from her forehead. Keeping the claws out was tiring, which filled Chris with hope. The entirely pink being before her was just as much her real self as the black and pink thing from earlier.

Chris got changed and walked downstairs. Her father was waiting in the kitchen, munching on some burnt toast.

"I manifested just now," Chris said.

"Can I see?" Cecil asked.

Chris raised her hand and revealed her claws to the open air.

"They're big, even bigger than Alice's. I'm so proud of you, Honey."

"How much more is there?" Chris said. "I tried to manifest as much as I could, but my face and body stayed the same."

"Fiends can manifest claws as far as their shoulder. There isn't anything else to manifest."

"There was a Beast in my dreams. It had these claws, but its face was twisted and disfigured."

"That's just the dreams, not reality. Don't worry, your pretty face will stay the same."

"That's good to know."

Chris shuddered when they pulled up in front of Alice's apartment. While she ascended the stairs, she babbled to herself, trying to figure out what could possibly defuse her sister. When she knocked on the door, she steeled herself, ready to launch into a string of apologies. Instead, she found herself gaping at Maxine. She hadn't expected the blonde to answer the door, and it ruined her prepared speech.

"I'm here to... is Alice here?" Chris asked.

Maxine rolled her eyes and turned her back into the apartment.

"Runt, the smaller, runtier runt is here to see you." Maxine soon turned back to Chris. "She said you should fuck off, and it would be wrong for me to get between such sisterly affection."

"Please, I need to apologize for last night," Chris said, edging her foot in the door.

"Sure, it'll be a good show." Maxine shrugged and let her in.

"What the hell are you doing here?" Alice shouted from the couch.

Chris tried to stutter out an apology, but Alice quickly cut her off.

"You're sorry?"

Chris nodded dumbly.

"You should be more than fucking sorry."

"I know. I didn't mean..."

"I got woken up last night by a war between my father and my girlfriend, and I had to push all my feelings aside to keep them both alive."

"Yeah, she cried for like two hours after you guys left." Maxine pointed at the black-haired girl. "Do you know how late it was when I finally got to sleep?"

"Not helping, Max," Alice shouted before pointing at Chris. "I trusted you. Were you waiting for any opportunity to let it out?"

"God no, it's nothing like that," Chris insisted. "I was going crazy yesterday, okay? I saw some people, and we got into a huge fight. One of them used to be my friend, and she wanted to murder me, just because of what I am. To top it all off, my fucking claws came out right in the middle of it and I couldn't figure out what to do. And when it was over I hated myself so much that I just started drinking until I didn't know what was happening."

"Don't start hiding behind self-pity again." Alice let out a frustrated groan. "You talk about not being able to trust Dad. How can I trust you?"

"What can I do to make it up to you?" Chris asked.

"You can't, Chris. God, why do you have to be so goddamn insecure? If you were normal, like me, you wouldn't have been freaking out."

"I'm sorry."

"I'll forgive you this one time. Luca's coming home, and we have to play nice. But don't you ever stab me in the back again."

"I can do that," Chris said adamantly.

"You'd better."

"Why am I even here?" Maxine asked. "Seems like you two are getting ready to make out." Maxine turned to Alice. "She's awful. I'm going to push her down."

Alice nodded, baring her teeth in a great grin.

Chris sputtered as the blonde's hand found her chest and shoved her with inhuman force. She landed on her rear and stared daggers at her attacker. Maxine was smirking with one arm possessively curled around Alice. Alice shared her girlfriend's smirk.

* * *

Luca was waiting in a wheelchair in front of the hospital with a nurse when Cecil pulled up. She did not look pleased. She was dressed in a moth-eaten t-shirt and a pair of baggy sweat pants.

"Wheelchair?" he asked.

"Shut up. They're making me sit in it." She slowly stood up and limped to the car.

"Thank you," Cecil said to the nurse, who was already on her way back into the hospital.

"How do you feel?" he asked.

"I feel weak, like my muscles have atrophied."

"Give it time." He laughed. "You'll be fine. Knowing you, you'll be in the gym within a week."

She looked out the window, flexing her arm and frowning.

"I don't like feeling weak. A bunch of kids shouldn't have been a problem for me."

"We both know you hesitated because of Chris. Besides, thirteen to one in close quarters is still really impressive."

"Did you talk to her?" Luca asked.

"I did." Cecil smiled.

"Who's behind the disappearances?"

"I don't know." Cecil's smile immediately vanished.

"Are her roommates involved?"

"I don't know."

"Did you find out anything?" Luca asked.

"No."

"I'll deal with it." Luca sighed.

"Thanks." He breathed in deeply. "Okay, so I've got to tell you something, and you're not going to like it."

Luca glared at him.

"Alice finally got herself a girlfriend."

"About damn time," Luca said with a smile. "What's so bad about that?"

"It's Maxine," Cecil said, shielding his face from the fallout.

"That butcher?" Luca barked.

"It's not our decision. It's what Alice wants, and, surprisingly, what Maxine wants as well," Cecil said before Luca had a chance to erupt further. "I don't like it any more than you do, but we don't have a choice. The last thing I'm doing is driving my other daughter away when I just got one back. And no, you aren't going to try to fight Maxine again," he added, wagging his finger at her. "I'm not taking you back to the hospital."

* * *

Chris was quiet on the ride back home and she winced when she saw the once-powerful woman limp into the house. Cecil ordered pizza as Luca lowered herself onto the couch. Alice had been all over the woman from the time they picked her up. When they got into the house, she brought out her claws.

"Look at these," Alice said, waving her hands around.

Chris glanced over. Her father was right. Alice's claws were about an inch shorter than hers. Somehow, that filled her with a perverse pride.

"Be careful. They're not toys," Luca said, the faint trace of a smile marking her face.

"Hey, Luca, do you have claws?" Alice asked.

"No." Luca sighed. "And no, I'm not showing you anything. I don't manifest on demand." As she spoke, she looked over at Chris, who was sitting silently in the chair opposite the couch.

"Go help your father, Alice. I have to have a talk with your sister."

Alice raced to the kitchen, skin forming up her hands.

"Not going to talk?" Luca glared at Chris.

"I'm sorry," Chris stammered out, expecting to be destroyed by Luca like she had been in her nightmares.

"Don't be sorry. If it wasn't for you, I'd be dead in some Skull Head's cabin."

Chris looked up at her, mouth agape.

"If anyone should apologize, it should be me," Luca continued. "It was wrong to bring up your mother."

Chris couldn't believe what she was hearing. After everything that happened, Luca forgave her. And of course she did – it was that powerful devotion that had snapped Chris back to reality in the cabin. Chris felt her cheeks pull into a wide smile.

"It's okay, Luca. Everything's okay. Are you coming back to work soon?"

"Yes," Luca responded.

"No, she's not." Cecil yelled from the kitchen.

"We'll talk about that later, Cecil," Luca yelled back.

Luca gestured for Chris to follow her. She led Chris upstairs to her bedroom and gestured for the girl to sit down. Luca stayed standing, a pillar of strength even in her weakened state.

"We need to talk about where you've been," Luca stated plainly.

"Now? This is your coming home party." Chris fidgeted in her seat.

"Yes, now. Your father, like always, has been putting this off, and we need answers immediately. Who is in charge of your group?"

"It's not his fault. He just doesn't understand."

"This doesn't work like that. You can't play both sides. Tell me everything I need to know, or I will personally take it out on the ones you're protecting."

"That's... that's a little harsh," Chris said.

"They are killing the people I'm supposed to protect, and they've been doing it under my nose for almost a year. I'm not being harsh."

"Have you thought of talking to them? Maybe you can convince them that you're not evil?"

Luca sighed and sat down next to Chris.

"We're past that point now, Chris. Even if I wanted to talk with them, and I don't, they've hurt enough people that we can't let them get away. Tell me who's in charge."

"Professor Glenn Moore. He's reasonable, just misguided – I swear."

"Reasonable people don't kill people."

"Then what about you?" Chris asked.

"I'm not a reasonable person. Your roommates, did they see you manifest? Were they part of the vigilantes?"

"Please don't do this," Chris begged.

"It's my job. I have to protect the city's demons – I have to protect you."

"They don't deserve to die."

There was a knock on the door frame. Both women looked over as Cecil stepped into the room.

"We don't have to kill them," Cecil said.

"Yes we do, Cecil." Luca groaned as she buried her head in her hands.

"Here's the deal, Chris. Tell Luca everything she wants to know. You do that, and then we'll consider finding an alternative solution."

"That's not a promise," Chris said bitterly.

"No, but it's the absolute best you're going to get," Cecil said, before leaving.

Luca turned to Chris, eyes steady, mouth flat.

"He was an interrogator for years before he became the Overlord. He could get you to talk in twenty seconds, if he wanted to, but he wants to be your friend, not your father, and certainly not the Overlord."

"Will he kill them?" Chris asked.

"We will. That's what I'm supposed to say. That's what I'd say to anybody else." Luca groaned again. "He's not going to kill them, and just this once neither will I."

Chris stared, wide-eyed.

"Do you trust me?" Luca asked.

"Y-yes," Chris said.

Chris realized she actually did. Luca didn't sugarcoat the same way her father did. Where he was prone to exaggerate or minimize everything, Luca would hit her with the hard steel of truth. Trust was becoming a scarce commodity in Chris's life, but Luca still had it. Cecil said he wouldn't kill her friends. That didn't mean much. But Luca backing him added certainty to the proposition. So, Chris told her everything.

Half an hour later, the four of them were lounging on the bottom floor. Cecil was trying to tell a story, but Luca interrupted every five seconds to correct it. Chris cherished the moment: it felt normal. It helped her forget what she'd done to her former friends upstairs. The doorbell rang, and Cecil left to grab the pizzas they'd gotten delivered.

"Why are you staring, Alice?" Luca asked as Cecil paid the pizza deliveryman.

"I've never seen you so dressed down before."

"They gave them to me at the hospital." Luca groaned, pulling at the ratty clothes. "Don't expect to ever see them again."

Cecil sat the pizzas down in front of the family before heading off to the kitchen. "You missed Christmas, Chris," he yelled from the kitchen.

Chris crossed her arms, unhappy about where this was going. She didn't want to be reminded of her mistakes any more that day. Cecil returned and threw a box onto her lap.

"We got you something," he said. "I've just been waiting for Luca to get back."

Chris opened the box. Inside was a tiny .32 revolver.

"You got me a gun?" she asked, staring up at Cecil.

"Only for your protection, of course," he said. "This is a dangerous world."

Luca leaned forward with a grunt. "Don't go flashing it around. It doesn't come with a license."

Chris looked at the present in awe. The whole time she'd been playing vigilante, this had been waiting for her. No matter how much she tried to forget her family, no matter how far she ran away, they never abandoned her.

* * *

After dinner, Cecil took Luca back to her apartment.

"You're picking me up for work on Monday," she said, staring him down.

"Fine." He sighed in defeat. "But you have to take it easy, okay?" Cecil handed over her only picture and her phone.

Clutching them to her chest, Luca turned away without answering. When she was safely inside her unit, she looked down at herself.

"Disgusting," Luca said as she pulled off the hospital clothes.

She ran her hand across the bandages on her stomach and legs. Limping over to the kitchen, she pulled three chocolate bars from the fridge and carried them to the bedroom. She threw the chocolate on the bed and carefully placed the picture frame in its old spot on the side table. Everything was back the way it should be. Groaning, she flipped onto her back and turned her phone on. There was another missed text from Julian. Against her better judgment, she texted the detective. All she wrote was the number eleven and the word tonight. She hadn't planned to see him again after the Ghoul incident, but he obviously wasn't too bothered by the episode. Besides, she needed a distraction from the bandages and a man who would come running at the snap of her fingers and never asked questions was a valuable commodity. After sending the text, she opened a news website on her phone. She'd fallen behind on current events. Browsing the news, she spotted a headline from a few days prior that jumped out clear as day.

The headline blared: *Another Body Missing – Did the Police Snatch the Wrong Snatcher?*

CHAPTER 49

Another body had been spirited away from its grave, and the police had been unable to keep the media from swarming all over the story. New detectives were quickly attached to the case. Larry had been reassigned and reprimanded for accepting Norman's confession. The dressing-down he'd received from the chief rankled him. Larry didn't think he would mind being yelled at so much if it was about sloppy police work, but it was about embarrassing the department, and he was the scapegoat they'd feed to the press. Nobody mentioned Julian. Larry saw to that. He turned over the official evidence to the new detectives on the case, but kept the letters he found in Norman's dorm room to himself. He knew anything he gave them would be delivered straight to Lady Black.

"What's wrong?" Larry watched Julian toss heaps of paper onto the floor.

"I'm trying to find the file on the Jacobs murder," Julian explained.

"Why? That case is closed," Larry said. "Another spontaneous confession, remember?"

"It's probably in storage," Julian said, ignoring his partner as he bolted out of the room. He'd been trying to follow Larry's advice and ignore everything related to the group bribing the police, but it kept swirling around gut like a piece of badly digested beef. He'd cracked. He needed to know.

Julian raced down the hallways of the police station, ignoring several attempts by other detectives to converse with him. He reached the basement storage area and fumbled for the lights. When the room lit up, Julian saw row after row of accountant's boxes, each one bursting with files. Julian checked the dates labeled on every aisle. Eventually, he found the one he was looking for. Retrieving a nearby stepladder, Julian pulled a box from the top shelf and rummaged through it, pulling the Jacobs file from its depths.

"Where are you?" he asked himself as fished out a sheet of paper. The name Christine Delacroix was at the top.

Julian ran back to his desk. Larry said something, but Julian was too excited to listen. He typed 'Christine Delacroix' into the police database. She had no police record, not even a traffic violation. Her file did list two living relatives: Cecil and Alice Delacroix. Julian started combing through Cecil's records. A sly but jubilant smile overtook his face when he pulled up a driver's license photo – it was the man from the warehouse, clear as day. The address on the license brought Julian to a two-story, yellow house on a hill. The pleasant neighborhood was a surprise to Julian. He wasn't sure what he'd been expecting, but it wasn't suburbia. He parked his car a few houses down the street and waited.

A few hours later, a car pulled up to the yellow house. Two girls climbed out of the back seat. Julian recognized one of them as Christine. Seconds later, Luca exited the car. Even from a distance Julian could tell she was badly hurt. His heart leapt into his throat. She didn't turn around. Julian watched in silence as she limped up the stairs into the house, followed by Cecil and the girls. Whatever Julian had planned for that evening was dropped the second he laid eyes on her, and he left the neighborhood thirsty for something to numb his mind.

Much later, Julian was sitting in the dark in his apartment. He faced the television, grasping his sixth drink of the evening. He felt an irritating buzz on his hip and realized he was getting a phone call.

"Hello," he slurred into the receiver.

"There was another grave robbery tonight." It was Larry.

"Yeah, what's going on?" Julian cleared his throat, trying to sound less drunk.

"Norman Argyle had a partner, H.W., and I think I know who it was. I'm going to confront the guy, see if he'll let anything slip." Larry paused. "I shouldn't even be saying this on the phone. It's big, Julian. Meet me on the corner of Fifth and Broad. I'll explain everything."

"I'm really busy, Larry," Julian said, pinching his cheek, trying to get more alert. "I can't meet tonight."

Larry began to protest, but Julian hung up the phone.

"What am I doing?" Julian asked himself as he nodded off in the chair.

His phone buzzed again, disturbing him from his nap. It was a text from Luca. She wanted to see him. A smile erupted on his face.

Julian sat in his car outside of Luca's apartment. He didn't remember driving there. His mind was prodding at him, telling him to follow Larry's advice and stay away from her, but he didn't care. He felt a desperate need to see her. By the time he knocked on her door, he had forgotten everything else. The door swung open and Luca re-entered his life in her familiar black suit.

Luca grabbed Julian by the hand and led him to the bedroom. She was still limping, but in her armor, she looked as strong as ever.

"Are you going to make this complicated?" she asked as she began undressing.

"It's already complicated," he replied.

He considered leaving, but he craved her company and he hated himself for it. Julian comforted himself that she was protected by the department, so nothing he did with her would make a difference. He wasn't the corrupt cop. That was everybody else.

"Where have you been?" Julian asked.

Luca unbuttoned her shirt to reveal a myriad of bandages.

"Sometimes accidents happen," she said.

"Are you okay?" He looked over her body with concern.

"I'm sick of that question. I'm fine. Just ignore them." She paused. "You aren't taking your clothes off."

Julian immediately fumbled with his shirt buttons.

As she moved toward the bed, Luca stumbled and fell. Julian rushed to help her up.

"I'm not some cripple that needs your help," Luca snapped at him.

"It's all right to need help sometimes, you know." Julian spoke against his better judgment.

She shut him up by covering his mouth with hers.

Julian lay exhausted in the bed. Strangely, Luca stayed beside him instead of getting up to get dressed.

"Do you trust me?" she said quietly.

He turned toward her and smiled.

"No."

"Good." She tapped him on the head.

"How's the girl in the picture?" He looked at her in the eyes, studying their shining green.

Her eyes shot away from his. They lay in silence for several minutes. Eventually, Luca took a deep breath and resumed eye contact.

"Better." She lingered on the word. "It almost killed me, but I think it's going to be okay." She groaned as she turned onto her back. "You should take his offer. It would make things a lot easier on my end."

Julian was shocked she'd even mention Cecil Delacroix. Luca had always been so secretive, he'd assumed she wouldn't want him involved in whatever it was she actually did.

"I don't take bribes. My job is to solve murders, not cover them up."

"That's cute. Maybe you should have thought about that before you literally got in bed with us."

"I didn't know anything about you."

"Don't pretend to be innocent." She slapped him in the chest with the back of her hand. "You saw my gun the first time we met without asking any questions, and you're here now. You knew what you were getting into this time. If you wanted to take the moral high ground, maybe you should have done that before getting off." She sat up and wrapped her arm around his shoulders.

"Take the offer," she said. "Loose ends don't stay loose forever, and I've grown attached to you."

CHAPTER 50

Cecil studied Professor Moore's image from the computer in Fen's office.

"Love that they post faculty pictures online. I don't even remember how we ever did this before the Internet," he said to Luca, who was standing to his right. "When I get this bastard on my table, I'm going to have so much fun with him."

"Work first, Cecil. Fun later," Luca said.

"Here's the plan. We stop by his office first..."

"Let's just grab him at home," Luca interrupted.

Cecil feigned being wounded, keeling over in his chair. Luca hated when he was dramatic.

"No, no, no, Luca. I want this to be personal. I want to meet Moore before we take him. It's much more fun that way. The spark of bare recognition in their eyes when I first turn on the light... just thinking about it makes me shudder."

"Why is it always complicated with you?"

"It's not my fault that I like to have fun at work. Should we bring Chris?"

Luca smacked him on the back of the head.

"That would go over just great," she said. "Making her an assistant is bad enough, but we're talking about kidnapping. Why don't we ask her to cut him up while we're at it? How did you survive without me?"

Arcadia Hall was quiet. It was just before spring exams, but few students took advantage of their professors' office hours. Cecil practically skipped down the hallway of the third floor. He stopped and laughed to himself at some of the occult cartoons and newspaper articles that were taped to Professor Moore's door before he knocked. No one answered. Cecil looked at the office hours, which were posted on the door, confirming that he was there at the proper time. He sauntered into the faculty lounge on the other side of the floor, asking the occupants if any of them had seen the professor. One of the staffers said he was out sick.

"How'd it go? Did you get to size him up like you wanted?" Luca asked upon his return, both eyes fixed on her phone.

"He hasn't been in for a while."

She looked up, tightening her jaw.

"I know," he continued. "There's a good chance that he's pulling a disappearing act." Cecil sighed, his previous enthusiasm gone. "Maybe he's just sick. Either way, we have to check his house now."

It was late afternoon when they arrived at Moore's home, a small, one story white house in the suburbs.

Luca gestured at a young man loading boxes into the back of a truck.

"I'll go check it out," Cecil said. He walked across the street, waving at the young man, who looked at him defensively. "Hey, there. Glenn asked me to come and help you pack up his stuff."

The boy's mouth hung gaped, while he examined the middle-aged man.

"The professor didn't say anything about help."

Cecil gazed around in feigned paranoia. "Glenn's worried that one of the monsters might get to you before you're finished."

"I'll show you what's left," the boy said, nodding in fear.

The inside of the house was empty except for moving boxes cluttering the floor.

"There's a bunch of boxes left in the kitchen," the boy explained.

"Gee, I'm pretty embarrassed about this," Cecil said, rubbing the back of his head.

"What's wrong? Never moved before?"

"No, that's not it." Cecil shook his head.

He grabbed the kid's head and slammed it into the wall twelve times. The kid yelled out in pain, but soon fell silent, leaving only the repetitive thud of skull hitting drywall. Cecil took out his phone and dialed Luca.

"I'm going to need help getting him into the car."

Minutes later, the two of them were speeding off to Tartarus.

"I can't believe we got to roll someone up in a carpet," Cecil said. "I've always wanted to try that. It's like we're in the mob."

"I'm glad you're happy, but we have a bigger problem." Luca rubbed her temples with worry.

"What?"

"Chris, Cecil. If her roommates warned Moore, Chris will be a target."

"He can't hide forever, and we can just keep Chris at Tartarus until we find him," Cecil scoffed. "With a bit of luck, our friend back there will tell us everything we need. Problem solved."

"You're the one telling her, then."

Cecil fished out his phone and pressed dial.

"Hey, Fen. We're coming through the loading dock. Tell Chris to meet us down there. We're bringing someone in."

"Disappointed?" Luca asked.

He looked up and gave her a half-hearted smile.

"I guess you could say that. I was hoping we'd be done with this stuff today." He cracked his knuckles. "At least I've got a new toy to play with."

* * *

Chris met them at the loading dock, located on the far end of the bronze area of Tartarus.

"Did you get him?" she asked nervously.

"No," Cecil said as he helped Luca haul their cargo from the car. "But we found this guy at his house." He looked back at Luca, who was struggling with her end of the carpet. "Hey, Chris, take over for Luca."

Chris went over to relieve her.

"I'm not an invalid, Cecil," Luca yelled at him.

"I want you to go see if Chris's roommates pulled a vanishing act, too."

Seemingly satisfied by the answer, Luca got back in the car and drove off.

"Don't worry, she's not going to kill anyone," Cecil said to Chris.

Chris was relieved for a moment, until a trickle of blood seeped out of the carpet onto her hand. She kept her end up, desperately trying to put the ghastly consequences of the work out of her mind.

"Where are we going?" Chris asked.

"Holding cells."

Whoever was in the carpet must be alive, Chris realized. She doubled her effort to keep her end in the air, although the load was far too heavy for the slight girl.

When they got to the holding cells, Cecil unrolled the carpet to reveal a bloodied youth, before dragging him into a cell and locking the door. Chris didn't recognize him. She wondered if he was a new recruit to replace the boys Luca had killed in the cabin. The knowledge of his likely fate made her feel sick to her stomach.

"We'll give him a bit to wake up," Cecil explained, "Then we'll find out what he knows."

"And just how do you plan to do that?" Chris asked.

Cecil smiled widely and gestured for her to follow him down the hallway. At the very end was a solid, metal door. Cecil quickly unlocked it and stepped into the room with Chris close on his heels.

"This is my favorite room in Tartarus," he said with more than a little bravado.

At the center of the room was a steel operating table equipped with black leather restraints. One dull, glass orb hung from a wire in the ceiling directly above the steel table. On a side table there were rows of terrifying blades, and, in the corner, lay the only other piece of furniture: a single, wooden stool. Chris retched at the sight and her heart rammed against her ribcage.

"Check this out," Cecil said, oblivious to her distress. He flicked a light switch behind the door. The ceiling lights turned off and the glass orb illuminated the room with a sickly shade of green.

"This color really freaks people out," Cecil babbled happily.

"I've been here before, haven't I?" Words spewed from Chris's mouth as she tried to check her rage. "I thought it was just in my dreams, but... you sat me on that stool over there, didn't you?"

"I... may have brought you in here when you were younger." Cecil offered a sheepish smile, hoping to defuse the tension.

You... you bastard," Chris cried. "All of this time, all of my nightmares revolved around this place. How could you do that to me?"

"I'm sorry, Chris. I couldn't find a babysitter and you were too little to leave by yourself," Cecil stuttered out.

"So what was the alternative? Did you torture somebody in front of me when I was a child? Please, please tell me you didn't."

"Honey, I swear, things just got out of hand."

"That's not an excuse and you know it!"

"I'm so sorry."

Chris stormed back to Elysium, leaving her father behind in his hellscape of a room. Her mind was flooded with images of Cecil, coated in blood. He was a monster. He had given her the nightmares, or at least filled their subject matter. He was her father, and she loved him, but she hated what he was. With every passing moment, she got angrier. Chris didn't know how she was going to reconcile the love she felt for her father with the disgust she felt at his actions. Perhaps it wasn't possible. But she wouldn't downplay the truth, and she wouldn't let herself be shocked anymore.

The Meridian Fiend

CHAPTER 51

Larry didn't come in to work. Julian called him a few times, but didn't get a response.

The older detective wasn't a stickler for time, but it wasn't like him to blow off work entirely. Julian put it out of his mind as he filtered through a backlog of paperwork. He even took Larry's absence as an opportunity to follow up on a few leads the older detective had been blocking from him because of possible connections to Luca.

Julian was in trouble and he knew it. He was the only one on the force who knew who Luca was outside of her Lady Black persona, but he was protecting her. He should rally the troops. All it would take is a few good men and they could raid her apartment and Cecil Delacroix's house, maybe break the hold they had on the police. Or maybe he should get closer to Luca, use her to get more work done. Larry thought she had something to do with the Snatcher crime spree. If he asked nicely, maybe she'd tell him what she wanted the bodies for, or direct him to some measure of closure. He shook his head at his own stupidity. Of course she wasn't going to be his informant – she probably expected him to be one of hers.

That afternoon, Julian finally made up his mind – he'd confide in another homicide detective about Luca, see if he could get the ball rolling on some real justice. He picked Ramon Menendez, one of his long-time friends, and the detective now in charge of the Snatcher case. The two chatted over lunch about nothing in particular as Julian worked up the nerve to get back on the honest path, knowing full well that outing Luca was, in effect, outing his own weakness. There was a lull in the conversation, Julian's mouth opened, ready to spew his confession forth. But Ramon's phone cut him off. It was a text from Lady Black. Ramon excused himself immediately and left. Julian slumped forward at the table and realized how futile his life really was. There was no escape.

On his way home that night, he got a call from Ramon. His suspicions were immediately raised when Ramon told him to pull over before he would reveal the reason for the call – that was never a good sign. There had been another murder at the West Blair Cemetery, Ramon explained.

"Do you need backup?" Julian asked, confused.

"No, Julian, listen," his friend replied. "The victim... it's Larry Saunders."

The cemetery was awash in oscillating blue and red lights when Julian's car screeched into the parking lot. He played his last interaction with Larry over and over again in his mind. His partner had needed him and he'd blown him off for Luca. This was all his fault. He was disgusting. Ramon met him at the entrance.

"This way," Ramon urged Julian forward.

At the back of the cemetery, behind several unkempt graves, Larry was impaled on the iron spikes of the cemetery fence. His arms were jutted obscenely over his head. Black ribbons snaked across his flesh where his wrists had been slit all the way to the elbow, draining him of blood. Larry's shirt was torn open to reveal deep cuts on his stomach. The murderer had sliced him open from hip to hip as if performing a perverted C-section. Glistening guts hung down from the corpse and decorated the ground.

"What the fuck did this?" Julian whispered.

"I think I have a good idea," Ramon replied.

Julian climbed up the fence next to the body, looking for a good angle of the back of Larry's head. There was an exit wound. Julian scanned the earth with his flashlight, but found no skull fragments or blood spatter.

"Looks like gunshot to the head," he said. "My guess is they killed him with a firearm somewhere else, and then dragged him here before cutting him open." He looked back at Ramon. "What do you make of it?"

"It's a message."

Hours later, Julian found himself on Luca's doorstep.

"You're late," Luca admonished Julian when he knocked at her door.

"I have a job, you know."

Luca moved away from the door to let him in. Julian pushed past her and blocked the path to the bedroom.

"Did you kill Larry Saunders?"

"No," Luca responded, her face expressionless.

"Would you even tell me if you did?"

"No."

"What do you have to do with the Snatcher?" Julian balled up his fists.

"That's not how this works." Luca crossed her arms. "You come here for sex. If you're here for a different reason, then you need to leave."

"What's wrong with you people? You stop us from catching criminals so you can protect murderers. You *are* murderers," Julian shouted, pouring out all his horror and frustration into Luca's unreceptive ear. "I can't even properly investigate a case if there's even the slightest possibility you might be involved."

"Goodbye, Julian," Luca said, gesturing toward the door.

"You're going to give me answers, damn it," he shouted. Enraged by her apathy, Julian pressed her even further. "Maybe I'll ask Cecil or Christine Delacroix. I'm pretty sure I can get the girl to talk. Last time I interrogated her she almost wet herself."

Luca punched Julian in the throat before he could make another sound. In an instant, he was on the ground with Luca crouching on his chest. She whipped her gun from its holster and pressed it to his cheek.

"Where did you learn those names?" she demanded.

He tried to choke out a response, but she hit him across the face with the butt of the gun.

"You don't get to live with that information, Julian. Why didn't you take the offer? This didn't have to be complicated." She slammed the gun into his face again.

Tears welled in Julian's eyes. He was going to die, just like Larry.

"You're going to forget those names and you're going to make sure nobody else stumbles upon them." Luca put her gun back into the holster and stood.

"Aren't you going to kill me?" Julian croaked.

"Don't make me regret this." Luca took a deep breath. She avoided his eyes. "If I ever see you again, I will kill you. Do you understand?"

He nodded.

"If you even think the word Delacroix, I will kill you, and I will make it as painful as possible."

He nodded again as he pulled himself up.

"Get out of here," she said, not watching him stumble to the door.

He didn't look back. Larry had been on to something. Julian needed to find out what. He didn't really care what happened to him anymore. If following Larry's trail led him back to Luca's apartment, so be it.

CHAPTER 52

Chris lay on her bed in Tartarus, staring at the barren, grey walls of the room, feeling more like a prisoner than someone in protection. She had been confined to the demon club for two full weeks and was going stir-crazy. It reminded her of rainy days on campus when she stayed in her dorm room, only then she wasn't surrounded by demons... or maybe she was? The thought of university gave her a craving for campus food. She marched into the corridor and dialed Alice.

"You're meeting me for food at Sullivan's in an hour," she stated, not bothering with any formalities.

Alice protested, referencing exams.

"I don't care. I'm starting to think the outside world was just a dream, and I need to see it to know for sure. You're going to be there." Chris hung up without waiting for a reply.

Chris walked to Elysium and found her father in his usual spot.

"I'm going to meet Alice on campus."

"You know that you have to stay here until we get Moore," he replied.

"I promise I won't be long, and I'll be careful. These guys don't grab people off the street. It takes them weeks of planning to make a move."

Cecil tapped his hand on the back of the couch. Chris had been trying to get out from the moment they'd confined her to the club and his resolve was starting to waver. He had never been good at telling his daughters no.

"Fine, but only for two hours, and I want you to call Luca immediately when you're finished."

Chris smiled her agreement.

"And don't call her before because she'll stop you and yell at me. And be careful," Cecil shouted as Chris ran off to freedom.

Sullivan's was loud, and the atmosphere was drunk with anxious students avoiding exams. Beating all odds, Alice was already there when Chris entered the bar.

"How'd you get Dad and Luca to let you out? I thought you were supposed to be on lockdown," Alice asked.

"It's just for a couple of hours. I hate sitting around in there with nothing to do."

"Stop moping." Alice flicked her in the forehead.

"Whatever. How's Maxine?" Chris asked.

"Perfect, as always. Are you flirting with any boys?" Alice asked, prodding her sister.

"Who am I going to flirt with? I'm stuck in Tartarus all day."

"That's no excuse. You're literally living in a nightclub."

"Oh, yeah, it's like a smorgasbord of eligible monsters in there," Chris retorted. "There's this one dude with a hot lizard tongue, but Dad's had all he can take of daughters dating coworkers."

Alice stuck out her own tongue at Chris's sarcasm.

"Still with the monster talk, I see," Alice said. "How's Dad taking that, smartass?"

"Okay, all things considered," Chris admitted. "I just try to avoid him as much as I can. That's not easy, since I'm technically working as his assistant."

An hour later, they left the restaurant, relaxed and full. Chris called Luca and giggled at the woman's outrage that she was out of Tartarus. Before Chris could explain, Luca had hung up and left to pick her up. Meanwhile, Alice texted Maxine for a ride. Chris didn't relish going back into quarantine, but she'd had her fun. She looked down the street for Luca's car and saw instead a ghastly sight - Michael was strolling casually in their direction. She immediately scanned the sidewalk looking for other vigilantes, but her eyes found none. Michael wasn't even looking at her, she realized. Maybe he hadn't spotted her yet. Without a thought, she grabbed Alice's hand and raced across the street.

"What the fuck?" Alice shouted, breaking free.

Chris shushed her. "I recognized someone on the street. We have to get out of here."

"We can lay low in the park until Maxine gets here," Alice suggested.

The sisters ran into Stanford Park, stopping to hide behind the hedges along the perimeter. They squatted down out of the moonlight, the skeletal shadows of spindly trees shrouding them in darkness.

"It might just be a coincidence, but we need to stay out of sight. How long will it be until Maxine gets here?" Chris whispered.

"I don't know, but we can keep an eye on the street from here."

Alice peered through the hedge. Six men were walking to the park in a line. The leader turned toward the hedges, scanning them for a sign of the girls. He took a step in their direction. So much for coincidences.

"Fuck!" Chris pulled Alice to her feet.

They ran deeper into the park. Chris frantically craned her neck behind her, hoping that they'd outrun their pursuers. The darkness of the park, and the pounding of her own heart, had her jumping at shadows as they passed bush after bush. After minutes of madcap dashing, Chris yanked Alice into the underpass.

"I think we lost them." Alice reeled, resting her hands on her knees.

"No. We fell for their trap. They're corralling us," Chris said with chilling clarity.

The unyielding concrete surrounded them like a tomb.

"I'm not running from these bastards for another minute." Alice peeled out her claws. "If they're still after us, we need to take them out. Do you have your gun?"

Chris pulled the tiny firearm from her bag. They both froze at the sound of approaching footsteps. Alice raised her claws in preparation. She was trembling with fear and adrenaline. Despite her boasting, she was terrified. The footsteps grew steadily closer. With every dull swish Alice grew more restless. She darted out of the underpass, claws at throat level, and slashed the first thing she saw. A quick spray of blood shot through the air, followed by the thud of the body hitting the ground. Chris peered out at Alice's victim.

There had been only a single pursuer, and she was lying in a pool of her own blood. It was Emily.

Alice stared in shock at the lifeless girl, unable to believe she had killed her. She felt bile rise up from her stomach and threaten to spill from her gaping mouth.

Chris rested her hands on her head as her mind spun out of control. Alice just killed someone. Her black claws were dripping with blood, but what was worse was how Chris wished she had been the one to do it. The itching in her hands was intolerable.

Shouts erupted from the trees.

"We have to go." Chris shook her stunned sister.

Alice's lower lip was trembling.

A bullet hit the concrete behind them, waking Alice from her shock. Chris yanked her through the underpass, but three men stepped out of the shadows to block the entrance. They grasped knives glinting in the dull lamplight. Chris pointed her gun at her assailants, shouting for them to back off. They ignored her pleas and kept coming. The urge to fire rushed through her, but she didn't pull the trigger. Chris lowered her weapon and ran with Alice close by. There was no one waiting for them at the other end, and Chris burst through the entrance, willing her legs to pump even faster. She didn't think or care about where she was running. All that mattered was reaching the busy city street on the other side of the park. When she thought she'd been running forever, Chris looked over her shoulder for advancing enemies. It was then she realized Alice was gone.

A shot rang out.

"Don't move," boomed a deep voice.

A burly man stepped out of the shadows. He was pointing a rifle at her.

"What do you want?" Chris stuttered and clutched her gun.

"Drop the gun, now," he yelled.

She threw her weapon into the nearby bush. Acting quickly, the man closed the distance between them and slammed the butt of his rifle against her head. Darkness ensued.

CHAPTER 53

Maxine was half asleep on the couch, wondering how she ever kept herself entertained before Alice. A strange whim came over her, and he dialed Cecil's number.

"Hey, Cutter. I'm bored, and I'm thinking you should take me out on Monday."

There was a prolonged silence.

"Not a date, stupid." Maxine continued. "I mean, you should take me, as your superior, out to a movie or something. I don't know."

Cecil hesitantly agreed.

"Good." She paused, "And you should know, I expect the best." She hung up the phone, pleased with herself.

That was, without a doubt, the most successful social interaction she'd had in years, possibly ever. Something about Alice made her want to be part of the world. Not an equal part of it, of course. She was still a Devil. Her good mood was bolstered by the arrival of a text: Alice wanted to be picked up.

The spring air was cool on Maxine's face as she sped down the street on her motorcycle. She parked near the bar and waited, but Alice never came. She tried texting the girl, but there was no response.

"You've got to be kidding me." She dismounted her bike and proceeded into the bar, to drag the truant girl out.

Alice wasn't there. Maxine stormed out and walked the street, searching for her girlfriend. Alice was nowhere to be seen, and she wasn't answering her phone. Maxine felt a surge of panic come over her. Luca or Cecil must have picked her up, Maxine told herself. She called the Overlord, but there was no answer, and, of course, she didn't have Luca's number. So she got on her bike and roared downtown.

In Elysium, she found Cecil talking to Kent about some bullshit she didn't care about.

"Where's Alice?" she asked, interrupting their conversation.

"Get out of here, whore." Kent roared.

Maxine placed both her hands on Kent's back and sent an electric shock through his body. Kent collapsed instantly, his muscles spasming.

Maxine repeated her question.

"She went to meet Chris for dinner near campus," Cecil huffed, looking down at a writhing Kent, who would surely be yelling at him later.

"I was just there, Cutter, and she was gone. No fucking trace of her or your other runt."

Cecil leapt over Kent's smoking body, called out for Luca, and ordered one of the guards to send out an alert for all available security to reconvene at Elysium.

Maxine impatiently shoved the sole of her boot into Kent's twitching ribs, while Cecil called his daughters' phones for the sixteenth time as they waited for Luca. Neither had any better idea of how to spend their time.

"What happened?" Luca emerged from the restricted areas. "Chris called me for a ride, but I couldn't find her at the restaurant. Did you pick her up?"

"She's missing. Alice is too." Cecil's gaze pleaded with her for a solution.

Luca nodded sharply and took out her phone.

"They're not answering," Cecil said.

"I installed GPS trackers in the girls' phones. Their attackers didn't break them. I have two strong signals."

"Where's Alice?" Maxine sidled next to Luca.

"Alice is at the port and Chris is in Stanford Park."

"Okay," Cecil declared, slapping Luca on the back. "Maxine and I are going to the port for Alice. I want you and a security detail to go to the park and get Chris."

"Give me your phone," Luca said. "I'll put the address in your GPS."

Maxine bounced back and forth between her feet. "Hurry up," she yelled, sweat dripping from her forehead.

* * *

"Wake up."

Alice's vision was hazy as consciousness returned to her. The last thing she remembered were hands grabbing her in the park, then some kind of chemical smell.

Someone slapped her in the face.

"Wake up, Monster."

Alice groaned through a drool-coated rag in her mouth. She jangled against thick, cutting rope that secured her hands above her head in a hook on the ceiling. Another slap brought her senses into focus. A brown-haired man stood in breathing distance. Behind him a few men looked on, witnesses to her fate.

"Disgusting creature," Michael spat.

Alice's eyes sought out aid, but none was forthcoming from the crowd, who were huddled around in the windowless steel room. Michael trembled with rage and righteousness. None but him would look her in the eye.

"Come on, Michael," one of the men pleaded. "Just kill her like the professor said."

"Shut up," Michael snarled. "This thing killed Emily. It's going to suffer."

"I'm happy you're alert for this, Monster," Michael said quietly. "You should know what sins you're being punished for. Emily was a warrior for good and righteousness, and you cut her down. You know what that makes you?"

Alice bucked against her restraints and swore at him through the gag.

"I see you still have some fight in you. Good."

Alice tried to kick him, but her legs were tethered to a bolt in the floor. She had enough slack to shift her weight from one foot to the other, but not enough to do any damage. The man in front of her smiled. The others kept their eyes to the ground.

"We were coming for you tonight," Michael said, cupping her chin. "We never thought in a thousand years that your sister would come out of the woodworks. You delivered her to us." He checked his watch. "She's probably dead by now."

Alice screamed behind her gag and thrust forward with every bit of strength she had, desperate to obliterate the man in front of her. The ropes yanked her back harshly.

"Don't worry," Michael said, brushing her tears away. "I'm sure you two will be reunited in hell."

Michael walked over to a table behind him and retrieved a three-foot length of steel pipe. With fury overtaking his sense, he reared back and slammed it into her ribs. Alice's eyes flew open in pain. He hit her again, this time on her leg. She tried to concentrate. Her hands were restricted, but she managed to loose one clawed finger. Though the rope was thick and she could barely move, she raked her claw against it, slowly and surely. Michael went back to the table to retrieve a heavy, black book emblazoned with a gold cross. He pressed it to his chest before hitting Alice across the face with it. He stepped back to open the book. The delicate pages fell open by habit on a familiar page.

"Matthew 10:1 - And he called to him his twelve disciples and gave them authority over unclean spirits, to cast them out, and to heal every disease and every affliction." He closed the book with a snap and pointed at the girl. "You're the affliction, Creature, and we," he spun around, gesturing at the other men, "Are the remedy.

"We've been following you for a while now, Beast," he whispered in her ear. "I'm going to enjoy performing God's work today, for Emily's sake."

He drew a hunting knife from the table, and ran the blade across his thumb as he gazed upon his prey.

CHAPTER 54

"They're all going to fucking die." Maxine fumed in Cecil's passenger seat, trying to remain in control of her emotions. "She's alive. They aren't tough enough to kill her."

"In all previous cases, they've killed the demon where they found them." Cecil was quiet, his voice devoid of emotion.

"They were in public. They couldn't kill her in public."

Cecil's hands twisted on the steering wheel. "As far as we can tell, they don't toy with their prey."

"What are you doing here then?" Maxine slammed her fist into the console, cracking the plastic. "If you're so sure she's dead, why even fucking bother?"

Cecil clammed up, unwilling to discuss reality anymore.

"She's not dead," Maxine repeated.

* * *

Tiny red beads escaped from Alice's chest as Michael's knife split through the fabric of her shirt. It was a shallow wound, but it burned.

"I'm surprised your blood isn't black, Beast. It would suit you better."

"Just do it, Michael." One of the men behind him stepped out to grab his shoulder. "I don't want to spend the rest of my night in your mom's storage locker."

While her tormentor was distracted, Alice desperately sawed at the rope with her free claw. The rope was thick and Michael's attacks broke her focus, which made maintaining her demonic manifestation difficult.

Michael turned. He was far past reason, or sanity.

"This monster must be exorcised. I want her dead more than anyone, but she needs to pay for her sins before we send her to Satan."

"Try to hurry it up." The man sighed.

Michael ignored him. He ran the side of the knife across Alice's face, smearing her with her own blood.

* * *

Clouds obstructed the moonlight over the port, casting a long shadow over the water. The lone security guard jolted awake by the sound of metal grating on metal. He leaned through the window, straining his old eyes at a middle-aged man.

"The port is restricted at night, sir."

Cecil grabbed the man's tattered uniform and hauled him halfway out of the window.

"If you want to see another sunrise, you should leave this place and go home. Understand?"

The old man nodded frantically.

"Good." Cecil released his grip and started walking away. "I also wouldn't recommend calling the police, for your own sake."

The old man didn't need any more prompting, and fled for his life.

* * *

Alice was covered in blood and bruises. Michael had grown tired of cutting delicate lines into her skin and returned to hitting her with the pipe, a smile etched on his lips. All the other men had left the locker, unable to stomach Michael's sadistic attacks.

"What the fuck's wrong with him?" one of the men outside asked.

"He's just pissed off about Emily," another responded.

"No, he's been acting like this for a while now. He likes doing this too much. We need to say something." The man stopped speaking and fell to the ground, clutching his throat. A short stick of metal protruded from his neck.

The others spun around to see Maxine bearing down on them, her palm outstretched. With a crackling boom, an arc of electricity shot through a man's chest, leaving a charred chasm where his heart had been. Cecil stepped out from behind them, taking advantage of Maxine's distraction. He cut a man's throat with a scalpel, while the last man ran for his life. Cecil threw a scalpel after him, but missed his target. Swearing, he gave chase.

"Where is she?" Maxine screamed at a corpse.

She looked down the rows of storage units, each one the same as the last. Which one held Alice? In a moment of insight, she reached into the pockets of the dead man at her feet. There was a key, but there was no indication of what locker it opened. Looking around, Maxine saw hundreds of identical storage lockers. Maxine ran to the closest one. She reached the handle and fumbled the key in the lock. It didn't fit. She moved to the next with blinding speed. Nothing. Sweat leaked down her face as she looked around. Alice could be anywhere. Maxine slumped forward, arms outstretched against the locker. What would she do without Alice? Her world came to a head when she heard the faintest noise. It came from the left - a scream, muffled through steel and distance, but a scream nonetheless. Raising up, Maxine ran in the direction of the noise, loudly swearing all the way.

* * *

Alice's muffled cries combined with Michael's righteous shouts nearly overwhelmed the locker, but the crash of thunder could be distinctly heard from outside. At the sound, Alice began laughing through the pain.

"What's so funny?" Michael pressed the knife to her throat.

A shout from outside broke his concentration. He slowly approached the door, keeping the knife high in front of him as he walked. He pressed his ear to the metal and waited, listening for signs of danger. All he heard was the faint click of the lock being turned. Michael sighed in relief. It was just one of his friends returning. He crossed over to Alice once more, not bothering to look when the door opened.

"Don't you fucking touch her," Maxine ordered.

Michael leapt behind his captive, brandishing the bloody knife.

"Stay back, or she dies," he barked.

Maxine advanced on him, undeterred.

"I mean it," he yelled. "You're going to let me out of here, or your girlfriend dies."

A snap rang out as Alice finally managed to sever the rope with her claw and plunged to the floor, knocking Michael backwards. In an instant, Maxine had him pinned to the ground.

"Get off of me you God-forsaken demon," he cried. She wrenched the knife from his hand and threw it across the floor.

"God boy, huh?" She pulled out his hand. "Our father." She snapped one of his fingers. "Who art in heaven." She broke another. "Hallowed be thy name." She reached up and dislocated his arm.

Maxine looked at Alice. She had cut away her remaining bonds, and was trying to wipe the blood from her face. Alice looked back through tears, her voice having vanished like so much of her blood. Maxine's eyes fell back at the man with the severity of an artillery shell. Her mouth hung open as she placed both hands on his chest. He jolted up as electricity coursed through his body. His teeth clenched shut and his muscles quaked. Skin sizzled and popped, and smoke rose from his chest for minutes after he died.

When the crackling of Michael's charred corpse faded, the storage locker was filled by the sound of Alice's sobbing. Maxine rose from the body and pulled Alice into a hug. They held each other like they couldn't let go.

"I knew they were too weak to kill you," Maxine said.

At that moment, Cecil rushed through the door. He had a small bloodstain on his wrist, a sure sign he had caught the fleeing man. At the sight of Alice, bloodied but alive, he fell to his knees with relief.

"Are you okay?" he asked, breathless. "Let me see." He reached forward and grabbed at Alice's cuts and bruises.

She recoiled.

"Please, Honey. I know wounds. I need to make sure you're all right." His hands moved quickly across her body. Pulling back he sighed and smiled. "You're going to be sore for a while, but you're fine." He gently reached out to touch the wound on her chest, his hands shaking as he took off his shirt and pressed it against the wound.

"I told you she'd be alive," Maxine said, slowly nodding her head.

Cecil raised his hands to his head in relief. Smiling, he helped Alice to her feet.

"We're getting out of here," he said. "Do you know where Chris is? Is she all right?"

Alice shook her head no.

CHAPTER 55

Luca arrived at Stanford Park with fifteen people in identical black suits.

"We're looking for Christine Delacroix," Luca said. "She is presumed to be in enemy hands. Spread out and keep in contact." She pointed at three people. "You're with me. We're heading directly to the signal. The rest of you, fan out."

They broke into teams and proceeded into the park. Luca gave her phone to the woman beside her, who took point. Removing her gun from her holster, Luca walked closely behind her. Luca had expected a welcoming party, but, instead, there was a distinct lack of commotion. She raised her hand, stopping the group at an underpass. She knelt down to examine a large puddle of blood, and a streak leading away from their target. There was a spray of blood staining the concrete wall. Luca had seen Cecil rip through enough throats to know that this was the work of a Fiend. Her eyes traveled to a bullet hole in the concrete wall. It hadn't connected with a body. She gestured for the team to continue through the underpass.

After walking for fifteen minutes, the woman in front stopped.

"The signal is coming from here," she said.

Luca raised her weapon and pushed forward. The area was empty. She heard a crunch underfoot. Under her shoe was a pair of broken glasses she recognized as Chris's. She ordered a man into the bushes. It didn't take long to find the abandoned cell phone, and a .32 revolver.

"All of you, canvass the area," Luca commanded.

When they disappeared into the trees, her phone vibrated. Pulling it out, she saw a hauntingly vague text from Cecil. Tense hands fumbled with the phone to dial his number.

"Do you have Alice?" she snapped.

"She's all right," he said.

Luca blinked in quick succession, fighting indolent emotion.

"And Chris?" she asked.

There was a long pause.

"Find her, Luca."

She enabled the speaker on her headset. "Burke, Manning, you two are staying here. I want the rest of you to meet me back at the cars. We're expanding the search."

* * *

Julian sat in the shadows, parked in the middle of a suburb. He had torn through Larry's evidence from the Snatcher case and turned up one name that matched the initials H.W.: Herbert Wright, the night caretaker at the West Blair Cemetery they had interviewed so many months before. It couldn't have been a coincidence that Larry was killed in that same cemetery. Julian sat with his arms crossed, knowing that he could lose his job for what he was about to do, but the image of Larry's mutilated corpse urged him out of the car. In front of him was a little house with a large garden ready to be filled with flowers. He placed his hand on his gun and knocked. No answer. Julian bent over and began picking the lock.

"Herbert Wright, this is the police," he called out upon opening the door. Dreadful silence taunted back at him. "I have a warrant," he lied. When there was still no response, he broke off the door handle and forced his way inside.

It was surprisingly clean inside, considering the massive collection of potted plants. They were outnumbered only by the faded, old pictures on the walls. Julian moved slowly through the home, his gun ready. With no computer, no phone, not even anything in the cupboards other than scraps of food, Herbert Wright's house was drearily un-notable. Julian cursed after nearly an hour of fruitless searching. There was nothing here, he concluded. But, just as he turned to leave, a picture on the wall caught his eye. There was a lineup of people, surrounded by lush ferns, tiny cacti, and dozens of bright flowers, frozen in time. He saw Herbert Wright next to Norman Argyle with his arm around him. There was a banner, which read 'Meridian University Horticultural Club.' At the end of the row, there was a familiar, well-dressed man, smiling brightly: Professor Glenn Moore.

* * *

Chris's eyes uneasily cracked open. There was a large, blinding light above her, not green, but dim yellow. The nightmares were long over, so whatever was happening was real. The room reeked of damp earth. There were blue tarps covering piles all around the room and gardening tools scattered across the floor. Chris tried to shift her body weight from side to side. She found herself to be bound tightly to a table. This could be a serious problem.

"Awake, are we?" she heard a voice from the side of the room.

Chris craned her neck to see Professor Moore, wearing a white, rubber apron and rubber gloves. He sat in the chair beside her and tapped her on the chest, shaking his head in disapproval.

"Oh, Christine." He shook his head. "You really had me fooled. I knew one of my students might someday betray me. I never guessed that it would be you."

Chris pulled against her bondage again, but there was no give. She felt a cool, hard edge dig into her wrists.

"Emily told me about your talons." Moore pointed at her hands. "That's why I used metal shackles."

"Professor," Chris said, her voice cracking as she spoke. "Please, listen to me. It's not what you think."

Moore's eyes didn't flash anger, pity, or even sadness; they were empty, devoid of anything.

"You're a demon, and you've been trying to trick me, just like the rest of your kind."

"I wasn't trying to trick you. Please, untie me and I'll explain. Things are a lot more complicated than you think."

Moore looked at her, as if he were deep in thought. Chris was certain she was getting through to him.

"If you just let me go, Professor, I can help you. I know a lot more about demons. I'll tell you. All you have to do is let me go."

"Christine, Christine, Christine," Moore muttered.

Chris tried to examine his face for some hint of his intentions, but it was impossible to read.

"You tempt me greatly, I must admit that. The chance to learn about your kind from a primary source is thrilling. But you're not a trustworthy narrator. You'd say anything to save yourself, and besides, you creatures like your secrets too much to ever talk to someone like me."

He smiled. Chris felt like she'd been slapped in the face.

"Still," Moore continued, "This has been a delight. I've never had a live specimen before. It's interesting how you attempt to make an emotional connection with me, to manipulate me into doing what you wish. Part of me really wants to take the time to study you, but I'm afraid, you'd lead me astray."

Chris clamped her jaw shut, anger filling her as she realized he had no intention of helping anyone.

"Not feeling talkative anymore? That's fine. I'm sure you'll perk up a little later. I was so surprised to hear that you resurfaced, Christine, that I just had to take you alive. My friend Herbert was very helpful, much more reliable than students." He looked at her confused face.

"Oh, you've met Herbert. He's the one that gave you this." He reached over to her face and rubbed his hand over a large bruise.

Chris felt sick every time he used her full name. He treated her like a toy. She'd thought of him as a mentor, and he'd thought of her as... nothing. Moore's casual attitude toward her, chained to this table, reminded her of her father. Her stomach churned in disgust.

"I know what will get you in the mood to talk." He smiled. "We captured your sister along with you. I gave her to Michael to finish off, and you know how he gets. I'm sure she's been dead for hours."

Chris screamed as she lurched against the restraints.

"Yell all you want, dear Christine. This used to be a bunker during the Cold War, and I made sure it was soundproofed."

Chris fell limply on the table. She couldn't bear the thought of Alice in the hands of Michael, that monster. She didn't know how, but she was going to make sure Moore paid for this.

"You're an idiot," Chris said between gritted teeth.

"Excuse me?" Moore leaned in close.

"You think you're helping people, but you're not. All you're doing is killing indiscriminately, and getting innocent men and women killed in the process. If you took two seconds to get off your goddamn high horse and actually thought about your plan for a second, you'd see that you're causing more problems than you're solving."

Moore laughed loudly. Chris could feel drips of his saliva as they tumbled from his convulsing maw.

"Oh, Christine. I don't care about saving people's lives. That's just the line I feed you students."

"Then what the hell do you want!?" Chris demanded, shocked by his cavalier confession.

"I want to learn about demons."

"But you won't even talk to them? You're fucking insane."

Chris was cut off by Moore's hand slapping her across the face.

"I don't need to talk to them. There's a little trick that will make you a much better research subject. I learned about this recipe when I was studying the occult in Louisiana." He went over to one of the tarps.

"You should feel privileged. I've never shown this to anyone else." He removed the blue plastic, revealing an industrial wood chipper.

"What are you going to do?" Chris asked, staring at the machine.

Moore flung himself onto the chair beside her again. "We're going to process your body until it's the proper consistency." He lingered on the last word. "That's the first step in making you into a proper research subject."

We see their influence throughout history, but human scholars don't know anything concrete about them. I learned about demons years ago, but you people are far too secretive to study. Besides, you're corrupted by human social structures.

"These other creatures - what I'm about to turn you into - are far more agreeable. My contact in Louisiana compared them to innocent children, and I can see why. They are like you, but pure. They don't shroud themselves in secrecy. They just behave naturally, the way all demons would if they could shed civilization. They make the best research subjects. I've already started writing a paper on them. I'd show you, but what good would it do a dead girl?"

"Those monsters are killing people, you bastard!"

"Of course they are." He slapped her across her face again. "They don't know any better. It's all part of my research project to see how demons interact with humans in a natural state, not held back by millennia of evolution. It's also enlightening to watch how the modern demons try to clean the mess up."

All this time Chris had thought Moore was just misguided, like she had been. But he wasn't. Her former idol was more twisted than anything in her worst nightmares.

Smiling, he raised large scissors in front of her face. "We have to get you ready now, Dear."

Chris leaned as far as she could to the right, away from Moore. He smiled slightly. When she could pull herself no further, she threw all her weight toward him. She felt the legs of the table rise slightly into the air. Bolstered by the shift, Chris threw herself away again and immediately lunged back toward Moore.

"Fascinating," he said. "Like a turtle on it's back. You are helpless, Christine."

Chris swung back again. This time, the table tilted even further with her, but it wasn't enough. She needed more momentum. She saw Emily's body beside her and thought of Cindy, now alone in the world. With a final surge of rage, Chris launched herself toward Moore. He leapt away just before the table crashed to the ground. The wood splintered and broke. Chris's arm was forced underneath the full weight of the table. She yelped reflexively, but felt no pain. She'd manifested. Her metal limb absorbed the impact without question. The bolts holding one of her shackles had broken loose on impact. She was able to yank it loose from the table with one mighty lunge. With the shackle still around her wrist, she reached over and tore the wood away from her other hand and legs. Her new limbs weren't just sharp, she was pleased to learn. They were also strong. Only Moore stood in the way of her freedom now, and he was made of far weaker material than the table.

He raised his hands in front of him as he slowly backed up.

"Wait a moment, Christine. Think about what you're doing," he said.

Chris pumped her legs forward. She reached out with her claw and spiked it downwards. Moore ducked, causing the claw to embed itself into the concrete wall. Chris tried to yank her arm free but it was stuck. As Chris's other hand worked on dislodging its sister, Chris heard a 'woosh', then felt a heavy impact on her side. She groaned and turned her head, just in time to see Moore slam her in the side with a shovel again. He twisted the shovel in his hands and pointed it at her. Grinning, he thrust it forward. Chris yanked her claw out of the concrete and dropped to the floor, narrowly avoiding the shovel's point. He brought the shovel down upon her, hitting her with the flat of the weapon over her shoulder.

Chris flipped over on her back and formed an X in front of her with her black metal arms. The next shovel blow clanked against them and sent sparks flying around the room. She grabbed onto the shaft of the shovel and pulled herself up with it. Moore's face was covered in grimy rage – a far cry from the serene care he pretended to have for her not so long ago. Chris reared back and sent her claw forward. It nicked past the shovel and tore into Moore's side. Moore gasped in pain as Chris jumped on top of him, knocking him flat on his back. She brought her right claw over his throat next and stopped.

"You're the real monster," she said, pressing her claw closer to his jugular.

Moore continued grimacing.

"Say it. Tell me that you're the monster."

"I'm the monster," he repeated in a dull monotone.

"And I'm not. It's about choice, asshole. You chose to murder dozens of people, and I'm choosing not to kill you."

"I don't," Moore started, but was cut off by Chris's other claw covering his mouth, its large black fingers easily covering his entire lower face.

"I'm sick of people lying to me. Say one word, and I'll cut your goddamn head off."

* * *

Julian climbed out of his car at the university. Glenn Moore's registered address was a miss, and he wasn't picking up his phone. He decided to check the horticultural club's greenhouse. As he sauntered to the building, a stout man with a rifle at the end of the path called out to him.

"Who're you?" the man asked, shouldering his weapon.

"Police. I need you to put your weapon on the ground, sir," Julian shouted back.

The man fired. The bullet twisted and boomed through the air, narrowly missing Julian, who leapt behind a nearby dumpster.

"Drop your weapon! Now, or I will respond with lethal force," Julian yelled.

Another bullet clinked off the metal dumpster.

Reaching for his gun, Julian peered out from his cover. The man was just standing there, in the middle of the path, an easy target. Julian ducked out of cover and fired four shots at the man before pulling back. He heard a thump, followed by light groaning. He cautiously looked out from behind the dumpster and saw that the man had fallen on the ground. Julian ran to the injured man and kicked the gun away.

"Herbert Wright?" Julian said as he finally got a close look at his assailant.

Herbert gasped. Looking over his body, Julian saw that two of his shots had landed in the man's chest. Herbert groaned as he choked out his last breath.

"What the hell were you guarding?" Julian wondered aloud.

Julian kept his gun at the ready, expecting more resistance when he entered the greenhouse. He looked around the room, but couldn't see anyone through all of the plants. The air was warm and damp as he walked through the rows of flowers. There was no one there. Julian started moving down the center row. Below his feet, he heard a soft clunk. Looking down, he saw the slight outline of a trapdoor, nearly obscured by dirt. Julian gripped the handle and pulled. He was surprised to find it opened easily. Quietly, Julian lowered himself into the bunker.

When Julian reached the bottom, he was in a small cavity. A dull light from an open door called out for him. With his gun at his side, Julian stepped up to the door. Moore was lying on his back, and Christine Delacroix was on top of him, her arms replaced with glinting metal claws. Julian was momentarily stopped in his tracks by the demonic manifestation, but quickly shook himself out of it.

"Police, freeze," Julian yelled.

Chris immediately threw her hands up in the air. Her body shook as she rolled off Moore, and took in the newest visitor. Julian saw the wooden fragments still clinging to Chris's shackles, the smashed table behind her, and realized how she must have escaped. Emily's lifeless body and the wood chipper told him how close she had come to a grisly fate.

"Put your hands behind your head," Julian said to Moore. "You," he pointed at Chris, "Just stay over there." He gestured toward the corner.

Moore scowled, but complied with the detective's orders. Julian cuffed him, then walked around the perimeter of the room, keeping his gun trained on the professor. He lifted the corner of a tarp with his shoe. Underneath, he found a pile of fresh corpses.

"You're the Snatcher," Julian said breathlessly. "Did you kill Larry Saunders?"

"Why would I tell you anything?"

Julian walked over to the man and kicked him in the face. "Tell me, you son of a bitch, or I'll tell everyone I found you here with a bullet in your head."

"I didn't kill him." Moore laughed. "I did send a friend of mine after him, though. He made some unsavory accusations. They were accurate, but unsavory nonetheless. I didn't hold the knife, but I made sure that it was used to rip the fat man open."

Julian slammed Moore across the face with his gun. The man laughed loudly.

"Now either kill me or take me in. I don't like to waste my time talking with idiots, especially ones too stupid to see they've got a police brutality charge coming their way."

Julian called the station, but he impulsively hung up the phone as soon as it connected. He had broken a lot of rules to get this far, and he'd be damned if he let this son of a bitch get off on a technicality.

EPILOGUE

A few days later, a still-bruised Chris sat at a student café on campus, trying to enjoy a drink while she waited for Cindy. She shifted uneasily in her chair, finding it difficult not to be paranoid in public even though Moore's group had been neutralized. Cindy had contacted her after Emily's body had been found by the police. Chris was afraid to face her, ashamed of her involvement in Emily's death, but Cindy deserved some closure. The café was full of students studying for their last exams. There were study groups trying to get work done, but failing in a sea of laughter, and there were solitary students, buried in their work. The whole thing was filtered through a nostalgic haze. Everyone was so content and happy. Chris looked forward to getting back to class in the fall, hoping to find a place in the world that didn't involve black metal and death, if that was even possible anymore. She hoped very much that it was. Cindy entered the café, and Chris breathed heavily, preparing for the worst.

"How're you holding up?" Chris asked cautiously.

Cindy tried to smile at her, but Chris could tell it was forced.

"I heard about Emily. I'm sorry."

Cindy looked down, but didn't cry. She looked like she'd been through hell.

"The police told me that Professor Moore killed her, and that he was one of the biggest serial murderers in Meridian history," Cindy said, "And that he likely skipped the country." She lowered her voice. "But we both know the truth."

Chris's heart fell. Of course Cindy blamed demons for what happened.

"That bastard tricked us," Cindy said, taking long, labored breaths, "He never cared about protecting people. He was just messing with us to get some sick thrill. And he killed Emily when he decided to run away. Michael was found dead, too. I think he was tying up loose ends." Cindy rubbed her nose. "I should have stopped her. I knew what he was saying didn't make sense, but... she was always the smart one."

"None of us knew what he was up to," Chris said.

"What do you think happened to him?" Cindy asked.

"I don't know. He's probably long gone by now, but if I ever see him again, I'll make sure he pays."

Cindy looked Chris in the eyes and leaned forward. "So, you're actually a monster?"

"Demon," Chris corrected. "Don't say monster, and keep your voice down."

"I'm so sorry. I meant demon." Cindy's eyes lit in a panic. "I don't care if you're a demon, Chris. I mean, it's not like that makes a huge difference. You're still my friend."

"How can you say that?" Chris asked, unable to comprehend Cindy's line of thought, now and always.

"I just know," Cindy said with undeserved authority behind her voice. "You always looked so sad when we went out. It must have been hard for you."

"I didn't find out until this year." Chris cleared her throat. "I guess I didn't take it very well. I let myself be controlled by that bastard. But aren't you scared I might hurt you?"

"You're way too uptight." Cindy smiled. "Besides, you wouldn't have shown up if you were a bad person. You'd probably have killed me back at the house. Actually, that brings me to why I wanted to meet with you. I'm moving into an apartment in Gloucester." Cindy fidgeted uncomfortably. "I don't know where you've been or if you're comfortable there, but I wanted to know if you wanted to move in with me?"

"Are you sure that's a good idea?" Chris asked.

"If I can deal with your night terrors, I can deal with claws and whatever else you have."

"Just the claws. The nightmares stopped when they came," Chris smiled. "And I only bring the claws out if I really need them, like for chopping tomatoes and fighting killer hedges."

Chris's attempt at humor once again flew far over Cindy's head, and she sat speechless.

"I'll move in with you." Chris shook her head.

"I was worried I'd be all alone," Cindy said with a sigh of relief.

"You don't have to worry about that," Chris told her. "I'm the one who's lucky to have you, not the other way around."

Chris took the bus downtown and headed back to Tartarus. When she opened the door to the storefront, there were two guards as usual, but it was still too early for anyone to be lining up for the club. The second she took a single step into Elysium, all she could hear was giggling. Looking over, she saw Alice straddling her sadistic girlfriend. Before Maxine could notice her, Chris turned around and proceeded into the staff areas. She headed for the employee gym. Sure enough, Luca was there, running on a treadmill in an undershirt and shorts.

"Where's Dad?" Chris asked the heaving woman.

"Interrogation room."

"So he finally started?"

Luca nodded.

In the hallway leading to the interrogation room, Chris grimaced at the sickly green light emanating from underneath the door, a sure sign that her father was working. Even as she became more or less accepting of her demon heritage, Chris still hated that room. She steeled herself before entering. Cecil was in his surgeon's outfit, sharpening a scalpel in the back. She didn't think she'd ever get used to seeing him that way. It sickened her, and she vowed to stay away from that room as a matter of policy. But today was special.

On the table, Professor Moore was strapped down and gagged. His eyes were bloodshot and frantic. He started yelling through the gag when Chris entered the room. Blood was dripping from his mouth. It was no surprise – there was a collection of bright teeth in a nearby tray. The sight of him, bloody and begging, gave Chris a little pinch in her stomach, but she didn't linger on it. Chris flipped the light switch, turning off the green light. Cecil jumped and took a meat hammer off the table. He slammed it against the table beside Moore's face.

"Quiet," he shouted. "What's going on, Honey?"

"I'm going to be moving into an apartment with my friend, Cindy, and you aren't going to do anything to her. She's been through enough."

Cecil gave an exaggerated nod and stretched his hand toward Chris, offering her his scalpel. Moore's eyes bulged in fear. Chris looked down at her former professor then back at the scalpel. Her hands itched terribly. They wanted something, but she wouldn't indulge them.

"No, Dad. You two deserve each other."

Cecil frowned as his daughter walked out of the room. He had hoped she would stay and learn from him the fine art of interrogation, but if she didn't want to see this man mutilated, who had hurt her so deeply, then more fun for him. He reminded himself that most people didn't have his tolerance for extreme violence before Moore's whimpering reminded him how much he loved his job.

* * *

That night, Chris had the first dream she'd had since the nightmares stopped. She was standing in Elysium, its pink and purple hues glinting off of the black metal covering her arms. She moved her right hand up to her face and flexed the joint-less metal, testing its strength. She didn't look around the room for the Beast with the Black Metal Claws. She didn't need to. It was there, whispering to her from within the dark recesses of her heart, and causing her hands to itch. The room was empty, but, as she walked forward, she could hear the laughter and clapping of invisible patrons, goading her on. She reached the back of the room, to her father's couch, and sat. Chris crossed her legs and surveyed the room and her world. Everything was clear, no longer obscured in a deep, green fog.

Chris leaned back, smiling at the long shadow she cast. It smiled back at her.

ABOUT THE AUTHOR

Nick Doyle is a former lawyer who grew tired of the courtroom and decided to do draft something a little less legal. He is a trained classicist and loves nothing more than reading about ancient Rome. He lives on the east coast of Canada with his wife and the blondest son you'll ever see.

You can visit his site at www.nickdoylewrites.com.

If you enjoyed The Meridian Fiend, please leave a review on Amazon

Made in the USA
Middletown, DE
17 September 2020

19074427R00203